D0408983

TIME FOR BED

TIME FOR BED

DAVID BADDIEL

LITTLE, BROWN AND COMPANY

A *Little, Brown* Book

First published in Great Britain in 1996
by Little, Brown and Company
Reprinted 1996

The author gratefully acknowledges permission to
quote from the following:
'Arsehole' by Craig Raine from the anthology *Rich*;
reproduced by permission of Faber and Faber Ltd.
Rommel? Gunner Who? by Spike Milligan, copyright ©
T. A. Milligan 1974; reproduced by permission of
Penguin Books. 'When the Girl in Your Arms is the
Girl in Your Heart' by Sid Tepper and Roy Bennette,
copyright © 1960 Pickwick Music assigned to
MCA Publishing.
Every effort has been made to trace
the copyright holders in all copyright material
in this book, and the author would like to
acknowledge the following sources:
'We've Only Just Begun' by Roger Nichols and Paul H.
Williams, published by Rondor Music; 'Love is Like
Oxygen' by Trevor Griffin and Andrew Scott, published
by Sweet Publishing

A CIP catalogue record for this book
is available from the British Library.

ISBN 0 316 87671 2

Typeset in Sabon by
Palimpsest Book Production Limited,
Polmont, Stirlingshire
Printed and bound in Great Britain by
Clays Ltd, St Ives plc.

Little, Brown and Company (UK)
Brettenham House
Lancaster Place
London WC2E 7EN

To my parents

I would like to thank: for their advice and encouragement, Bruce Hyman, Nick Hornby, Alexandra Pringle, Roddy Doyle, Tracey Macleod, and Alan Samson at Little, Brown; for diverse reasons, Frank Skinner, Janine Kaufman, Jon Thoday, James Herring, Boothby Graffoe, and Ivor Baddiel; and, for everything, Sarah Bowden.

'When the girl in your arms
Is the girl in your heart . . .'

Girl In Your Arms, Cliff Richard

1

2:17. Don't have to get up until, latest, half twelve. So, let's see: two hours of scrabbling irritatedly in the sheets (4:17), then maybe three? hours in a blank coma, if I'm lucky (7:17), followed by an hour and a half of adamantine wakefulness (8:47), and then, at last, the luxurious morning, when I rest copiously, dreaming and drifting as if these actions were easily in my gift, gives me . . . six hours and fifty-three minutes of sleep altogether. Not quite the mythic eight hours, but not bad, considering.

This is my problem. I nurture it somewhat – sometimes I give out my card at parties: hi, Gabriel Jacoby, *Insomniac* – but we all need our negative hallmarks of identity. I don't mean self-deprecation – that's just knots in the pattern of awkwardness – but a real maladjustment, a big fuck-off flaw, a therapeutic black hole through which we can present ourselves with the subtext *I am interesting, dangerous and romantic*. However: this one – at the end of the day, it's just not worth the trouble.

2:19 now. Insomniacs are relentless about time, about night-time, because each minute is another grain of sand through the hour-glass and into your head for the next day. But 2:19 – that's nothing; oh no, 2:19, that's still the best part of the day, lots to look forward to. A world-class insomniac doesn't call it a bad night until at least, *at least* half five, and only then if it's accompanied by anxiety, bone-ache and two hundred visits to the toilet.

I sleep, or rather I lie in cold hyperthought, wearing a blindfold and earplugs, a kind of pathetic but portable sensory deprivation tank. An old airplane blindfold inscribed with the legend *Virgin* – and it is a legend, God's joke to stamp over my eyes like blackmail the name of the consciousness I so desperately crave – which I tie tighter and tighter round my eyes every night, tight enough to hurt, and leave me blinded by psychedelic lights for twenty minutes every morning. I achieve this tightness by tying knots in the two strands of elastic you fit round your head; but I've done that so often with this one it now has a huge, hard lump of elastic round the back which sometimes, when I'm finally about to find an exit from insomnia, will press into my skull and wake me up. I need a new one, but blindfolds, you can't get them from shops, you have to go on a bloody plane to get one, and I haven't been on a plane for years; nights there are, though, when I get so desperate I consider saving up my dole money and splashing out on a trip to, I dunno, Australia, Bermuda, Fiji, *anywhere*, just to get a new sodding blindfold. The earplugs, pink, waxy balls like rabbit scrotum, I force deeper and deeper into my ears every night, in the hope, I think, that I might faint: now I couldn't hear if Metallica decided to play a surprise one-off gig in my bedroom, but the thumping of the blood in my head keeps me awake. One night they'll get stuck and I'll have to call the fire brigade out.

What do I yearn for in the slow, slow dark? When I was twelve I had my tonsils removed, and I can remember the anaesthetist counting backwards, ten, nine, eight, seven, six and at six I fell asleep. That is what I want: I want to know the moment of sleep. Stupidly, because that's the self-reflexive centre of the whole mind-curse – the light in my mind, the one that keeps me up, *I've* left it on, so as not to miss the moment when someone comes in to switch it off. I am a moron in a blindfold trying to pin down, once and for all, the tail on the sleep donkey.

There is a woman here. When I'm on my own, counting backwards through the night, that's often what I think I most desire. Yeah. So then, when the bad night becomes the strung-out soul-splitting night from hell, when the psychic demons come out for their regular 5.30 a.m. morris dance on my skull, then, oh lord thank the lord, *there's someone else here*: and, hey, whaddya know – they're asleep. And then I just think: you bastard. Lying there, fatuously snoring – yeah, don't tell me, innnn, ouuuuut, innnnnn, ouuuuut, each rattle of your breath saying, 'It's a doddle this sleep business, no worriezzzzzzzzzzzz' – YOU'RE TAKING THE PISS!!

Actually, I tell a lie. There *was* a woman here. She just left, in what I can only assume to be something of a huff. The truth is, things didn't go too well. And then they got worse.

You see, you have to be empty to sleep. A trick – one of the millions that don't work – is to imagine your body as an empty glass shell, into which a relaxing yellow gas is pumping, slowly, filling every corner and releasing tension. But it's difficult to imagine your body as an empty glass shell when some warped neuron in your awareness ventricle is picking up every millilitre of urine in your bladder, every trickle of sperm in your testicles, every tiny hair lying twisted up against the grain on your skin. When I get up to go to the toilet for the two-hundredth time, it's not that I *need* to go to the toilet again, it's that I've realised, through cleverly controlled sphincter spasms, that if I was poised above the toilet, I *could* go: and that's enough to get me out of bed. Straining, straining, every last drop: only when I'd have to undergo a Caesarian to get any more out do I feel voided.

And it's ten times worse with sperm. It just *has* to be got rid of, surreptitiously if need be, especially when things haven't gone too well and I've built up a huge backlog of the stuff. But do women, especially women who I thought had gone to sleep twenty minutes ago, understand that? Do they fuck.

If only I hadn't put the blindfold and earplugs on first. I only just about heard the door slam.

Next morning, Nick is up before me, for a rundown.

'Well?'

'Brilliant. Three-nil. Some dispute over the third goal but the action replay showed it definitely crossed the line. Handball in extra time.'

'What was the state of the pitch?'

'Waterlogged.'

Nick is my flatmate; he is thirty-five, and balding. He is the sort of man who farts, and is pleased about it. This would not bother me, were it not for the fact that his farting sounds painful to me, as if his anus is cracking with the effort, and I really don't want to be there when it finally gives way. My flatmate and myself, a dream for unposted feminists, tend to deflect our obvious fear of the dark complexities of sexual intercourse by talking about it as if it was football. Nick is a Bradford City supporter.

'Gabe?'

His dressing-gown is black, mine is burgundy. He wears a pair of enormous slippers with a three-dimensional upright Zebedee from *The Magic Roundabout* on each of them. Zebedee has his arms outstretched, as if appealing for clemency. My feet are bare and cold on the kitchen floor. I adopt the attitude of a man reading the newspaper, but the words – some committee, some child abuse, some inflation figures, some psychokiller in America, some new motorway – bounce off the blindfold-induced light show in my eyes.

'Yeah?'

'I thought I heard the door slam. Round about two o'clock.'

'Mmmm . . . no. Must have been the wind.'

'She still here then?'

I pretend I haven't heard this. One thing about being known for not sleeping, it allows you to act distracted all the time. I look out of the window. London is so pallid all the time; or perhaps it's just my windows going yellow.

I say: 'You going out today?'

'Yeah, in about ten minutes.'

'Where you working?'

'Camden Road.'

'The big traffic lights?'

'Yeah.' He smiles evilly. 'Word has it they've got a fault – stick on red for ages . . .'

The reason he's smiling is that Nick makes his money cleaning windscreens at traffic lights. Yeah, he actually is one of those terrible blokes. £350 a week he makes; £350 a week, not a penny of which anyone ever really wants to give him. I put the paper down.

'Doesn't anyone ever say to you, "Sorry, but – would you believe it – I just happen to have something on my car called a windscreen wiper"?'

'No,' he says, getting his bucket and sponge out from beneath the sink.

'"And – do you know – when it's dark, I don't actually need anyone to lie on the bonnet holding a torch either . . ."'

He gets up. 'Is she in bed or what?'

'Yeah. I said I'd make her breakfast.'

'Hey. Must be serious. Alice'll be beside herself.'

Ten minutes later, as his footsteps retreat down the stairs, I spatula two eggs, two sausages, one lean rasher of bacon and three lightly grilled tomatoes into the swing-bin. I could've eaten it myself, but I'm trying to wean myself off that sort of food. It's always the same: the first six mouthfuls are heaven, paradise in the mouth, but then it all starts to go wrong, and by the second sausage I've got a headache. End of the meal without fail I want to vomit, and the whole affair leaves me deeply depressed for the rest of the day. Greasy-spoon hangover. Next morning I fancy the same again. It's worth it for those first six mouthfuls.

The swing-bin, because it's overflowing, won't swing-bin open, so I have to take the top section off but then – CHHHHHHHAAAAA – the Gehenna inside roars its smell at me. I should change it, but instead balance the food from my plate precariously on a blue, green and furry mound that was once food itself, but God knows what food, although some sections of it are definitely descended from batter. Even on this pedestal of death, one of the sausages just looks too appetising, all brown and black and available, so, brushing off a fragment of my ruins, I eat it, but the mental effort of blocking out the fact that it's just been in the bin robs me of my cut of joy.

What time is it? I look at the microwave. 6:20. No, that can't be right. Then I remember what's happening. For some time, I had begun to notice that it was dark outside at one o'clock in the afternoon, and still light at eleven at night. I had just assumed that this was some by-product of the ozone layer going a bit thin on top, and was preparing to board the boat to the mountains ready for when the sky actually fell in, when I realised that time itself was actually moving, that one second it would be 4:20, the next it would be 8:20. I thought, *it's too late, this is it, the space–time continuum has gone down, we are skidding along the curve of eternity, any second now Stephen Hawking is going to come crashing in through my roof*. Then I noticed that each change of time was accompanied by a twitch of antennae. That's when I worked out that there is a fly living in my microwave clock.

I don't know how that can happen, a fly living in my microwave clock. It's not just that now I have to plan my day around when this fly decides to take its daily constitutional. It's more the fear that, at some point, I'm going to put a steak and kidney pie on for five minutes, open the door, and out's going to burst some huge mutant steak and kidney fly, a great big piece of pastry with gossamer wings and a thousand eyes, vomiting all over my cat before it eats her. I sense the fly, though, is smug about it. It thinks it's got a flat in bloody Piccadilly Circus.

Unable to restart my life until I know what the time is, I go into the living-room, do a quick glissando on my battered old upright piano, and sit down on the sofa. I look round: our flat takes up the second floor of a Victorian house in Kilburn, but it seems hard to imagine that, once, stiff-collared gentlemen traded remarks about Palmerston on this biscuit-carpeted floor strewn with old copies of *Complete Car* and Yellow Pages got out for phone-calls made months ago. The only two house-plants that I've ever bought – a yucca and one I don't know the name of, but it's meant to have big yellow leaves – stand limply against the wood-chipped magnolia wallpaper at either side of the room's one window, looking out the back of the house onto Abrakebabra on Willesden Lane. Idly I notice that, again, there are a couple of cigarette butts pressed into the soil of the big yellow-leaved plant's pot. No amount of asking Nick not to do this makes any difference. He once told me that it was good for them, an argument he used on another occasion when I found him urinating into the yucca.

Swinging my legs up and along, I stretch out and lie down. This is not difficult on our sofa. Our sofa is the biggest sofa in the world, fact. The reason I bought it is probably related to growing up in my parents' house, which contained only one comfortable chair, a fat red leather one in the telly room, the sitting on of which was a source of much bitter dispute, and some not inconsiderable domestic violence; so our sofa, with its space to seat The Roly-Polys and their families if need be, is probably a psychological compensator. A once green now grey monster, curved or possibly warped into enormous concavity, getting it up here was like *Fitzcarraldo*; but it was a bargain at £150, plus a matching armchair, from Powers of Kilburn. At the far, far end, the back cushion has become stained, but not like you sometimes see on white sofas – a little oval puddle of grease spread from an over-Brylcreemed head; virtually the entire cushion is overlaid with a picky brown film, half an inch thick, etched with lines like a particularly troubled forehead. I'd hate to get the lab results on it back.

I lie there for some indeterminable time, staring aimlessly at the rust discs and amber twines of the small section of Persian rug which pokes out from beneath the great wedge of sofa. A bald square patch stands out on one corner of the rug, like the area round the scar of a cat that has just been spayed, and one of the rust discs has been discoloured brown by coffee stains, and again I'm struck by the way that history incongruises objects: I see the sackclothed weaver, his loom, by his side a small curved glass of brown-black tea, hear the noise of the souk outside, and wonder what he would say if he saw this rug now. 'That one was made in Luton', probably.

It starts to rain. If it gets hard and driving, water will start to pour through from the windows, and from a grey crater just above the piano, where the ceiling has sunk in the shape of a small wok. Luckily, the two saucepans needed to collect it are still in place from the last time; as indeed is the rain-water inside them.

I'm still trying to work out what the time actually is when my cat, Jezebel, bites my ankles. I have this relationship with Jezebel: I am prostrate before her. She is beautiful beyond belief. Sometimes I see her curving like a Matisse in a shaft of mote-sparkling sunlight and I believe in God, I do, I believe in God.

She bites my ankles. And sometimes, if I'm lucky, she punches me in the face. I give her food and, breakdancing, she chucks it up. Not Whiskas, oh no, not Choosy – *Sheba*, fucking *Sheba*, she chucks up. Sheba that sometimes I open and wish that someone would make me such a delicacy once in a while. And all I want from Jezebel is that, every so often, she comes and sits in my lap. But she doesn't. I sit on the sofa for hours, patting my lap until my thighs start to smart, cooing like an idiot, in the hope of some spontaneous affection, and then finally, stung by her ability to ignore – animals, they really can ignore, can't they? – I go over to the radiator, pick her up and place her on my lap. A reassuring warm weight settles into my body-hollow. Two minutes later she realises what has happened, punches me in the face, and goes back to the radiator.

Back in the kitchen, I give Jezebel some Sheba – tuna with prawn, it smells fresh as the sea itself – and think about making myself some coffee. Let me see: I have a filter coffee maker, two cafetières, an espresso machine that does cappuccino as well, one of those Italian silver stove kettles, coffee bags, coffee beans, ground coffee, Lavazza, Lyons, Kenco, Nescafé, Gold Blend, Red Mountain, one jar, unopened, of Mellow Birds, and three sachets of various makes stolen from hotel-room baskets over the course of the last five years. Coffee is very important to me. Don't tell me: 'perhaps that's the root cause of your problem?' How clever of you to spot it. You are King Aha! for the day. But, you see, God has shat in my Italian silver stove kettle: drinking a lot of coffee means I can't sleep, but *because I haven't slept I have to drink a lot of coffee*. I make myself an enormous ceramic bath-bowl full of Lavazza Super-Speedy Head-raper. The phone rings, disturbing my narcotic consciousness. I hesitate before picking it up, as my phone has started humming and fizzing under all conversation recently, making me suspect, quite unjustifiably, Interpol. I watch it ring five times before I lift the receiver. It is my brother, Ben.

'Cunt?'

'Speaking.'

'Did I wake you up?'

This is something people on the telephone ask me at any time of the day.

'No. Well. No. I haven't been asleep.'

'Have you thought about my offer?'

'I'm sorry, I can't accept less than two billion for that amount of crack.'

'Funny. You know what I mean.'

I pause. This is a difficult call.

'Look. Ben. It's a brilliant offer. You're a brilliant editor.

Over The Line is a brilliant magazine. But I can't even string three sentences together without overusing the word "brilliant". You'd be better off with someone else.'

'Bollocks. All I want is a weekly column. Something funny and incisive and perceptive and satirical about sport.'

'What about something tedious and rubbish and shoddily written and not-thought-through about sport?'

'Sounds great.'

'But I don't *want* to work. I like not working. I especially like not working for my brother.'

'You wouldn't be working *for* me, you'd be working *with* me. A partner.'

There is a short croak on the line: Interpol logging off. 'I dunno, Ben. I'm thinking of maybe going travelling for six months—'

'You're not going to.'

This is such an obviously correct statement that it requires no supporting nor will bear no contesting. All my adult life I have planned to go travelling – big travelling, China, Greenland, South-East Asia – and I never have. My arguments are starting to flag: I can feel my hidden agenda burgeoning inside me.

'Listen,' he says, after a brief whirring silence, 'd'you want to come round tonight? Alice says she'll cook something.'

Right. I pause, to imply that I have something else I might rather do. In actual fact, if I had an appointment to have my undergroin smeared in oil by Kathleen Turner, I would cancel it.

'Er . . . well, I was . . . no. OK.'

'You sure? 'Cos we could make it next week.'

'No. It's fine. It was nothing.'

'All right, see you about eight thirty.'

'Yeah, see you.'

'Cunt.'

'Cunt.'

I replace the receiver. My soul fills quietly with the yellow gas of joy. I am to see Alice. I feel light returning, a sudden surge like a goal in extra-time; hope spreads in my heart like fridgeless Clover on white white bread. Even my cold toes become warm. Then I realise that Jezebel has been sick on my feet.

2

Yes, that's right. Alice is my brother's wife. I am in love with my brother's wife. *I suppose this is something I've come to accept*. This is the sentence I rehearse in my head to deal with the situation. *I suppose this is something I've come to accept*. I have to rehearse this sentence in my head to stop me saying the other sentence, the one that goes, 'Howl, howl, howl, howl, howl!!!'

This is why I don't want to work with Ben. He wants this column for the back page of *Over The Line*, the hip, glossy sports weekly he edits, and I get the impression Ben genuinely thinks I've got something to offer the magazine, it's not just him being charitable to his layabout brother. But, although I love him, I can't spend that amount of time with Ben: because he'll nonchalantly mention Alice, I know he will, in minor anecdotes, in future plans, even, maybe, in occasional sexual asides, which will deeply, deeply underwrite my isolation from her. There's only so many cuts to the flesh I can take.

I first met Alice three years ago. Ben had been going out with her for two months already. This, at the time, was astounding. Ben used to be unable to sustain a relationship for more than twenty-five minutes. It was not that he was promiscuous: he just had these ridiculous standards. To go out with Ben, you had to pass a series of mental and physical tests so rigorous many of his exes went on to devise challenges for *The Krypton Factor*. As far as I could make out, the basic qualifications you needed to last past the next morning with Ben were five or six A Levels, a degree, preferably in English, but French or Biochemistry might be acceptable, some sort of post-graduate qualification on top of that, MA or Ph.D., an extensive analytical knowledge of film, television and all other aspects of current popular culture, an ability to toss off Thurber-like *bons mots* at will, and enormous great big tits. Unfortunately, most of the time, the women he actually went out with tended just to fulfil the last requirement (but extremely well some of them – oh, with flying colours). Then, suddenly, three years ago, he turned up one evening with Alice and the conversation, which I've *précis*ed a tiny bit, went something like this:

'Gabe. This is Alice.'

'Hi, nice to mee—'

'She's got four A Levels, done a Ph.D. on Racine, and she writes for *Sight And Sound* magazine.'

'Really? And . . . wait a minute, you're a double D cup as well, aren't you? Bingo! House! Housey-housey!'

Well, no, I didn't say that, but it's what I was thinking. It's what I was thinking for a millisecond, before I thought: *I am in love. I have seen the face of Helen.* A thousand doves flew out of my heart, and I believed in God, I did, I believed in God.

'Ben,' said Alice. 'D'you get a hard-on reciting my CV?'

Or words to that effect. Now, it wasn't exactly Thurber, but you don't know something, you will never know something, about Alice. She has the voice of a sex angel. Some women have this voice: I don't mean the sperm-breathed whispers that pass for sex across the 0898 lines, I mean a voice that makes you want to care for the speaker, to hold her forever, and yes, to fuck her, but to fuck her gently. Listen: you can hear the soft moan; and, sometimes, the plangency of a child crying.

Seeing and hearing this woman, I was moved to anger that Ben should have her – in fact, that anyone should have her. She was not a person, she was a Platonic ideal of womanhood, a slacker-styled embodiment of fantasy. And *such* fantastic tits. Ay, there's the rub: for all my reveries about Alice, I have never not thought about her tits. Men, sometimes they go into a state about a woman, and so they stop thinking about her sexually: the mark of their love is that they don't wank about her. But sometimes, when you're wanking, and you're approaching climax, your imagination goes out of control, shooting off the roller-coaster of memory-bank and make-believe into a whole cluster of people down below, causing untold damage. In the 1970s, there was a children's programme called *Vision On*, for the deaf, which had these collage sequences, broken up by a speed-wheel flicking from image to image. When you're doing *Vision On* in the head, the one for those about to go blind, suddenly there comes a point where there's no access to the brake on the speed-wheel – it spins wildly, flickflickflickflickflick-stop! coming to rest on the face of whosoever *actually* lives at your sexual core (ninety-nine times out of a hundred *not* your partner – blasted with ecstasy, you face that guilt). From this moment on, that face, for me, was always Alice's: the girl of my dreams.

They got married last spring at a register office in Marylebone. There was some talk about them getting married at a synagogue, but because Alice is half-black, and no fraction Jewish, the rabbi panicked and they were forced to go secular. I've got a slight problem with marriage at the best of times (the service, I mean, although the evidence seems to be that the institution isn't flawless either) – there's always such a deep smugness emanating from the seated relatives that the young'uns have finally come round – but, funnily enough, I had *major* problems with this one. They'd done their own vows, for a start, which I thought was twisting the knife a bit – isn't bloody 'love you and keep you till death do us part' enough, for heaven's sake? – and when it came to the bit about 'if any man here has any reason why these two should not be joined in matrimony, let him speak now or forever hold his peace', a point at which it's well known that everybody in the church or register office or wherever *always* feels some urge to shout out anyway, I was biting my tongue so hard my mouth began to fill with blood. My only consolation from the whole affair was that, being a Nineties woman, Alice decided to retain her maiden name – Friedricks – which, sometimes, in my stupider moments, I can pretend demonstrates a level a little below total commitment.

That night, before going over to my house of pain, I spend a lot of time trying to make myself look attractive without looking as if I've spent a lot of time trying to make myself look attractive.

The largest fraction of time is taken up attempting to make my hair correspond to what I'm sure it looked like before I looked in the mirror – kind of messy but symmetrical, falling over my eyes in a mixture of freedom and vulnerability. The image in the mirror, however, is more a mixture of twat and ponce: it's all curling upwards and away from my forehead, like I've got a circus strongman's moustache on my head. I try to remedy it but apply far too much gel, so then have to apply water to stop it sticking to my skull like a burst black shower cap. I'm cursing Ben for not inviting me last night, so that I could've shaved then, and by tonight had some attractive, but still apparently uncaring, stubble. It's not that I want to give off an 'I've made no effort but, hey, I still look great' vibe; it's because even though I'm desperate for Alice to feel just the slightest twinge of desire for me, more desperate than hungry men lost amongst the icebergs, I'm even more desperate that she should never discover my obsession. This is the salt sprinkled into the wound of my insomnia, as night after night I lie and watch the ceiling play and replay the disaster film that would follow: my bond with Ben, my brother, my door back to the burnished days, would crumble. But more, much more, I could never see Alice again comfortably. Now I can see her, and it hurts, it hurts my heart, but at least there is no wall between me and her, no grille of awkwardness, no sense that perhaps it would be better if I left; I am crying, but I am crying backwards, the tears are running down the inside of my face where I know she can't see them. When I am with her, my love is locked and manacled; but I sing in my chains, quietly.

So before I leave, Nick says to me: 'Fuck me. You going to meet Michelle Pfeiffer or what?'

Clearly the cover-up has not been as comprehensive as it might be.

'No, I'm just going to—'

'Ben and Alice's?'

Nick knows about Alice. I unburdened myself to him one night, late, sitting in a bucket of tears and vodka: there we were, swapping the usual crap confessions – childhood homosexuality, hatred for parents, how we could both have been professional footballers (if we'd wanted to) – when suddenly, God knows why, I cracked the safe in my heart and produced my jewel. Now, of course, I wish I hadn't, and am terrified that, one day, he's going to make a leading remark in Alice's presence, something like, 'Did you know Gabriel's in love with you?'

'Might be,' I say.

'Right,' he says, with an air of all-knowing complacency.

I feel suddenly outraged by his air of all-knowing complacency.

'Will you fucking do some clearing up in here while I'm gone, you absolute cunt?' I say.

'Oooooooooo!' he says, lilting the middle 'oooo' in cod sarcasm. 'Just because you thought you looked really casual and uncaring.'

'No, actually, it's because it's filthy in here.' I cast around for some objective correlative of this. Not hard to find. 'Look: what's this?'

'Some orange peel. What does it look like?'

'Some orange peel in a cup with two butt-ends and . . . oh for fuck's sake, bits of your *toe-nails* in it! I could've drunk them.'

'Oh, stop sounding like an old woman.'

'You're the old woman.'

'No, you're the old woman.'

'You are, you wear a big greying bra.'

The big greying bra stops the flow of argument. I can't bear arguments. Most of the time, I would rather choke on my resentment than give vent to my feelings. Which is a mistake, as every time I think 'I won't say anything about that', I'm stoking the coals of cancer. Sometimes I can feel my future tumour glowing in the dark, like E.T.'s heart.

So, meanwhile, I go back to the bathroom and worry my clothes a bit, pulling a button loose here and shirt-flap free there, all the time repressing the fact that, in the last ten minutes, my hair has mutated into an Indian waiter's bouffant. I check my watch – 8:15. Nothing I can do about it, I have to go. It takes twenty-five minutes to drive to Ben and Alice's, and it's important, for the appearance of casualness, not to arrive on time, but, obviously, not too late – obviously, because I calibrate time spent with Alice in milliseconds: I hoard them in my heart, those milliseconds. Bidding a curt 'Cheers' to a suspiciously smiling Nick, I put on my brown bomber jacket, lined with something that looks like a sheep, and go outside. A thin mist, a mist that can't be bothered, doesn't hide the street, but renders it a bit out of focus; my car, a Triumph Dolomite, sits on the other side of the road covered in droplets like it's been sweating. My car is a portable rubbish dump. To sit down, I have to move ten boxless cassettes – The Carpenters, Dusty Springfield, The Cranberries – a packet of chewing gum, an empty bin-liner, and four ravaged copies of the A–Z. Pages fall out of my A–Zs, I've noticed, quicker than leaves from a suicidal house-plant. You could reforest whole sections of the Amazon out of the aerial visions of London scattered over my car. So many times I've set off for some virgin destination without checking where it is beforehand, and then it's only when I'm lost in some Godless section of hard-pub London that I open the book to realise that the relevant page has pissed off somewhere into the quagmire of the back seat, never to be seen again. The back area of the car is a total no-go zone. Underneath the front seats, however, is quite a lucky dip; rummaging around in it the other day in search of page thirty-seven, my hand alighted on what turned out to be a box of dominoes. I have never in my life owned a box of dominoes.

It's so cold inside the car that gripping the steering-wheel shocks my hands like biting into ice cream does my teeth, but it still starts OK, thank God. It's very impressive, the Dolomite. Never serviced, never had an oil change, certainly never been washed, but still it always opens up with a big reassuring *vrooom*. It's taken to stalling now and again at traffic lights, but one twist of the ignition and it's fine. I stop off at a KwikSave in Queens Park to get a bottle of wine. As I go in, a lumbering shadow of a man, previously on a perfect trajectory out of the door, lurches to the right and bumps into me. He leaps backwards melodramatically, his fists raised.

'Come on then. Let's fucking 'ave yer! Let's 'ave yer! 'AVE YER!!'

'Hello, Barry,' I say, and carry on inside, leaving Mental Barry's fists to circle in slow motion around each other for as long as it takes him to realise I've walked off. Poor Mental Barry: rumour has it he's so disgusting the other tramps in

Kilburn have taken a vote and asked him not to hang out with them any more.

Once inside the shop, overlit with its always openness, I hit the usual wine wall. What's the deal here? I have an image in my head, corresponding to a taste on my tongue, as to what a nice wine should be like. All those words – *oaky, buttery, vanilla, spicy, matured* – they're all part of that image; I know, when I hit that elusive taste sensation, that it will combine all these things, and I wait in happy expectation of the day when I sit down by my fireside with a glass in my hand, quaff, and feel spicy matured oak vanilla butter slide down my gullet as I turn to Alice and say, 'This is it, darling. This is our drink.' And yet, despite continually upping the price bracket I'm prepared to enter looking for this wine, the words that come to mind when I actually pour the stuff into my mouth are always *sour*, *off*, *thin*, *Ribenary*, and *leading to shivers and a tingling pain around the gills*.

Looking at the labels in mute incomprehension, the words of a thousand ignorances float up before me – *Australian always good value, can't go wrong with a Hungarian Merlot*, *Chilean meant to be very good one year* (but what year? Are there people who actually know, d'you think?), *Valpolicella a good drinking wine*. I dunno. I try an old ploy.

'What would you recommend?'

Like the bloke behind the counter at the Queens Park KwikSave is fucking Albert Roux. He says nothing, just looks at me with tired refugee eyes, his whole being saying, 'Please, I just want to betray my entire life doing time in this overlit soul-vacuum: don't make it harder for me.' So I tell him not to bother, and do what I always do, which is head for the label which looks like it might at some point have had some dust on it, in this case something called St Auberge 1987, £6.99, because a dusty label, well, that means, yes, that it's been in a cellar, probably, and that's got to be good, hasn't it? I mean: I'm not one of these people who thinks that it's a quality wine if the bottom half of the bottle is a basket. Not any more.

Outside the KwikSave Mental Barry's fists are still circling as I walk past him. 'You've got no *bollocks*!!' he shouts. Perhaps he's right. Or perhaps he just doesn't realise that I chose to wear mine *inside* my trousers.

I'm still well on course for arriving at Ben and Alice's at twenty to nine, when, at the Harrow Road, halfway to their Ladbroke Grove house, I hit a traffic jam. I can never understand why traffic jams. Presumably, at some point further down the line, cars are moving, unless you're in some kind of total world jam. So why should there be a point where traffic is not moving? It's all the same line in space. But perhaps gridlock is not stagnation, but salvation. I remember being in a jam on Hammersmith Roundabout once, and after twenty minutes it became clear that this *was* it, the total world jam, and so people started getting out of their cars and walking about, smoking, lolling, joking with and talking to other drivers; faces that usually peered through glass at other traffic in fixed own-world bitterness cracked and smiled and responded, and car-versus-car hatred, for a second, disintegrated: it was like Christmas Day 1914. Back at the Harrow Road, I think about this positive, healthy image of traffic jams in between shouting 'CUNT!!! CUNT!! AAAAARRRGGH, CUNTING CUNTINESS!!' and banging my forehead repeatedly on the steering-wheel, until I realise that a woman in the car next to me is pointing me out to her friend.

I arrive, eventually, at 8:51, eleven minutes past my planned requisite lateness, eleven minutes lost into the Aliceless ether. I check the mirror: I still look like I've made too much effort, so I ruffle my hair, but the bastard stuff simply won't fall into that happily mussed look – I've just made myself look stupid, but I can't waste any more time. I get out, knock on their door, and adopt a pose of detached interest in the night sky. It is a beautiful night: stars are the freckles of God. Then Alice opens the door, and the night sky is revealed for the cold, ugly dot-to-dot pattern it is. What constellation has soft eyes and black hair and breasts to make you weep? Freeze her: freeze her as she is.

'Hello!'

'Hi.'

A more muted exchange than my screaming feelings fancy.

Alice really is beautiful, y'know. I'm not fucking you around here. Just her hair alone – hundreds of soft, black tunnelettes piled three inches high on her head, falling in occasional, heart-breaking ringlets across her forehead, like Medusa's heavenly obverse – the sort of hair that, from the back you'd think, shit, she can't match that from the front, the face must disappoint, *surely*, not to mention the bod. And so you'd catch up with her, quickly, and disappointment would disintegrate. How can I describe her face (look at the hair stuff, I'm clearly at full stretch as it is)? Her eyes are large, very large, but *just* not too large; that is, they're as large as they can be without going over into looking a bit thyroid: right at the edge of the envelope. They're brown. Not enough? OK. They are mahogany suns, ringed at the core with black. Her nose is small, small enough for me to wonder how she manages to fill her lungs through it without hyperventilating. (I like small noses; it's a self-hating thing.) Her nostrils curve slightly downwards, but hit her face flat, with no hint of the unnecessary extra depth that so often creates the snotbucket. The bald cushion below leads down to her upper lip, that I've never kissed. Like her eyes, her lips are full to the brim, but held there, their shape the shape of that meniscus. When she smiles, as she does now, she shows her one flaw, her teeth. Although very white, they are both higgledy *and* piggledy: pointed, and with no symmetry of line, like the Himalayas seen from a great distance. When she was younger, she should have worn a brace, but hated the taste of aluminium.

What else can I say? Large eyes. Small nose. Fangy teeth . . . she looks like Jezebel. Alice looks like Jezebel. Only she scratches me in the heart, rather than the face.

I hand her the wine, and she kisses me on the cheek. I don't want to make too much of this. You know – she kisses me on the cheek, it's no big deal. I mentally time the entire event, from 'hello' to the trace of eye-meeting, a dream of sexual consciousness, that follows the drawing apart of our faces – partly to work on the details later: 6.3 seconds, well, that's almost a personal best for the lad, just .9 of a second short of the European and Commonwealth record of 7.2 set when meeting outside the cinema before *Henry: Portrait of A Serial Killer* – but more just to elongate it, to slo-mo the movement of her face to my face, to freeze-frame her lips on my skin, holding it on pause, hold it, hold it, ah . . . the screen flips back to gibberish. It's no big deal.

I follow the back of her neck through the terracotta hallway; when the light around her hair turns blue, I know I'm in the living-room. The room smells fresh and clear, as if recently shaken and vacuumed; surfaces are reflective, books are in controlled lines on the shelves, the windows are transparent, the cushion covers are of the purest white, and, in the corner near the television, newspapers and listing magazines are stacked neatly together in a fucking *rack*, would you believe.

'Sorry the place is in such a mess,' Alice says, and goes out through the doorway, at the same time as Ben comes in, squeezing past her with no sense of great privilege. He too has a rich mop of curly black hair – I've always thought that that was probably the point of similitude around which their attraction initially curled – and caught in the frame together they look suddenly comical: a shot that Robinson's would use on their labels if only they were still allowed to. He kisses me as well. This is something I would rather he didn't do. I don't like men kissing me. 'Oh, that means you're actually a repressed homosexual.' Yes, yes, yes: every subconscious desire is a simple reverse of your conscious abhorrences; and I'm a Freudian Chinaman. I mean: when just the slightest element of down on a woman's upper lip is enough to sour my vision of her forever, then it is surely the truth, the not particularly broad-minded truth, that an entirely emery-papered male chin is not something I secretly crave resting human on my faithless arm.

'Drink?' he says, his large frame pulling away from mine with gravitational force. Ben's face is simultaneously gaunt and jowly, like . . . oh, what's his name? That American magician bloke.

'Don't mind if I do,' I say, wiping my cheek.

Drink/Don't Mind If I Do is a running joke of ours, a playing-at-being-adults joke; it's something we think of our parents as saying, *we* only say it ironically. Me and Ben, now into our late twenties, continue hard at these playing-at-being-adults jokes, but they are starting to have a ring of desperation about them.

He gets me a beer, a Sol, and a slice of lime to go with it. I marvel at the sheer order, the sheer total command of the known universe, that allows these people who do not live in a wine bar to actually have slices of lime on hand to go with Sol, as I probe it into the bottleneck and watch it fizz up in a matter/antimatter burst. I'm aware all the time of Alice's absence from the room. I swig the beer: as it hits my tongue I feel the usual immediate revulsion, followed by the usual deep instinctive crying-out for Tizer.

'Been to the gym today?' I say, sitting down on their unspeckled white sofa.

'Yep,' he says, falling into the armchair opposite. 'Do I look like it?'

'No. I would. If I'd been to the gym yesterday, I'd still look like it.'

He grins; Ben likes it when I confirm our positions, him Tarzan, me Janus.

'I've been working on the "pec deck",' he says, sticking a very clear pair of inverted commas around "pec deck".

'Aren't they uncertain about you down at that jockbox?' I say. 'I mean . . . look at you. Glasses. Obviously Jewish.' He frowns. 'Furrowed brow. Probably a copy of Dante's *Inferno* tucked into your sweatpants. Aren't they suspicious? Don't they think you're a spy?'

'No,' he says, his thickset nose, that looks as if it must have been broken once, but never has been, tilting upwards. 'They see through me. They know it's all a pose.'

'Going to the gym?'

'No. Pretending to be . . . an intellectual.' He looks me up and down. 'I haven't got the spindly body to carry it off.'

'Fuck off,' I say. 'You're not that narrow-minded. You can be thoughtful with pectorals.'

'Very good.'

'Thanks. And anyway, a proper meathead would never have used the word "spindly".'

'What word would he have used?'

I consider this for a second.

'Scrawny,' I say eventually.

He nods, and takes another swig. He seems to be thinking about whether or not to mention something.

'Gabe,' he says finally. 'D'you know where I went on Saturday?'

'White Hart Lane?'

'Before then. In the morning.'

'No. Should I?'

'Synagogue.'

Blimey.

'Synagogue? Which one?'

'The United.'

'In St John's Wood? Where we got barmitzvahed?'

'Yeah.'

I let out a whistle; which, to be honest, I'm not very good at, so it comes out as more of an overloud breath.

'Is Louis Fine still the rabbi?'

'Yeah. Still doing sermons about how it's not good enough to come just on Rosh Hashanah and Yom Kippur.'

'So . . .?' I say. 'What did you go there for? To discuss the bit of Torah you sang when you were thirteen?'

'No. I never knew what I was singing meant anyway. He taught it to me parrot fashion.'

'Better than him teaching it to you doggy fashion.'

Ben does a quick David Letterman-style rim shot on the arms of the armchair with his palms.

'Ho-*ho*!'

'But why did you go?'

'I dunno. I just wanted to see what it was like.'

'Don't you remember?'

'Yeah, 'course. I remember being really bored. But I wanted to see what it was like now I'm old enough to appreciate it.'

'Did Alice go with you?'

'No,' says her voice, instinctively making me turn round. She's come back into the room. 'They don't let coons in, do they?'

'What about Sammy Davis Junior?' I say.

'He's dead,' says Ben.

'So are most of the people in the front row, aren't they?'

'Yeah, yeah.'

'No, honestly. What are you thinking about? Aren't we clear about this? Jewishness, what's its value?'

'I know what you think.'

'What *I* think? Suddenly this is just my point of view?'

'Stop asking rhetorical questions. If you're going to denounce it you could at least stop sounding so Jewish.'

'Being brought up Jewish has one great value,' I say, carrying on with my well-rehearsed thoughts regardless. 'Finding Jewish stuff—'

'Really funny when you get older,' intones Ben with his eyes closed.

'It's true. Once you get a bit of distance from it, you realise what a hysterical religion it is. A creed of funny hats, silly vests and singalongs. Alice, you might have a very wide range of experience, but you'll never know what a laugh it is to sing Hud Gudyor—'

'The last song you sing on Passover,' says Ben to her, helpfully.

'—what a laugh it is to sing Hud Gudyor now, with the memory of how seriously you took it when you were four.'

'Oh dear,' says Alice, laughing. 'How bleak my future seems. Food'll be two minutes.'

She goes out again. Ben is looking at me with a strange mixture of weariness and apprehension, trying to suggest I am being tiresome but too unsure of his own position really to carry it off.

'That's why I'd bring my children up Jewish,' I say. 'I wouldn't want them to miss out on all those laughs.'

I look at him. (David Copperfield. That's it.) He runs his fingers through his teeming hair. Something is bothering him more deeply than this skittish conversation allows for; I sense he doesn't want to continue it.

'So have you given it some thought?' he says.

'What?'

'The job.'

I'm about to refuse categorically when Alice comes back in. She's wearing the black leggings and the big white woolly jumper. This is basically how I think women should dress all the time; clothes I associate, sentimentally, with sitting in front of the fire, or stumbling to answer the door after sex, or reading the papers together on Sunday morning. Alice really suits all that as well; despite all the order in the house, she always seems a bit rumpled, her smile the smile of a loved one just waking up and recognising you.

'Yeah, Gabe,' she says, 'it's a really good idea. I was thinking about it. You're the best person for it . . .'

'Why?'

'Because you're so opinionated. You'll say lots of stuff that people'll hate, and that'll be good for the magazine. Besides, the two of you working together, you'd have a laugh.'

She has been thinking about me when I'm not here. My face and name have been inside her brain.

'And I love you and I want to marry you. I'm sorry, Ben, I should've told you, but since I've been thinking about Gabriel while he's not been here, I've realised what a fantastic guy he is and, well, it's been a great three years, but goodbye.'

All right she doesn't. She says, 'Anyway, the food's ready, if you want to come through.'

In Gabriel Garcia Marquez's *Love in the Time of Cholera*, a suitor does not reveal his love for a married woman until her husband dies, and by then they are both in old age. They think it's all over, but then, in Marquez's vision, the pensioner lovers triumph over time, finding in their closing chapters a new narrative, happy news made more happy for coming through at the last minute, in life's PS. I take no comfort from this. I cannot conceive of joy made more supreme for coming at the close of play. I don't want to fuck in the five-minute warning; and besides, then there's floppy necks and enlarged earlobes and bald genitals and gravyish armpits and cold breathless death to think about. Try keeping a hard-on through all that when your prostate's already gone down. In the time of cholera, there just isn't the time. That's the trouble with thinking it's all over: it is now.

So fuck it. It'll bring me three millimetres closer to Alice; and, when I see her together with Ben, that's quite a sizeable fraction of my penis.

'All right, I'll do it,' I say, sitting down to eat. Dinner is some sort of Thai-style fish and noodle thing, absolutely brilliantly cooked.

'Grea—'

'But I can't come in to work before twelve. Ever. And I'll do it under a pseudonym, for cash, so I can keep signing on.'

'Oh, don't be such a tight wanker,' says Ben, filling up my glass. 'We'll see you all right.'

'Who the fuck *likes* signing on?' says Alice.

'You meet a lot of great guys down the dole office. It's a bit of a social club for me. And the lads down there, they've come to rely on me. Morris, what would he do without me?'

'Morris?' says Alice.

'Morris who once offered me thirty pounds to let him watch me urinate.'

'Well, perhaps we could take him on as well,' says Ben. 'Water sports editor.'

Alice laughs at this, short, breathy laughs across a trembling tongue. Through my jealous rage – *what about all* my *jokes that've made you laugh, have you forgotten them all suddenly, you slut, you whore* – I'm struck again by how well Ben and Alice gel, how there seems to be no trace of even the slightest couply tension between them. Unbelievable. Even the best of us, holding hands in front of the mirror of love, have seen one partner turn in a moment cross and sullen over nothing, over a follicle out of place on the itchy scalp of the relationship, an exasperatingly methodical way the other has of attaching the seatbelt, or of sitting, with lung-crushing complacency, too close to the television. But with Ben and Alice, it's not, as with most healthy couples, that any friction is quickly resolved into mutual forgiveness: there just isn't any friction.

'All right,' says Ben. 'We can do it that way if you like. Although if people start talking about how fantastic the weekly column is, I *know* you'll out yourself quicksmart.'

'Quicksmart?' I say.

'Yes. I don't know why I said it either. Did you buy the last edition?'

'No. I tried sliding it in between four copies of *Shaven Ravers*, but I was still too embarrassed.'

'I'll get you a copy,' he says, getting up and leaving the room.

There are always these times, when Ben leaves the room. The times when my Tourette's consciousness starts pressing at me, urgently, to shout, almost in surprise, almost as if it had never occurred to me before, 'Wha— Alice! Hey! Let's *fuck*!' To try and recreate, in two and half minutes, a lifetime's secret intimacy. But no, no: the best I can hope for is something which in fevered reminiscence five hours later I can transform into flirtatiousness. Once, in a restaurant, Ben having gone to park the car, the waiter asked Alice what dish she would like and she nodded in my direction and said 'This dish here.' There was, in my direction, I admit, as well as me, an open menu, and her nod may therefore have been directed towards the words *Lamb Dhansak* rather than to myself, but you're such a deeply encrusted cynic, you are, if you forbid me to surf for at least a second on this flutter of ambiguity.

There is a silence. I refer to my internal notebook of things to say.

'Ben?' she calls out, preferring (it seems to me) to speak to him even when he's in a different room. 'Can you get those sheets out for when Dina comes? They're in the airing cupboard.'

'Dina?' I say. 'I thought she was in America.'

'She's coming back, day after tomorrow. First time for five years.'

'God. What should I think of her as?'

'Pardon?'

'Relative-wise. What is she to me?'

Her eyelids beat rapidly for a second. 'Errm . . . she's a sort of cousin, I suppose. Your sister-in-law's sister. Is that a cousin?'

'It's a cousin by marriage,' says Ben, coming back in. Time's up. Visiting minute's come and gone. He chucks a copy of *Over The Line* down on the table in front of me.

'So how long she coming back for?' I say.

'Oh, for good, I think,' says Alice. 'New York's exhausted her, she says. And she's split up with the bloke she was going out with over there, so . . . y'know. She's staying with us until she finds somewhere else to live.'

'Right.'

Right. There's so much semiotics you can stick into a 'right'. When someone tells you it's over, meaning all your inner softness and misty yearning, all that's not being reciprocated, OK, our love is dust, the first thing you often say is just that: *right*. A flat deadpan *right* holding down the huge pressure of wrong. Purely linguistically, though, it's just a response, a tick, an empty agreeable echo. That's the end of the *right* spectrum I try and hit with this one – void of suggestion, a humdrum nod. Boiling over into it, though, is the feeling I am overcome by, of being a lifer, who, moving his bunk bed a couple of feet to the left, suddenly uncovers an escape tunnel. Sometimes, rarely, but in this instance with the certainty of a lost man at a fork in the road being pushed by an angel, I know exactly what it is I should say.

'Ben? Did you video *Match of the Day* last week?'

'Yeah. Newcastle were fantastic. It's incredible how much difference it makes, having a manager who was a very skilful player.'

I can't carry on talking about Dina, it'll seem pressing, probing, the reasons for doing so forming a visible scum on the surface of my conversation, so I head off, off into the safe secure world of football, the pre-charted discourse, where I can talk and talk and talk and give nothing away.

Alice seems lost in thought for a moment, but then interrupts, 'I think Keegan should've got the England job three years ago. You remember Jimmy Armfield recommended him to the FA, but they went with Venables anyway?'

Alice, you see, completes her royal flush with this ace, an unfaked passion for football. As a man, this is the range of emotions you go through when you meet a woman who professes to be interested in football: suspicion. That's it. The conviction lurks inside your sexist stomach that it can't be a pure interest, there's gotta be a sub-text – either she's doing it to be different, or, more likely, she's doing it to please her man, or, most likely, she's been ground down by years of her man constantly watching football and talking about football, and has decided that it's better to take in a bit of what Alan Hansen says than spend half her allotted time on this earth in silence. But Alice, it seems, has loved football since her father took her to watch Leyton Orient when she was four, and anyone who can recover from such a deeply scarring experience must have a real penchant for the game. She really does know about football, I can tell you, because I know about football, and I know about football for a reason she doesn't even have to worry about, which is that, in the late twentieth century, football trivia tests have replaced killing mammoths as a test of masculinity. 'What was the name of Port Vale's only capped player?' 'Which team has got the shortest name in the league?' 'Which six England captains played in the same Southampton team?' These, and many other questions, all actually mean, 'Do you have a penis?' It's terrible when the football trivia bully corners you in a bar and says, '*Right then. FA Cup winners since the war*', and you're meant to name them, and the losing teams, and the scores, and if he's a real psycho, the attendance figures, and if you get one wrong, you are poof of the month. The most appalling moment of all comes when he says, 'So what d'you think about Brian Harkness?' and you think *who the fuck is Brian Harkness?* but you can't admit you don't know, so you have a stab, you go for something that covers all possible ground, something like 'I think he's an interesting player', and then the football trivia bully says, 'He's the England *physio*', and you can see in his suddenly contemptuous eyes the image you've so lovingly projected of yourself curling black at the edges and burning up.

'. . . and Mick Channon?' Ben is saying.

'Yup,' says Alice, on her way out of the room with a pile of plates. 'That's the six.'

Ben turns his heavy head to me and smiles. He is proud, I think, of Alice's football nous; it is the trophy part of his wife.

The evening continues apace: I have a good time, eat twice as much as either Alice or Ben, we talk about people we've talked about before, the usual subjects are given slightly varying treatments, the air hangs still with familiarity. 12:48, I leave: too early for me, but I've noticed that others will start doing things like yawning and stretching round about this time, and that generally means the night's over. I leave without a kiss, from either: tired and smiling, they show me to the door. As I walk down their driveway, I turn back to see them silhouetted in the hallway light, and am overcome with a fierce urge to confess, to say stuff that all night has been swallowed. Honesty, it's such a pile-driving energy. I force it all down, and feel my future tumour glow on and off, once.

As I draw up to the kerb outside our house, I see The Man Who Lives Downstairs opening his door and going in. There are two flats in our house, and whatever used to be the front door has now been made into two separate doors, which allows The Man Who Lives Downstairs to come and go without ever saying a word to either me or Nick. He wears, as always, an ill-fitting fawn wool suit and black wide-brimmed hat, a sort of funereal sombrero, which he pulls down over his eyes whenever he sees anyone who might possibly say hello to him approaching. I've no idea what his name is, or what he does, but we know the phone number for the flat from the people who used to live there, and once, completely pissed, me and Nick rang him at three o'clock in the morning for a laugh. He just picked up the phone and said, quietly and carefully, as if he'd been waiting for it: 'Out.' *Out*. Ditching our plan of singing *What An Atmosphere* by Russ Abbott down the line, we replaced the receiver in silence, and sat there, sobered up with shame.

Out of charity, I wait for him to vanish inside before I get out of my car. I look up: the light in our living-room is off, but there is a flickering blue. I know what this means; as I come into our flat, I hear the whirr of the video being switched off, and the TV returning to its own programmes.

'*Poltergash*?' I say, hanging up my coat in the hallway.

'No,' says Nick's voice indignantly. '*Buttman's European Holiday II*.'

Ah, pornography. Sweet, sweet pornography.

When I go in, Nick is sitting topless in the big sofa's one matching armchair, methodically picking fleas off both the chair and himself and drowning them in a small willow-patterned cup of water. Jezebel does not have fleas, or at least she doesn't any more; I've got the scars from various collar fittings to prove it. But the chair in which Nick is presently sitting still has them. Presumably, Jezebel sat there at some point when she did have fleas, although, judging by their complete imperviousness to any of the powders on the market, I suspect she didn't just sit there, she spent some time there genetically designing a whole new breed of super-flea. If the powders don't work, what else can I do? I can't get a collar for the chair.

Nick, of course, could sit somewhere else, but he likes this chair: says it's got the best view of the telly. I suspect that what he likes, secretly, is killing fleas.

'How was it?' he asks, brushing his hands.

'Not like *Buttman's European Holiday II*.'

'Bad luck.'

I sit down on the big sofa, staring at the late-night screen. *The Equalizer*. Edward Woodward balancing the scales of justice. Perhaps I should give him a call.

It's probably best not to tell Nick anything about Dina. So I say, 'Her sister's coming back to England.'

'Whose?'

'Jezebel's. Who d'you think?'

'Alice's got a sister?'

'Yeah.'

'You never mentioned it.' He looks idly down at his left forearm, then moves his right hand to just below the elbow, the thumb and index finger poised to pinch. A second later, they shut, faster than a fairground dip. He picks up the willow-patterned cup and surveys the surface of the water, black with bloated fleas.

'So . . . ?' I say.

'So, is she fit?' he says, opening his thumb and index finger and flicking the flea into the cup.

'I've never met her.' *Except in my dreams*.

'Hmm. She must be all right if she looks like Alice.'

'I'd have to go along with that.'

'But what if she looks really like Alice, but she's mentally disabled?'

'Oh fuck off, Nick.'

'No, I mean it, what if she looks like your fantasy woman, but she's got a mental age of four?'

'Then I suppose she'd have to go out with you. Night night.'

Normally, I'd stay up till three watching TV with him – we've got cable TV, so anything at all – German game shows, Spanish discussion programmes, commercial presentations. Commercial presentations are brilliant, whole half-hours on the miracle of television devoted to Closet Maximisers and Juice Tigers and Perfect Presses, hosted by English salesmen and women, in front of American studio audiences who, remunerated for their efforts, clap and cheer and whoop the products along their road to saledom. As another one comes on, the moles feel the tremors and reassure their young, 'Hush. It's only John Logie Baird spinning again.' Naff to the point of art, sales techniques cruder than a Millwall fan's foreplay, and yet, at the end of them, all you want is a Closet Maximiser, or a Perfect Press, or a Juice Tiger. You'd kill your own mother for one sophisticated party drink from a Juice Tiger.

But tonight, I'd rather just get straight into the sheetless vigil: there's a lot to think about. I reckon four and a half hours should just about cover it.

3

Talking about killing your own mother . . .

'Hi, lover! How's things? I'm just glad we're able to touch base. I've been trying to dovetail things together with you and there just hasn't been the time, has there? The thing is what with the HAC meeting and going up to Harrogate for the aeronautical auction, I've been literally rushed off my feet. Quite literally.'

'WILL YOU FUCKING SHUT UP, YOU STUPID CHATTERING OLD WANKBAG!'

I'm round at my parents' house, 22 Salmon Street, Wembley Park. My mother is talking as ever about two things: herself, and The Hindenburg. The Hindenburg, or LZ 129 to give it its technical name, was the last great Zeppelin ever to be built for commercial use, and it exploded disastrously over Manhattan during its seventy-third Atlantic crossing on 6 May 1937, killing twenty-two crew members and twelve passengers. My grandfather, my mother's father, was one of the original designers, before he lost his job, his house and later all his brothers and sisters because he was Jewish; but my mother has made it her life's mission that he and his work should not be forgotten, and she is both President and founder member of the HAC: The Hindenburg Appreciation Circle, formerly a sub-section of the Zeppelin Remembrance Society – the acronym ZRS was the serial number of some other big blimp – but which broke off from its parent association following an enormous row at an East Finchley branch meeting over the airspeed of the Graf Zeppelin (four knots slower than The Hindenburg, according to my mother).

The HAC – originally it was the HAS, The Hindenburg Appreciation Society, but at a vote taken at the second meeting it was decided that four people only really constituted a Circle – meets every two weeks, normally at my parents' house, although recently there has been talk of one of the other members perhaps providing the tea and cakes for a change. My parents' house is a good setting for the HAC, as the walls groan from the weight of a thousand pictures of the great rigid dirigible, from tin-plate models of it, from books about it, 500 or so of which are in fact copies of my mother's own *The Hindenburg And Me*, and from various actual bits and pieces spewed out from it over Manhattan Island that fateful day, including Kapitan Lehmann's hat, and the original black bakelite radio. At the meetings, they talk about The Hindenburg a lot, I guess; they have readings from aviation history journals about it and related subjects, especially if Irene Jacoby happens to be the author; they cluck over new pieces of memorabilia; they have heated debates about whether the passenger cabins included private showers or just WCs; they even discuss the Nazi Party's use of the airship as a propaganda icon; but there is one Hindenburg-related event they never, ever mention: the crash. A Martian could land on Earth at an HAC meeting – not really a lucky turn of events for the Martian, to be honest – and never find out that The Hindenburg ever exploded; he could come again and again and again, and still never find out, although obviously, by that time, there may be talk of him perhaps providing the tea and cakes for a change.

Everything my mother does is in some way Hindenburg-related. Her car number-plate is LZ 129; the one band I was never allowed to bring any records of into the house was Led Zeppelin (check out their first album cover); she has a T-shirt – this is true – that says *I heart The Hindenburg*. Combine all this with a tendency to overuse the phrases 'dovetail' and 'touch base': that's my mum.

My father shouts at her. That's all he does these days. He shouts at my mother. All right, be fair: he doesn't just shout at her. He shouts and swears at her. And, to give him credit, he does comes up with some corking swearing. My father is the WBC (Wanking Bastard Cunt) Heavyweight Champion of Swearing. The appellation 'wankbag' is just at the beginning of his range. 'Cunthead', 'Tossturner', 'Fuckslob', 'Hairy Great Pudding-Face Arsewank' – thirty-two years with my mother has really stretched his linguistic invention.

'Shush, Stuart.'

'DON'T TELL ME TO FUCKING SHUSH, YOU INFURIATING SHITBASKET!!!'

My mother laughs. It might seem strange, but I suppose it's the obvious defence, not only against being called a shitbasket, but also against facing up to thirty-two years down the shitbasket.

'SHE'S LAUGHING! SHE'S BLOODY LAUGHING NOW, THE RIDIKALUS OLD BOLLOCK-WAGON!'

My dad cannot pronounce the softish 'c' in ridiculous, perhaps because the whole idea of softness is alien to him, so it always comes out like this: *ridikalus*. The furrows that run from his trumpet-shaped nose to well below his always slightly blistered lips cut deep into his patchily shaven cheeks as he shouts; and then relax a little as he stomps off into the hallway, expressed, I think, fulfilled.

'Dad's in a good mood,' I say.

'Isn't he?' says my mother, agreeing. 'I think he's happier now he's moved to the new offices.'

Actually, when I say swearing at my mother is all my father does these days, what I really mean is that's all he does these mornings and nights; days he works as some kind of sales manager for Amstrad, although the idea of him as a salesman, as someone who sweet-talks anyone into anything, is unimaginable to me.

'I think those tranquillisers the doctor prescribed for him have helped as well,' she continues, unironically. Irony is not part of her remit. In her vision of things, one of a million rays of darkness refracted through her prism of self-delusion, the man on her left calling her a bollock-wagon has just been rather charming.

She takes off her big white glasses. As she raises her face again, I realise that these too are a defence, a shield: for a second, the hole they leave shows her old and troubled, the scars visible at least on her outer layer even if the lead coating underneath is thirty-two years thick. Inside her oval nostrils the skin is pink as chicken flesh.

'So,' she says, pausing deliberately, a deliberation I've felt irritatingly often before, always signalling a gear-change into serious talk now, 'have you had any job news?'

I have an instinctive desire to hide developments in my life from my mother, because if I tell her, and it pleases her, then, perversely, immaturely, I feel defeated. Or perhaps not so perversely: because I know she will take it and transform it, somehow, to fit in with her own narrative. She will take it into her parallel universe of how everything should be and then, forever, part of it will not exist any more.

'Yeah,' I say over-wearily, in the hope that by sounding unbothered about it she will leave her strange emotional money uninvested, 'I've got a job doing some writing.'

'Really!' she says excitedly.

'On Ben's magazine.'

'Oh.' Her disappointment, for a second, is entirely obvious; then it gets shuttled, like all her other disappointments, the big ones and the daily ones, into her readjustment mill. 'That's good. Of course that might lead on to all sorts of other things.'

'Like what?' I say, harshly. Sometimes I just have to sadistically corner her. But she of course is boxing in a round ring.

'Well, you know, loads of things. I mean, the first thing I ever wrote was just a little piece in *Aviator's Weekly* about the aluminium piano in the starboard side saloon, and, I can promise you, Gabriel, I never thought that would lead to anything. But – it's amazing, really – it was that article that interested Joy, and next thing you know she was on the phone and I was starting work on *Lighter Than Air*. Well, as you know, Peter Blandham didn't like it at first . . .'

No, of course I didn't know. I don't know who the fuck Peter Blandham is. But this never stops Irene Jacoby. She has wrapped herself so warmly in her solipsistic cloak that she assumes everyone is born already intimate with her weird cast of Hindenburgabilia characters. Peter Blandham, Carrie Rosenfield, Jeremy Elton, Derek – Derek I know so well we're just on first name terms – Patsy White, Laurence St Hilaire, and the Tinderfields: names that pass on the conveyor belt of my mother's conversation like prizes on *The Generation Game* – you don't know where they've come from, or where they're going to, you just know you're supposed to remember them.

'. . . and so I told him, "Rolf. If that's the way you want to play it, so be it. But don't come crying to me when half the HAC demand to examine these so-called 'propellers'."'

Perhaps she has told me who half these people are at some stage. It's difficult to tell, because once she's started talking to me properly, my faculties go into shutdown. Sometimes I have to be fed intravenously.

'Right,' I say, nodding like a local news reporter doing a reaction 'noddy'. Another pause, another heavy sense of something significant about to be said.

'WHAT HAVE YOU DONE WITH MY BLOODY SHOES, YOU UNBELIEVABLE SPUNKERCHIEF!!!'

Even from upstairs, my father's voice threatens to draw blood out of my eardrums. Or possibly he's shouting from inside my head.

'They're inside the cupboard, darling,' she says, unstruck by the imbalance between *darling* and *spunkerchief*. 'So . . .' (This to me, resonant) '. . . still no girlfriend?'

If I strangle somewhat before telling my mother about odd little career developments, how much less breath do I have in my lungs to reveal to her the contours of my desire. I mean, y'know, I tell her how long it took me to drive here and it feels like she's got something on me.

'You know, Gabriel, if there's anything you want to tell me about, you always can. You can always come to me first.'

'What do you mean?'

'Well, it turns out the Rosenfelds' boy is gay, and—'

'I'm not gay.'

'Oh.'

'There might be somebody . . .' I say hesitantly, not knowing why I'm telling her, except, perhaps, because I've formulated the hope in my mind and expressing it out loud seems like it'll make it happen: only wishes you actually *tell* the genie come true. Although I could've hoped for a less suburban genie.

Her eyes flick into life. 'Yes?'

'Oh, it's probably nothing. There's a woman I know who's coming back from America and . . .' *time to lie* '. . . we got on really well before she went, so maybe something'll happen. Then again, maybe it won't.'

'Who is she?'

'Her name's Dina.'

My mother has two pairs of diagonal lines set, with almost fastidious symmetry, on either side of her brow, which, while she remains untroubled, resemble, I have always thought, the badge a police sergeant wears on his upper arm to indicate his rank; but when she frowns, as she does now, these lines curve to meet in the middle, hovering above her eyes like two seagulls, or rather, like a doodle of two seagulls.

'Dina?' she says as if the name rings a bell, which indeed it should; I feel a pinch of dread, as I have left out a vital piece of information about this woman who, apparently, I got on really well with before she went to America. A second later, however, and my mother pushes her lower lip over her upper and shakes her head: if only Dina had had the sense to own, I don't know, an authentic *Deutsche Zeppelin Reederei* compass, it would've been such a different story.

'She sounds lovely,' she says, on what basis I'm not sure. 'What does she do?'

Already I'm pissed off that I've told her; her questions feel like incest. I say, with a hard face, and a hard voice, 'Look, there's no point in telling you a lot about her. If something works out, you'll meet her. Otherwise it's just a waste of time.'

She looks down, hurt. I am much too harsh with my mother – I'm struck by this often, now, and feel guilty. It's a tic, a gene-tic, driven deep into my DNA by my dad – I should fight it.

In the filial silence, I stare blankly round the dining-room. Different size models of The Hindenburg sit fatly on far too many shelves. Pride of place is taken by the 1:1000 scale model originally made by my grandfather, which hangs as a mobile from the middle of the ceiling, correct in every detail except for the lack of swastikas on its tail; as a child, I was terrified of its continual circling. By the way, in case you might be wondering: I don't think my mother's obsession has a phallic basis. I don't think so. Well, I'd rather *not* think so. It's too simple, apart from anything, too – once again – nursery Freud. Bloody Freud: that Oedipal Complex stuff – one hundred years from now, historians will look back on that theory as we look back on the medieval idea that all being is composed of four humours, earth, air, fire and water, as a quaint but misguided kit of the human psyche.

'Look, I'd better be going,' I say to my mother.

'So soon? Don't you want to stay for dinner?' she says.

I feel I should, at this point, offer some redeeming feature about my mother; unfortunately, her cooking is not it. My mother's idea of cooking is to put an enormous vat of water on the stove for two or three days, occasionally throwing in some giblets and the odd claw: this she then scoops out into bowls and calls chicken soup. Everything else she just overcooks wildly. For her, cooking a steak blackened, well-done, and dry as a boot is essentially doing it *tartare*; by the time she gets to medium rare, it's as hard as a housebrick. Steak, though, isn't really part of her repertoire; most the time she makes stews, which is what my dad likes – Stu's Stews, my mum calls them, only to be told not to be such a cack-brained whore – that, again, spend two or three days on the stove until the inside of each bite-sized morsel turns to sand.

'Well, y'know, if I'm ever gonna get any of this writing done for Ben . . .' I say, getting up.

'Have you ever thought about getting what I call a "word processor"?' (Another odd habit – thinking some entirely standard terminology is peculiar only to her.)

'I can't afford a word processor.' My coat's on. 'Bye, Dad!' A wordless grunt from upstairs. My father doesn't really swear at anyone else except for my mother, but seems to have got to the stage where he doesn't know how to communicate in any other way: so if it's not my mother, he just grunts.

She kisses me at the door. As her face moves backwards, I catch her eyes, lit through the glass of the porch by the setting Wembley Park sun, and feel, through all my instinctive irritation, the pull of blood. I should apologise, I think, for everything – for cruel dismissive thoughts, for taking the piss, for my father, for never, ever listening. It doesn't matter how silly your life is: you made me, I should have more respect. It is *her* mouth, however, that opens, and it seems as if I won't have to say the words, that she is about to frame them for me, and we'll part, for once, having truly spoken.

'Don't be a Jewish post office!' she says. I've never quite understood what this means.

'I won't,' I reply anyway.

4

I've met Dina. Just now. She's in the living-room, now.

Last night, I struggled for over two hours against insomnia's secondary tumour, known medically as early morning wakefulness. This, an addition to my night-timetable that first developed about five years ago, normally kicks in with menaces around 7:00, although not always, as it works on a kind of satanic flexi-time: 7:00 is based on getting up at my normal time of later than ten, but if I *have* to get up at say, 8:00, the wake-up call will then come around 5:00 – if I have to get up at 6:00 it will come at 3:00 – and so on and so forth, my body clock, which hates my body, cleverly readjusting around my alarm clock. But it is, in evolutionary terms, a relatively new thing. Previously, my insomnia used to take the form of simply being hell to get to sleep. But once asleep that was it. So it was just a question of getting through the two or three hours before unconsciousness woke up and that'd be that. Piece of cake. But now I've still got the two or three hours to get through and then four hours after that I'm up, my eyes are open and my brain is running full-pelt towards the wall, strung out on a loop tape of whatever is number seventeen in the charts. Consider: the stuck needle is not even a possibility any more on modern music formats, and why, why, I'll tell you why, because it's too frightening to imagine some of this music repeated over and over again for more than five seconds. So, please, have some sympathy, think for a moment about the Bosch-like torture of hearing the needle in the brain snag on one phrase of a Two Unlimited track again and again and again and again and again and again and again and again and again and again and again and again and again and again and again and again and again and again, each time more frantically, for an eternity.

The early morning stuff having been particularly bad last night, I got up even later than usual, at one. I put on my dressing-gown, which, despite being the only item of clothing I wear for most of every single day, I never ever wash – sometimes I find sperm stains on it that make me feel *nostalgic* – and went downstairs. The answerphone's red light flashed seven times like a teacher's staccato reprimand – *How. Many. Times. Must. You. Be. Told.* – but I'd heard them all; nothing gets past me when I'm fast asleep. One from my mother, thanking me for coming over last night, and reminding me, above the voice in the background, to keep an eye out for Brian Truscott, two that just rang off (so heart-breaking, the expectant beep, full of hope and polite inquiry, crushed by the mundane macho *burrrrrr*), and four from Ben, in increasing degrees of exasperation, telling me to fucking get up and start writing that article.

I made some coffee. Because it expends two calories less energy than using the kettle, I poured some Nescafé into a cup, added cold water and stuck it in the microwave for one minute thirty seconds. As it cooked, to upset the fly, I put on *Away From The Numbers* by The Jam.

The phone rang. Even though I knew who it was, my heart-strings vibrated, as always, to the electronic bell-ring of possibility. I picked it up.

'I'm doing it.'

'No you're not. You've just got up.'

'I'm doing it now.'

'No. No. You're sitting around coming out of a coma for two hours now. Look, you said you'd have something for me by twelve today.'

'Twelve? I've never said I'll have something for anyone by twelve on any day.'

'Oh God. Ring me when you've written the first sentence.' Then, winding up, 'I'll speak to you this afternoon—'

'Ben. Hold on.'

'Yeah?'

Sometimes, in the morning, with my consciousness still marinated in dreams, I won't stop myself. I'll say things.

'Has Dina arrived?'

'Who? Oh, Dina, yeah. She's getting through jet-lag, so Alice has stayed at home with her.'

'Right. Cunt.'

'Cunt.'

So two hours later, I was still sitting in the kitchen. I was working out a graph of difference, Alice on the *y* axis, Dina on the *x* axis, estimating how much identity I could stomach. Then I thought, *OK, as long as the voice is the same basic sin wave*. Then I panicked, feeling my motivation to be transparent. (Consider this scenario. Dina looks like Alice. I ask her out. She says no. I'm no better off, with the basic ball-park of my heart's secret desire revealed.) Then the doorbell rang.

I opened the door to this tableau: my brother, my heart's secret desire, and a kind of version of my heart's secret desire on distort. Take whatever picture you've got of Alice so far and run it through a pixillator – widen the nostrils two millimetres, blue the eyes, short and blonde-dye the hair, round out the cheeks slightly, curve the corners of the mouth down six degrees: that's Dina. These differences made my heart stutter a bit towards her, to be honest; she was an electric magnet with Norman Collier's contact switch – I was drawn and then stopped (oh, the jaw's rounder), drawn and stopped (oh, longer fingers), drawn and then sent running back (oh, the breasts are smaller). Her clothes, though, suggested more extreme polarities: while Alice stood there in jeans and a suede jacket, Dina was wearing a green satin shirt with huge pointy collars, a transparent plastic mac, and white patent leather knee-length platform boots.

'You know, Gabe,' said Ben, 'I do like that dressing-gown.'

'Cheers.'

'Thought I'd pop round and pick up that article.'

'Ah. Right. Hello,' I said, turning to Dina, 'I'm Gabriel.'

'Hi. Dina.'

Little men in my head, very similar to The Numbskulls in *The Beezer*, went to work processing her voice against Alice's.

Timbre: similar. Pitch: very similar. Breathiness/sibilance ratio: more data required.

'Very nice to meet you.'

'Um . . . yes. You too.'

OK?

Yeah, hold on.

'So, can we come in?'

Breathiness/sibilance ratio: similar enough.

'Yeah, definitely. Sorry, I just got up.'

Inside the kitchen, I pulled some cups out of the sink to make them all coffee: Douwe Egberts, espresso. Absent-mindedly, I scanned the cork board hanging above the sink, full of reproaches, demands that have moved through the whole spectrum from blue to red, some even edging on to an as yet undiscovered colour; pinned, they jostle for position there amongst endless Polaroids of Nick, topless, grinning, and pointing to various different blonde women.

'Are those cups clean?' said Ben, sitting his bulky but fat-free frame on the cracked Formica kitchen table.

'Yeah, yeah.'

'He never used to wash anything up at home.'

'Ben, I *have* written something,' I said, pointing him towards three sheets of A4 lying next to the empty-but-for-one-wrinkled-orange fruit bowl. 'It's not finished. And it's probably shit.'

'You write for the magazine?' said Dina absent-mindedly, her head on a slow spin round the kitchen, taking it all in like a health visitor about to write a very depressing report.

'Sort of. A columnist. A ranter.'

'Oh. What's it about?'

'Matthew Le Tissier.'

'Who?'

Ah. There goes the curve of difference, up into the black.

'He plays for—'

'Southampton,' said Alice. 'Venables wouldn't play him, 'cos there's a myth about him that he's lazy; but that's just to do with what he looks like – he actually created and scored more goals in the last three seasons than any other midfield player.'

'That's more or less *précis*ed what you say here,' said Ben, putting the article down.

'I know.' I turned to face Alice. 'Why don't you just be the columnist?'

'Naaah. I'm sure you've expressed it much better.'

'You have actually,' said Ben. 'I like this bit: *Seeing Le Tissier in the Southampton line-up is like finding a Matisse amongst a row of Rolf Harrises*. I think this could be the making of something, this column.'

'When's it going in?'

'Next week. Would've been this week, but Ruth won't work late Friday nights any more, so the typesetting all seems to take that much longer.'

'Tell her to stop seeing that rabbi.'

'He's not a rabbi. And she has stopped seeing him.'

So here I am, in my bedroom, putting some clothes on. I take my dressing-gown off and, as I bend into my boxer pants, I catch sight of my naked body in the mirror. My genitals hang complacent, oblivious of the drama they're responsible for. As often, I get seized with the urge to cut them off and be done with it.

The rest of my body I notice is going the way of all flesh; three lines cut into the contours of my bend. Fuck. *Three*. It used to be two. My stomach is *corrugating*. I stand up straight and force it out as far as it will go. I look pregnant. This is a good move though, because when I relax and the muscles fall back into place, the waist size seems somehow more acceptable. That's how rotundity works. It creeps up on you, and day by day you accustom yourself to it, your physical self-image adjusts, and then you're fine, except for that terrible, truth-trapping moment when you catch yourself suddenly in a strange mirror, a shop, a friend's mantelpiece, and then it's: How did I get like *this*? And I'm not a naturally fat person. I don't tend to fat. So instead of putting on weight equally all over, I'm getting it in pockets – y'know, a hammock-chin, a clay-mould-belly. I'm sure the other day I noticed my *elbows* were plumper. Diet, you say. Thank you. But the thing is, I get terrible hunger pains if I don't eat. And if I do eat, but I don't have any pudding, then I get a terrible tingling pain along both sides of my jaw. It doesn't seem fair to me that because of this disability I should be punished by getting fat.

So, of course, *of course*, none of the clothes that make me look any good are clean. I have to scrabble around for ages in my weird-smelling laundry basket (it doesn't smell horrible, it's just in a different dimension of smell, like a Time Lord's dirty washing) and eventually fish out the baggy black T-shirt with a red stripe down the middle that I always plump for in emergencies. I put on my black jeans, but can't get the top button done up on them, so I leave it undone, covered over by the T-shirt. I even consider wearing my hat, this little pointy green thing with a black African band round it I bought from Camden Lock, but hats: you know, you just can't wear them nonchalantly, can you? It's not like: this is just something I've thrown on, a hat. It's really saying *I'm wearing this*; 'hat', it's saying, in a way that trousers never say 'trousers' – where trousers say 'trousers', a hat says HAAAAT – it's the nearest thing we have to a codpiece. And anyway, I can't find it.

Some sort of cry from downstairs – I'm missing something, I'm missing something. One last look in the mirror – oh good, my hair's decided to reconstruct some of the later work of Henry Moore – and I'm in the living-room.

'What's happened?' I say. The three of them are crouching in a tight huddle at the base of the great sofa, like American footballers planning their next play.

'Dina tried to stroke Jezebel,' says Alice, without looking up, her gaze intent on her sister.

'Oh God, no. You OK?'

Dina turns to me. Enticingly, her face betrays less complacency than Alice's. She is not so emotionally sure, I think. Her eyes are a shallow blue, like a rock pool you wouldn't chance diving straight into. The lashes are vulnerably long. Her nose looks ever so slightly squashy, as if there is no bone in the tip. Her lips are not entirely symmetrical: the top left-hand section is fuller than its opposite number on the right. There is, devastatingly for me, just the merest hint of Jolene-bleached down underneath her nostrils, and again on both sides of her mouth. Her cheeks are round and full. She has a faint scar reaching from the top of her forehead to just above her right temple. Well, she does since she tried to stroke Jezebel, anyway.

'I think so,' she says, dabbing at her wound gently with her right hand. 'She's not rabid, is she?'

I look at Jezebel, who is scowling in the corner of the living-room, less as if someone has tried to stroke her and more as if a tribe of wild Manx are pinning her there while their chief eats contentedly from her bowl.

'Well . . . I wouldn't know.'

'If we base it on character alone,' says Ben, 'I'd say she passed the rabid stage about two years ago.'

Dina gets up from her crouching position, quite quickly, quick enough to convey a slight sense of irritation at Ben and Alice's concern, and moves to sit down.

'Er . . . not there,' I say. 'The sofa's much more comfortable.'

She halts in mid-sit, and raises her eyebrow at me. Properly, classically, she raises her eyebrow. Goodness. This is a fantastic ability if you can do it. It's just a muscle thing, of course, but a really good, genuine raised eyebrow is a better weapon in your comeback armoury than a hundred plagiarised Oscar Wilde-isms. I can't do it. I've practised in front of the mirror, but it always comes out as a twisted squint, and, in truth, the rebuttal value of a cross between Patrick Moore and David Blunkett is virtually nil. It immediately appears to add about fifty points to her IQ.

'Honestly,' I say, trying to fend off a terrible vision of her covered in enormous bubonic bites. She shrugs, but thankfully moves away from the chair, to join Alice and Ben on the sofa. I sit on the floor, not, obviously, because there is no room for me on the sofa, but because I feel we'd look a bit ridiculous all sitting in a line.

'So, Dina,' I say, adopting a let's-get-to-know-each-other tone that I realise straight away sounds naffer than Peter Frampton on eight-track, 'how was America?'

Oh my God, she's raised the other one. She can do both! That I've never seen before.

'Good,' she says. 'It was good. It was America.'

And instantaneously manages to invest this otherwise meaningless remark with a sense of weight, of significance left unstated, of, y'know, enigma.

'Have you been there?' she says.

'Uh . . . I was born there.'

'You were born there?'

'Yeah. Upstate. Place called Troy. Do you know it?'

'No. Well, I've heard of it. But I've never been there. How long did you live there?'

'Oh . . . four months. Our parents lived there for a couple of years soon after they got married.'

'So . . . was Ben born there too?'

'Yeah,' says Ben.

'I never knew that, Alice.'

'You live and learn, Dina,' Alice replies.

There is a silence. Then Dina says brightly, 'Maybe that's why you're an insomniac.'

'Huh?'

'You're an insomniac, right?'

'Yeah . . .'

'What time d'you normally get to sleep?'

'Um . . . I dunno. It varies. About five o'clock, I think, on average.'

'Right. How far behind is New York? In time.'

'I don't know.'

'Hey,' says Alice. 'Yeah. Five hours.'

This is not dawning on me. 'So?'

'So . . .' says Dina, with the force of someone whose point is at last in their sights, 'that's how much your body clock's out of joint. Presumably it was set, originally, for American time, when you were a baby – and for some reason, got stuck like that. Five hours behind.'

Fuck. I can't believe it. I've thought and thought about insomnia. I've spent every minute of my waking night turning the subject on a spit in my head – and that's never struck me before. I'm speechless.

'But then Ben would be an insomniac as well, wouldn't he?' says Alice. Then, turning to him, 'And he sleeps like a baby. Don't you, darling?' She puts her arm round his shoulders, ironically. But she doesn't mean it ironically. That's just the late twentieth century – all public utterance must be couched in a crude, basic irony. Check it out next time you listen to Radio One. I know she doesn't mean it ironically.

'Not necessarily,' says Dina, clearly a bit miffed at this easy trashing of her big theory. 'Obviously, it might not affect everyone the same way. Y'know, other factors might have to be in place as well.'

'Oh, Dina . . .' says Alice.

'What?' says Dina tersely. I detect some tension between them.

'Why are you always convinced that you can figure people out, just like that? You've just met Gabriel.'

'I don't think I can figure him out. I'm just making a suggestion, that's all.'

Ah, hold on. She has the faintest trace of American in her voice. That's OK: that's sexy. It doesn't sound contrived, it sounds genuine, like it's actually got there by osmosis. There's really nothing worse than English people who go to America and within weeks are talking like Casey Kasem. It's a kind of physical law, that, I think: if you're English, the depth of your soul is calibrated in inverse proportion to how quickly you start sounding American in America. I remember on *The Word* once seeing Amanda de Cadanet in Los Angeles pick up a full American accent *during* an interview with Keanu Reeves.

'No,' I intervene. 'I think it's a great suggestion.'

Alice looks at me in blank surprise. Perhaps, unconsciously, she is aware of the fact that I've never contradicted her before.

'You might be right, Dina. That means, then, that if I went back to New York, I wouldn't have insomnia!'

'Yeah . . . I guess so.'

I feel, strangely, that some sort of bond between me and Dina has come out of this conversation. A bond which seems to have something to do with a collective annoyance at Ben and Alice, and their infuriating happiness. She looks at me somewhat slyly, and drinks her coffee, and once again raises her left eyebrow. I think I may have got somewhere. Then she starts coughing, violently.

'Oh. Ah! Oo. Aaaaha. *Caaaaahaaa!*'

'Oh my God, what's the matter?' says Ben.

Dina quickly stuffs her fingers inside her mouth. Two seconds later, she brings her hand out, and twists her palm upwards. She looks down, then looks up. Her eyebrows remain resolutely down.

'For fuck's sake, Gabriel . . .' she says, struggling to shout against the thickness of the hump-backed toad in her throat '. . . whose are the *toe-nails*?'

5

Something really weird is happening.

You know Nick? Nick. My flatmate. The Bradford supporter. Yeah, that's right, him. You've got a take on him by now, I presume. Superlad. Porn, football and lewd remark king. All that. Well, he's had a bit of a funny turn.

The day Alice, Ben and Dina came round, he stayed in his room because he'd just gone on some massive bender with the Bradford supporters club. Then, yesterday, at 12:20, I got up, went to load the espresso machine, and suddenly Nick bursts in and starts telling me how, while on the bender, he'd got really, really stoned. Now, I'm not much fussed about drugs anyway, but I'm considerably less fussed about drug stories. I mean, I'm not averse to the odd altered state now and again, but nothing seems more shit, unoriginal and fundamentally 1981 to me than long anecdotes about how out of your tree you were on Saturday night, how you ate forty-five Dime bars, how the police stopped you for driving too slowly, and how it was so funny. So I wasn't really listening properly – I was concentrating on the espresso machine which, recently, has started producing far more steam and noise than liquid – until suddenly, above all the boiling and toiling, I heard him say '. . . and I saw into the heart of light, the centre of all things.'

'Eh?' I said, not unreasonably.

'The heart of light,' said Nick. 'I saw . . . with new eyes. The world as it's meant to be seen – fresh, naked, real.' He paused, as if building up to something. 'Y'know that tree halfway down the road?'

'Tree?'

'Y'know, the poplar.'

I looked at him. Had Dr Johnson been there at that point, he would have noted my expression, got out his quill, opened his enormous compendium, and completely rewritten his definition of the word 'blankly'.

'You know the *names* of different kinds of *tree*?' I said incredulously.

'Um . . . well, I think it's a poplar.'

'Isn't that a really big tree with a pointy top?'

'It's not important,' said Nick hurriedly. 'What I mean is, there's a tree down there, right? And I looked at this tree, and I thought: This is The Tree. With a capital T.'

'What?'

'Eh?'

'The or Tree?'

Nick thought about this for, literally, ten seconds.

'Both, I think. But it was, it was like, the perfect tree, the Platonic idea of a tree.'

The espresso machine gave out a huge Falstaffian belch. Steam billowed from the shower-head like a little man inside it had just put his tiny wet dungarees into a miniature industrial laundry-press. And drop, drop, drop – three aromatic black tears fell sadly and individually into the silver jug below. God. My espresso machine is constipated.

'Nick,' I said, '*where* did you get stoned?'

'At The Red Pheasant.'

'They smoke dope at the London Bradford club outing?'

A strange light came into his eyes. 'There was this . . . *woman* there. *Fran*. She was passing round a pipe. And she was fucking incredible. Saying incredible things.'

'About trees?'

'About everything.'

'She supports Bradford . . .?'

Nick frowned. 'Um . . . I dunno. It doesn't matter.'

That was when I first started to worry. Nick has never not known someone's attitude to Bradford City. He is possibly the only person in history to have sent off a lonely hearts appeal which included the reply condition 'must be season ticket holder at The Valley Parade'. He has *Cec Podd 502* – Cec Podd, whatever else you might think it is, is the name of the player who holds the record for most league appearances for Bradford (yes, you've guessed it, 502) – tattooed on the back of his knee (a deliberately painful place for a tattoo, demonstrating hardness and commitment). I felt my normality twisting.

'Nick,' I said, 'are you OK?'

Nick looked at me intensely, one of those American 'I really really care' kind of looks. 'Gabe. I'm more than OK. I'm beyond OK. I'm . . .' And here he paused, and looked down, as if searching for the *mot juste*. Lying against the leg of the breakfast table was one of his slippers. He picked it up and held it proudly above his head with both hands, like it was Kunte Kinte. 'I'm *Zebedee*,' he said emphatically.

And then jumped two-footed into the air. He dropped the slipper, and, holding his arms outstretched on either side of him, bounced out of the room. Two seconds later, he bounced in again.

'From *The Magic Roundabout*,' he said helpfully.

Then, this morning, round about 2.15 p.m., I couldn't find Jezebel. I was looking for her because I'd just bought a new scratching-post, part of my regular programme of trying to get her to work out her anger on something else other than people; it's not been successful so far – this is her third scratching-post, and she's shown no interest in a whole stream of clockwork mice, bits of fluff on strings, and dangling spiders – however: this one is stuffed with catnip, so you never know. But I couldn't find her; I was calling and calling for her in the street. I'd started to contemplate putting up one of those heart-breaking notices you see on London trees – something like 'Lost: female tortoiseshell maniacal death-claw killer. If seen, do not approach without all-over body tarpaulin' – but I've always associated those notices with a basic admission that your cat's already dead. So, fearing the worst, I'd got to that familiar cat-owner's crisis-point – a place somewhere between utter total despair and idle contemplation of how sweet a new kitten would be – when suddenly, from Nick's room, I heard, quite clearly, a low, muted purr.

Initially I thought it was some sort of aural mirage brought on by desperation. You see, firstly, Jezebel never purrs. She'll hiss, obviously, a reptilian, visceral slow puncture; and regularly, after she's chundered, she'll give a short, crisp mew, which I think means 'clean that up, will you?' But purring isn't really in her nature; she may even have been born without the throat-motor. And secondly, Nick is not fond of Jezebel. He's one of those people who doesn't fundamentally understand the concept of living with animals, which, considering his anus, is kind of difficult to fathom. I sometimes wonder whether the whole problem of Jezebel's aggression might be something to do with the negative vibes given out towards her by Nick, a thought that first occurred to me about a year ago when I found what looked suspiciously like an old discharged banger, somewhat embrowned at one end, under his bed. So the idea of Jezebel being in his room, and, moreover, being pleased to be in his room, seemed unlikely. But the purring continued. Gingerly, not wanting her to run off, I opened the door to his room, pushing two plates of left-over jacket potato sandwiches – Nick only ever eats things between two pieces of bread; he even has meat pie sandwiches, even though, as I've tried to explain to him endlessly, pastry is essentially bread already – forward along a bobbled length of carpet. And there, sitting perched on all fours in the middle of the bed, looking somewhat bemused, was Jezebel. And facing her, sitting perched on all fours in the middle of the bed, looking fiercely focused and concentrated, was Nick. Purring.

He stopped, and turned his head around his left shoulder to face the door.

'I'm talking to her,' he said. 'She's unhappy. She wants to be a big tiger. She wants to roam free in the jungle.' He put his face close to hers. 'Meow,' he said. 'Meow.' He paused. Jezebel looked at me, deadpan. 'She says she knows I am a kindred spirit.'

There was a moment's silence. Then he turned to me and said, 'Gabe. D'you know where I can get a penny whistle?'

'No idea,' I said. 'Why don't you ask Jezebel?'

He nodded, neutrally, unironically, a 'yeah, good idea' type of nod, and turned back to the cat. Jezebel punched him in the face.

I dunno. I'm worried about it. He might just be pissing about, of course, but the fact is: falling in love with a tree, claiming to be Zebedee, and having deep conversations with the cat – I tell you, that way madness lies.

6

I'm going to phone Dina. I am. A man owes himself a certain amount of adventure.

It's tough, because I've never asked anyone out, as such. All the women I've ever got off with have seduced me. All five of them, including the one pushed out of my bedroom eight nights ago by my frantic deaf and blind hand-movements. I can't initiate sex; the cliff you leap off when you try to kiss someone for the first time is just too high. That's why I never think about moving to America, even though I've got the passport. Because if you live in America, you have to own a gun. And when that moment comes, when, in Seattle or Louisana or Blackrock, I, shitting myself, shift my head forward with my eyes closed and my lips puckered, and Mary Lou, or Peggy Sue, or Darlene, turns her face away, and says, firmly, *no*, or, *what d'you-all think yer doing?* – I'd just get the gun out there and then and shoot myself.

And as a close mate of Oscar Wilde, not as well known as him, once said, there is only one thing worse than trying to initiate sex, and that's trying to re-initiate sex. One of the five, Lucy, I met at college, and sometimes, in the night-ache, I can still taste the newness of her body and the grey Leicestershire weekend I spent trying to swaddle myself within it. I didn't see Lucy again until four years later, desperate for a shag, I phoned her, and we arranged to meet. Come the night, she was ultra-nervous, fidgeting at the pub table and not drinking her drink, until eventually she came out with it.

'Look. Why did you want to see me again?'

I couldn't say: because I'm desperate for a shag. So I went for the euphemism. 'Well, y'know. Just to meet up and talk, see how you are.'

'Is that it?'

I shrugged my shoulders. 'Yeah.'

She breathed a huge sigh of relief. 'Thank goodness for that. I thought you had AIDS.'

Great, I thought, do I look that fucking bad? But as she explained: a guy she has sex with four years ago suddenly rings her out of the blue, says we must meet up, he's got things he has to say to her. What else was she supposed to think? Love in the Nineties: it's paranoid.

But I have to phone Dina. I can't stand all this sexual loss. Alice, she's just the tip of the iceberg. This world, it's crammed, I tell you, absolutely *chocka* it is, with fantastic women that I'm never, *never* going to sleep with. How am I supposed to live with that? It's bad enough just doing the survey. Sometimes, when I see a woman walking in the street from behind, and she looks like she might be attractive, I have to get in front of her, I *have* to know what she looks like. And you know what I want, what I really want? I want her to be a fucking dog. I want her to be Bella fucking Emberg. Because then – phew – at least that's one more smuggled out of Never-never Land.

(I hate never. Never's a real problem for me. I once thought about getting rid of the Dolomite. I was gonna splash out, get an Austin Metro automatic. The cheque-book was on the table, the dealer nearly had me: then he made his mistake. 'Of course, once you drive an automatic, you'll *never* go back to manual.' The Biro froze in my fingers. Never. There's no going back. This will be the last time. Suddenly, I saw myself speeding down a long, floodlit tunnel toward death *in an automatic*. 'Hey, isn't this fantastic, I don't even have to change gear on my way to the grave.' I shut the cheque-book in silence and left. As I went through the glass revolving door, I telepathised the flummoxed salesman: never say never again.)

The telephone sits accusingly in the centre of the breakfast table, its left-hand corner blackened by some drying spilt Arabica. My fingers itch. Let's think about this. Who's gonna answer? What happens if it's Ben?

'Cunt.'

'Cunt.'

'Er . . . listen, Ben . . . can I speak to Dina?'

'Huh?'

'Can I speak to Dina?'

'Sure . . . why?'

'Oh nothing.'

'Nothing?'

'Well, no.'

'It's because you fancy her, don't you? Or rather, you fancy my wife, don't you? Or rather, you love my wife! But you know she's never going to leave me – and so, pathetically, you've decided to have a bid for her sister, because you're so miserably obsessed you're prepared to settle for a pale genetic shadow of love. Isn't that right?'

Well, it might not go exactly like that. But I still feel it's a giveaway.

'Hello?'

'Hi. Alice?'

'Hi, Gabe.'

'Is Dina there?'

'. . . Sure! I'll just get her.'

'Oh don't! Don't bother! It's you I love! You, you in full, not some eighty per cent version of you, with eighty per cent size breasts, you, wonderful you, marvellous you, beautiful you!!!'

Maybe I won't bother. I stretch my hands together palms-upwards above my head, pulling new oxygen into my sleepy muscles with my fingertips. Never put off till tomorrow anything you can leave till the day after that, that's my motto. I am the Procrastinator General. In medieval times, I'd have had a cloak and sceptre, and peasants would've come to my court to beg for my wise decisions – on the crops, on the war, on whether to raise their children in penury or give them away as servants to the king – and, after a fanfare, I would've risen in state and solemnly declared, 'Umm . . . dunno. Best to leave it for now. Er . . . Sleep on it for a couple of days and then ask somebody else. All right?'

The phone rings, frightening me.

'Hello?'

'You're home at last! Well! I thought I was going mad the number of messages I've had to leave on your silly machine. You're the slowest person I know at getting back to me – apart from Hugo, of course.'

'Hello, Mother.'

'I just want to touch base, that's all.'

'Right.'

There is a pause. The snarling on the line seems to have transmuted into a faint, constant background ringing. My espresso machine is constipated, my A–Z is a leper: now my phone has got tinnitus.

'So what about your new lady?' says my mother, as nonchalantly as someone trying to be nonchalant can, which is about the opposite of nonchalantly.

'She's fine. I met her the other day.'

My mother is silent for a second. 'I thought you said you two had got on really well before she went to America.'

Did I? Damn.

'Oh, yeah. I mean, I met her for dinner.'

'Oh!' she says joyously. 'The two of you went out for dinner!'

'Yes.'

A pause. I think I can guess what's coming.

'*Nu?*'

Nu is Yiddish. It means 'So? Yes? What else? Tell me more. And . . .?', only more probing.

'*Nu* nothing, Mother. We had dinner.'

'Are you going to have dinner again?'

'Yes. We're hoping to set up a supper club.'

'Really?'

'No. It was a joke.'

'Oh.'

I very much hope Interpol *aren't* taping this. I may be arrested on some trumped-up espionage charge just so they don't have to sit there any more, the ears underneath their little World War II headphones turning red in fierce empathetic embarrassment.

'You'll never guess who I bumped into the other day,' says my mother.

That is true. I will never guess. 'Jim Deacon? Michael Bunting? Wally? Indira Mutchenflacken? The Tishner twins?'

'No,' says my mother triumphantly. 'Nick.'

'Nick? Nick as in Nick?'

'You know, your friend.'

'Where on earth did you meet him?'

'At Wembley Market. I didn't know he could play the penny whistle.'

'He was *busking*?'

She laughs, as if nothing could be more ridiculous. Stretching the phone flex to its full extent, I go over to the kitchen window, steamed up from the radiator beneath, and pull my dressing-gown over my hand to rub a small hole in the condensation with the edge of my wrist. Through the smeary circle, I can see that frost has coated the tree-tops grey and white, as if during the night the earth had received some terrible news.

'No, darling, don't be silly,' she continues breathlessly. 'He was being the Pied Piper.'

'Oh, of course. *What the hell are you talking about?*'

'Really, Gabriel, there's no need to swear.'

No need to swear? My father shouts 'buggery-arse-cunt-bugger!!!' when he can't find his car keys. What would *he* say if the person he's living with turned out to be mental?

Actually, it's all starting to make sense . . .

'I just thought it was one of your little in-jokes,' says my mother, sounding a little crushed. Clearly, she'd been thinking of this anecdote as a nice chuckly mother–son interface, maybe leading to a bit of light belated bonding. She hadn't shored up for psychodrama. 'He's always been a bit of a joker, hasn't he?' she adds, almost pleading, a hand across the abyss, groping desperately for some shred of communion.

'Well . . . yeah,' I say, taking pity, grasping a little finger. 'But I don't think he's joking at the moment. I think he's gone a bit crazy.'

'Is he on drugs, perhaps?'

Incredible, isn't it, how the most unoriginal thought can sometimes be the right one?

'Umm . . . not bigtime.'

'What sort of drug is that?'

'I mean, he's not taking loads of drugs or anything. Or even very hard drugs. But I think . . . yeah, that might have something to do with it. So . . . what exactly was he doing?'

'He was walking up and down playing the penny whistle.'

'And you decided from that he was being the Pied Piper?'

'Well, he was wearing a little green hat.'

'But that doesn't make hi— What sort of little green hat?'

'I don't know, Gabriel.'

'Did it have a black band round it with an African pattern on it?'

'Er . . . I don't really remember. Yes, I think so.'

'Right. Did you say anything to him?'

'Just hello. How were you, you know. We touched base.'

'What did he say?'

'He said hello. Then . . .' She laughs, but slightly uncertainly, remembering that but a second ago the light in her heartedness had been suddenly switched to heavy '. . . he did a funny thing. He opened his arms – I really thought for a moment he was going to hug me – and he said, "No more bouncing with my arms outstretched. Now I'm walking with my arms outstretched." Then he went into Safeway's.'

And still she didn't think anything was seriously wrong. But then I suppose if you live in the Venn diagram 'Nice', there's no space in the circle for 'Seriously Wrong'.

'How could he play the penny whistle with his arms outstretched?'

'I'm not sure it made much difference, really. He was just sort of blowing it. He wasn't really playing a tune, you know.'

The earpiece, mistaking its role in the whole phone set-up, rings. I feel we've exhausted the subject. I walk back over to the kitchen table: the beige console seems to cry out to me to fit the receiver snugly back into its two empty squares.

'Well, anyway,' I say, adopting a wrapping-up tone, 'I'll speak to you soon.'

'Yes. Don't be a Jewish post office. And . . .' Mode: self-conscious playfulness . . . 'be sure to let me know if you and Dina go out to dinner again.'

'Yeah, yeah.'

I put the phone down. So now I've told my mother I've

already gone out with Dina. The thing I want is now inside the thing I least want – my mother's consciousness. This, and the fact that, as you've seen, I'm shit at lying, impels me. I press the quick-dial button marked 'A/B'. The phone rings in the terracotta hallway.

7

One of the thousand paradoxes about insomnia – and it is, after all, a paradox, not being able to sleep at night – is that all day I want to lie down, all day the only sitting posture that feels comfortable is practically prostrate, every part of my body sunk into the sofa parallel to the floor except for my head, propped against the back cushion (a five-chinned special, this), and yet the minute I lie in between sheets on a mattress when it's dark, my whole body will start to itch, every cell willing itself up and moving after a space of eight seconds.

This convulsion, and all the other sore disorders and disarrangements of this stupid sleeping sickness, always, always hit their peak whenever I've got something really big going on the next day. Every significant night-before in my whole life it's been the same. Barmitzvah? Not a wink. Finals? Eight hours fighting with the pillow. Playing as a ringer in a charity game for *Over The Line*'s football team against a team of real ex-pros, including Stan Bowles? Four wanks and two Horlicks. And thus, I've basically gone into every important thing in my life at about forty per cent.

Tomorrow I'm going out with Dina. She said yes. Now I'm not even sure I'm pleased. At least if she'd've said no I might've had a chance of getting off.

It was her who picked up the phone, thank God.

'Hello?'

'Dina? Hi, it's Gabriel.'

'Gab . . .? Oh, Ben's brother. Hi. Sorry, they're not here at the moment, they've gone to the doctor's—'

'No actually, it was you I wanted to speak to.'

'Me?'

'Yeah. Listen, I was wondering . . .'

Such an old, old trope, isn't it? The guy nervous and flustered and not knowing what to say to a woman he wants to ask out. Practising into the mirror, hearing it over and over in his head, all that shit. Unfortunately, the fact that something is really deeply embedded in the cultural landscape doesn't make it any easier to do.

'. . . I mean, say no if you want to, y'know, I just wondered if you fancied just going out for a drink or something.'

There was a pause. The phone's internal ringing got so tumultuous, I thought for a second she'd put me on hold and I was listening to Mantovani.

I wonder if I'd've been this nervous just asking her out; y'know, if it wasn't all painted in with the Alice-backdrop. If it was just a boy–girl thing.

'Um . . . why?' she said, after some time.

'Why?' Why? Why? What did she expect me to say? *Because eventually, after some customary preliminaries designed to suggest that there's more to it than this, I hope to put my penis inside your vagina. OK?* 'I just thought it might be nice. I really liked what you said the other day – about my insomnia.'

'You liked it?' said Dina over-incredulously. This appears to be what Dina does: incessant questioning. I don't know if that's an American thing, or what. It seems aggressive, and defensive, if that's possible.

'Yeah,' I said, slightly flatly, trying to inject a bit of 'look if you're not bothered . . .' weariness into my voice. Works every time.

'I don't think I'm really bothered about going for a drink with you, actually,' she said coldly.

'Oh. OK.' I felt two things: intense cold humiliation, and an overwhelming urge to shout, 'But I'm brilliant!!!' I took a deep breath for a short goodbye.

'I got a bit too drunk yesterday with Ben and Alice. I think I'm going to lay off drinking for a week or so.'

A lifeline. Fantastic: I didn't want to go to the pub anyway, I hate pubs. But suddenly I couldn't think of anything else. All the potential of our modern leisure culture wrote itself out before me on a very small notepad. What is there, really? Maybe . . . *four* basic activities? Three, if you don't count rollerblading.

'Um . . . what about going to the cinema?'

'To see what?' She wasn't making this at all easy.

'Uh . . . they're reshowing *Henry: Portrait of A Serial Killer* at the Phoenix.'

'No.'

'No, you're quite right. I don't know why I suggested it.' Then, I remembered something. 'QPR are playing Barnsley on Saturday.'

'And . . .?'

'Oh, you're not into football, are you?'

She paused. 'Well . . . no, not really. But to be honest, Ben and Alice go on about it so much I wouldn't mind going to a game for once. Maybe then I wouldn't feel so out of it when they're droning on about Matthew Le Mesurier.'

'Le Tissier.'

'Whatever.'

'. . . So . . . would you like to go?'

'Sure.'

That was it, really. 'Sure' was intensely matter-of-fact, very much in line with the overwhelming functionality of her reasoning. It was strangely anti-climactic. Sometimes women will clearly signal: there's nothing sexual here for you. But at least in doing so they'll acknowledge that sex has been in the arena. Dina seemed to have framed her tone to go even further than that: as if it had never occurred to her that a man asking a woman out might have a hidden agenda. My lust felt not so much barred as unrecognised, in the political sense – if she was Iraq, my lust was Israel.

I'm meeting her at Ben and Alice's tomorrow at 1:30. What to say to them, what to say to her: tonight's extended scratch sample. Lifting up my blindfold, I watch the brightness of the screen behind the curtains go up a notch. I take my earplugs out, and wait for Nature's final signal that I've lost the battle. Ah. There you go.

Do you know what it's like to *resent* the sound of the birds starting to sing?

8

I knock on the door. Ben and Alice don't have a doorbell: they have a big lion's head of a knocker, so heavy you often worry that one really hefty whack would take your hand splintering through the plinth and into the hallway. It's probably a main cause of subsidence in this street. Now the knocker adds to the portentousness of the moment. *Booom. Boooom.* Then nothing. Then, slowly, a sound like the shuffling of papers, gradually mutating into something identifiably clearer: footsteps. What's happening? Why has this moment suddenly turned into the bit from the Hammer Horror film when the innocent couple wait in the pouring rain at the castle door? The door is opened, slowly and deliberately it seems to me, as if the person behind is keen on producing the usual elongated creak, and yet it opens revealing not, however, a mutant hunchback servant, but the most beautiful woman in the world.

'Hello,' I say. Then, adopting a cod cowboy accent, 'I've come fer ya sister.'

Why did I do that? That's so shit. Sometimes, lying in bed at night, scanning the newsprint of my day, I'll look back at something embarrassing I said and actually get a slight shiver of distaste, as when you drink gin. This time, though, I think I shivered straight away, maybe even before I hit the word *sister*. My brain: it censures, but it doesn't censor.

Alice, bless her, takes it in good part. I mean, she doesn't slam the door in my face. But she does look at me slightly strangely, and I don't think just because I've made a shit joke.

'Hi, Gabe,' she says. 'Come in.'

She turns – oh, her arse in white trousers! – and goes into the living-room. I follow, and then they're all there, Ben, Alice, and Dina, looking at me (I feel) like a McCarthy committee.

'Hello, Gabe,' says Ben. He looks uncomfortable. Dina doesn't say anything, just nods at me. God. She might be simply too much trouble. I look at her. She's wearing a skinny red tank-top that comes down just below her waist, and a pink mohair cardy.

'Looking forward to the game?' I say.

'Not really.'

'Dina. What kind of attitude is that? I thought you'd have got kitted out with scarves and everything.'

'Why? It's not that cold.'

Alice laughs.

'Dina,' she says, 'people wear scarves at football matches whatever the weather. They wear their team scarf.'

'Oh,' says Dina, as if she still hasn't really understood – as if Alice really now needs to go on and explain the concept of 'team scarf' – but also very much as if she can't be bothered to pursue the matter any further.

'A red top, though . . .' I say.

'Yeah?' says Dina sharply, primed for incoming abuse.

'Barnsley play in red . . .'

'So?'

'So we'll be with the QPR fans.'

'So?' Impatiently.

'Forget it, Gabriel,' says Ben, laughing. 'I think Dina'll give off such a strong vibe of not giving a fuck, no one's going to mistake her for a Barnsley fan.'

Dina looks irritated at all this exclusion. 'Look,' she says, getting up, 'I'll go and change if it matters that much!'

'No,' I say, holding out a hand to stop her, but it's too late, she's walked. The physical differences between her and Alice may be pretty slight, but the psychical differences are vast. What happened to the laid-back gene? She didn't seem this tightly wound when I met her.

'Don't worry about Dina,' says Alice, following her. 'I know she seems pissed off with everything. But really she's just pissed off with her ex-boyfriend.' She goes out. I hear her tread going down the hall to the spare room. I look round. Ben is staring at me quite hard.

'What?'

'I spoke to Mum yesterday.'

My stomach pings, like it does when I'm a passenger in the front of a car going over a small bump in the road at speed.

'Nice. So did I.'

'I know.'

'How was she?'

'Mental.'

'Of course.'

'She seemed to think . . .' He pauses, searching my face for some precognition of what he's about to say, knowing that'll prove my guilt. But my features are dead. '. . . that you were already *going out* with Dina.'

'Eh?' I say. Archetypal of my mother to pump up the lie. She will say what she wants. She will always make damn sure and say it. 'She must have got it wrong. You know what she's like. I told her I was going out with Dina today. She must have thought I meant "today" in the documentary sense.'

'Huh?'

'As in "these days, nowadays". "This is the way things are today."'

'She's not an idiot.'

'I beg your pardon?'

'Oh fuck off, Gabriel,' he says, with real annoyance. 'You shouldn't treat her like shit. You never give her a chance.'

'You're the one who said she was mental.'

'Well, she is mental. But so are you.' He frowns. 'Anyway, she said you'd told her you'd already been out for dinner with Dina. And that you *hadn't* told her that she was Alice's sister.'

'Oh, for God's sake. You know she's always on my back about getting a steady girlfriend. She wants to believe it's already happened. So she's told you it as if it has. And I just forgot to tell her about Dina being Alice's sister.'

Ben looks at me, taking me in, trying to see my over-familiar eyes afresh.

'Maybe,' he concedes. 'But you have asked her out.'

'Yeah?'

'Don't you think . . .'

'What?'

'Well, I dunno. That it's all a bit . . . incestuous. You, my brother, trying to shag my wife's sister.'

'No, Ben. Incest is when I, your brother, try to shag you. And anyway, for fuck's sake, we're just going to see QPR. I'm not going to give her oral pleasure in the middle of the Ellerslie Road stand. Not unless it's a *really* dull game.'

His mouth does not curve. 'Gabriel. That's my wife's sister.'

'Oh, for Christ's sake!' I say, turning away from him. 'What stopped you from adding "you're talking about"? A sense of how pompous you sounded?'

Ben reddens. He will always back off if I really go for it. I am only technically the younger brother.

'Well, anyway,' he says, shrugging off his sense of self-confusion, 'be nice to her. She's had a rough ride with men recently.'

I'm about to ask how when Alice and Dina come back into the room. Dina has changed into a blue zip-up velvet top and jeans.

'Nearest thing I've got to a QPR kit,' says Alice, smiling. Dina stands there, with her hand on her hip, slightly modelling, aware of being the object of surveillance. She raises her left eyebrow. But then she smiles too; it's the first time since our phone call that she's done anything at all friendly. 'Blue is the colour,' she says sardonically.

In the car and on the way to the game, I say, 'Look, I'm sorry about that. I didn't mean you had to change your clothes. It doesn't make any difference.'

'That's OK,' she says, looking straight through the windscreen. The one atom of relaxed atmosphere we'd created between us appears to have had its half-life.

'What time is it?' I say.

She checks the bulky silver arrowheads of her old-man's watch. 'Quarter past.'

Still forty-five minutes to go to the game, when at least the football will fill the silence.

'Can you not ask me again?' she says coldly.

'Sorry?'

'That's the third time you've asked me.'

'Oh. Sorry, it's just . . . I like to get there in good time. Sit down, read the programme, get settled in – y'know – at least fifteen minutes before the game starts.'

'Haven't you got a watch?'

'No. I always end up losing them. Perhaps because they're telling me something I don't want to know.'

She turns three-quarters around, her left eyebrow arched towards me like the finger on an *I'm With This Idiot* T-shirt.

'The time?' she says, with just that level of incredulity which borders on contempt.

'The fact that it's passing,' I say, and realise straight away that this 'I'm a bit of a mystical type, given to enigmatic sayings' approach has not impressed. Hmm: you can just see the beginnings of black roots in the crown of her blonde hair. I try another tack. 'Would you like to hear some music?'

'If you like.'

Holding on to the steering-wheel, I bend down to rummage around in the cassette swamp beneath the driving seat; in doing so, I accidentally press the accelerator, and the Dolomite roars, although luckily, being the Dolomite, doesn't really speed up. I get a tape out and look at it, trying to keep one eye on the road. As ever there is no title on the white sticky. In fact there's no white sticky; all of my tapes stubbornly cling to their anonymity, refusing any form of classifiable identification. When trying to find a particular one while driving, I'm always forced into a long process of trial and error, putting one after another into the machine, dropping them back under the seat as I go – well, I say, one after another: normally it's just one, then another, then, always, the next one I pick up and play turns out to be the first one again, and then normally the next one is also the first one again. This means that I'm chancing my arm putting this one in the machine. It could be anything. I take a deep breath.

> '*We've only just begun*
> *To live;*
> *White lace and promises . . .*'

Ah. My finger hovers over the brutal eject button. I look over at Dina. She is staring at me; both of them are raised.

'Not a Carpenters fan, then?'

'Umm . . . no. Correct me if I'm wrong, but aren't they shit?'

Now that's just unnecessary. I'm not going to pander to that. I know I can pander a lot – sometimes so much a voice in my head starts saying, 'Ming-ming! Ming-ming!' – but there is a limit.

'No, they're not. Karen . . . I mean, obviously, they're sort of naff, but she . . . she had the voice of an angel. I mean just listen . . .'

'*Before the rising sun . . .*'

'Lovely.'

'No it is, really. She has this lovely crack in her voice, and it really . . . OK . . . listen to this . . .' I press the FF button, still talking. Karen's voice speeds up to an android's yodel. '. . . on the last note of the song, you can really hear it. You can hear her voice kind of . . . give.'

She looks out of the window again. I press harder on the FF button.

'*fwwwomgggopoooomgggggg* . . .' (I release my finger) '. . . *only just beguuuuuuuuuhuuu* . . .'

'There it is,' I say.

'Karen Carpenter's lovely crack,' she says, still looking out of the window.

'Yes,' I say, feeling myself flush somewhat – whether through surprise at Dina suddenly coming out with such a brash sexual reference, or through outrage at my poor anorexic angel's name being taken so in vain, I'm not sure. I press the eject button. As I do, the engine makes a strange sound I've never heard before: a kind of cough. Oh shit. Now hold on – what are those things again, that coughs are usually followed by? Oh yeah, thanks, engine, that's right. Splutters.

A couple of bumps and grinds, and we finally come to a halt at the corner of Westbourne Park and Ledbury Road. 2:23, by a surreptitious glance at her watch.

'It's OK,' I say. 'It's just stalled.'

I turn the key. Nothing. Nothing at all. Not that slight shudder and slow dying fall you get when there's something quite wrong; that *nothing* you get when there's something very wrong.

It's so jarring, for a modern human being, that; to make the technological gesture, throw a switch, press a button, turn a key, and for the machine just to ignore you. I mean, what are they playing at; who the fuck's in control here?

'Great,' says Dina. 'A car that breaks down when you eject a cassette.'

'It's very fond of The Carpenters.'

'It might be the battery,' she says, getting out.

'Huh?' I say.

She is bending over the bonnet, which in another universe might be quite a good thing. From the other side of the street, a crop-haired man in a rather military-looking brown crombie looks across as if contemplating coming over to offer assistance, but then thinks better of it and walks off.

'Open it,' I hear her shout mutedly. I wind my window down and stick my head out of it.

'How?' I say.

She looks up. 'How? Push the bonnet release lever.'

'I don't know where it is.'

She comes round to my door. 'What do you mean?'

'I mean,' I say, halfway between exasperation and embarrassment, 'that it's never broken down before. So I've never lifted the bonnet up.' Behind her, a car strewn with blue and white flags and scarves whizzes by.

'What about changing the oil?' she says.

'I've never done that.'

Dina's left eyebrow hits the roof. Then she leans in through the window, stretches her arm into some nondescript area beneath the steering-wheel, and, after a couple of seconds' rummaging, pulls something. The bonnet comes up. She stares at me again for a couple of seconds, and then turns on her heel back to the front of the car. Absent-mindedly, I rearrange some of the cassettes, empty envelopes and A–Z sheaves piled on the dashboard into an order no more useful than before, until, stung by a sense that perhaps I should be doing something, I get out, into the cold Westbourne Park air.

'Any ideas?' I say.

'I think it's the distributor,' she says, pointing to some bit of the engine that looks like every other bit of the engine.

'So how do we fix that?'

'Get a new distributor.'

'Isn't there anything else we can do? Can't we . . . hot-wire it or whatever?'

She looks at me like I'm some sort of an idiot.

'Explain something to me,' she says. 'You're a man. You like football. Doesn't that mean you're supposed to know something about cars?'

'I'm Jewish.'

'Oh, right. Silly of me.'

'We could walk to the match from here.'

She looks up, incredulous. 'And then what?'

'Well, get a taxi back afterwards.'

'And just leave the car here forever?'

'Um . . . well, I could come back here and sort it out and you could get a taxi back to Ben and Alice's.'

'Are you an AA member?'

'No.'

'So when you said "sort it out", what exactly did you mean? Push it all the way back to Kilburn?'

2:34.

'And anyway,' she says, pointing at the left front wheel, 'look at that.'

I look down. Wonderfully, the car has come to rest on one of those road spaces where the authorities were simply not content with basic 'no parking' stuff. It's on a *triple* yellow line, with extra chevrons painted into the kerb, and I can see the bottom of a silver pole as well. I don't bother to look at the sign – I know it says, 'NEVER. AT NO TIME. ANYWHERE ELSE IN LONDON, BUT NOT HERE. IT WON'T JUST BE CLAMPED, YOU KNOW. OH NO – STRAIGHT TO THE SCRAP. NEXT TIME YOU SEE IT, IT'LL LOOK LIKE A BIG RUBIK'S CUBE.'

'So,' I say. 'Are *you* an AA member?'

'Yeah, of course, Gabriel. Regular as clockwork I used to renew it from Manhattan.'

She turns away, digging her hands deep into the pockets of the blue velvet zip-up top. The last vestiges of hope within me decide to follow the example of the engine, and give out.

'Wait a minute,' says Dina, still facing away, but her tone suddenly up. 'What's this?'

She turns round, holding a small yellow patent leather purse, out of which she has taken what looks like a credit card. She hands it to me: on it are written the words 'Green Flag', Dina's name, and a membership number.

'How have you got this?' I say.

'Check the name again,' she says.

I scan the bottom of the card: A. Friedricks. Alice.

'It was in the pocket of this top,' says Dina before I can look up confused. 'What the fuck is "Green Flag"?'

'They're like the AA. They sponsor England matches – Ben's probably got him and Alice free membership in return for advertising space or something.'

'Right. Well . . . I could probably pass for Alice, couldn't I?'

Can you give me a couple of months on that one?

'I mean,' she continues, 'they're not going to ask for ID, are they? And even if they do, I've got stuff with "Friedricks" on it.'

Reprieved: those same last vestiges rumble and turn over, shakily.

'So . . . d'you think they'll tow us to the match, then?'

She looks at me hard. 'Gabriel. Accept it. We're not going to the match. The match stopped for us when you ejected that fucking Carpenters cassette. I'm going to look for a phone booth.'

Twenty minutes later, we're sitting in the car, waiting that within-the-hour wait. I turn to Dina. Her cheeks have reddened with the cold in the now heater-less car.

'Look, Dina. I'm really sorry.'

'Yeah.'

'No, I am.'

'Yeah, I know you are.'

This is starting to grate.

'Dina,' I say, with a certain weight, the steam coming out of my mouth seeming not frost, but cartoon anger, 'I love QPR Football Club. I've supported them since they came second in the league in 1976. That's a lot of time invested for very, very little return. But, that aside, going to Loftus Road is extremely important to me. You, however, are coming along to this match because of an idle sense that you'd like to join in with your sister and brother-in-law's conversations about football. Now, it seems, we're going to miss the game. And yet you are the one who's much more pissed off. Why is that?'

She turns to me. Her eyes are weary, bereft.

'Fuck off,' she says. There is a pause. 'As soon as I put the phone down to you I thought this was a stupid idea,' she continues. 'I don't want to see . . .' she looks away '. . . men, at the moment, OK? Ben's just about all right, but men in general – I just don't want to see them. So I forgot – somehow you talked me into going somewhere with about fifty thousand of them.'

There is another pause.

'Capacity's only twenty-four thousand at the moment. Until the new Loft stand is finished.'

She stares out of the window. A green sports car zooms past like a satire on our stasis.

'And at least a couple of thousand of them must be wom—'

'Gabriel.'

'All right. But look – we're not going now. So why are you still pissed off? It's not like you've cheered up since the car broke down.'

She doesn't answer. Her face is set hard into the dashboard. Hearing a tapping noise from my window, I turn round; it is a moustachioed man in a green tunic, his face streaked with black. The Green Flag man.

'Hello,' I say.

'Hello,' he says. 'Mr Friedricks?'

'No,' I say, pointing to my re-shaped love. 'That's him.'

A shadow seems to pass across the Green Flag man's murky face.

'Hm,' he says to her. 'Could I see your member's card please?'

Dina reaches over me to give him the Green Flag card produced from her handbag, glancing Stanley knives at me as she does so. He looks at it for a second, then trudges off to his van.

'You fucking idiot!' hisses Dina.

'What? What have I done now?'

'You're sitting in the driver's seat! He knows the driver isn't the name on the card now!'

'So?'

She opens her mouth, but then shuts it again. The Green Flag man is back at my window.

'I'm sorry, sir and madam, but I've run a check on this card, and the member in question – A. Friedricks—'

'Me!' says Dina, rather too eagerly.

'. . . drives a *Volkswagen Polo*,' says the Green Flag man, focusing on her, telling her off. 'And since, madam, you have not taken out our special personal cover we cannot come to your aid whilst you are in a non-member's vehicle. As for you, sir, we can't of course repair the vehicle of a non-member, unless you join here and now, which will cost sixty-seven pounds.'

£67? Not on your Noah and.

'Sorry. You've obviously misunderstood. I'm not Mr Friedricks, although . . .' I say, laughing like I imagine a Young Conservative laughs and putting my arm round Dina '. . . barring anyone changing their mind, come next June I very much hope that *Miss* Friedricks here will be Mrs Jacoby.'

I look at her and smile nauseatingly. She looks at me. I don't think I've ever seen anyone so clearly think I'm a cunt.

'Eh?' says the Green Flag man.

'This is my fiancée,' I say. 'We're *engaged*. I'm sorry we . . .' (that laugh again, plus a quick wink to Dina) '. . . didn't get around to informing Green Flag, but there you go. You see,' I continue, extricating my arm from her unhappy shoulders and getting out, 'I gave Di . . . Alice this car. It was mine from – oh, years ago. So it's her car, but I'm still insured to drive it.' Then, sotto voce, confiding, 'She wrote off the Volkswagen. To be honest, she's not really that at home behind the wheel.'

'Well, sir,' says the Green Flag man, after some consideration, 'not many of 'em are, really. If truth be told.'

Gotcha.

'Let's see what the problem is then.'

He moves to the front of the car, pausing briefly to pop his head down to the window and smile patronisingly at Dina. She, clearly, has died inside.

'Could you do the bonnet for me?' he shouts.

'Certainly.'

I smile, reach through the window, and stick my hand under the dashboard. Holding the fixed grin, I angle my head slightly to see Dina; she raises her eyes to heaven, and then nods slightly to the left. Ah. That's it.

'Why'd you say that?' whispers Dina, with some hate.

'Because I had to,' I say, out of the corner of my mouth. 'Why else would I be driving your car?'

'We could've just been friends.'

Above the raised edge of the bonnet, I see the blackened balding crown of the Green Flag man's head.

'I'm not sure men and women just being friends is part of this bloke's experience.'

'D'you mind coming here a minute, sir and madam?'

We get out and crowd round either side of him, looking once more into the engine.

'It's your distributor,' he says to me. Then, to Dina, pointing, 'That's that little johnny over there, madam.' He wipes his hands on his tunic. 'I haven't got one of those with me, I'm afraid. As David Mellor once said to Antonia de Sancha, it's a tow-job.'

I laugh heartily at this (Don't hate me, I'm in character); the Green Flag man's face lights up like his mobile phone receiving a call. He goes off to get what looks like some mountaineering gear from his van.

'We're going through a rough time,' says Dina to me, quietly.

'Well, I know that.'

'No. I mean, in our engagement. It's not going too well. Therefore,' she says, fixing me, her shallow eyes deepening, 'we're not touching each other that much at the moment.'

I do my best to return her stare. 'Look,' I say. 'This isn't a ruse. I haven't planned all this – I didn't rig the distributor to burn out halfway through the journey – just to get into your pants.'

A light spatter of rain starts to fall. Dina turns away and hugs herself; distantly, a crowd roars.

'I could just go, of course. Tell him it's all bollocks, get a taxi home, and leave you here.'

I look at her. 'Please don't do that.'

She looks back at me, uncertain how to take this sudden vulnerability; her eyes flicker over my face, looking for sincerity.

The moment passes; she shrugs and looks away again. The Green Flag man, blacker in the face than before, emerges from round the back of the Dolomite.

'There you go. We'll drop her off at a garage I know in Ladbroke Grove. Then I'll take you to . . .?'

'Hamilton Road,' says Dina. 'It's near Ladbroke Grove station.'

No. No. I sense a problem here.

'Oh, darling,' I say petulantly, 'you don't *still* want to go and see my brother and his wife?'

'What?' says Dina, staring hard at me, her look clearly spelling out to me: *if you think I'm coming back to your house* . . . All right then. Have it your own way.

'Actually, yes,' I say to the Green Flag man, 'could you drop us there?'

'Certainly,' he says. 'You two lovebirds'll have to sit up with me in the truck, I'm afraid. Unless of course,' he adds, his pale green eyes, the colour, presumably, of the flag, twinkling in their charcoal sockets, 'you want to go and have a quick frolic in the back together!' His head jerks to and fro between me and Dina, hugely grinning; I can't work out whether or not he's missing some front teeth or whether they too are covered over with black. I laugh, comradely. His head stops jerking suddenly and fixes on Dina. 'Cheer up, love,' he says. 'Might never happen.'

The tension on the journey back is so palpable I wonder the Green Flag man doesn't just stop the truck and suggest we break it off. We drop the Dolomite off at a place called Moran's SuperDrive and then stop again at a Jet garage so that he can refuel. You know Jet garages – the ones that achieve the incredible feat of taking the all-night garage downmarket. I take the opportunity to get out of the Green Flag van, saying I've got to stretch my legs, but actually to escape the electrified force-field that has sprung up in the tiny plane between me and Dina on the two-person passenger seat. Leaning my back between 'R' and the second 'E' on the van's side, I notice a blue plaque on the wall opposite: Alfred Hitchcock, the film director, was born here, 19 December 1909.

'True, that,' says a voice beside me. It is the Green Flag man. 'He was born here.'

'In a Jet garage?'

'Naah. His house was here. Got bombed during the war.'

'Bit pointless putting up the plaque then, wasn't it?'

He looks at me blankly. 'Why?'

'Because it's changed so much. You know . . . if you're going to commemorate something – I mean, what's the point of that? To come over all goose-pimply, right? Teary. In the presence of greatness. Well, y'know,' I say, looking around, taking in the sack-clothed pumps, the drizzle, the bad Jet yellow, '. . . it doesn't really happen for me here.'

He looks at me somewhat piercingly; I can tell I'm losing it for him now. 'What's happened to the nice bluff uncomplicated fellow?' is the thought he's orbiting.

'Not to worry, eh?' I say, before it's too late.

'No,' he says, eyeing me slightly askance, as if to say, *careful: if you're not the person I thought you were spiritually, perhaps you might not be the person I thought you were Green Flag-ly.*

Back at Ben and Alice's house, Alice says a typically Alice thing, through the higgle and piggle of her smile.

'Look, if you've towed them all the way back, you might as well come in for a cup of tea.'

So here we are, the five of us, in the spotless living-room, with the Green Flag man sitting on Ben and Alice's white sofa like some particularly sprawling Rorschach test ink-blot across the centrefold of a piece of shining A4. Luckily, communicating to her with my eyes that there was good reason for it, I've got away with introducing Alice to him as 'Dina', if a confused, somewhat upset look from Alice and a hateful one from Dina counts as getting away with it.

The Green Flag man it taking two or three millennia to drink his tea; or at least something defying the laws of physics is going on, because each time he drinks a bit, I check the rim of his cup and, despite a seemingly endless amount of glugging and slurping, the level of liquid never seems to have sunk at all. Although Alice actually offered him coffee, mineral water, orange juice and even, if I heard her right, Aqua bloody Libra, the Green Flag man, of course, has stuck with tea. I'm not sure it's possible for the labouring classes to consume any other beverage, just as it seems to be part of the social contract they have struck with us bourgeois that, as they mend things in our houses, we must make them endless cups of the stuff. I don't have a problem with that; I don't even have a problem with running out of sugar; it's just, on each offer of each cup, having to smile through the terrible tea banter: 'Tea? Tea? Is it my birthday?! As long as it's hot and wet! Get the kettle on (it won't suit you)' etc etc. This time, at least, he just went for 'Thought you'd never ask!' and thankfully left it there.

There is an awkward silence, almost as if, y'know, a fucking Green Flag man is in the room or something. Suddenly, he grins; the tea, I notice, has washed the grime off his teeth, so he looks, in so doing, like a badly dressed Black and White Minstrel. I think I know what's coming.

'These two, eh?' he says, nodding and winking – something only the truly plebeian can properly do at the same time – in the direction of me and Dina. 'Ha!' He shakes his head. 'These two!' This very much corresponds to what I thought was coming. 'The path of true love, eh?'

Ben and Alice exchange glances.

'The path . . .?' says Ben, smiling helpfully, his tone one of polite inquiry but with just a hint of expecting the answer to be rubbish.

'Never did run smooth, did it? Unlike . . .' he says, scratching his moustache thoughtfully, '. . . a Lexus GS400.'

'I'm not quite with you,' says Alice.

'The thing is . . .' I say, then realise I've started the sentence without any idea of how I'm going to finish it. 'Ha-ha!' I say pathetically.

'Well, they've had some sort of a barney, 'aven't they? Can't you tell?'

'Um . . .'

'Hope it doesn't mean they're gonna call off the big day!'

You know when you read stuff in the tabloids and it says something like 'Bobby Davro, or Princess Diana, or whoever, *joked* . . .', and then something which isn't really a joke as such, but perhaps counts as an uncly quip? That's how the Green Flag man is speaking. He jokes.

Ben leans forward in his chair. 'The big day?'

'The big day when we go and pick up the car!' I say desperately, knowing that I'm only postponing things.

'Naa!' he says, looking at me as if I am very foolish. 'The wedding!'

There is an audible silence.

'Oh right,' I say grimly. 'For a moment there I thought you might've meant the big day when we go and pick up the car.'

Dina glares into her Aqua Libra. Clearly I'm not as yet in tune with her sexual preferences, but, for what it's worth, I shouldn't imagine the arrival of Johnny Depp with his pants off would make her look up. Ben and Alice look at me with open mouths. I fax them telepathically, *To: Ben and Alice, From: Gabriel. 1 page including this one. Obviously, I told the Green Flag man we were getting married, because we were in my car, but Friedricks is the name on the card. Obviously. Oh, for heaven's sake, don't look so fucking mystified. Can't you work it ou—* It's not happening. Their minds are engaged, mainly, I think, with the idea of me and Dina being so. It occurs to me that I could just blow the whole thing – after all, he's towed us here now, there's not much he could do if I tell him we're not actually engaged, except maybe blacklist anyone with the name Friedricks from further road rescue. But something holds me back from that, something which, despite whatever other racial gene you might expect to be the dominant swimmer in my ethnic swamp, I would have to call Englishness.

'That was quick,' says Ben, to me. 'So I guess it *was* a really dull game then?'

9

I get the bus back from Ben and Alice's, not so much because it's the only way of getting back, but more because the top deck of the 31B feels almost exactly like the place to be right now. The itchy grey check of the seats, the smell of cigarettes smoked in 1973, the tickets on the floor creased with DM-print: objective corollary or what. It's good to be somewhere that matches your mood. How did I leave it? Badly. I mumbled something to the Green Flag man about trying to keep it a quiet affair, before instantly realising that no affair is so quiet you don't tell the groom's brother or bride's sister. We sat there in silence for a couple of long seconds, as the Green Flag man's coordinates of time and space started to slip – about, I could tell, to rearrange themselves into the configuration 'Hold on . . . I've been had!' – when, thankfully, God deciding at last to clear up this terrible mess, his mobile phone rang. The thought of another Green Flag member in trouble on the highway fought off all other impulses. Just stopping to tell Alice that if her tea was always this good he'd be back tomorrow, forty seconds later he was gone. Relief informed Ben and Alice's hysteria at my explanation.

But I might've left happy if Dina had smiled. There was an opening, I thought, to transform the base metal of our first date into the gold of a good time through the alchemy of laughter, possibly leading into a nostalgic projection of the two of us together in the future looking back fondly at what a silly time we had when we first went out. But she just scowled through Ben and Alice's giggling, and carried on scowling – it was like she was starring in that great unreleased comedy classic, *Carry*

On Scowling – until I was out the door, with not even a hint of a goodbye kiss. Perhaps she's distantly related to Jezebel.

I get off the bus outside the big Iceland on Kilburn High Road and walk up Streatley Road to the flat. 5:22. I'm tired. I'm often at my most tired round about this time, even when I haven't chanced my arm emotionally and had it twisted round my back. It comes with the unsynchronised body clock, which releases the go-to-sleep hormones deliberately early, so that they're all used up by the time I actually want to go to bed. Once inside, I throw my unused scarf on to the hallway floor and head straight for my bedroom. I think I'm going to try to sleep. I don't often sleep during the day, even though it's often easier than at night, because my insomnia gets so outraged at the fact that I've nicked some sleep from behind its back, it completely cancels out any time I've got owing to me for the night ahead. So I'll regret it later, no doubt, when I'm trampolining the mattress with restlessness, but, hey, you only live once.

I take my clothes off on the way to the bedroom – my baggy black T-shirt with the red stripe down the front, my 501s with a tear in the left leg that at certain times I have tried to pass off as a deliberate trendy tear, but is actually just a tear, my Next Y-fronted undershorts that I'd specially selected that morning with a certain amount of optimism – chucking them all over the flat in angry rejection, an ostentatious expression of their failure to help me pull. My bedroom is dark, the curtains still shut from this morning when I stumbled out of bed in a walking coma, but I don't even bother to switch the light on, just fumble for my blindfold and earplugs at the side of the bed and get in. I lie there on my back for a couple of seconds and wait for my senses to diminish. Sight and Sound clock off as normal; oddly though, two of the junior ones, Smell and Touch, start registering acutely. I can feel something really, really rough on the side of my arm, like the hairiest hair shirt in Hair Shirts R Us. And – hold on – I can smell something. Something . . . appalling. Something appalling which corresponds very directly with a new sensation just sent in by Touch: a warm wetness spreading across the sheet.

'AAAAAAAAAHHHHHHH!!!' I scream, not knowing what I'm screaming at, or why, but just immediately consumed with absolute terror. I leap out of the bed without even stopping to take off the blindfold and earplugs, hopping about naked, blind, deaf and screaming. Then I hear it, just perceptible through the thick soft wax.

'Come on then. Let's fucking 'ave yer. 'Ave yer! 'AVE YER!!!'

The most intense fear, I find, often stems from an unspecified object, some nightmare in the dark, some formless unfamiliar lurking in the mist, and, once you sense the presence of such an object, all you want is for it to melt into shape, any shape: anything is preferable to the unknown. Anything, that is, except Mental Barry – in particular, sleeping naked with Mental Barry in a bed he's just wet – who, as I take off my blindfold and earplugs and switch the light on, stands before me now in his enormous stinking greatcoat, his fists circling in slow motion. There is a very short pause. Then I start shouting.

'Get out!! You fucking tramp bastard!! How the fuck did you get in? Get out!!'

'You've got no bollocks!'

Barry's fists stop circling for a moment. It's not often that this favourite statement of his is contradicted by the evidence of his own eyes. Then they're off again.

'Come on then! Let's 'ave yer! Let's fucking 'ave yer!'

'All right then!' I say, and pile in. Seems to me at this stage I might as well ignore my natural instinct to avoid close physical contact with Mental Barry. I jump over my bed and leap on top of him, pummelling my fists into his head. My knuckles sink deep into the matted ginger bale of his hair.

'Wharriggghaalliiaa!' says Barry. 'Ooooh! Help! Lordy! Help!'

He gets down on all four and tries to cover his head with his hands. I climb on to his back. Then Nick bursts through the door.

'It's not how it looks!' I say.

'What?' says Nick.

''Ave yer!'

'Fucking Mental Barry's got in here! Phone the police! He must've broken in! He was in my bed! In my *bed*!'

'I know,' says Nick.

'Quick, get his legs . . . you *know*?'

'Hm.'

Slowly I pick myself off Mental Barry's back. Where's my . . .? Ah. Barry doesn't move as I slide my burgundy dressing-gown out from beneath him like a magician slipping a cloth from an overladen table.

I walk over to my flatmate, tying the band as I go. 'You *know*?'

'Yes,' he says, his eyes meeting mine defiantly. His eyes. Fuck. His look isn't *far* away, it's light years. 'And don't call him *Mental* Barry. That's just a label society has given him.'

'Mental Barry is mah name, Men-tall-ing is mah game!!' sings Barry.

Nick flashes me a contemptuous look, and then goes over to the still on all-fours Barry. He kneels down and wraps his arms around the tramp's belly, distended like a Rwandan child's.

'Warrroigggh! Noooo! Help!!'

'It's all right, Barry. Let's get up now. Come on.'

'Nick, what the fuck are you doing?'

'I'm helping him up.'

'Can you leave him for a moment, please, and just explain to me what's going on?'

Nick lets go and wheels himself round to face me, his eyes glittering with some terrible surface energy.

'You think you know what's mad and what's sane, don't you?' he says. 'It's all clear to you, isn't it? People who live in houses, who go to work, who use the car and the phone and talk about what they saw on TV last night and who the boss is sleeping with, they're sane. But people who live in the air, who shout in the street, who don't care about whether they're doing well or doing badly in life, who sing and dance whenever and wherever the mood takes them, they're mad. Well, perhaps, Gabriel, just maybe . . . *it's the other way round*.'

'But he pissed in my bed!'

Nick, just for a second, looks taken aback by this. Even through the thick mist of all his unadulterated hippie bullshit, part of him has to concede that this isn't very nice. The smell rising gradually into the room, which I'd locate on the scratch 'n' sniff somewhere between Jezebel's never changed litter-tray and a nineteenth-century distillery, works here to my advantage.

'Well . . .' he says, 'I'll pay for some new sheets, if you're that bothered.'

'No, I'm not bothered. I've always wanted to sleep in tramp's piss.'

'Ha! *Tramp*.'

'He *is* a tramp.'

'He's a free spirit.'

'No, he's had some free spirit.'

'Yeah, yeah. Do what you always do when you can't deal with something, Gabe – make a joke of it.'

'Oh, for fuck's sake, of course I can't deal with it. I touched his shitty coat. I was lying naked right next to his shitty coat!'

Nick nods, in smug self-righteousness. 'That's OK. Be angry. Just let it out.'

I take a very deep breath. 'Are you telling me that you invited Barry in, then, just to make some sort of sub-R.D. Laing psycho-point?'

'No,' says Nick, clearly lying. 'I just thought he might fancy a cup of tea.'

I look over at Barry. He's gone to sleep. It is true, of course, that if you take much of what Barry has said over the years at face value, you might think that what he often fancies is a cup of tea.

'Did you give him one?'

'Yes.'

'Did he drink it?'

'. . . No.'

'So then what happened?'

'We had a talk. About . . .'

'Whether or not you had any bollocks?'

'No. About many things. About his childhood in Limerick, about his wife leaving him, about the time he murdered a park keeper, about the—'

Something occurs to me. 'Was the Bradford game abandoned then?'

'Huh?'

'Bradford. Who were they playing today?'

'Stockport.'

'So . . . how come you're back here so early?'

'I didn't go.'

'Pardon?'

'I didn't go.'

'Why?'

'I dunno, I just didn't. Other things to think about.'

I have no touchstone left for this bloke now. He may just as well be someone else.

'Anyway, I just went off to practise the penny whistle for a bit, and when I came back, he was gone. I thought he'd gone out again.'

'Let's see if we can work out what happened,' I say, pushing him through the bedroom door, and out into the hallway, past my scrambled clothes. In the living-room, as I suspected, the one bottle of wine and three bottles of spirits that once formed our not especially well-stocked drinks cabinet lie scattered and empty around the carpet, like used shell-canisters on the Somme. I look at Nick. He starts laughing. But not proper, 'you must see the funny side' laughing, no: mad laughing, robot laughing. It is not infectious. I grasp him by the shoulders; my stare rebounds off his overlit eyes.

'Nick, mate. *Nick*.' His body shakes and his breath catches with giggling. 'Where have you *gone*?'

10

Who are all these people? Peter Peter Tao. C. Hook. Bafnia Software Consultants. Ugo Cindetta, Ph.D. Smidgy. Today, in our mail, there are letters for all of them. There's always an envelope addressed to at least one of them, sometimes two, but today it's the whole set. As time and piles of their unsent-on post have built up, I've created in my mind images of them all. Peter Peter Tao, a quiet unassuming Korean gentleman, whose parents were desperate to Westernise their children, but had only ever heard of one English Christian name. His letters are always formal, never personal, like his life. He wears a Magritte bowler hat and works for Unilever. C. Hook, the receiver only of red final demands, is a woman – Catherine. A junkie, she dropped out of college to play bass in the band that, some time after they booted her out for bursting into tears on stage, became Elastica. Bafnia Software Consultants chose the big-company-sounding name – Bafnia – to disguise the fact that they were working out of a second-floor flat in Kilburn. '71b Streatley Road Software Consultants . . . I'm sorry, Jack, it doesn't quite work.' They only get letters very occasionally. Their last days were almost certainly plagued by intent young men from *Watchdog* banging on the door shouting 'Mr Bafnia? Mr Bafnia! We know you're in there, Mr Bafnia!'

Ugo Cindetta, Ph.D. has returned to Italy after a somewhat controversial marriage to one of his students broke down irretrievably. The name on his envelopes sometimes looks shakily written – she is still trying to contact him, unaware that he's put most of a continent between them. Writing out her scars, I suppose; would they deheal, though, if she knew her letters lay unopened on top of our fridge? And Smidgy, who only ever receives letters from one source, a correspondent in Burma, is, I am sure, the nickname of an ex-public schoolboy, whose old school-chum – Flipper, I should think, or maybe Basho – now working in the diplomatic corps, writes him brisk but occasionally satirical diatribes about bureaucracy and corruption in South-East Asia, the nicknames retained as just a trace of what passed between them during those cricket-green days.

I put the letters, unopened, on top of our fridge. We're going to have to start a new pile soon. From them, I sort out the two that are actually for me, one, which I instantly recognise, from the old age home in Edgware where my grandmother lives, and the other a postcard of George Best, George Best when he was the coolest person on earth – when he was *Elvis* – turning round to grin at a cameraman on the touchline, knowing full well that, in the resulting picture, the football in the background would be eclipsed by his smile. The words on the back are written in an ordered hand, with sloping I's and romanesque e's.

> *Gabriel. I'm sorry about the other day. I was a touch, much as I hate the word,* hormonal. *Also, to be honest, I suspected your motives a bit. But now I'm not so sure. Give me a ring, love Dina.*

No X's. That's a turn-up, though. Not quite swinging myself round lamp-posts time yet, but positive. I even attempt a little whistle, but, stupidly, start before I've decided on an appropriate happy tune, and so it just comes out like a nondescript bit of pan-pipes.

The letter from my grandmother is less cheering.

> *My dearest Gabby,*
>
> *Hello my love. How are you? I'm not so well. My liver problem has got worse, and my arthritis is terrible. Also, I have cataracts now, which means soon I won't be able to*

see much, but feh! who wants to see in this place, anyway? I don't want to see a lot of old cuckers spilling tea all over themselves. Mrs Hindlebaum sends her love. Mummy tells me you have started seeing a young lady. Mazaltov! At long last! Jewish? Anyway, you must bring her to see me, if you ever come again. Please do come, Gabby. Sometimes the day passes so slowly.

All my love,
Mutti XXXX.

The hand is so old and spindly the letter looks already like an antique; only the unyellowed blue of the Basildon Bond reminds me I'm not reading it through a glass case. She writes, as ever, with no sense of distinction between speaking and writing – I hear her Polish/German accent clearly: she was saying the words out loud as she wrote. She sounds, of course, like a terrible hypochondriac, but then you do, don't you, when you're eighty-three, and your body winds up its parts, one by one. Thinking of someone at that age as a hypochondriac is just a way of telling yourself they're not dying.

I put the letter down by the microwave and go over to the filter coffee machine (I looked into the espresso machine yesterday and discovered a potentially mineable quarry of limescale). As I do so, my bare right foot goes into something soft, wet and squidgy, unlike Flipper/Basho who, years ago, presumably, went into something soft, wet and Smidgy. I look down. It is a sodden piece of dark green pondweed. Jezebel has started carrying these in recently and depositing them on the floor. Cats bring things into their owners' houses – mice or birds or whatever – as gifts, I read once, thank yous for feeding and stroking them. But what sort of gift is a piece of pondweed? 'Oh thank you, Jezebel, just what I've always wanted.' And where does she get fucking pondweed from in Kilburn? Oh, wait a minute. There is a place nearby that the council laughably refer to as a park, called The Grange, where, in fact, me and Nick dropped off the still fast asleep Mental Barry back on his favourite bench the other night, despite the protestations of the other tramps who clearly thought he'd gone for good; and I think it does have a sort of cesspit surrounded by a circle of broken bricks, which, if you were perhaps commissioned to landscape-garden Hell, you might use as a reference point for a pond. Personally, I think it's a bit dangerous for Jezebel to go there by herself at all times of the day and night; just think what might happen to those poor tramps.

I smear the piece of pondweed on top of the two layers of food and cans poking out of the swing-bin. It looks pretty at home there. Then, swinging my leg round like a spastic Kung-Fu artist, I stick my foot into the kitchen sink and turn the cold tap on. The water system thinks about it for a couple of seconds, and then blasts out a freezing jet, washing off the green slime-mark. Still in this position, I bend over backwards to open the fridge door for some milk. What's that? A new fridge magnet?

Ah. Zebedee. From *The Magic Roundabout*. He is crucified against a small crayon drawing, a badly drawn sun shining on some upside-down houses, out of which stick-people are falling and smiling. Using Zebedee's arms as a cog, I turn it round. The stick-people jump into their houses and frown. On the top of the page, now the bottom, is written *A Souvenir from Nick*. Then the phone rings: my foot jumps instinctively upwards, hitting the tap hard. Water spurts everywhere from around my instep. As I bring it away, an upturned fork inside a dirty cup spears my heel. For fuck's sake. Giving up the ghost, I choose – choose, mind – to fall over.

The phone rings for the third time as my head bangs on the fridge door. Zebedee springs into my left eye. I always think that if you are, in real life, suddenly put through some slapstick, you may as well follow its rules to the end, and so I lie there momentarily looking deadpan. The answerphone clicks on.

'Hi, this is a message for Gabriel, from Dina. That's some answerphone message, by the way. Scary. Anyway, I hope you got my card and—'

I just pick up the phone in time. 'Hello!'

'Hi! You screening your calls?'

'No, I was just . . . I was in bed.' Always plausible.

'Oh, sorry.'

'No, it's OK. Thanks for the card! Where d'you get it?'

'In Camden.'

'Great,' I say, immediately realising that there isn't anything particularly great about this. A moment of embarrassed silence sets in. Well, not silence exactly.

'Gabriel? Are you growling?'

'It's just the 'phone. Listen, why don't you come round tonight? I'll cook you dinner.'

'Uh . . . sure. Why not? But there's one thing you should know.'

'AIDS?'

'Pardon?'

'It's just the 'phone.'

'I'm a vegetarian.'

'That's OK. I was vegetarian for a while.'

'Really? How long?'

'Four hours. Then I got too depressed about never having sausages ever again, and so I had some.'

'How many?'

'Seven.'

She laughs. It's the first time I've heard it. A quivering, breathy laugh. It reminds me of someone. Oh yeah, her.

'I'm sorry about lying to the Green Flag man and stuff. It was the first thing that came into my head.'

'That's OK. I overreacted. We'll laugh about it when we *are* married.'

''Scuse me?'

'A joke, Gabriel.'

First laughing, now jokes already. Such an effect I could wish my hormones to have. (Sorry, sometimes I think very Jewishly.)

'Well, great,' I say again, not having learnt my lesson.

'OK, I'll be round sort of eightish.'

'Eightish?'

'. . . Yeah?'

'Is that like . . . before eight? Or at eight? Or something like five or six minutes past?'

'I'm not coming if you're a psycho.'

'Great. Eightish it is, then.'

'See you.'

'Bye.'

I put the phone down and feel, well, great, I suppose would have to be the word. Then I feel not so great. Our answerphone message just says 'You've reached the number for Gabriel Jacoby and Nick Munford. We can't get to the phone just now, but please leave a message and we'll phone you right back.' What's scary about that? Admittedly, it is said over *What An Atmosphere* by Russ Abbott, but . . . I press the outgoing message replay button. The tape whizzes backwards, clunks, then slowly moves forward.

'Tell the truth,' says Nick's voice, his flat Bradford syllables measured out in a slow metronomic tone. 'Tell the real truth. Look into your *soul* – and leave a message from there.'

Beeeeeeep. Yes, that is scary. Particularly because he still chose to say it over *What An Atmosphere*.

The Liv Dashem retirement home is a large semi-detached house in Edgwarebury Lane which lines its crazy-paved front pathway with a series of pairs of ever-larger chrysanthemum bushes: a sort of Seven Ages of Chrysanthemum Bush effect. To the right of the path is a standard two-car-sized driveway, at the front of which stands a handwritten 'Car Park' sign, and, in which, without fail, someone will have always parked some type of Volvo estate. The sun shines hard for the first time I can remember this year as I wait for the figure of a nurse to shimmer into view through the frosted fire-glass of its front door.

After making the arrangement with Dina for tonight, I felt at a bit of a loose end. I looked at my atlas, torn out of a 1960s *Encyclopaedia Britannica*, and started writing down a list of destinations that me and her could cover if we ever went on a world trip together, but got depressed halfway through writing down 'Bechuanaland Protectorate' and threw it away. Then, on my way back from getting two packets of Quorn and a jar of tandoori paste in Foodworld on the High Road, I started to feel guilty: here I was, in a state similar to that which I often feel just before entering a party, halfway between anticipation and panic, while my grandma sits lonely and letter-writing in a scuffed armchair hoping that soon, seven or eight hours will be over. Where's her pre-party feeling? Liv Dashem House does have a party, actually, at Chanukah, but I can't imagine that extra-large portions of Kneidlach and the opportunity to light a few candles induces in any of the residents a feeling halfway between anticipation and panic, and even if it does, I'm not sure they'd be able to tell this apart from the normal, everyday antici-panic brought on by encroaching death. So I mixed the Quorn and tandoori paste and left it to marinate (the trick here is to leave the pan open so that the paste dries crusty, then, when it's ready, quickly slip a top on to it and put it in the microwave: comes out just like a proper one from an Indian restaurant) and, seeing as the road to Edgware lies just at the bottom of my road, I decided to go and visit her.

She's a good old girl, my gran. I would come and visit her more often, actually, were it not for the fact that Liv Dashem House, as you might expect, is a bit of a reminder of my own mortality. I don't really need reminding of this, as I've never forgotten it, right from the day I found out about it. 'Death,' my mother told me at the age of five and a half, completing a conversation about what that big black car that just went past was, 'is like a long sleep from which you never wake up.' Thanks, Mum. No wonder I never fancied doing that sleeping thing again. It's supposed to pass over you at about forty, isn't it, that shadow, that genuine concrete awareness of your end? I remember feeling it that night, staring terrified at my bi-plane wallpaper, and most nights since.

The nurse that opens the door is a tired-looking black woman in her late thirties. A lot of the staff in Jewish old age homes are black, which gives them the feel of mini pre-Mandela South Africas.

'Yes?' she says suspiciously.

'I've come to see Eva Baumgart.'

She nods, withdrawing to let me in. An old man holding a walking stick sits on an orange plastic chair in the hallway. There are more comfortable places in the house, but I imagine that once sitting becomes all you do, after a while you think, 'S'pose I'll sit here now, for a change.'

'She's upstairs, visiting the Frindel sisters. Room Seven.'

Oh no. The Frindel sisters are two ninety-three-year-old twins who're convinced, completely wrongly, that Liv Dashem House is one of those old age homes where the staff beat up the residents. The nurse points me in the direction of the lift, but I take the stairs, because I can. Helps to fight off that reminder.

Outside Room Seven, I can hear my grandmother talking loudly in German. I knock on the door.

'*Ja?*'

I open it. As the Frindel sisters have often told me, all their belongings are holed up in a flat in Acton, and so their room is pure institutional, just a linoleum cell with a sink at one end. The two of them are identical in every respect, except the older one, Lydia I think, has got a wobbly brown mole large enough to hang your coat on in the hollow next to her right nostril. Her and her sister Lotte have both worn only black since their father died in 1952. Now they sit, very close together, on two school-classroom style wooden chairs set neatly in between their twin lilac-quilted beds; on the right bed, hair completely white, dress navy blue as always, sits my grandma, her feet not touching the floor.

'Hello, Mutti,' I say.

She looks up. For a few seconds, her face is ugly, distorted by fear and loathing, by memories of other large, indistinct men who smashed through the doors of her parents' home. Then light finally squeezes through the interstices of her cataracts, and her face clears into a smile, an incredibly welcoming smile.

'Gabby!' she says, and, forgetting she's eighty-three, makes to leap up. 'So nice of you to come!'

I go over to help her up: I'm only 5″ 9′, but even without her natural stoop Mutti comes up only to my solar plexus. I kiss her on her softly wrinkled cheek.

'How *are* you?' she says. She doesn't wait for a reply. 'Well! That was a quick response to my letter, I must say! Lotte! Lydia! *Es ist Gabby! Mein Enkel!*'

'Hello!' says Lydia.

'Hello!' says Lotte.

'Can you help us?' says Lydia. 'They come into our room without knocking. They don't tell us when our friends have telephoned.'

'Don't worry,' says my grandma to me in what I suppose you

would call a whisper, but, as she's almost completely deaf, it's more like a very breathy shout, 'it's not true.' I know this, but nod as if it's news. 'Well, ladies,' she continues, 'if my Gabby is here I must go.'

'But all our things are in Acton!'

'Well, goodbye,' says my grandma, tugging at my sleeve. I back out of the door, smiling vacuously.

'But, Eva! Young man! You must help us!'

We begin to move down the corridor. Holding her arm, I have to force myself to take extra-small steps to keep my speed down. She tuts, and shakes her head.

'Those women! I don't know what they want! But I'm so pleased you came. What—'

'They won't let us use our own toilet!!'

I turn round. I can just see the edge of Lydia's zimmer-frame poking round her door.

'Come on,' my grandma says, her face set. We move off at about ten yards an hour; Lydia emerges from her doorway at about two. Perhaps the slowest chase in the history of chase-sequences is on.

'They won't do Lotte's laundry!!'

The William Tell Overture plays in my head; it's all I can do not to turn round and stand waiting for her, and then, when she gets within an inch of me, run off again, holding Mutti above my head, waving. Two and a half minutes later and we're just about round the corner. Lydia has gained no ground on us, but I have a terrible feeling as I look back towards their door that I can see the first spoke of Lotte's wheelchair. It's like some terrible 4 by 400 metres.

'Quick!' says Mutti, absurdly, as to be honest I could go quicker. The lift is in sight.

'It's just off the North Circular Road! You could go there tomorrow!'

We're there. I press the button. The silver circle lights up. Stupidly, I press it again a few more times, as if this is going to make any difference to the lift. Come on, come on: we've only got thirty-five minutes. It arrives just as Lydia makes the corner.

'No!' she says, seeing us go into the lift. And I feel a bit bad, really, because even if, as my grandma says, it's not true, it's probably just Lydia Frindel's way of saying please stay.

In the lift is an old man with glasses so thick they make his eyes look like novelty pop-out ones.

'Are you from the council?' he says to me.

'Don't worry about him, he's mad,' says my grandma matter-of-factly.

The old man looks at her sharply. 'Don't bother talking to her,' he says. 'Deaf. And crazy.'

I look back at my grandma. She nods in his direction and taps her right temple. We're standing in a triangle, both of them looking at me.

'You'd better take her back to her room.'

'We'll tell the nurse to come and get him when we get out.'

'Very difficult when you get to her age.'

'I only thank heaven, Gabriel, that *my* mind hasn't gone that way.'

We get out on the ground floor and little-step towards the TV room. The TV room is so called because there is a huge old Ferguson colour TV in the centre of it, not because anyone in there actually watches it. As we go in, it is, as ever, on, but I can't believe that any of the five or six pensioners in the room are big fans of *The O-Zone*. Three of them are asleep. Another, Mr Susskind, glares at the screen in mute fixed intensity, but his eyes, I know, see only a man in an SS uniform carrying away his sister.

'Mrs Hindlebaum!' says my grandma. 'Mrs Hindlebaum!'

Mrs Hindlebaum, an even smaller woman than Mutti, with a ridiculously squeaky voice and a moustache Joe Stalin would've killed for, is already looking benignly in my direction, but this makes no difference to my grandma. 'Mrs Hindlebaum!' she says, much louder. 'Look who's here! Gabriel! Irene's boy!'

'Yes, yes, I know,' says Mrs Hindlebaum. 'How nice to see you.' Mrs Hindlebaum sits on a red mock-velvet sofa pressed against the far wall behind a reproduction antique coffee-table, its glass top franked by the circular marks of many cups; my grandmother has known her for over thirty years, but I'm buggered if she knows what her first name is.

'Sit down, Gabby,' says my grandma. 'Would you like some tea?'

Drinking and eating at Liv Dashem House I can't do. This is stupid and prejudiced of me – everything seems entirely hygienic – but the fact is, no matter how much Roseglade they spray round every room, you can still smell just a little bit of incontinence. Just the merest hint.

'No, thanks.'

'So,' says my grandma, settling herself down on the sofa next to Mrs Hindlebaum, 'tell us all about this young lady. Tina!'

I draw up an orange plastic chair. 'Dina.'

My grandma frowns. 'Your mother definitely said Tina.' For my grandma, this means that her name must be Tina. As far as she's concerned, my mother, in two distinct ways, is like the Pope: born in Poland, and infallible.

'No, honestly, it's Dina.'

'Well, never mind,' she says, with a sense that, obviously, I'll come round eventually. 'And you've been seeing her for two months!'

'Not *quite* two months . . .'

'You should've brought her! I'd love to have met her!'

I consider how this would've looked. First date, a day out coming back from Loftus Road with a Green Flag man. Second date, a day out at a Jewish old-age home.

'A Jewish girl?' says Mutti, her voice rising like a ski-jumper to the end of the sentence.

I pause. Then I do something stupid: 'Yes.' Oh well. If it ever happens, I'll teach her some Yiddish. And say her dad was one of those Ethiopian Jews – what are they called? Oh yeah, Falashas. Or Sammy Davis Junior, of course.

Mutti is so overjoyed she claps her hands. 'Oh, Gabriel!'

'Mutti, it's only just started. Nothing's happened yet.'

'Two months and nothing?'

'Nothing serious.'

She looks to Mrs Hindlebaum and shrugs. 'After two months, my Josh had proposed.' She holds the shrug for so long it looks like the last frame of an American sitcom: any minute now I expect to hear the closing theme-music of *The Eva Baumgart Show*. My grandma is pretty big on shrugging, although, to be honest, her repertoire consists only of this one, the 'what can you mach?' one.

'Ah yes, Eva, but your Josh was like that,' says Mrs Hindlebaum. '*Voreilig*.'

My grandma nods, smiling regretfully. 'Impulsive,' she tells me.

Yeah, he *was* impulsive, except in death, I remember: my grandfather was an unconscionably long time a-dying. He thought about it, he mulled it over, he deliberated and cogitated, as Loyd Grossman would say, he ran it past the rest of us over and over again, he tried out a number of different routes – cancer, heart failure, Alzheimer's Disease – before, finally, settling on some sort of total body meltdown. Thank goodness we're not Catholic, or by the sixth time, I think the last rites priest would've instituted a call-out charge. It's a shame, in a way, because, you know what it's like with death, it kind of blows everything else out of your head; and so, now, that's the main memory I have of my grandpa: constantly dying. Now, when I see him in my dreams, he doesn't appear as he's meant to, healthy again, robed in white, riding on a cloud: he comes back more literally from the grave, like a moaning staring zombie, bits falling off him and everything, crying for help like the Undead do.

'The Reverend Oshor Rosenberg, rabbi of Redbridge Synagogue, announced in a shock move today that from next Shabbat, all prayer services would be accompanied by a Hammond organ, to be played by Mrs Nesta Mayer, already well known in the community for her sterling work at the piano-keyboard for the Redbridge and District Good Companions production of *Yentl*,' says my grandmother, in a loud and distinct voice.

She has picked up a copy of *The Jewish Chronicle* lying on the coffee-table and read a random bit of it out loud, as is her wont. Putting her chained-round-her-neck reading-glasses back on her disturbingly large bosom, she looks up and does her shrug again, injecting into it just a little element of 'fancy!' She puts the newspaper down, finished with it.

'How are you sleeping at the moment, Gabriel?' says Mrs Hindlebaum. That I have insomnia is one of the three things

Mrs Hindlebaum always remembers about me, the other two being that I like Smarties – bit out of date now – and that I could've done very well for myself if only I'd been prepared to work a bit harder.

'Not very well, Mrs Hindlebaum, but thanks for asking.'

She lays a finger, made angular by arthritis, across her grey lips, and pauses, as if she is about to say something momentous.

'Have you ever tried Kalms?'

I've made it my policy always to be truthful about the state of my insomnia, whatever trouble it brings me. This, however, *is* the trouble it always brings me: well-meant but bloody useless advice. People cannot hear that I am an insomniac without offering some apparently entirely foolproof, it's-always-worked-for-me remedy, and they honestly seem to think, these people, that I must never have *tried* switching the light on and reading for a bit, or having a hot bath before I go to bed, or a cup of hot milk, or counting backwards from a hundred, or one of the hundreds of low-level herbal remedies available without prescription from the chemist, none of which have any effect on proper, fuck-off insomnia, and the most popular of which, with people who don't know what proper, fuck-off insomnia is but who perhaps have had a little bit of trouble dropping off once or twice in their lives, is always, without fail, Kalms. This is maybe the twenty-sixth time Mrs Hindlebaum has offered me this advice.

'No, I haven't actually, Mrs Hindlebaum,' I say. 'I must give it a try.'

'It's available from Boots.'

'Is it? Good. Great.'

My grandmother's misted-over eyes drift back from nowhere. 'So *nu*, Gabby?' she says, picking up her thread. *Nu*, remember? 'How do you see it going with this young lady? What do you feel about Tina?'

Um . . .

Someone taps me on the shoulder. I look round.

'*And* . . .' says Lydia Frindel breathlessly, 'they force us to eat pork!!'

* * *

Back in the flat, 7:10. Fifty minutes to go till eightish. My need for specificity in time has never been more acute than now. The thing is, I've got the horn. No point in saying this poncily. I've got the horn. And so, I'm going through that particular dilemma that men go through fifty minutes before a hot date: do I conserve all my resources for later on, or do I have a quick wank now? Here are the pros and cons of the latter option.

Pros: 1. I won't be in a terrible state of hyped-up sexual excitement all through dinner, spilling things and speaking in tongues.
2. Should sex actually occur, I may be able to hold back for longer than otherwise in the manner so often prescribed in video sex manuals.
3. It'll feel quite nice.

Cons: 1. Halfway through dinner, realising that I smell like a Maltese brothel.
2. Should sex actually occur, my prostate exploding.
3. The doorbell going halfway through.

I check my watch. 7:17. Sod it, let's have a look in the library. I open the drawer above the TV: *New Wave Hookers, Anal Eccentricity, Spunky Birthday, Pissing Party, Heisse Titten, Wet and Willing, Inside Desirée Cousteau, Anal Anal Anal, Max Hardcore, Buttman's Big-Tit Adventure*. I really must file them alphabetically at some point. Second layer: *Schoolgirls Disciplined, The Jumping Jizz of Ed Powers, Gandhi*. I don't know how that got in here. The third layer is mainly terrible British soft-core – *Electric Blue* and so forth – plus three untitled tapes where that little hole in the video which stops it being recorded over has been covered with an enormous piece of brown gaffer tape.

A difficult choice. They all hold so many different meanings for me. *Wet and Willing*, the first tape I ever got, which I bought from Julian Ng at school for £3.95 and a copy of *Exchange And Mart*, and which I was able to play hundreds of times without getting bored: now of course I'm lucky if I'm still interested before the end of a new tape's first run-through. *Max Hardcore*, which I found broken on a rubbish dump round the back of Cricklewood BR, and nursed back to playability like a pigeon with a broken wing. *Heisse Titten*, given to me by my dad. *Anal Anal Anal*, which sounds so much like a remake of *Tora! Tora! Tora! Spunky Birthday*, the title of which so cleverly allows you to infer what the plot might be. *Inside Desirée Cousteau* (no relation, I think) which always makes me wonder if, at breakfast next morning on the set, anyone accidentally ate that hard-boiled egg.

That's it, I'm going for that one. I reach in for it: there is a snap, and a sharp, direct pain shoots through my right hand.

I bring my hand out quickly. My finger, red and throbbing, is attached to a mousetrap, which is attached, with Blu-Tack, to the back of the video. A fucking *mousetrap*. I did buy some of these a few years ago, because, perversely, the only thing Jezebel never seems interested in killing is mice, but I can't believe that she put it in there: even her venomosity doesn't stretch that far. With my left hand I delicately pull the metal bar back and away from my fingers. Underneath them is written, in black Magic Marker: YOU'RE CAUGHT IN A TRAP.

Nick. The fucking hypocrite. I suppose he thinks now that he's gone mental, all previous character records are erased. For heaven's sake, Nick's spent more time watching pornography than the British Board of Film Censors. If I ever acquire a new tape, I might watch it once, then again maybe three hours later, and that's it for the day; Nick once told me that he'll watch it, make a cup of tea, then watch it again, then make another cup of tea, then watch it again, then make another cup of tea, then watch it again, until, basically, he runs out of tea. And when I say watch, I don't mean a purely passive, non-interactive kind of watching.

Actually, it strikes me, as I wait for the cold tap to condescend to run over my fingers, this sort of pomposity wasn't beyond Nick even when he wasn't mad: it just had the opposite objective. We have a house rule that we never watch pornography together – what kind of men do you think we are, anyway? – and so, often, there have been times, towards the end of the night, when both of us would sit humming and haaing on the sofa waiting for the other one to go to bed. Normally, I'd be the one to give in – after all, he had, as I've just explained, more to get through; but once – I think it was just after *Buttman's Big-Tit Adventure* had come in – I refused; I thought, no, have some will-power, some self-control, and stayed there, pretending I was waiting up to watch *The Hitman and Her*. And Nick just cracked: he got up and started shouting about me being selfish and inconsiderate, and what a hard day he'd had on the windscreens, and how some people thought about other people apart from themselves now and again. Incredible, isn't it? He actually tried to claim the moral high ground for having a wank.

I would have it out with him, but he's off on some stupid New Age weekend with this Fran woman he keeps going on about. Well, he's not going to beat me this time. No, I can do that perfectly well myself. I put the tape in the VCR, go back to the sofa, loosen my trousers and reach for the remote.

Damn. It's not on the arm of the sofa. If I can't find the remote, I might as well not bother. I only watch pornography on fast-forward. A couple of times in my life I've stayed in hotel rooms, and once, one of these had a porn channel, from which most of the actual porn had been painfully dissected, making a very worthwhile channel, I must say. But I remember watching it for no more than five minutes before my free hand instinctively reached for a phantom video remote. Because my eye is trained. It is a crack eye. Most people, you see, think of good vision as an ability to spot detail in the first dimension – in space, at length; but what about those of us who are able to spot detail in the fourth dimension – in time, at speed? The merest pucker of brown; the slightest trajectory of white; a momentary sideways tug of fabric – I can read all these at 150 frames a second. And bom! My finger's on normal play. Then on slow.

The trouble is, if you watch too much pornography – and I do, I watch too much pornography – then what you find is that suddenly, you never take your hand off FF. Images flash by in pink piles, straight sex, lesbian sex, two-, three-, and seven-way sex, oral sex, anal sex, oro-anal sex, golden, golden showers, enemas, and still your thumb remains unmoved. The whole video is about to fly by. And then eventually the thought comes: *what the fuck am I looking for?* Or, to put it another way, what fuck am I looking for?

Where *is* it? Hmm. 7:22. Oh, there it is. No, that's the bloody CD one, that I never ever use. Has Nick hidden it as part of his moral cleansing programme? Oh heavens to Betsy, she'll be here in a minute. Why do I spend so much of my life looking for things that I've lost? In between two cushions on the sofa . . . under these old copies of *ES magazine* . . . ah, here we go. Right in front of my face, on the coffee-table.

I settle down in the seat, pull my pants down to my ankles, and click on play, then FF before the image has even come up. It spools through, two women–one bloke, standard intercourse, one woman–one bloke, standard intercourse, one woman–two blokes . . . oh yeah. This bit. Incredible. Not so much an erotic treat as a magic trick, but we'll start here anyway. I grasp my – I believe the word is *straining* – member. Then I hear this noise.

'Wibbit.'

I mean, that's the only way I can write it down. Obviously, it wasn't exactly 'wibbit'. It was just a croaking noise. Then again.

'Wibbit.'

Still holding on steadfastly to my – I believe the word is *proud* – member, and still refusing to take my eyes off the screen, I become aware of something else, something in the corner of my vision, something, which, to be honest, fits in quite logically with all this wibbiting. Tentatively, unhappily, I turn my neck away from the pyramid of flesh on the TV to see, sitting on the far edge of the living-room rug, looking at me somewhat curiously, a small frog.

I leap up in fear, into a crouching position on the sofa. What's a fucking *frog* doing in here now? Is this more of Nick's crazy shit?

I crouch there, trousers round my ankles, watching the frog, the frog watching me. Perhaps he thinks I'm doing an impression of him. Then *flap!patpatpat*: Jezebel comes through the door, looks at me contemptuously, picks up the frog, and goes out again, the frog's legs hanging out of her mouth like some sort of aquaphibian moustache.

I draw my pants and trousers up over my – the word, without any doubt, is *wilting* – member. The people on the screen grunt, moan and go 'oh yeah, baby' a lot; I reach for the remote and turn it off.

It was Jezebel. She brought it in. So . . . presumably, it's another gift. Having brought in the green pond-slime for a while, and perhaps realised that it hasn't been greatly appreciated, she's thought, 'I know. I'll bring him some of that state-of-the-art green pond-slime that moves.' Either that, or she's working her way up the evolutionary scale, and next thing I know she'll be dragging The Man Who Lives Downstairs kicking and screaming through the cat-flap. Then she comes back, without the frog.

'Where's the frog?'

She looks at me as if to say, 'Frog? What frog?' I look over at her new scratching-post stuffed with catnip – pristine, not a mark on it – and lose my rag a bit.

'I DON'T WANT FUCKING FROGS!! DON'T BRING FROGS IN HERE!'

Jezebel looks a bit startled. Then she starts cleaning herself, slowly, methodically, meaning: what you shouting at me for? I'm a cat. I raise my palm out to slap her across the head, and she looks up at me like: don't even think about it. I don't even think about it. Then the doorbell goes.

'Anything except for The Carpenters.'

'Right.'

I check the CD collection. I'm sure I've got some Barry White somewhere. Perhaps that's a bit obvious. I settle for Miles Davis's *Kind of Blue*, like I always do when I want to appear a bit sophisticated.

'Oh, I hate this café music,' says Dina. I look a bit crushed. 'Sorry,' she says, smiling. 'Still instinctively aggressive.'

'Why is that?' I say, adopting my serious face. She raises her left eyebrow, and takes a sip from the drink I've just poured her. Her face contracts.

'Sorry about the wine,' I say.

'No, it's fine,' she says, picking up the bottle. 'And maybe afterwards you could use the basket as a fruit bowl or something.'

Dina's wearing a pair of purple velvet hipsters, and some kind of gold lamé polo-neck top. She looks like a curtain hanging in St Mark's Cathedral. When I opened the door, the street lamps lit her from the back, and for a moment I thought it was she, come at last. Strange, really, because ever since I met her, I've been aware of this possibility, that I might at some point see Dina through a glass brightly, refracted by my desire into Alice; so aware that the contours of difference between her face and Alice's have, if anything, become exaggerated. Only in this moment, when, for once, Alice wasn't in my thoughts at all, live as they were with hope and fear and possibility purely about Dina, did her features morph softly sideways: only when I forgot how much I want her to look like Alice did she look like Alice.

'I dunno where it comes from sometimes.'

'But it's normally induced by men . . .?'

Dina puts her drink down on the coffee-table, next to the video remote.

'So,' she says, changing the subject, 'what was Ben like as a kid?'

I fall backwards into the far end of the sofa. 'Um . . . serious. He worried about stuff you don't expect kids to worry about. I remember he was very uncertain about whether or not Britain should join the Common Market.'

'How old was he then?'

'Five. Too young, I suppose, for him to have had any significant influence on Ted Heath's thinking. But I remember by the time he was ten he could recite the Periodic Table.'

'So he was a swot?'

'Well, it wasn't anything to do with school. I think he wanted our parents to think he wasn't just a meathead.'

'At ten?'

'At ten he already looked like Israel's entry for Mr Universe.' I pause. 'What about Alice?' My stomach lurches, like when you feel someone may have spotted you lying; but I say it nonchalantly.

'Oh, happy. The sort of little girl who spends a lot of time on a swing attached to a tree in the back garden.'

'Did you not get on?' I mean, do you not get on now, really, but I think it's a bit early to ask that.

'Well, just sister stuff, you know. I always thought our mum much preferred her. After all,' she says, raising her right eyebrow, 'she is the beautiful one.'

She says this straight; not, I think, with an eye towards a gushing contradiction from me. Which, craven though I am at times, I might've found hard to do.

'Don't all kids think their parents prefer their brothers and sisters?'

'Well . . . when I was four, our mum let her open my Christmas presents before I'd got up, just because Alice wanted to see if I'd got anything she would've liked.'

'No!'

'I hadn't, of course. All her presents were just slightly better.'

She says this with a smirk of bitterness. I'm getting a signal off Dina, a sense that the world has let her down, and an expectation that it will again.

'But I got my own back. I used to beat her up.'

'Really?'

'Yeah. Once I tied her to the tree using the ropes of the swing.'

'Wasn't that a bit difficult?'

'I cut it down first.'

Oh dear. I can't get the image of Alice tied to a tree out of my head.

'Sorry,' says Dina, relaxing her features. 'I love her really. It's just I had a bit of a row with her tonight.'

'About what?'

'Oh, nothing.'

'How long are you planning to stay with them?'

'Just until I can find a place of my own. I need to get some work.'

'God, I don't even know what you do . . .'

'Well, I did . . . in America, I ran a paintball site.'

'Paintball? What, like . . . people who can't make it into the Territorial Army running about shooting each other with Dulux?'

'Basically.'

I try to process this information and get nowhere. 'That's amazing. Sorry, but I sort of had you down for being PC.'

'PC? Well, I'm a feminist. Not fashionable, I know . . .'

'And you're a vegetarian: that makes you about the most PC person I've met since I was a student.'

'Oh, bollocks!'

'Well, not someone who organises paintball. Isn't paintball a terrible expression of male aggression?'

'Well, yes and no. Lots of women do it as well. But I gave it up anyway. Round about the time I became . . .' she says it with a hearty slab of eyebrow-induced irony '. . . PC.'

'Is it big in the States? Paintball?'

She blinks. I feel somehow that this blinking is a form of sighing. 'Yeah, huge. You can buy all sorts of high-tech paint-guns there.' There is a short pause: she looks out of the window. An Asian man comes out of Abrakebabra loaded down with doners. 'Actually, can we talk about something else?'

My answer – yes – is blocked by the ringing of the phone. Dina looks at me. I don't pick it up, meaning, very clearly, *I'm interested in you.* If I was really brave I'd pick the receiver up, press the button down without answering, leave the phone off the hook and turn back to her with a James Bond smile. I don't. The answerphone clicks on.

'Hi, lover! Just ringing to touch base!'

Oh no.

'I was just putting some dinner on for your father, and I was wondering if you wanted to come and join us. Why not bring Tina! It's about time we met her, I think. Just joking, lover. See you soon.'

'WHAT ARE YOU DOING ON THE PHONE, YOU TWITTERING OLD BUGGERNAUT!!'

I can just hear the beginnings of her 'what a card your father is' chuckle as she puts the phone down. I look at Dina. I think I'm blushing.

'Buggernaut?' she says.

'Yeah. It's a new one on me.'

She smiles to herself. We both know she deliberately hasn't picked out the real key word of the message.

'Who's Tina?'

Now she has. I have a choice here. I could claim it was . . . I dunno . . . my cousin: what a coincidence! Or I could tell her at least half of the truth. I feel I'm standing in a hallway facing two doors, one marked *Beginning Of A Beautiful Relationship*, the other, *Nightmare*. I don't know what to do, so I call up in my mind the one person who really knows about love. She appears in a mist of light.

'What shall I do?'

'Can you not bug me now?' she says. 'I'm still really pissed off about that Bitty Maclean cover of *We've Only Just Begun*. D'you know he changed the opening lyric from "We've only just begun to live/White lace and promises . . ." to "We've only just begun to live/*Life's full* of promises"? What, did he think that people don't know what white lace is?!'

'Karen . . .'

'Why not change it all! "We've only lust, big one!" Eh?'

'Please. Karen. I'm relying on you.'

She tuts, and picks a book out of the mist. It is the size of a wedding register, and leather-bound. On the front, in gold-embossed Gothic lettering it says *Love*.

'Let me see . . .' she says, licking her finger and turning the pages by the corners, '. . . Lads and lasses . . . Laughter . . . Length . . .' She looks up. 'You wouldn't have a sandwich on you, would you?' I shake my head; she sighs. 'Ah, here we are: Lying.' She leans back and clears her throat: vapour cradles her neck. 'Best not to.' She looks up at me. 'OK?' And she's gone. I look at Dina.

'She means you.'

Dina nods. She turns her face away and scratches the back of her neck thoughtfully. Without turning back, she says, 'I suppose it is about time I met your parents. After all, we have been going out for ages. For all I know we might be married.'

'Look, Dina. You know when you said on your postcard that you suspected my motives . . .?'

'Yeah?'

'If you meant that I want to sleep with you, then yes, I have got those motives. But I don't see what's *suspicious* about that.'

Goodness. I've never been so straight-talking in my life. Thanks, Karen. Dina turns back to me, holding my gaze now in a way that means 'I'm holding your gaze.'

'That still doesn't explain why your mum thinks we're an item.'

'Oh, she's desperate for me to get a steady girlfriend. So I just stuck your name on her dotted line. Probably because I wanted to think it was going to happen. I'm sorry.'

Dina frowns. 'When?'

Ah. Before I even met you. Because I was so convinced that you'd look like your sister. 'Couple of days after you came round here the first time.'

In the stellar distance, a leather-bound book slams shut angrily. I'm so craven. I'm so craven. Just call me John.

'Look,' says Dina, getting up, 'perhaps I'd better go. It's all got a bit candid for this early in the evening.'

'Dina,' I say, 'I *am* sorry.'

'The thing is,' she says, picking up her handbag, a black, permanently sunken, 1940s doctor's bag, the leather so lined it appears to be frowning, 'it wouldn't work, would it? Be honest. You're Ben's brother. My brother-in-law's brother. What are we trying to create here, the Waltons? Men.'

That pisses me off.

'What? What men? Why do women like you always say that? "Men." As if it's self-explanatory. What thing is it that men always do that I'm doing now?'

'Not thinking about the consequences of a fuck.'

Her eyes are the opposite of Nick's eyes the other day: burning *with* meaning, *with* reason. She turns to go.

'That's not true,' I say. 'It's just wrong. I wish I *could* dive into bed with anybody and not worry about it. I wish I *could* be happy-go-lucky in love. I hear people – men *and* women – talking about changing their partners all the time in a matter-of-fact way, and I'd really like to be part of that . . . merry-go-round. But I can't. Every time I get into a relationship, I can't face getting out of it. Nothing seems to be worth that much pain.'

Dina turns round, putting her bag on top of the piano. 'So why are you still single?'

Because I'm in love with your sister.

'Oh, I get chucked. All the women I've ever been involved with have ended it, normally just about the time that I'm deeply wrangling with myself about how on earth I'm going to end it.'

'Well, that's OK, then. Saves you the bother.'

'Not really. As soon as they do it, I desperately don't want them to go.'

Dina looks at me searchingly, like she did when she threatened to blow my story to the Green Flag man and I pleaded with her not to. I think she's not used to men freely admitting to weakness. She sits back down on the sofa and picks up her drink. 'Do you know why I left America?'

'No.'

'No reason why you should. Only Alice knows here.'

She pauses, as if uncertain to continue. Then, somehow managing to make it look real and not just an action copied from seeing 'secret about to be divulged' scenes in the movies, she knocks back the remaining wine in her glass in one go.

'I was running the paintball site on a patch of woodland at the back end of Queens. I ran it with my boyfriend – a guy called Miles. Miles Traversi. It was his idea, he was really into it. We started, oh . . . summer 1993. And basically, I did the business and commercial side, and Miles did the creative stuff.'

'Creative?'

'He thought of the name – *Rampage*. He designed the site: it had a big wooden fort, bunkers, hides, tree-houses – he even got a batch of bombed-out old Ford Zephyrs from a scrap dealer and strewed them all over the place for the guerrilla games. And he worked out all the games, all the wars: guerrilla, trench, jungle, all-out combat. *And* he used to run the games on the day. He'd lead one group against the other, and then, because he was so good at it, he'd swap round.'

'Why was he so good at it?'

'He'd been in the Marines. Served in the Gulf War, but left the Army soon after that because, he said, it wasn't like he imagined. It was just people pressing buttons: all long-range death. Anyway, at first we did really good business. People came, I think, because of Miles. He was a born . . . leader, and people who wanna be soldiers like that. They liked following all his strategies, jumping to his orders. But then we started to get complaints. If a paintball pellet hits you, it hurts. It can bruise if you get shot at close range. That's why people wear reinforced masks. D'you mind if I smoke?'

'No. But I'll open the window.'

We move in a little pincer, me to the window, her over to the piano to get a packet of Silk Cut from her bag. The window, of course, sticks; strips of paint fall off as I jog it haltingly upwards, desperate not to appear too much of a weakling in the face of this revelation that her previous boyfriend was Steven fucking Seagal. When I turn somewhat breathlessly around, Dina is standing a little smirkingly by the sofa, with one cigarette in her mouth and another sticking out of the packet towards me: I turn it down. She sits down, lights hers, and takes a deep breath, exhaling the smoke through her nostrils.

'The complaints were about Miles. People who'd got shot by him would come into the office literally splattered with paint. If he got someone in his sights, he wouldn't give up. They'd be telling him to stop firing and he'd just carry on until they fell over and started screaming. He'd even deliberately shoot people from the side so that the pellet would hit them on the temple, behind the mask. I spoke to him about it, tried to tell him it was bad for business, but he wouldn't have it – told me that was why people came to *Rampage*, because they knew it was as close as they got to the real thing, to proper danger.

'Round about the same time, he started upgrading the guns. As I said, you can get some pretty high-tech paint-guns in the States – long-range ones, rapid-fire ones, all that stuff. The more you paid, the better the gun you could hire. Some people came with their own ones, customised. And Miles had his own gun. He made it himself. Some days, that's all he'd do, sit in our apartment and work on his gun, trying to get it to fire faster, and more accurately.'

'He sounds like a terrible man.'

'Well, that's just the point – he wasn't. Away from the site, he was a real sweetie – caring, loving . . . y'know. Really good with the kids.'

This makes me start. 'The two of you had kids?'

She looks up. 'Me? No. I can't have them. Well. I don't think so. Too many woman problems.'

'Oh . . .' She's clearly on a confessional roll.

'His kids, from his marriage. A girl of four and a boy of six, Bryony and Spike. Fantastically sweet; he used to see them every other weekend.' Her melancholic smile melts away. 'But by then it was like he was *never* away from the site. He'd even get angry about regulars who he thought were trying to steal his thunder. One guy, Jimmy, who used to come every weekend, and who was pretty well as good as Miles at the games – he hated him. Used to go on about him all the time. And one day, unbelievably, Miles accused me of sleeping with this guy. That was it. I cracked. I told him he was crazy, obsessed, that he'd put his stupid fucking war-game before us, and I walked. Washed my hands of the whole thing, me and him, *Rampage*, everything. And before I left I chucked his gun into the trash.'

'No!'

'Yeah. I just hung around to see it go into the back of the garbage lorry, and then I went to stay with friends.'

Something about all this starts to prickle at my memory in a way I'm not sure I like. Dina stubs out her half-smoked Silk Cut and lights another one.

'So . . . that was it, I thought. I did the usual stuff – cried on my friends' shoulders, looked in the local papers for a new apartment, got a part-time job, thought about ringing him. Then a couple of days later I turned on the TV and my world collapsed.

'Miles had gone down to the site as normal without me. He'd started the game up: all-out combat, I think it was. Only with one difference. He'd taken along a real gun.'

Now I remember. *Some psychokiller in America*. I wish I bothered to read the papers properly.

'A fucking Kalashnikov.'

'Shit! Where did he get that from?'

'You can get anything in New York. Guns in particular are not a problem.'

Her blue eyes blaze with the telling.

'So what happened?'

'He killed three people, and injured five. The cops were called, but, obviously, it's the middle of the woods, on a war-site he's designed – he's got the advantage. He's the Viet Cong.'

'But they got him eventually.'

She draws on her cigarette. 'No, actually. Jimmy got him eventually. With his paint-gun.'

'Really?'

'That's who Miles was after. But like I said – Jimmy was as good as him, and so he kept dodging him, covering his tracks, hiding. And something Miles didn't know is that Jimmy had built a couple of his own hides on the site, just using rocks and trees or whatever. He was hiding in one of these when Miles appeared screaming and shouting for blood. Jimmy stayed put. Eventually, Miles sat down on a tree-stump and took his mask off.' She stops for a second and looks into the middle distance. 'Some newspaper reports suggested he was crying.' Her eyes snap back into place. 'Jimmy came out of his hide, spraying Miles with paint as he ran. He blinded him long enough to get the Kalashnikov off him, then led him out of the woods with it. As soon as they got to the edge of the site, the cops peppered Miles with bullets.'

Dina looks at the floor. *Kind of Blue* fades to black. Silence pumps into the room like Zyklon B.

'I'm really sorry, Dina. Jesus.'

'Yeah.'

'I . . . um . . . I did read something about this, I think.'

She looks up. 'Yeah, it made page two or three of the papers here. But none of the American papers knew where to find me, and I left for England the next day, so . . . I got out of all that. None of them mentioned Miles having a girlfriend, anyway, it was just all, y'know, about Jimmy being a hero, and who's going to make the movie of it, and all that stuff, with some of the better papers printing long leaders about whether or not paintball should be banned. And no one here knows about my involvement with it at all, apart from Ben and Alice and now you.'

I don't really know what to say. So I say that.

'I don't really know what to say. It's like . . . I mean, every two or three months you read about something like that going off in America, but it's not . . . real, y'know? You don't really believe it, not . . .' I press my swelling lower gut '. . . *here*, not the way you believe Securicor men getting clubbed or Dyno-Rod unclogging drains filled with rent-boy flesh. Those are the things that bring our own crimes home to us, y'know – Securicor, Dyno-Rod, Hungerford, a closed-circuit camera in a shopping centre – some touch of mundanity.'

'Yeah, well, I left out the mundane details. Sorry.'

Perhaps a deconstruction of how this story sounds ludicrously glamorous to me wasn't appropriate. 'God, how awful' might've gone down better. But it did actually feel real, because, I suppose, the mundane detail now is her, just sitting here telling me this, with my mind occasionally wandering off towards how I can steer all this towards sex, just like it does when I hear about Securicor men getting clubbed on the news.

'Why did you decide to tell me?'

'I dunno,' says Dina gloomily. 'I already wish I hadn't.' Something in my face must show a little hurt, because she continues, 'No, sorry, I didn't mean that. I think I really wanted to tell *someone*, and . . . I guess I was feeling that we've been in a few situations now where my behaviour must've seemed a little . . . antagonistic, and so I suppose I just didn't want you to end up hating me without realising why I was being . . .' she casts around for the words '. . . such a cunt.'

'I thought you were a feminist.'

'I am. Thus I believe that women should be allowed to express themselves in any way they want.' She pauses. 'And also . . . you were being really honest with me about your . . .' her eyebrow twitches just a touch upwards '. . . intentions. I felt it was only fair to let you know what and who you were trying to get into.'

I check my watch: 9:23. Oh no, the Quorn'll be getting over-encrusted.

'Listen, d'you wanna eat?'

'Not half,' she says, smiling. 'Thought you'd never ask.'

This chirpy Brit-response takes her away from being the star – and paint-spangled victim of her story. It seems to lift the mood in the room. I leap up and out into the kitchen. I think I may even be rubbing my hands together, Robert Carrier-style.

'What is it?' she shouts from the living-room.

Just you wait and see, is presumably the flirtatious response. But I'm not that much of a tosser. 'Tandoori Quorn. It's one of my secret recipes.' Oh dear. Seems I'm very nearly that much of a tosser.

I check the Quorn. It looks very crusty, almost warty. Lovely. I slip a cover over it and put it in the microwave: two minutes, thirty-four. From the living-room comes the sound of Russ Abbott singing *What An Atmosphere.*

'Take that off!' I shout from the kitchen.

'No!' she shouts back.

I smile to myself. Suddenly, it all seems to be going well. What was it she said? 'What or who you were trying to get into'? That's pretty positive, isn't it? Isn't that just saying, we *are* going to have sex? She may as well have said come on you little tart you know you want it. I get the impulse to punch my fist in the air in a Coke-advert manner. Time to give myself the once-over; I pop into the bathroom.

Now, let me see. Quick clean of my pits: bugger, there's only a butter-pat of soap. Have to do. I take off my black T-shirt with the red stripe down the front and rub vigorously. The wiry black hair goes white. I let it soak in for a while, undoing my trousers. Hmm. No soap left. I douse my genitals with water, then crane my cupped hand underneath to scrape the odd drop into my arse-crack. As I towel myself dry, I panic: not good enough. Let me see. Ah, yes. Inside the big enamel sink-cup that holds five or six old toothbrushes and a tube of Brylcreem gel – Nick's bottle of Old Spice: the mark of a man. I sprinkle it liberally over my front parts, then put it down, then think, fuck it, and sprinkle it liberally over my back parts. *Ting!* Oops, Quorn's done.

Coming out of the bathroom, I just catch Dina's eye through the living-room door. I smile, which I hope covers my tracks as far as what I was doing in the bathroom goes. She smiles back. I go into the kitchen and open the microwave door. I put the big red pan and a couple of plates on to a wooden tray with yellow handles that I made for my woodwork O Level and rush into the living-room.

Dina sits expectantly on the sofa, having drawn the coffee-table up, assuming, correctly, that we don't have a dining-table. I put the tray down on it. I'm thinking of saying '*Voilà!*' Stop yourself, stop yourself.

'Hmm! Smells lovely,' she says encouragingly. I smile bashfully and lift the cover off the pan. She looks into it. Something big and red jumps out of the pan and hits her in the face.

'OH MY GOD!!' she screams.

'Fuck!' I scream. I look down. By the side of the coffee-table, blinking and steaming, is a tandoori frog. Shit. No wonder the Quorn looked a bit warty. Dina runs off screaming into the bathroom. My head spins: I start to feel an enormous rage building up within me. Looking at the frog, I see red.

I cast around for a weapon. Right. I go over to the window and tear the stalk of the yucca plant out by the roots. Soil sprays everywhere. Hmm: smells a bit pissy. No time for that now. I stomp back to the coffee-table, raising the dismembered trunk above my head. I bring it down on the frog, only the frog moves, leaping surprisingly high in the air. '*I love a party with a happy atmosphere*,' sings Russ. I try and hit it again: again the frog jumps out of the way. Then it starts to emit a high-pitched noise, a kind of distress-signal, which, y'know, is fair enough: it hasn't had a great day either. I try sweeping the yucca plant along the floor towards it instead – the frog leaps sideways, but cleverly I keep the yucca moving so the terrified reptile lands on it, just at the point where the two branches fork. I lift the frog to eye-level: its distress-signal gets so loud, I expect any moment to see hundreds of other frogs come crashing through the door dressed in little firemen's outfits. It looks at me. Bits of its tandoori-coating have started to flake off, revealing a slightly blackened green skin underneath. Sorry, mate: wrong place at the wrong time. I swing the yucca backwards like some sort of absurd sling-shot, then hurl it forward with all my might: the frog flies straight off its branches and out of the open window. Taking a deep breath, I sit down on the coffee-table next to the rapidly cooling Quorn. Strangely, I can still hear the frog's screaming distress-signal. Then I realise that Dina's come back into the room.

'You SWINE!!' she says, screaming, just a tiny bit of tandoori paste still stuck to her right eyebrow. 'What sort of joke is that?!!'

'It wasn—'

'And now you've killed the poor thing. I saw you! I'm a

vegetarian, remember? You disgust me! Don't you think I've had enough of killing?!!'

'Well, I hardly think—'

But it's too late, she's off. I stay sat on the coffee-table, looking at the unused plates. For the second time in recent months, I hear the particular slam our flat door only makes when an outraged woman goes through it at vehement speed. Not knowing what else to do, I pick the tray up and take it into the kitchen. What time is it? The microwave clock reads 1:92. Great. You'd think that, while it was in there, the frog could at least have curled out its tongue and eaten the fucking fly. Second slam. That's the front door.

I'm not having this. None of this was my fault. All right, perhaps I should've hunted high and low for the frog after Jezebel went off with it. Perhaps I shouldn't have left the pan open for five hours. Perhaps the frog was sent by God as an image of my own disgustingness, masturbating to vile images only minutes before Dina came round. But I am a man more sinned against than sinning – I do a quick mental calculation – just about. I slam the tray down on the sink and run out of the kitchen and down the stairs.

As I open the front door, Dina is sitting with her back to me on our front garden wall, crying. The Man Who Lives Downstairs is standing in the middle of our front garden path. For the first time ever, he does not avoid my eyes. His, which I've never seen properly before, are black and full of sadness. As they dock with mine, this sadness is covered over, like a fresh corpse, with a new look: reproach. I return it with one of pure confusion. What's his problem? Then he does his familiar action of tipping his head down slightly, normally designed to dispel eye-contact, although he does it in a particularly pointed way, as if something else is involved. Then I see what else is involved: the frog, looking fairly OK, considering, sits lumpily on the brim of his funereal sombrero like an outrageous red hat-badge. Head bowed in this manner, he pauses for two or three seconds to allow me to take in the terrible reality of the situation: the frog begins to slide down the gently angled brim. Then, The Man Who Lives Downstairs looks up and walks, in a slow, stately tread, towards his own front door. As he goes in, he flashes me one last look, again of deep sadness, subverted only slightly by the fact that the frog is looking at me at the same time, perhaps just a pinch more sadly.

As his door closes, I go over to Dina, still sitting shaking on the garden wall. Only she's not crying. Laughing uncontrollably, she falls into my arms.

11

My bedroom is painted quite an intense shade of blue. I did it myself, getting the colour I wanted by mixing 'Blueberry' and 'Violet' until the paste became cerulean. Blue is the best colour in the spectrum after black for soaking up light, and that's why I chose it – black being an impossible option for bedroom walls past the age of fifteen – because early in the morning it postpones the penetrating sunshine, giving me an extra twenty to twenty-five minutes of night to play with. At this moment, however, the blue has soaked up all the light it can; in fact, to be honest, light is starting to spill out of the walls like a bad case of damp. Leaning my back against the bare wall which forms the headboard of my bed, I watch the shapes in my bedroom evolve into familiars (I took my blindfold off twenty minutes ago in one irritated grab – always the sign of total defeat): the posters on the wall, one a framed Man Ray photograph of a Louise Brooks lookalike, resting her head sideways on a table and holding, direct to camera, an African tribal mask (underneath the photo it says *From The Israel Museum Collection*, and this was why it was bought for me, by someone who thought, being Jewish, I'd like that), the other a Rothko print, dark red on purple; the white fireplace, blackened inside from its once ever use, now a storage area for two wooden juggling sticks I bought four years ago with an idea towards doing a bit of street theatre at some point, never realised; the large oak second-hand wardrobe, with its full-length oblong mirror that I spent so long angling towards the bed; my desk, also second-hand, a relic from when the middle classes were mainly clerks, made out of grey heavily scratched wood with an ink-well and separate under-section for the drawers, sitting in the corner below a sloping section of the ceiling, a hundred different bits of paper hiding a Brother electric typewriter; the bedside table, a black self-make thing, £19.99 from IKEA, on which stands an old Goblin Teasmaid, broken now for two years, and my domey black bedside light, designed as an ultra-violet sun-tan lamp, but then given an ordinary bulb fitting, broken now since last night, after I insisted on turning it on for the fifth time; my clothes – baggy black T-shirt with red stripe, 501s plus tear, Next Y-front undershorts, lying in a contained pile slightly smugly, slightly 'we told you so'; next to them, a gold polo-neck top and a pair of purple velvet hipsters; and next to me, an unfamiliar, Dina Friedricks, breathing regularly and quietly, her delicately rounded face half-smothered in my spare pillow, that I never use, my own being one that I've had since I was a child – despite having to put three cases on it now to stop the foam stuffing falling out, my head always feels uncomfortable resting awake on any other.

I didn't think about Alice. Not once. I had too many other things to think about (not least the fact that I never managed to have that wank). That's the thing about sex, or at least one of the many things about it: I remember Holly Johnson, in his uninfected prime, saying that Frankie Goes To Hollywood celebrated sex because it was the only unself-conscious act left – the only one where people behaved perfectly in tune with their true selves, without considering how they were supposed to. But that's so wrong. Sex is the *most* self-conscious act, crossed and criss-crossed in the practice by millions of dissenting voices, telling you how to do it, how not to do it, how to keep doing it with the same partner for years, how to do it if you do or don't want to have kids, how to do it after you've had kids, where and when, how and why, in books, in poems, in newspapers, on video, on film, everybody from Denise, the agony aunt on *This Morning*, to Saul Bellow. How on earth is anyone supposed to perform this supposedly most natural of acts naturally in the face of all that? Only Kasper Hauser could, and he probably had trouble pulling anyway because he smelt like a forest.

But yet, but yet: despite all these people giving you directions, there *is* a place, hidden away at the centre of sex, where you can lose yourself after all. It is a maze within a maze. Sometimes, you can't find your way into it at all, but mostly it's a question of chancing upon the door. If, like me, your erotic appreciation has been roughly planed down by pornography, then too often you go route one, via the eye – the buttocks-stretched-apart-tits-pressed-together gateway to oblivion. This gets you somewhere – I can't say it doesn't – but even in my hardened, desperately visualising desire I know it's not the key. I have found it before in a smell (although, to be fair, it was a smell that came with a buttocks-stretched-apart-tits-pressed-together moment). And many times in a touch, a hand snaking through my moving thighs to cradle my testicles, a fingernail drawn down the soles of my feet, a tongue jabbing gingerly at the ashen dent of my anus. And once in a sound, a shh, a whisper to me to be more quiet or parents would hear.

With Dina, it was her skin. Falling into Dina was like stepping into a bath of flesh. Even in our preliminary touchings, through the thick gloves of awkwardness, I became aware of a tactile oasis waiting for me, no mirage in this Sinai of uncertain approaches and mistried stumblings. Plumper than Alice – when I first met her one of many problem deviations – I realised, as I moved to press as much of me against as much of her as I could, that this plumpness registered on Dina not as an oozy collection of fat, but as a wealth of skin spread like butter on top of her bones. I wanted to glue myself to this woman, to wrap myself in her security blanket, flesh of my flesh, finding forgetfulness in her soft fleecy covering. Perhaps, I thought, as I came into her and out of my touch-based trance, I have found at last a comfortable bed.

My cold sperm lies coagulating in a condom underneath the bedside table. I get up to deal with it. My method is to fill the condom with water, tie it in a knot at the top, and flush it down the toilet. It's best to go through this process before the morning, I think. Once I filled a condom with water, tied it up, and forgot about it, left it on the side of the sink, and later, after a visit from my mother including a wholesale spring clean, found it carefully rearranged with my toothpaste and shaving equipment inside the big enamel cup.

The bathroom mirror with its harsh strip-light surround throws back a haunting image: a tired-looking man with short brown-black hair lying in flat asymmetrical sections on his head, blinking as if surprised, naked all the way round his jutting convex belly, holding the emblem of his ecstasy in a dribbling balloon. I turn on the tap: the rushing water forces the white jelly into floating strands. I tie the knot, and a surge of panic goes through me as a tiny jet of water seems to emerge from the dug. I remember the packet's assurance: *Tested To BS Standards*. Yeah, I think, so was the fucking Hindenburg. But as I hold the condom up to the light, it stops, and then I remember anyway that Dina is sterile. I flush the toilet, and watch yet another chance of recreating this fat tired-looking man for future generations swirl away to the sea.

As I turn around, I notice in my reflection a glint of light above my right temple. No, tell a lie, it's not a glint of light: it's a bit of head. Webster, it is said, saw the skull beneath the skin; I, recently, have started to see mine beneath my hair. At the corners of my forehead, my hair, maybe – not definitely, but definitely maybe – is starting to move backwards. I bend my head towards the mirror and look up, pulling my hair backwards into a tight ponytail at the top. Some four or five millimetres in front of my increasingly straggly hairline, at the centre of my pate, I've actually got one rogue hair, an outpost from less virile times. I have decided to use this hair as a benchmark. If the massed ranks of its brothers retreat any further away from it, I'll know for sure: I'm going bald. Not thinning out, not losing a bit on top, no: going bald. Fuck. As Winona Ryder says in *Dracula*: 'take me away from all this death.'

I get back into bed, colder, less content. Rummaged in her sleep by the draughty whoosh of the duvet, Dina turns away, burbling some dream-words; I feel her body-heat like an aura. I quell an instinct to hug her and warm myself against her somnambulant fire: you have to know someone pretty well to get away with waking them by lowering their body temperature that much. Immediately after sex, I lay on my back, and Dina, unprompted, crawled up my chest to rest her head on the inside of my shoulder. She said 'Your knob tastes of Old Spice' and fell instantly asleep. At the time, lying there, with her head growing heavier on my side, the weight of her leg on mine cushioned by her compulsive skin, I felt she'd closed a gap in my soul. Now I'm not so sure.

I don't know what I want from this. I thought, maybe, that it would be like sleeping with Alice, but then, I only know what sleeping with Alice is like in fantasy, and it was different from this, mainly because no one else was involved. So now, if I end up going out with Dina, I'm in a *relationship*, not in . . . I dunno what I thought it might be – some shadow-play. And then, perhaps, I'm further away from Alice than ever. My thoughts bat back and forth inside my head, held tight in the vice of early morning wakefulness.

12

Where I went to school – the John Lyon School in Middlesex, one of those petit-bourgeois institutions that try desperately hard to imitate Eton or Harrow, but just end up attracting too many damn *Jews* – it seemed to be on the syllabus to own, by the age of sixteen, a flash car. Failing this, it was of crucial importance, from the word go, to at least know about cars. I have seen boys who would not legally be allowed to drive for another decade argue amongst each other, with all the specifications at their fingertips, as to whether a Cavalier or a Carlton is the classier motor (most of this information was garnered from a game called *Top Trumps*, which allowed you to pretend to be playing cards, when in actual fact you were learning about cars). Not knowing about cars qualified you, paradoxically, for the term of abuse *spanner*. It was unmanly, but not just in the masculine sense; car ignorance demonstrated that you were still a child, whereas at my school it was necessary, from your first day in the first form, to appear as if you were, in actual fact, twenty-six. Knowing about cars equated with knowing about sex: the knowledge may have been redundant, as far as putting it into practice was concerned, but it still inspired in your peers that craved-for sense of awe. I remember John Ostroff, through brilliant deployment of such knowledge, was able, before he'd passed puberty, somehow to imply that he was both driving and having sex regularly in some parallel universe.

And that's why, as I stand on the forecourt at Moran's SuperDrive in Ladbroke Grove listening to the mechanic explain why the Dolomite still hasn't been fixed, I curse, not for the first time, the fact that at school I was such an outsider.

'It's the tappets,' he says, his stiff psychobilly quiff moving slowly from side to side in tune with his conciliatory headshake.

I have two choices here. I can put on a quilted smoking-jacket, raise my eyes to heaven and say, in a voice of ultimate weariness: 'And what on earth would tappets be, you grimy little oik?'; or I can nod knowingly. I nod knowingly.

'So d'you want 'em squared or repointed?' says the mechanic.

I continue to nod. 'Um . . . which . . . which would you suggest?'

It's no good, I'm sussed. All over the forecourt, green boiler-suited men are downing tools and staring contemptuously in my direction. I see myself clocked in the mechanic's eyes: *spanner*. Then I think I see some dollar signs.

'Well . . . I'd *suggest* . . .' (he says the word with a heavy ironic emphasis, as if to imply that the concept of suggestion is entirely alien to the man who really knows about cars) '. . . getting a whole new set.'

In the dimness of my memory, I recall something the Green Flag man had said that doesn't quite square with this. With a sense of launching my plywood canoe into an unknown part of the rapids, I say, 'Er . . . I'm sure I was told that the problem was the distributor.'

He looks at me sharply, like *don't try it. Don't come it with me*. You could cut the testosterone with a knife. 'We've already fixed the distributor,' he says, his tone so much adding the word *spanner* I'm sure I can actually hear it, 'but it's the tappets that burnt it out in the first place. See?'

No, I am as a blind man, crying in the wilderness.

'You could take it away as it is, but unless you get the tappets sorted the distributor'll just go again in a couple of weeks.'

Then I remember: of course. Garages don't mend cars. They don't. They just find other things wrong with them. Fixing the brakes will involve the discovery that the accelerator cable is leaking; mending the headlights will somehow screw up the exhaust; if they really can't find anything else, they'll tell you the *feu d'orange* is knackered.

'How much will it be?'

'What?'

'A new set of tappets.'

The mechanic walks away towards the especially nasty reception area, in which the sole woman in this phallocracy sits bored and permed flicking through *Marie Claire* while three separate phones compete for her attention. A few seconds later, he comes back holding an enormous blue file. He opens it and flicks through a couple of hundred oil-smeared invoices, presumably to suggest that the price he's about to come up with is in some sense not his responsibility.

''Bout two hundred quid,' he says, slamming the file shut.

'Two hundred quid? But I'm on the dole!'

The mechanic shrugs: the same basic gesture as the one that my grandmother did the other day, but so unjewish, so *yokishe*, that it seems like a different action altogether. Her shrug said 'Life! Love! Time! Suffering! Who knows?'; his shrug says 'Not my fucking problem, mate.'

I leave the garage, having pledged faithfully to come up with the two hundred quid necessary to replace what sounds to me like a Bavarian side-dish. Better write some of those columns.

'And so what *would* you accept?'

John Hillman, my Restart officer, looks at me scornfully. He remains stock-still, leaning forward, his hands clasped together at the far edge of his Formica desk so tightly that the tips of his knuckles have yellowed, but his name-badge, perched daringly just a little too high on his lapel, quivers slightly, as if despite the attempt to seem unruffled, his identity is in fact marginally shaken by my disinterest in any of his Restart options.

'Honestly, John, I don't know.' Although, when I speak to these people, I try not to be bolshy or condescending – it's not their fault what they do – I cannot resist calling him 'John'. Even though everything about my Restart officer – his 'you don't surprise me, y'know' bearing, his Burton's suit, his blue shirt with the white collar, his Alan Whicker glasses, his obliviousness to nose-hair as a problem, his slightly acrid BO, his tendency to press repeatedly at the button of his Parker biro before writing anything down, his (I'm guessing now) separate bedroom arrangement with his wife so much more exciting really because he can creep across the landing when he's in the mood and surprise her – bespeaks *Mr* Hillman. You know the way that most people – you, me, everybody you know – actually feel about fourteen? And yet sometimes you meet people who just are the age they are: like Mr Hillman. But I call him John, much to his obvious inner rage. Seems to me he knew the risks when he pinned the name-tag on.

'Just not,' I continue, '. . . what were they again?'

Mr Hillman unclips his hands and picks up the green sheet of A4 that had been lying within the 'V' formed by his arms.

'Packing, Safeway, Holloway Road, 7 p.m. to 7 a.m., Mon–Sat, £170 pw.' He reads in a clear precise voice, using all the abbreviations. 'Tinning, Peek Frean Factory, Walworth, 9 to 5.30, Mon–Fri, £155 pw. Bricklayer's apprentice, Dagenham site, part-time, Mon, Tue, Wed, £90 pw. Waiter, Jenny's, Walthamstow, lunchtime and evenings, £70 pw basic plus tips.'

He looks up, his face entirely uncreased by irony. I have cupped my face in my hands and am drawing my eyelids down to the red.

'Are you all right?' he says.

'Yes,' I say, releasing my face. 'Just a bit tired. I don't sleep very well.'

He pauses momentarily and scratches his right temple. 'Have you tried Kalms?'

'John,' I say, relaxing into my chair as I relax into his name, 'do you *like* working here? In this partitioned cubicle in the middle of Willesden DSS office?'

His brow furrows – what else can a brow do, I wonder – like *don't try it. Don't come it with me.* 'I don't see how that's relevant.'

'I'd just like to know.'

He pushes his chair away from his desk, continuing to eye me suspiciously.

'No, not really,' he says. 'I'm here to help. Help people find employment. But I don't get much thanks for it. I have to put up with all sorts – people who come in drunk at ten o'clock in the morning, people who tell you that they're looking for a job when all they're doing is going into the betting shop all day, wasters . . . abusive types . . . and worst of all,' he leans forward back across the desk, 'obnoxious smart-alecs who think they're too bloody clever to do an honest day's work.'

'Point taken, John,' I say, nodding. 'Fair dos.' I feel I'm speaking his language. 'So why don't you leave?'

'Leave?'

'What did you really want to do when you were a kid?'

He blinks at me. He reaches for the Parker in his jacket pocket, then leaves it. I think – I honestly think – that what's stumping him here is not 'what did you really want to do', but 'when you were a kid'. Perhaps he was never a kid: perhaps he sprang fully-formed, Burton's suit and bird's-nest nostrils already in place, from the furrowed brow of his father, Mr Hillman.

'An astronaut,' he says. 'I wanted to be an astronaut.'

Naaah. You made that up. It's not an actual memory. You just know it's the sort of thing kids say. And to think they named an Imp after you.

'But unlike some,' says Mr Hillman, his sallow grey eyes suddenly switching on with the realisation that he's fallen on to a point-making possibility here, 'I grew up. I realised that that was unrealistic. And so I knuckled down and got myself some work. I may not always like it, but we can't all be astronauts, y'know.'

That's true. We can't all be astronauts. Who would run Mission Control?

'The thing is, John,' I say, '– and this may sound immature to you – it may sound like what I'm saying is we *can* all be astronauts: I don't think people should spend most of their lives doing what they don't want to do. I think . . .' taking a leaf out of Mr Hillman's folder, I lean in close to him, 'it's a betrayal of God's gift to us. The gift of life.'

Mr Hillman, without breaking my gaze, sighs audibly. Ah, he's thinking, loony. I knew I could sound like one; Nick going mental has had its advantages. The fact that, in my sixth-former soul, I actually deeply believe the speech I've just made is beside the point: I've still dressed it up to sound like any second now

I'm going to be standing on his Formica desk singing *Jerusalem*. He wants me out of here.

'But the other thing is,' says Mr Hillman, leaning in so our noses are almost touching, like one of those head-to-head sketches in *Alas Smith and Jones*; 'Mr Jacoby, pretending you're some sort of lunatic will not prevent me from going ahead with our normal procedure with regard to claimants like yourself who fall into the long-termed unemployed category.' He leans backwards and pushes the green sheet of A4 over the table towards me. 'Either you take one of these jobs, or you get yourself some other work in the next four weeks, or I'm recommending your benefit be withdrawn. Good afternoon.'

Shit. Sussed again. If only I could switch my life around a bit and apply the Restart option to my car. Better write some of those columns.

13

It's three o'clock in the morning. Yeah, I know you're used to it being that time by now. But I'm not in my livid bed, staring at the ceiling. I'm not in the lounge, staring at the screen. I'm in the Casualty department of the Royal Free Hospital, staring at an exhausted nurse telling me for the fourth time just to be patient, the doctors will see us when they're ready.

Earlier this evening, me and Dina had just begun our first meeting after our first coupling. Again it was at my flat, probably because neither of us wanted to confront the strange light that the presence of Ben and Alice would've thrown on to the rippling surface of our relationship. Dina wanted to go to the pub.

'Where?' I said hazily.

'The pub. You know. Your local.'

Again the possibility of the quilted smoking-jacket floated into view. *I'm afraid, my dear, I don't have the faintest idea what you're talking about.*

'I don't have a local. I never go to the pub.'

'You never go to the pub?'

'I'm Jewish.'

'Will you stop using that excuse for everything!'

'But it actually *is* an excuse for everything!'

I was secretly pleased at this minor argument – when she first arrived the air had hung heavy with discomfort, with eyes refusing to meet, and kisses uncertain where to land. Any second now I'd been expecting the 'look we made a mistake' speech to begin. Suddenly, though, we'd connected, even though we disagreed; and the pub in the abstract had become for me something it never has been in reality: a breathing space.

'And also, the pub's responsible for everything that's wrong with this country.'

'How do you figure that?'

'The three worst things about this country,' I said, snuggling deeply into the safety of the discussion – if I broaden this out enough, I thought, it could be anything up to quarter of an hour before either of us wonders what to say to the other again, 'violence, terrible food and shutting down at eleven thirty – they all stem from a culture based on the pub.'

Dina stared at me impassively, her tubular *Ready Steady Go!* black and white striped dress making her look like a zebra-crossing – deceptively, because she clearly wasn't about to be walked over.

'Stop slamming the back of your hand into the palm of your other hand,' she said. 'You've got a bit of a sermonising side, haven't you?'

'It's just so joyless in there! And I don't even like beer.'

'Oh, don't be such a poof!'

'I thought you were meant to be P— Oh, never mind.'

'We could always go to a club.'

'Great idea – a really dark pub that plays house music from hell.'

'I like that sort of music.'

'Oh, Dina. You might as well dance round a car alarm.'

She took a deep breath. I began to realise that our liberating disagreement had turned the corner into being just a disagreement, and an irritating one at that.

'Gabriel,' she said, 'is it worth our seeing each other at all, d'you think? When you actually look at what we've got in common? Apart from our in-laws, of course.'

We had come very quickly from smooth ground to sticky. That's what happens if you get over-into your own stupid opinions. The ball was so squarely in my court it seemed to have been served there by Jim Courier.

'Let's go to the pub,' I said, putting my jacket on.

After just a tiny bit of 'I'm not sure I want to go anymore'-ness from Dina, we made it to the front door. At the gate, I paused for a second, thinking *where*? There are a thousand pubs in Kilburn – more per square metre than anywhere else in the world – but it suddenly struck me that I had no idea which one to head for, and, perhaps more importantly, which one was safe to drink in. *Biddy Mulligan's, The Black Lion, Sir Colin Campbell, McGoverns, The Cole-Pitz* – there's something that connects all these establishments, and it isn't orange décor. I was just checking my pockets for some loose change in case there should be something in the way of a collection at the end of the evening, when I heard it. A whimper.

'What was that?' I said.

'What?' said Dina.

It came again, a muffled low cry, rising and falling in pitch like a distant and rather badly executed yodel.

'Is it Jezebel?' said Dina. The fact that she said 'Jezebel' and not 'your cat' made me feel momentarily uplifted at how far inducted she was becoming into my life.

'No. It's too vulnerable.'

I looked around. The four working street-lamps threw their intermittent sodium rays along Streatley Road. Nothing. Just some kids whose parents can't afford Play Stations jumping on and off the opposite house's garden wall, and the distant noise of the High Road. Remembering that it was Friday night, I made a mental note to try and leave the pub before the High Road got out of hand. The first time I got a night bus late back along Kilburn High Road on a Friday night about three years ago, watching from the top deck I thought: there's a riot going on. This'll be on the news tomorrow. Men lurching across the road oblivous to traffic, police chasing cars along the pavement, dark figures making desperate love in back doorways of dance-clubs. I got off the bus and walked home through the blazing bins expecting at any point to see Mad Max. But, as time went by, I realised that's what happens every Friday and Saturday night in Kilburn. So if you leave early enough it's all still contained within the pub.

'Gabriel,' said Dina, raising me from my reverie, 'I think . . . I think it's coming from your bin.'

I looked over at the big black dustbin, just inside our gate next to the neighbouring wall. Fear stabbed at me. I'd felt this type of fear before, in horror films – the tension, the sudden revelation, the monster lurking in wait – and then I've known what to do. But here, I couldn't lift off the lid with my hands covering my face at the same time.

'Oh, let's leave it,' I said, and started to walk off.

'Gabriel!' said Dina, pulling me back via my jacket-sleeve. 'Don't be ridiculous!' Her voice, for no apparent reason, lowered to a whisper. 'See what it is.'

'But I'm frightened,' I said. I've never been one for butching this kind of thing out.

'Oh, don't be so stupid,' said Dina, and walked over to the dustbin. For a second, she hesitated, and then, mustering all the inner strength of someone who's come through her previous lover being shot dead by New York police after a four-fatality paintball siege, she lifted the lid. From my standpoint six feet away, I heard the whimpering grow louder, but not break, as if the whimperer hadn't noticed the lid being removed; and I saw Dina look down, start, and back off in fear.

'Look,' she hissed at me. 'Go and look.'

'Can't you just tell me what it is?'

'GO AND LOOK!'

Unhappily, I walked over to the bin at about half the average pace of Lydia Frindel. When I got to its edge, I was still looking straight ahead at Dina, but then the need to know overtook me: I felt the hand of curiosity pushing my head downwards through my fear like I've sometimes had gently to do to timorous women. And, as my chin reached my chest, I saw Nick, naked and whimpering, his eyes shut tight against the outside world, hunched in our dustbin like a foetus in a particularly dank and rotting womb. I stared at the tip of his shivering scalp, discoloured by some carrot-coloured smudge, and the thought crossed my mind that if only I ever emptied the swing-bin he wouldn't have been able to do this.

'Shall we call the police?' said Dina, still whispering.

'Er . . . no. I don't think he's actually committing a crime, is he?'

'Well, indecent exposure for a start. And trespassing on your property.'

'How do you mean?'

'Well, it's your bin, isn't it?'

It was then I remembered that she hadn't met Nick yet. What a fine introduction.

'Yeah. I'm afraid . . . the thing is . . . it's *his* bin as well.'

'How?'

'He's my flatmate.'

Dina's face contracted, except for her right eyebrow. I knew what she must be thinking but she spelt it out for me anyway.

'For fuck's sake, Gabriel,' she said, turning away and raising her voice straight from a whisper to a scream, 'I thought going out with someone who turned out to be a psychokiller was as bad a date as I was gonna get!' She was starting to sound very American in her anger. 'But no. I should move in with fucking Charles Manson.' She was nodding her head furiously, in the seventh gear of sarcasm. 'I should. At least I wouldn't have to put up with instant engagements, frogs jumping out of my dinner, and now *this* – this fucking . . .' she searched for the words '. . . nudist production of *Endgame* in your front garden. BY YOUR FLATMATE!'

'Dina . . .'

'Gabriel?' It was Nick's voice: an anaemic, hollowed-out, transported version of his flat Bradford brogue. I went over to the dustbin. He was looking up out of it at me with his mouth open, like a baby bird emerging hungry from an egg: tears rushed from his eyes, outpourings of his crashed soul. When he saw me his memory seemed to turn over: something in my image turned a key, and for a second we met on the plane of recognition, him recognising me, me recognising shreds of him floating about in his watery pupils. Then he said the obvious, the heart-breaking thing.

'Help me.'

So we brought him into Casualty. We brought him into Casualty suffering from mental illness. I didn't know what else to do. The men in white coats, the ones who rush on in British comedy films in the 1960s whenever a character starts ranting and raving, they didn't appear. I didn't know what else to do.

Piecing together Nick's scattered speech, once we'd got him dressed and into a minicab – I considered calling an ambulance but felt that it wasn't exactly a sirens and stretcher-bearers sort of emergency (it's really more of a *long-term* emergency, isn't it?), and besides, I didn't fancy waiting four or five hours – it became clear that he had decided, at last, to go back to work on the windscreens. It being a sunny day, however, he'd decided to do it naked. Two or three major accidents at Camden Road traffic lights later, the police had been called. Somehow – it's not entirely clear how: Nick's version involved astral planing – he managed to get away from them, and had been hiding ever since in our dustbin, convinced that a dragnet had been thrown across London for him. At this point, the moustachioed Cypro–Greek minicab driver, who didn't appear to have been listening, stopped the cab and ordered us all to get out – 'Bloody fucking loonies, what I am doing with them in my car?' – but Dina, having come down from her exasperated peak via what had seemed suspiciously like *motherly* sympathy for Nick's obvious helplessness, swore at the man so loudly, and rattled his wooden-beaded seat-cover so violently, that he drove off again in terror.

So here we are, me and Dina – Nick, who, worryingly really, seems to have taken on an impossibly oxymoronic state of manic calm, has gone off, he said, 'to make some phone calls' – continuing my orange plastic chair life by sitting at the front of a phalanx of them facing the Casualty desk. To the left of me sits a tall blond man with jigsaw pieces of a bottle of Beck's stuck to his face and neck, and, behind us, a dumpy shawl-wearing woman, with a black eye and a bleeding mouth, being tutored into a story of greasy floors and unfortunately positioned doorknobs by her enormous red-faced husband. Behind them are others with less visible traumas, but all wearing the same sad sitting-in-Casualty expression. We've been here since 11:30. In my hand, I hold the crumpled remains of the pink numbered ticket the nurse gave me on arrival; it's just like the supermarket deli, except here they probably see more red meat. It says '43'; the number-changing thing – fuck knows what the proper name for *them* is – hangs above and just to the right of the Casualty desk at a resolute '38'. It's been like that for sixty-seven minutes.

Dina has fallen asleep on my right shoulder. Strangely, this doesn't feel like a terrible parody of her action three nights ago. If anything, in fact, her doing it here, in this accident-house, this bedlam, feels like the greater display of trust: it shows a deeper sense of security in my shoulder. I sense an unusual mantle creeping on to the same shoulders, that of protector; even though if you look at it in the cold light of the waiting room, it's just that she can fall asleep and I can't. Occasionally, she slips down my chest, but each time puts her head straight back on my shoulder without waking up, a level of sleep I can't even begin to imagine.

The whole experience – the antiseptic smell, mingled with patients' green-tongued breath, the continual pumping sound of the hospital generator, the winking cursor of the staff nurse's computer monitor – is wrapped in a basket of sensation so muffled by tiredness that it seems already a memory, even though it's happening now. Earlier, I tried to get a cup of coffee out of a Gold Blend machine opposite the toilets, but once the brown water had evacuated violently into the beige plastic cup, I found I couldn't walk it back to my chair, every movement causing a spillage, and each spillage invoking an involuntary hand-shake causing a greater spillage, until, by the time I got back to the Casualty desk, I was considering admitting myself with first degree burns of the mount of Venus.

An Asian man in his early twenties, who had come in earlier with what looked upsettingly like a Union Jack carved on to his forehead, hobbles out of the double-doors by the side of the Casualty desk, his brow ornately bandaged. The '8' on the number-changer falls forward like a much slowed down time-passing sequence in a 1930s film, revealing a '9' behind. I hear the couple behind shuffle up out of their chairs, and the husband's low grumble of a voice asking her if she's got it straight what she has to say. Nick pushes through them on his way back from the phones, and sits down next to me, oblivious to the fact that the red-faced man has turned and is staring at him in an *any time* sort of way. Luckily, his dumpy wife tugs at his sleeve, giving him an excuse to turn his face away, which otherwise would have stayed staring at Nick forever.

'Who were you phoning?' I say.

'A friend,' he says, not looking at me. Since we got here,

his momentary vulnerability has passed, and he's been shoring up the self-righteous aggressive side of his madness, possibly because he can sense the asylum beyond.

'At three o'clock in the morning?'

He continues staring straight ahead. 'Some people don't obey the laws of night and day.'

Ignoring the stark staring irony of him saying this to me, I decide to lodge one last appeal.

'Nick. You wanted to come here, remember?'

'Did I?'

'You wanted help.'

'That's true,' he says, turning to me finally, '*but what type of help?*'

He emphasises every word, imparting as much enigma to the sentence as he can. That's the trouble with Nick's madness: it's a thick bloke's madness. In our culture, we're so convinced about the interface between madness and genius that nothing prepares us for vacuous, clichéd lunacy, for the madness of non-Maupassant man. Thick is perhaps too strong a word for the sane Nick Munford – he had the sharp wits of the superlad – but he was not a vastly original thinker. Not an enormous problem when all you think about is windscreens, *Heisse Titten* and Bradford City; but once a chemical imbalance in your brain starts you thinking about life and death and madness and sanity – into thinking like Hamlet – without, however, giving you the expansion of *intellect* necessary to contain this broadening of subject-matter, then all that happens is you come across like an angst-ridden sociology student desperately trying to sound serious. Bit like Hamlet, in fact.

'Psychiatric, I thought would be the best bet.'

'Ha!' says Nick. He actually says 'Ha!', which of course no one ever says. '*That's what I need, is it?*'

'Just asking questions in a significant tone doesn't make me think you possess some sort of great insight,' I say wearily.

'Oh, but he *does*,' says a whispery female voice I don't recognise. I look up. Standing in front of me is a thin, olive-skinned woman, her pupils encased in bright turquoise contact lenses, with a long C-shaped nose, the effect of which she appears to be trying to counter by arching her chin upwards, allowing me an unashamed view inside her nostrils; she's wearing enormous Persian trousers, a top that could easily double as a potato sack, and . . . hold on a minute . . . would you credit it: my little pointy green hat with the black African band round it. She looks at me with a face that says, clearly, 'I understand.'

'Fran,' says Nick, hushed. 'Thank God you've come.'

Fran holds her palm out flat to him without taking her eyes off mine, and without adjusting her face from 'I understand.' She doesn't fucking understand whose hat that is, though. I'll tell you that for nothing.

'Hello, Fran,' I say, holding out my arm. 'I'm Gabriel. I've heard a lot about you.'

Still looking me straight in the eye – is she playing that kids' game, where eventually one of you starts laughing? – she twirls her held out palm around, a bit like Ted Rogers used to on *3–2–1*, although I don't think that's an intended reference, and slides it into mine, grasping my fingers and bending them into hers as she does so. She smiles knowingly – I get the impression this is something she does a *lot* – and finally looks away from me, towards Nick. He is on his feet.

'Hello, Nicholas,' she says, and they embrace, sexlessly. She is such a waif, and Nick is so comparatively hulking, and his spiritual bearhug so forceful, that for a second Fran loses her apparently armour-clad composure and looks a bit startled: I hope against hope that she will start saying 'yes . . . all right . . . thank you . . . that's enough hugging now . . . put me down. PUT ME DOWN!!' But she doesn't. They part, but continue to hold hands.

'I'm sorry Nick phoned you so late,' I say.

Fran takes her smiling stare off Nick and places it on to me. She is unnerving to look at: it's strange that someone who obviously bases much of her projection of self on eye-contact should *wear* eye-contacts, especially bright turquoise ones. Does she see a turquoise world?

'Nicholas knows he can call *me* at any time. Whether by phone or . . .' she looks back at him significantly (I'm not sure she can look any other way) '. . . by *other* means.' She speaks in a constant hushed tone, which must make emphasising every other word a bit hard on her throat.

'Right,' I say. They carry on looking into each other's eyes. God. It's a bit slow, being with Fran. Then, without a word passing between them, Nick nods gently; she does the same, and, breaking her gaze but not releasing his hand, she swivels and crouches down to my seated level.

'Gabriel. Me and Nicholas had a long chat on the phone, and . . . do you really think it's a good idea to bring him here?'

Oh, these people. If they're so convinced that they're operating on a plane that the rest of us have no access to, why are they so damn *predictable*?

'Yes,' I say.

She takes this monosyllabic punch without flinching. Behind her, I see the red-faced husband and his now stitched up wife slide by towards the exit, him whispering in her ear, soft-breathed words that make her shiver, promises, promises.

'Why?'

'Because he was naked hiding in the dustbin, you fucking cretin! And what business is it of yours? Who the fuck are you?'

Ah, Dina's woken up. Sometimes it's useful to have someone who's spent a long time in America on your side.

'Hi,' says Fran, holding out her hand, pleased that this outburst allows her to demonstrate her unruffability. 'I'm Fran.'

Dina has backed off from my shoulder and is sitting upright next to me. She ignores her hand. 'Gabriel? Do you know her?'

'She's a friend of Nick's.'

'What, a proper friend or just some nutcase who came running to the sound of his penny whistle?'

Dina knows Nick's whole story by now, both his own Messianic version and my undercutting commentary. The answer to the question, I think, is that Nick came running to the sound of Fran's penny whistle, but, even though I have already developed, over the period of our very short acquaintance, a deep and well-nurtured hatred for Fran, I can't talk about her in the third person in front of her face like Dina can: Englishness again.

'I'm a friend. A *good* friend,' says Fran. Fucking hell. I'm going to break the italic button soon.

'Did you know him before he started having this breakdown?' says Dina, interrogatively.

Fran smiles to herself, as if she's been expecting the question. 'I prefer to call it a break-*up*,' she says.

'AAAAAH!!!'

At first, I think: that's probably just someone who's been listening too closely to Fran. Then one half of the front row of the orange phalanx of chairs collapses, throwing me forward into her: I hit her awkwardly in the face with my shoulder, upturning her nose even further. She rolls backwards from her crouching position, and I end up lying sideways on top of her like I'm trying to front crawl my way to her other side. From this position, I crane my neck round to find out what pushed us over and see Nick kneeling on top of the second row of chairs, now the first, with both his hands pressed flat against the face of the man covered in pieces of Beck's bottle.

'AAAAH,' says the man.

'I can heal you,' says Nick, loudly. 'I can heal you.'

'You bastard,' says Fran, still lying on the ground staring upwards, to me. 'You attacked me! You violent *bastard*!'

For the first time, her emphasising sounds real and spontaneous.

I tell you, they're used to fights breaking out in Casualty. Within seconds of Nick knocking over those chairs, five or six male nurses had appeared from all corners, pulling him off, pulling me off Fran, carting the Beck's man off somewhere, and restoring order. So that's where they were, the men in white coats.

Marvellously, though, we got promoted as a result. Numbers 40, 41, and 42 looked on, incredibly peeved, as the staff nurse made a snap decision to have Nick seen straight away, before he could cause any more trouble. So it's all worked out rather well, really, except perhaps for the man with the bits of Beck's now rather deeper in his face.

'And how do you feel about these thoughts?' says Dr Prandarjarbash, the Royal Free's on-call psychiatrist.

'How do *you* feel about them?' says Nick, the fifth time he's used this tactic as an answer. Dr Prandarjarbash pushes his glasses a little way back up his nose, sighs ever so slightly, and scribbles a couple of notes on to the sheet of paper attached to his black clipboard. Nurses come and go behind the blue, trollied curtain drawn in an L-shape across this small section of the consulting room.

'Is it OK, Mr Munford, just for the moment, that I ask the questions and you answer them? You can ask me some questions later on if you like.'

'I'm mad, aren't I, Doctor?' He throws his hands in the air and waves them around, Al Jolson-like. 'Wheeeeheeeeheee!' He draws his index finger up to his dry and cracked lips and vibrates it across them. 'Wubbawubbawubbawubbawubba!!' He stops. 'Bonkers! You'd better put me in the loony-bin with all the others . . .' and here he leans forward, his whole body straining towards one really big bit of emphasising '. . . *who think differently from you*.'

Nick leans back smugly, with a 'put that in your pipe and smoke it' expression on his – without doubt – completely mental face. Fran, sitting in the chair next to him in our little circle, squeezes his hand: a look passes between them, a look that I suppose, wearily, you'd have to interpret as 'that's told *him*'.

'Do you think, Mr Munford, that running naked in the streets shouting . . .' Dr Prandarjarbash looks to me to refresh his memory.

'Words for windows,' I tell him.

'. . . "words for windows" is just you thinking a bit differently from me? Sometimes I think very differently from the majority of people.' He smiles to himself at the memory of some personal unorthodoxy that, perhaps, had rocked consensus thinking in North London's psychiatric community. 'I even think very differently from the way *I* think I should sometimes. But I never think to run naked in the streets shouting "words for windows".'

'It was my new policy,' says Nick. He leans in again, but this time unaggressively, just as if he's about to betray some great confidence. 'You see, most people who work on the windscreens – they do it for money.'

'Yes, I see.'

'But today, I decided to do it for words! Words are much better than money, don't you think, Doctor?'

'Of course.'

'I'd clean a windscreen, and then I'd say: OK.' He holds up his palm. 'Put your cash away. Just tell me something about yourself. Anything. Or maybe, hey, recite a poem. Sing a song!'

Fran laughs at this, the loud, cardboard laugh of the rigorously humour-free.

'It wasn't, Mr Munford, I think, your method of payment that was the problem, but the fact that you were doing it naked.'

Nick looks a bit surprised about this, as if it genuinely is the first time it's occurred to him.

'Oh. Well . . . it was hot.'

It wasn't, of course. It was about 5°C, but maybe madness acts as some sort of furnace to the blood. Dr Prandarjarbash, paid to spot signals, has picked up on Nick's surprise. 'You realise that's why the police came to get you? Because you were naked?'

Nick looks at him, then at the rest of us. He laughs.

'No! No,' he says, shaking his head. 'That's not why. Is that really what you think?' He laughs again, adding to it a large dollop of man-of-great-wisdom-speaking-to-the-young. 'No.' Another lean-in. '*They were coming to stop people talking to me.*'

He leans back again, but before he can frame his features once more into victoriousness, Dr Prandarjarbash says, 'So why didn't you just talk to them?'

Nick's twisted smile stops in its tracks. 'Huh?'

'The police. Why didn't you talk to them? They're people. Why did you go and hide from them in the dustbin?'

Nick looks frightened now. 'What dustbin?'

'Don't you remember hiding in the dustbin?'

He turns to Fran, his face crumbling. 'What's he talking about, hiding in the dustbin?'

'It's OK,' says Fran, grasping the side of his head and drawing it down towards her potato-sacked bosom. 'Shhh.'

Nick closes his eyes and trembles; Fran looks at Dr Prandarjarbash fiercely, the dial that controls her eyes switched all the way round from *I understand* to *you are the enemy*.

'All right,' says the psychiatrist, clipping his pen back into his breast-pocket and turning his clipboard around so it rests shiny black side up on his knees. 'Let's leave it there.' He gets up and walks over to the white metal table with a variety of bottles on it that formed the only furniture when the curtain was drawn across and this space became a room. He puts the clipboard down on the table and turns back towards us: only then do I realise how small Dr Prandarjarbash is – under five foot, at a guess – his physical diminutiveness coming as a shock after his psychical largesse.

'Mr Munford, I wonder if you would mind going and waiting in the Casualty area for a little while? I just want to have a quick chat with your friends.'

'What, by himself?!' says Fran, outraged. I'm not sure that's a good idea either.

'Hmm . . . now you mention it, Miss . . .?'

'Fremantle. Fran.'

'Perhaps it would be better if someone went with him.'

Telling him off with her eyes, Fran does three slow, patronising nods, and then gets up, taking the shattered husk of Nick Munford, still clinging to her side, out through the curtain, completely unaware that Dr Prandarjarbash has tricked her into making her own exit. He stands looking at his soft brown loafers for a few seconds until the blue material stops swishing.

'Your friend has first strike symptoms of schizophrenia,' he says, looking up.

Dina looks at me, eyebrows steady, probably because her exhausted eye muscles are too set on moving down to lift them. I want to put my cheek against her cheek and rub the side of my face on her soft bulwark like a cat against its feeder's leg. *First strike*: isn't that some sort of Cold War term?

'There are a number of options as regards treatment,' Dr Prandarjarbash continues. I feel a tiny sense of relief, as I always do when I come to the doctor and some form of illness is actually diagnosed, that at least I haven't been dismissed as a complete time-waster. 'We can prescribe him chlorpromazine, an anti-psychotic drug. If that doesn't work, we can suggest that he admit himself to our psychiatric unit as a voluntary patient.'

'What if he doesn't fancy that?'

Dr Prandarjarbash ticks his tongue against the roof of his mouth thoughtfully. 'The problem is, he's a euphoric. Schizophrenia can manifest itself like that, as a sort of manic energy, a frenzied elevation of the spirits, a strange, feverish . . .'

'Joy?' I suggest.

'Exactly. And in those cases, the patient doesn't tend to see himself as requiring treatment. Now, under the conditions of the Mental Health Act, to commit Mr Munford against his will would require the presence of a psychiatrist, a policeman and his GP, all of whom would have to agree that he presented a danger to himself or to the public at large. He would then not be allowed out again unless those same three people agreed that he was no longer a danger.'

He pauses, as if expecting me to comment, but my mind is stuffed with strait-jackets, black pads pushed towards temples flinching away, loose-fitting trousers pulled down flailing legs to make way for the needle, the naked stutterer committing suicide at the end of *One Flew Over The Cuckoo's Nest*.

'It's generally thought of as something of a last resort. I wouldn't at this stage recommend it for Mr Munford.'

'But Gabriel has to live with him!' says Dina. 'How do you expect him to sleep at night with a lunatic in the next room?'

'Probably no worse than usual,' I say.

'How do you mean?' he says.

'I'm an insomniac.'

He frowns. 'Have you tried Kalms?'

'That's not the point!' says Dina.

'I don't think Mr Jacoby is in any danger.'

'Didn't you *see* him out there?'

'As far as I understand it, he wasn't actually trying to hurt the other patient. Quite the opposite.'

'Yeah, right,' says Dina, her chair screeching backwards against the hospital parquet as she suddenly gets up, 'and he probably won't be *trying* to hurt Gabriel when he puts the pillow over his face for his own good.'

Although I really think this scenario she's painting leaves out the fact that I never go to sleep, I must say it's nice to hear that she's so worried about me. I look at her, gratified, but, as she returns my look somewhat coldly, I realise that it all just stems from a sub-text of her previous experience with Miles. She knows the dangers of leaving lunacy to escalate unpoliced. Which reminds me.

'Doctor,' I say, feeling slightly stupid as soon as I've said it, slightly 'what, are *the daleks* gonna appear in a minute?', 'I think we've forgotten to tell you something.'

Dr Prandarjarbash inclines his head politely, a somewhat sub-continental gesture, equivalent to me shrugging with my hands held open.

'The day this all started, Nick told me that over the weekend he'd smoked some dope. Cannabis.'

He takes off his black heavy-framed glasses, and rubs the corner of his left eye with his index finger, quite violently, like he knows exactly at what point rubbing your eye becomes dangerous and will stop before he gets there.

'You should have told me that before,' he says, extracting his finger. His eyes were bloodshot enough before not to register the impact. Clearly, he thinks I withheld that information. He thinks we're like those kids on anti-drug adverts who, when asked if their friend on the operating trolley has taken anything untoward look shifty and say, in stage-school cockney, 'Pills. I dunno.' But I didn't, I just forgot. It's three o'clock in the morning, for Christ's sake. That's the trouble with therapy-infested thinking – nothing happens by accident. But that's wrong: most things happen by accident.

'But he's smoked it before, I'm sure, and nothing like this has happened.'

'That doesn't matter. If it's a cannabis psychosis, he—'

'A what?'

'A cannabis psychosis.'

You ever heard of that? Dina, for all her American encounters, shrugs her shoulders when I look at her.

'Is that common?'

'More so than you might think. Anyway, my point was that the fact he's smoked it before, even regularly, is neither here nor there. If he's prone in any way to mental imbalance, then that can come on suddenly after a build-up of drug-use over many years, or maybe because there are some other stresses and strains in his life at the present time which might cause nervous breakdown and so the drug acts as a catalyst. Or perhaps it was just some different, new type of . . .' he pauses, young enough in his late thirties to want to seem comfortable with the terminology, aware though how out of place the vernacular is going to sound within his detached medical vocabulary '. . . dope.'

He picks his clipboard up again and tucks it under his arm in a winding-down kind of way.

'So how long might it last?' I say.

'Depends. I'll give you a prescription for chlorpromazine, and, as long as you can make sure he does genuinely take them . . .'

Despite her tiredness, Dina's eyebrow lifts at this, and mine too, at least internally; the doctor's deliberate over-stressing of the potential difficulties of administering the drug, obviously a product of experience, leads into an entirely new imaginative arena, all mortars and pestles, stews sprinkled with bluish dust, Jezebel at the vet having her mouth forced open for a worming tablet (it took three of us and don't even ask what happened when he tried to take her temperature).

'. . . he may come out of the psychosis, if that's what it is, in a couple of weeks. But it can last anything up to two years.'

'*Two years!* I can't carry on living with a lunatic for two years. *I'll* have a nervous breakdown.'

'You could always move out,' says Dina.

'What, and just leave him there, mentalling it up all day with that . . . that *herpe*.'

Dina frowns. 'I think you mean harpie.'

'It was a deliberate contraction of hippie and harpie.'

'Oh.'

'And besides, it's taken me *four* years to get the DSS to pay my housing benefit for the place we're in now.'

'Get a job?' says Dr Prandarjarbash.

I look at him: although his head is down and fixed on to the prescription he's writing out, I can still make out the merest speck of a smile playing around the indents of his mouth.

'I'm sorry,' he says, finishing off his signature, a flourishing, confident, adult one, redolent of a sorted self-image. 'It's none of my business. It is true, I'm afraid, that in cases like this, it can be harder on the people around the person who's mentally ill than for the patient himself.'

He holds out the prescription. With his other hand, he lifts a section of the blue curtain for us to go out through.

'Yeah,' I say, taking the prescription, 'I could use a bit of euphoria myself.'

Walking back to the Casualty waiting-room in fear of whatever Nick may be doing in there, I say to Dina, 'Thanks for coming down here.'

She smiles at me. I'd like to put my arm round her or peck her cheek or something, but I find myself uncertain whether it's the right thing to do: amazing really when I was absolutely sure a few nights ago about putting my penis in her mouth. But smaller displays of affection take longer to come by.

'That's all right. What sort of person would have left you on your own with your flatmate naked in the dustbin?'

'A person who didn't want to get involved,' I say, without meaning this to sound quite so pointed as it does. I really mean 'didn't want to get involved' like a man walking past a gang of white youths carving a Union Jack on a young Asian's forehead doesn't want to get involved.

She stops and looks at me. 'Are we *involved*, then?'

Typically, I shrug: I defer. 'I dunno. What d'you think?'

'I thiiiinnnk . . .' she says, 'that if you get it together to organise a date for the two of us that's just, y'know, a date – nothing complicated or anything, maybe just getting a video out or something; but at the end of it, no one's died or gone crazy or whatever – then, on the basis that we will at last have spent some normal time together, I'll be able to assess whether or not we are actually involved. OK?'

'OK,' I say, and act immediately on my correct realisation that now is the time to peck her on the cheek.

Back at the re-built phalanx of orange chairs, Nick is sleeping on Fran's shoulder in a similar arrangement to Dina sleeping on mine earlier. His mouth is open, and although there is no fishing line of spittle hanging out, a darkened patch on her upper potato sack stems from the edge of his lips in the shape of a small map of Ireland, like a 1916 *Punch* cartoon about Home Rule.

'So what did your *psychiatrist* tell you, then?' says Fran, whispering, I think – I mean, I think she's actually whispering now, because Nick's asleep – although it's hard to tell.

'He gave us this,' I say, showing her the prescription. She looks at it through her turquoise lenses.

'I wouldn't bother with that,' she says.

'Oh, wouldn't you,' says Dina fiercely. Much as I quite fancy the idea of them having a fist-fight, I step in.

'Look, Fran. I'm sure you've got Nick's best interests at heart. But I think we should do what the doctor says.'

She tilts her nose up at the prescription, allowing me to see quite into her brain. 'That stuff makes people into zombies.'

'How do you know?'

'I'm a pharmacist. And I used to be a psychiatric nurse.'

Eh?

'Eh?'

'I worked at the Maudsley, in South London.' She speaks slowly, as if teaching a simple but important lesson. 'It was there that I realised that our society's whole concept of . . .' she makes finger inverted-comma signs, jiggling Nick's head slightly in so doing '. . . "mental illness" is mistaken.'

I look at Dina, uncertain how to take this, but she is unblinking.

'A lot of people who work in mental hospitals end up going crazy, don't they?' she says flatly.

Fran turns to her, her head moving suspiciously like Robocop's. 'At some point, you really should take some time out to talk to someone who can find out what's really bothering you.'

'Well, I can't see much point in paying a psychotherapist thirty quid an hour for five years to come up with the answer . . .' she points her finger directly at Fran '. . . *you*.'

Fran nods, as if to say: *interesting. More data for the case study I'm compiling*. It is perhaps the most infuriating gesture I have ever seen. Quelling an impulse to punch her in the face, I say, lowering my voice, 'Fran . . . I remember Nick saying that when he first met you, you were with some people passing round a pipe with some dope in it?'

'Um . . . yes, maybe.'

'What sort of dope was it?'

'What sort? Just hash, I think.' Then she closes her eyes suddenly. 'No, wait a minute . . . my friend Mandy had just come back from Nepal with some killa bud.'

'Killer bud?'

'Kil*la*,' she says, opening her Dulux eyes. 'With an "a". It's wonderful stuff. Looks quite different from ordinary dope, more like a little green flower. It's beautiful, really. Why? Do you want me to get you some?'

I shake my head. Dina, I can tell even out of the side of my vision, is bursting to tell her how it's all her fault, how her stupid drug is responsible for the disintegration of my friend and flatmate, how she can stick her killa bud up her consciousness-expanding arse. I grab hold of her arm to stop her: she looks at me, confused.

'There's no point,' I say. 'Forget it.'

I mean this. Fran is clearly one of those people who never accept blame for anything, and besides, while she is of the opinion that what's happening to Nick is essentially a positive thing – a break-*up* – she's only going to celebrate the idea that her silly drug is directly responsible, and I'd rather not give her the pleasure. Fran continues to look at me in innocent inquiry: even this action has a certain self-consciousness, a certain studiedness, a certain 'Here I am looking at you in innocent inquiry'-ness.

'Is something bothering you, Gabriel?' she says, in tones moulded to match her look.

'Yes,' I say. Her features adjust subtly, into 'open up to me, that's what I'm here for.'

'Where did you get that hat?' I say, not singing.

14

'Happy birthday to you! Happy birthday to you! Happy birthday, dear Mutti . . .'

My grandmother, smiling, hair newly rinsed the colour of her Basildon Bond, lowers her head towards the candles on her cake, brilliantly decorated with icing-sugar models of the major monuments of pre-First World War Gdansk. She takes a professionally deep breath, as only those for whom breathing is no longer quite taken for granted can.

'*Happy birthday to you!!!*'

Her wrinkles smooth for a second as her cheeks puff out: the precious air comes out of her lungs in something of an asthmatic trickle, but proves to be powerful enough to blow out the candles, of which, thankfully, there are only four, rather than eighty-four. Only the pink twirly one on top of the *Marienkirche*, Gdansk's towering medieval cathedral damaged in the onslaught of Russian artillery throughout 1945, turns out to be troublesome, flickering into life again just after the little puff of smoke from the wick seemed to spell the end for its flame.

'Oh!' says my grandmother, through the applause of her immediate family. 'It's like the Maccabite candle.'

Still applauding, Alice turns her mahogany eyes instinctively to Ben.

'The Maccabite candle,' he says, bending his mouth to her ear, in a way suggestive to me of his licence to continue that parabola all the way in if he so desired, 'was a holy candle that continued to burn miraculously all through the siege of the second temple by the Romans, even though we had no fuel left.'

The applause dies down. The other inmates of Liv Dashem House who are in the TV room look over resentfully, maybe because my family's singing is not of the best, but more likely because here, where, in terms of status, visits from your relatives is hard currency, is fags in prison, having twelve of them standing around clapping your every move is perceived as ostentatious. The man with the thick glasses who I met last time in the lift – Mr Fingelstone I thought I heard one of the nurses call him – sits as far away as possible in a blue flannel-upholstered rocking chair, looking particularly peeved; he grunts in audible dissatisfaction as my mother, responsible for the cake, hugs my grandmother, making them look together like one two-headed Jewish mother monster.

'We?' I say to Ben. He is standing next to me, Alice on his other side.

'The Jews,' he snaps back without looking at me, implying 'you knew very well what I meant.'

I keep looking at his profile, wondering how much it's like mine. 'Did you remember that from primary school?' Although we both went to (different) secular secondary schools, we shared kosher custard and compulsory yarmulkas at North West London Jewish Day School for five to eleven year olds.

'No,' he says, turning to me at last, 'I read about it last week in a book.'

What light bedtime reading was that, I wonder, but get no chance to pursue the matter, as my Auntie Edie – actually my Great-Auntie Edie, but she prefers us to drop the prefix – is wafting everybody into line to kiss and present presents to Mutti. I use the word waft, because that's what her hand movement is like, similar in many ways to a type of self-satisfied waving upwards to the nose that the pre-mad Nick used to do following a particularly pungent fart.

All Auntie Edie's movements are performed in super slo-mo, by which I mean more than just, like Mutti and Lydia Frindel, slow; she seems to have pockets of air swirling under her limbs at all times – she gestures when story-telling like a batonless conductor in a permanent adagio, and she glides across a crowded function room like a small Jewish hovercraft. She is tanning-machine orange in colour, and if you were to cut off and stretch taut all the loose flesh she has hanging between her chin and neck, you could reskin Phil Collins' biggest drum-kit.

Ben and Alice, I notice, have brought a proper present, wrapped beautifully in gold metallic paper with a red lace bow. This is because Ben, although only a couple of years older than me, is about fifteen years more adult, and has grown out of thinking that because Mutti is the grandmother, she's the one who's got to come up with the presents on the birthdays and we don't have to bother on hers. I haven't grown out of this way of thinking at all, even though I live just off the Kilburn High Road and can walk perfectly well, and Mutti lives half a mile from the nearest shops and only just makes it to the toilet some nights. I have however bought her a card, *To A Wonderful Grandma*, with a colour drawing of a kitten on it. And when I give it to her, I know she'll be entirely satisfied, because, even though eighty-four might seem very adult indeed, her understanding of who buys presents for who in the grandparent–child relationship is essentially the same as mine.

In front of Ben in the queue is my cousin Simon, Auntie Edie's boy, who is patently gay. This is stark bollock-nakedly obvious to everybody except Auntie Edie – I think even Mutti, if you asked her, would say 'Poof. Definitely', or words to that effect – who is always going on about how she can't understand why he never gets married; although to be fair to Edie, when she's around, Simon snuggles so deeply into the closet that you could open it, get five or six blankets out for visiting friends, and still not spot him hiding behind the boiler. As he lives with his mother, he's presumably become very used to breathing in that cramped and restricted air-space. Looking at him now, I think, as I often do, that if I was gay, I wouldn't fancy Simon. Getting into his early forties, I guess – I once asked him, and he pouted and said 'Mind your *own*!!', which I felt was a bit of a giveaway – he wears his dyed black Brillo-pad hair in a side parting and has a face so elaborately pock-marked that all he'd have to do is suck an American flag and he'd be the spit of the surface of the moon.

The rest of the queue consists of members of my family always called upon to make up the numbers on these occasions: Uncle Ray, who has a revolving left eye and smells of cabbage; his wife Avril, five foot three and four foot across, who only returned to Ray six months ago after running away with Maurice Gross, a psychic investigator from High Barnet; their two children, daughter Tanya and son Maurice; and Auntie Bubbles, who only ever says the word 'marvellous!' I say members of my family – what I really mean is members of my mother's family. My dad has no living relatives, but even if he did, I doubt he'd have invited them today; he doesn't get on with my grandmother – obviously, he doesn't get on with my mother, either, but in a different way – and sits in an armchair on the other side of the reproduction antique coffee-table deliberately not joining the queue and scowling into *Rommel? Gunner Who?* by Spike Milligan, which he's been reading for about fifteen months. Each time I look at him he appears to have buried himself slightly further into the armchair's cushions.

'Thank you, Tanya! Thank you, Maurice!' says my grandmother, holding up a gold circular brooch enclosing the star of David. Uncle Ray's neck muscles tighten ever so slightly at the mention of his son's name, as they must do ten, twenty times a day; if only Edie's husband Henry was still alive to run off with someone called Simon and save her the price of a face-lift. Maurice and Tanya, who have a disturbingly intimate relationship, break their enchanted gazing at each other for a microsecond to smile bashfully at Mutti, almost as if they'd actually paid for the thing themselves. Then they lock back into using each other as a mirror.

'So, how's Nick?' a cello of a voice asks me.

I look at Alice, leaning under Ben's head to speak to me. This is the first time I've seen her since my dalliance with Dina – *My Dalliance With Dina*, a Thirties music-hall song – and, knowing she'd be here, I had been wondering if my growing, indefinable feeling for her sister would take the edge off my adulation; certainly, she hasn't been stitched into my waking thoughts like a backcloth so much this past couple of weeks. I even felt a certain optimism, as I got off the bus and walked up Edgwarebury Lane, that perhaps I wouldn't feel so trapped by desire any more in her presence, so under the cosh of my brother's possession. But, of course, I hadn't bargained for her breasts.

Not true, actually. I just said breasts for the bathos, for the alliteration, although they do form maybe thirty per cent of the impact of Alice. What I mean is, *her*. I hadn't bargained for her (much as I'd like to at some point – 'All I've got! All I've got in the world I'll give you!') You know how, inside, you've got an inexpressible yearning? Lying dormant most of the time, erupting every so often with a bursting swell in the chest, like when the city suddenly ends and you drive past a field with the right music on the radio? It feels abstract, that yearning, like it's not actually *for* something, it's just yearning, just the soul howling. But it is for something, let me tell you: it's for Alice.

'It's a Chanukah plate, Mutti!'

'She *knows* what it is, Avril.'

'Marvellous!'

'Not great,' I tell Alice. She nods concernedly, her mess of black ringlets bobbing against my brother's forty-six-inch chest. Even though she may know already, I feel an urge to tell her about having slept with Dina, to confess my strange adultery.

'Is he taking the anti-psychotic drugs?' she says.

I'm always astounded when Alice knows anything about my life. This is partly because no matter how one-to-one, equals-in-conversation, me chatting to her may appear on the surface, inside, I'm grovelling, pathetically thankful that she can even be bothered to talk to me: anything else – starting with her remembering my name – is a bonus. But also, she does have a certain *insouciance*, Alice, stemming not, I think, from arrogance or disdain, but from serenity, from having drawn a circle round her life out of which she need not step: the natural incuriosity of the entirely content.

So first I'm surprised that she knows the name of my flatmate, then more surprised because she knows what's wrong with him: when it comes to knowing the nature of his medication, I'm like a duck in thunder. Then I realise where the information's coming from.

'Dina told you?' I say, disguising in a heaviness of tone, meant to be indicative of the pain Nick's causing me, a secret pleasure in this unlooked-for side effect of being involved with her sister. Alice does a stoically affirmative smile, raising both her eyebrows. Uncle Ray and Auntie Avril move off from the front of the queue, five or six feet apart.

'Yeah, he's taking them, I think,' I say, shuffling forward. Simon bends down to Mutti, smiling, a box in blue crêpe paper sitting ready prepared on his palm. 'It's difficult to tell, I can't force them down his throat. But he's been much quieter these past few days. Fran might have been right about them.'

'Fran?'

'Didn't Dina tell you about her?'

Alice frowns. I feel sure Dina *would've* unburdened herself to her sister about Fran – only my father describing my mother compares to the way she talked about her after we got back from Casualty – so this is either an example of the limits of Alice's interest or . . .

'D'you mean The Herpe?' says Ben.

. . . they know her by some other name.

'Is that what she called her?' I say.

'Yeah. A mix of hippie and harpie, she said.'

Alice shakes her head, laughing. '*So* Dina.'

'Right . . .' I say.

Mutti holds aloft cousin Simon's present, a framed print of The Wailing Wall. I'm beginning to detect a theme here. I consider asking Ben and Alice where Dina is, but think better of it. It's obvious why she isn't here, at least. This is a family gathering, an arena where your identity is at its most three-dimensionally constructed, seen, like a technical drawing, from seven or eight views: e.g. Auntie Edie is my Great-Aunt/Mutti's sister/Simon's mother/Ray's aunt, etc, etc – but who is Dina? Ben's sister-in-law? Or my girlfriend? The last thing you want at a family gathering is that kind of slippage. Especially when you've got all the uncertainty that Maurice throws up already.

My dad laughs, loudly. Everyone in the room takes their attention off Mutti and looks at him. He looks up from *Rommel? Gunner Who?*

'What?' he says.

'Stuart . . .' says my mother.

'What?!'

'Oh, Stuart.'

'WHAT!!?'

The veins on my father's bald head bulge with swearwords. But he doesn't say them: he's pretty good like that, my father – he'll only swear at my mother in private. It's true that Uncle Ray once asked him not to call his sister a piss-bag full of pile-juice, but that was something he heard in the background while talking to her on the phone. Once out the house, he keeps himself pretty much to himself; which is not to say he isn't just as irritable.

'Can't you just join in for once, Dad?' asks Ben, saying the words for my mother. Ben has always been sadder about the sorry state of my parents' relationship than myself; I of course am rather ironic and post-modern about it all, and not at all as a defence mechanism.

'I am . . .' I can see his vocabulary struggling down, through 'fucking', past 'sodding', and into 'bloody', before realising it has nowhere to go '. . . JOINING IN!!!' He says it as loud as possible, to compensate for the missing swearword.

'What is he saying?' says Mutti to her friend Mrs Gildart, the only non-family member at the party, sitting beside her. Mrs Gildart, Millie as most people know her, is not an inmate of Liv Dashem House – she is an old friend of Mutti's from when she used to live in Wembley, and although eighty-two herself has refused to be incarcerated in an old people's home. She wears a beret and is old in the other way to Liv Dashem House and queueing in the post office and photos of grandchildren and enormous underwear and smelly hallways – in the Spanish Civil War way, the W.H. Auden way, her face like one of those black and white portraits so lined the beauty in it has turned full-circle and come back out again, her mind as you hope against hope yours will be, full of truth and sadness and stories. Refusing to go gentle, she has just, she told me earlier, enrolled in a computer course at night school.

'He says he is joining in, Eva,' says Millie.

'How is he?' says Mutti, raising her voice to that frightening level you never imagine older people have. 'He sits there not speaking to anyone. He doesn't say hello to me on my birthday, he just nods at me, like . . .' She nods, pulling the corners of her mouth absurdly far down as she does so. 'He doesn't sing, he doesn't bring anything!'

Chucking the book violently down on the table, my dad stands up and walks out. Uncle Ray's right eye follows him, his left follows some invisible gyroscope; Auntie Edie floats her hands around and purses her lips as if about to say 'b-b-b-b-but . . .'; Tanya and Maurice continue looking at each other, oblivious; Ben and Alice look down, embarrassed; Auntie Avril smiles to herself, smug in her bitterness, her conviction that marriage is a sham consolidated; Millie sighs; across the room, Mr Fingelstone tut-tuts loudly and shakes out his *Jewish Chronicle*; Simon rests his chin on his hand and drums his fingers repeatedly on his cheek; Mutti stares straight ahead sullenly, her face set, the corners of her mouth pinched tight, daring anyone to question the validity of her outrage; I cough; my mother takes her glasses off and starts cleaning them.

'Marvellous!' says Auntie Bubbles.

'"Something kills everybody in time",' says Mutti, pronouncing each word carefully. '"Take my grandmother, she died of deafness." "Died of *deafness*?"' she continues, reading both parts of the dialogue in exactly the same voice. '"Yes, there was this steamroller coming up behind her and she didn't hear it." "She didn't die of deafness . . . she died of steamroller."'

A short silence, and she puts *Rommel? Gunner Who?* down, looking a touch confused. My mother and Auntie Edie smile encouragingly, as if they have learnt much from the reading; Mutti shrugs. The atmosphere has lightened a bit since my father's walk-out. We've split up into discussion groups, sprinkled around the sofa; the Gdansk-cake has been divided up, and hundreds of lime-green institutionalised cups and saucers have appeared from nowhere to house burnished tea. My father has even come back into the room, muttering something under his breath about not even being able to sit in the corridor without some old bag coming up and telling him how to get to Acton. I'm sitting with Ben and Alice, and Simon, who's playing his 'I may be in my early forties, but obviously I categorise myself as one of the young people here' card.

'*What* did you get her?' I say to Ben, picking up the book. '*A Dictionary of Jewish Lore and Legend.*' I read it slowly.

'Well, y'know,' says Ben, trying to shrug off any further implication of deepening Jewishness, although he should know you can't do that in a *shrug*, 'she likes all that stuff.'

'Yeah,' says Simon, deliberately, as opposed to saying 'yes'. If he does it any more, I may suggest he goes to sit with Tanya and Maurice. 'Doesn't she just?'

They're right, of course: she loves all that stuff. But still I suspect Ben's present. I feel, looking at him, that he's taken the opportunity of buying this book undercover as it were; he's exploiting the context, using Mutti as an alibi. After all, he didn't have to read the bloody thing.

'Have *you* read it?' I say to Alice. She shakes her head, but doesn't, as I expected, smile, acknowledging the absurdity of the idea. Instead, she looks somewhat confused, and a glance passes between her and Ben the like of which I have not seen before. Well, I *have* seen it before – I've *perpetrated* one half of it before – but not between Ben and Alice: it is the frazzled look of a couple who, having had an argument, are now having to deal with the subject-matter of that argument being brought up coincidentally by a third party.

Just to prove what a topsy-turvy world it is, the air of embarrassment is actually broken by the interruption of my mother.

'So! Isn't it nice to have the whole family together for once! I don't think I can remember the last time we sat down together for what I call a "family occasion".'

'Yes!' says Simon, slipping on, for my mother, his adult hat. 'And that fabulous cake! Where on earth did you get it?'

'Oh! Marks and Spencer's.'

'No!' says Simon, his eyes wide.

'No, of course not. Hahahaha!'

'Hahahaha!' says Simon.

My wrists itch for a razor blade.

'No,' continues my mother, 'I'm being silly. I made the cake-base myself, and then had the top of it – you know, all the monuments etc? – flown over especially from a woman in Poland.'

'That's so thoughtful of you.'

'Well . . .' she says, looking up into an imaginary sky

'. . . when one gets to eighty-four, I think that you deserve that little bit of extra effort. Don't you?'

She smiles wistfully. I often think that my mother, like many women of her generation, works on the basis of this mathematical equation: saying something patently apparent to everyone + wistfully smiling = saying something really quite perceptive.

'Tea, Irene?' says Alice, holding a lime-green institutional teapot up to the air.

'*What* a good idea!'

'Is there any coffee?' I say.

'I don't think so.'

'OK. I'll have tea, then.'

'So, Alice,' she says, snapping into an 'all-girls-together' voice, 'what do we think about Gabriel and Tina?'

'Dina,' Alice says, pouring.

'Dina!' she says, flapping a hand at her in apology.

Alice looks at me, and, once again, does a stoic smile. Even though my mother's tactlessness is symptomatic of the terrible way parents never take their children's sexual quandaries seriously, no matter what age they are, it's great the way that the issue of Dina has opened up all sorts of new lines of communication between me and Alice. At last, we have a secret meeting-place.

'I mean – does she look like you?' my mother asks.

'Why should she?' asks Simon.

'She's my sister,' says Alice, a little bashfully, trying to play down the thousand implications of this.

'Oooooooooooo!' says Simon, doing his façade no favours. 'Gabriel!' he continues, his palm flat against the side of his face. 'What *are* you playing at?'

That's quite a good question, in truth. Leaning over to hand me my cup of tea, Alice's face comes close enough to mine to pull the supportive grimace of the jointly put-upon.

'Me and Dina have . . . gone out a couple of times, that's all,' I reply. 'We're being cautious.'

'Should hope so this day and age.' Simon nods his eyes knowingly at my mother, perhaps forgetting who she is.

'Yeah, well . . .'

'*Does* she look like you?' he says to Alice, sniffing scandal, and, with a homosexual's quick instinct for polymorphous motivation, *all* the potentially juicy angles on my interest in Dina.

'I can't see it, really,' says Alice. 'People have told me she does.'

'What do *you* think, Gabriel,' says Simon pointedly. Now another type of over-emphasiser to deal with. The opposite type: where Fran and Nick hit words hard to imply huge unspoken depths beneath, Simon does it to spike the surface, to glitterise, to show how serious he is about superficiality.

'A bit,' I say, after a carefully judged moment's thought, 'Dina's got dyed blonde hair. And she's sort of rounder. Couple of inches taller as well, isn't she?'

I've pitched it as best I can. To say, her nose is four to five millimetres longer, her mouth curves six degrees further downwards at the edges, her eyes are maybe four per cent narrower, her chin ends closer to her bottom lip, I've never seen your breasts, Alice, but I estimate hers to be at least a cup smaller, and, sorry about this, but I'm going to have to press my body naked against yours to work out the exact difference in the texture of your skin: this, I feel, would imply an unhealthy degree of know-how on the subject.

'Not really,' says Alice. 'You haven't allowed for those ridiculous platforms she wears, have you?'

I have, of course: that was my deliberate mistake. I freeze the upward movement of my cup of tea, and close my eyes and tut and nod smilingly, before letting it continue to my mouth. Urrh. The flat unmediated dullness of the drink indicates that Alice has, as usual, forgotten to put sugar in it. This fresh example of her continual inability to remember that, although I drink coffee without, I take tea with, breaks my serene self-satisfaction about our new and secret communion, reminding me, as it always does, that this is exactly the sort of tiny lifestyle detail that she would know if we were lovers. Less is more: I'd swap all her recently acquired savvy about my terrible torments with Nick for her remembering that I drink coffee without, tea with.

'She wears *platform shoes*?' says my mother, laughing. 'I used to wear those twenty years ago!'

My mother wears green ski pants and a red sweat-shirt with

an embroidered picture of The Hindenburg on it. When she says twenty she means more like eleven – my mother resolutely carried on dressing like she was in a porn film until well into the early Eighties. (I mean porn film in the classical sense, that is – moustachioed men, women in spangly evening-dresses, wobbly sound, wah-wah pedals, long velvet curtains, sex in saunas and forests – not the sort of stuff I collect.) And I think she only actually threw out most of her flared Lurex jump-suits and patchwork hipsters about two years ago, at which point – who knows, maybe *because* my mother threw them out – they became violently fashionable again.

'Alice?' I say. 'Can you pass the sugar?'

'Oh, platforms are very in again now, Irene!' says Simon. 'So is she a bit of a clubber, then?'

This question is, cleverly, not asked to anyone in particular, so as to provoke an awkward uncertainty about which of us is the information-carrier about Dina. Me and Ben and Alice look three ways at each other. It's clear. Knowledge, in this case, bespeaks possession; whoever speaks first, it seems, is saying, *she's mine*.

'I'm going now,' says Millie Gildart, suddenly appearing on the edge of our group, looking, in her black overcoat and beret, like a terrorist from the military wing of Age Concern. We all move to get up.

'Don't get up, for God's sake,' she says. 'Goodbye is no reason to get up. Hello, maybe.' She walks round to my mother. 'Goodbye, Irene.'

'Millie, have you got a car home?' says my mother, with that air of slight reproach often adopted towards old people which is meant to indicate concern.

'Car?'

'A taxi. Look, I'll order you one.'

'Will you stop getting up! The bus is fine.'

'But you have to change at Golders Green!'

'Shut up, Irene. I'm not going to get mugged. It's Golders Green, not The Bronx, for heaven's sake.' She moves on, with an air of having said a resolute 'no' to nonsense. 'Bye, Ben. Bye, Alice.'

'Bye, Millie. We'll come and visit you sometime,' says Ben.

'Yeah, yeah,' says Millie sarcastically. Ben appears somewhat hurt, and looks for a second as if he wants to explain that although he may have said this as a platitude in the past, this time he really means it. 'Bye, Simon. We haven't talked again, but then we didn't last time.'

Simon grabs her hand, puts his other hand over it, and gazes deeply into her eyes. 'We will next time,' he says.

'I don't know if there will be a next time.'

'*Millie!* I won't have you talking like that. You're not getting into heaven just yet.'

'Why?' says Millie flatly. 'Have they changed the door policy?'

Simon's face fills with blood like a drip bag. She moves off, leaving him holding his palms together in the air in the pose of an Olympic diver.

'Goodbye, Gabriel,' she says. Then she halts, squinting at me. 'It is Gabriel, isn't it?'

'Yes,' I say.

She nods, and leans down so that our faces are touching, her whorled cheek like Braille against mine.

'When you get to this age,' she whispers, 'the light plays terrible tricks with your eyes.' Then she kisses me, and, without bothering even to check my reaction, shuffles off to say goodbye to Mutti, still on the other sofa.

'Well!' says my mother, shaking her head and smiling. 'The things that little old lady comes out with!' We all nod in spurious assent, apart from Simon, who looks at his piece of Gdansk-cake in mute rage. 'So what were we talking about?' There is a short pause.

'Jerome Mandle,' says Ben inspirationally.

'Were we?' says my mother, uncertain for a second, before not worrying about it. 'Well, his new book on the maiden voyage to Lucerne – don't quote me on this, by the way – but I'm sorry, it's just got too many simple errors. The captain's cabin on the port side? Excuse me!'

As long as Simon continues to sulk, there's no chance of anyone bringing her back on to the ticklish subject of Dina. I look over to the other sofa, where Mutti and Millie are standing facing each other like two beardless garden gnomes.

'Goodbye, Eva,' says Millie.

'Goodbye, Miriam,' says Mutti. Their hands meet for a second. This farewell, I notice, has a different tenor to all Millie's others, more restrained, yet with a sense that more rests on it; a knowing look passes between them, not smirky or supercilious, but knowing in the purest sense, as of being possessed of a particular knowledge; and then suddenly I realise that they are saying a particular type of goodbye, the goodbye that old people who do not live that close to one another, and who therefore cannot visit regularly, say to each other – the opposite perhaps of all our other goodbyes, with their nonchalance, their ease of saying, their synonymity with 'see you', 'later', 'au revoir'. Words change their impact with age, goodbye more than most, I suppose; imagine, every time you say goodbye, knowing that it could really be just that, and die more than a little. I can hear it now, in the restraint, in the gaps, like Lord Haw-Haw, eternity calling; brave though Millie is, this time the old savante has left the sub-text unsaid, although perhaps she hasn't, as all the sub-text really is is silence.

'. . . frankly, I'm surprised it hasn't got worse reviews. Barry Beam was especially generous, I thought, in *The Dirigible*, although he is a friend of Jerome's – who wouldn't be after the review *Jerome* gave *Airships and Airmen*?'

Ben, probably against his best intentions, has started staring into the middle distance. Simon has just *gone*: there he is, over by Auntie Edie, standing in a completely new way. Only Alice is paying attention, genuinely, and not because she's interested – fourteen or fifteen family dinners in, I think The Hindenburg crashed again over her boredom threshold – but because she's polite to her bones. Politeness for most of us is entirely a question of appearances, mainly of looking like you're taking in information when you're not, but that leaves out those who can't, in any way, lie, and who therefore are condemned actually to take in all sorts of terrible rubbish. Alice is like a method actor: to appear to be listening, she has to listen.

I see Millie Gildart pad by and out of the door, getting a grim nod from Ray, before he goes back into a hissy-whispery head-to-head with Avril, the size of their gesticulations completely out of proportion with the level of their voices.

'"Randolph Churchill: When I grow up, I'm going to sue everybody for a living. Evelyn Waugh: I'm braver than you. Randolph: No you're not, my daddy's Winston Churchill."'

Mutti, having taken the time out to say goodbye to Millie, has sat down and become aware that, for a second, everyone is in their own groups and no one is talking to her: she is combating this lack of attention by reading once more from *Rommel? Gunner Who?* in a loud voice, one of Milligan's short comic playlets, a dialogue between Randolph Churchill and Evelyn Waugh. She pauses, extending her arms to hold the book at full stretch away from her, as if this will make its point clearer. The room resumes its general murmur; Alice nods artlessly at my mother.

'Ben?' I say, wrenching my eyes from his wife, 'can you give me a lift back?'

'When?'

'Soon.'

He shakes his head. 'I think maybe we should stay a bit longer.'

'Naah, we've done our bit. No one'll be upset if we go now.'

'But I *want* to stay longer.'

'I thought you just said "we *should* stay a bit longer." "Should" is not "want".'

'It's not diametrically opposed to want, either.'

What on earth does *that* mean?

'You can *want* to do things that also happen to be your duty,' he continues. 'Like . . .' he searches for a moment, then catches sight of Mutti still holding the book at arm's length '. . . fighting the Nazis. If we'd be alive then, it's something we should've done, *and* something we'd have wanted to do.'

'Speak for yourself.'

'Sorry?'

'Well, you're a big lad. You'd look great in camouflage gear. Me, I'd have got killed. Probably in training.'

'But if everyone thought like you—'

'The world would be a much better place?'

'No. Then no one would've fought and you'd definitely have been killed. In a gas chamber.'

'Look. All I bloody asked for was a lift home.'

'"Waugh: I'm braver than you, I wear a woolly outer garment."' Mutti is off again, in her stentorian reading voice. '"I'm braver than *anyone*! When a German plane comes over, I never take cover, you know why? Randolph: Yes, you're a cunt."'

The word pierces the air like a scud missile. Not just the rest of the room – everyone in *Edgware* seems to look round. It's like an H.M. Bateman cartoon: 'The Old Lady Who Said The Word "Cunt".' My mother's hand, holding a last piece of cake, freezes on the way to her mouth; Auntie Edie's face goes from orange to white, like a speed-sucked ice lolly; Uncle Ray looks confused, as if perhaps thinking his wife's voice has suddenly developed an echo; my father, still sitting buried in his armchair, looks directly at Mutti for maybe the first time in his life, with an expression halfway between anger for all the years he's had to control his tongue, and sheer, unadulterated respect. The only person not looking up, round, or askance is Mutti, her eyes still resolutely fixed on the end of that sentence.

'*Cunt*,' she says again – I'm sorry, it describes the way she says it, but honestly, honestly, no pun intended – tasting the word. She looks up, innocently. 'What's that?'

Various members of our party eye each other in panic; others cough; my father, for a second, looks as if he's about to answer.

'Oh, that's terrible!' says a voice from the other side of the room. It is Mr Fingelstone, his *Jewish Chronicle* open on his lap. 'I haven't heard language like that since the *trenches*.' He folds his newspaper and leaves the room in an attitude he imagines resembles high dudgeon, but which is clearly readable as triumph.

Mutti, sensing that she may have said something out of place, shuts the book, like Pandora once did her box, too late. The clap of the pages meeting together reverberates around Liv Dashem House's TV room. Then she notices something on the back, a quote about the book.

'"'I resign.' General Montgomery",' she says. The room breathes a collective sigh of relief; just a comedy quote.

'Hm,' says Mutti, looking up sombrely, 'I'm not surprised after reading this.'

15

'*Ghost*?'

'Yes.'

'The one with that man with the blow-wave? Looks like a gay bricklayer?'

'Patrick Swayze. Him there.'

Dina's face, lit hard by the strip-lights of the Kilburn High Road branch of Blockbuster Video, reflects off the gloss cover of *Ghost*, halfway between Demi Moore and Whoopi Goldberg. 'This is your *favourite* film?'

'Yes,' I say defensively. 'Well. One of my favourites.'

Quietly, she replaces the empty video-cover back on the shelf. A peal of overloud, demonstrative laughter comes from a group of four adolescent boys, hunched in the 'Adult' section behind us. All around, on TV monitors, *Home Alone* plays.

'Is this the same kind of schtick as with *The Carpenters*?' she says, turning to me. 'Sort of a post-modern ironic love of all things kitsch and schmaltzy?'

Schtick? Kitsch? Two months at Ben's house and already she's speaking in bloody Yiddish anagrams.

'No. I genuinely like The Carpenters, and I genuinely like *Ghost*.'

Dina looks doubtful. The boys behind us make *Beavis and Butthead* noises. 'What about . . .' her eye roves across to another rack '*Manon des Sources* . . .?'

'Oh, I don't want to see that subtitled bollocks.'

'Aha! I knew it.' She turns away, her arms folded.

'What?' She is looking down at the car-seat-colour carpet, smirking.

'*What* do you know?' I say, feeling the first creeping tones of couply irritation in my voice.

She looks up. 'It's not just an objective preference for *Ghost*, or films like it, is it? You're making a statement. An anti-art-film statement.'

'No . . .' I say, battling uselessly, like a fly against insecticide, against a burgeoning self-realisation brought on by Dina's words '. . . no . . . yes, I suppose in a way. But it's not some stupid *Modern Review* "I love Arnie" anti-art-film statement.'

'*Speed*!' shouts a blonde woman, facing the adjacent wall. She turns round. 'Y'know . . . with that Paki bloke!!'

'He's not a *Paki*!' shouts back her also blonde friend, breaking off her chat with the Asian man, glazedly putting tapes into covers behind the counter. 'He's Hawaiian!'

'What is it, then?' says Dina.

'Well . . . when I was eighteen, art films were all I'd go and see,' I say. 'Y'know – Godard's *Passion*, I saw that. *The Marriage of Maria Braun. The Draughtsman's Contract.* I think *The Draughtsman's Contract* was my favourite film at the time.'

'So what happened?'

'I saw *E.T.*'

'*E.T.*!!'

'Yeah.'

'How come, if you only ever went to see art films?'

'For a laugh. I thought, in a superior, bohemian kind of way, that it'd be funny.'

'And . . .?' says Dina.

'And I've never fucking cried so much in my life.'

It's true. Ten minutes from the end of *E.T.*, my face was not wet with tears, it was awash with them – fierce, fierce tears, wrung out of me through divine emotional manipulation. Steven Spielberg had burst a dam in my heart.

'And so,' I say, picking up *Ghost* again, 'that's all I really want from films now: to make me cry.'

'But you're just being manipulated.'

'I know.'

'What's good about that?'

'It's great. It makes me feel better. Look, if you didn't want to be emotionally manipulated, we could've stayed in and watched *Countdown*.'

She's right, it is a protest against art films. Because art films are all about making the viewer more aware of themselves, themselves in the act of watching a film, or some other such post-structuralist nonsense; whereas great cinema is all about *losing* the self, that's why – videos aside – it happens in a large, dark arena, hundreds of small I's swallowed up by the big screen. And the greatest loss of self is tears – serious crying, really uncontrollable weeping at the breakdown of love or restored happiness or death of a fictional character, someone who, deeply, is *not* yourself. It's quite different from crying at one's own misfortune, or at starving people on the news – the self cannot be lost in those tears, because it is, in one way or another, responsible. Crying at films is a giant, freely-given I-relinquishment; sometimes I can feel myself being syringed out of my eyes in bucket-loads.

The adolescent boys have settled on *Suburban Sex-Slaves*. Stifling giggles, they carry it like natives would a captured white explorer to the counter. I could tell them: it's a poor 1970s documentary about wife-swapping in an over-explicit cover, but I won't bother. Better to let them travel by themselves the long road to pornographic consumer wisdom.

'What other films have made you cry, then?' says Dina. 'Apart from *Ghost* and *E.T.*'

I look round for reminders, but see only rows and rows of the films that always seem to be depressingly available in video shops: *Jumping Jack Flash*, *The Breakfast Club*, *The Butcher's Wife*, *Flatliners*, *St Elmo's Fire*, *Look Who's Talking*, *1*, *2*, and *3*, *Jacob's Ladder*, *Serial Mom*. In my revolve, I catch sight, in the long window, of Mental Barry stumbling past, a fleece of toilet roll stuck to his foot like one of those Russian girl gymnasts who dance trailing ribbons. He stops and stares in, but not, I think, at me, suddenly jolted by the sight of someone who once he shared a bed with: he just stops and stares in, like he does at every other shop along Kilburn High Road.

'*Edward Scissorhands*,' I say. '*Green Card. Play It Again, Sam*.'

All love-stories, with different shaped lovers; all bittersweet, ending with the lovers going their separate ways, yet no matter how separate these ways are – between planets, between continents, between life and death – there is always a sense that somehow, somewhere, they'll reunite. Is that what makes me cry? Love barred, but living in hope – or more, in certainty?

'*Play It Again, Sam*?' she says, frowning. 'That's a really *funny* film.'

'Yeah, his funniest,' I say, and notice her clock my definiteness, my reflex absenting of the words 'I think' from a critical judgement, with distaste. 'I got it out of here again quite recently, actually. They've always got loads of Woody Allen stuff.'

'But why does it make you cry?'

'Well . . . there's a bit, at the end, where Woody Allen slips into a speech which sort of sounds familiar but you can't immediately place it, and Diane Keaton says – she's crying – she says, "That's beautiful," and he says, "It's from *Casablanca*. I waited my whole life to say it."' I pause. 'Sorry, it makes me go a bit wobbly just telling you about it.'

She looks at me, again, that look: the one that doesn't believe you can both admit softness and have testicles. Is it a ploy, she's thinking.

'But *Ghost*,' I say, looking down at it still in my right hand and tapping it with my left, 'was one of the best. I cried so much at the end of *Ghost* that I started to laugh.'

'Well, it still looks shit to me,' says Dina, taking the video out of my hand and putting it back in the rack. 'But, y'know – choose whatever you like,' she says, with a hint of weariness.

'Well, I *like* Ghost,' I say, going through a certain amount of internal alarm at the thought of spending £2.50 on something I've already seen, 'but it's up to you.'

'No, honestly, you decide.'

A blast of hot noise sweeps in from the High Street as the two blonde women exit with a copy of *Wild Orchid*. Surely, if tonight is, as Dina said in the hospital, about finding out whether or not we're involved, we can stop it here: we're having a 'you decide – no, *you* decide' moment in the video shop – how much more of a couple can we get?

'What about this?' she says, picking up a video with Sandra Bullock and some bloke I've seen in many films but don't know the name of on the front cover. '*You* should like this.'

'*While You Were Sleeping*? Just 'cos it's called that, you mean?'

'Well, it's a weepie, I think.'

I hate the word 'weepie'. Films that make you cry should not be relegated so.

'Or what about this?' she says, picking up another with Barbara Hershey and Bette Midler cuddling all over it. '*Beaches*. I remember hearing this was supposed to be stupidly tear-jerking.'

'What happens?'

There is a film review cut out and stuck to the cover. Dina glances over it, her mouth just pursing slightly as she reads.

'Barbara Hershey dies,' she says, looking up.

'I don't normally cry at someone dying.'

'Don't you? Doesn't Patrick Swayze die in *Ghost*?'

'Well, yeah, but that's not the bit that you cry at. And he doesn't really die.' I feel I'm not doing it justice. 'Let's have a look,' I say.

My eyes scan the review. It isn't actually a very good review, which makes it odd that they've stuck it to the video. Plot description . . . character summaries . . . usual tendency of film reviewers to refer to the characters by the names of the actors, presumably to demonstrate how they the professionals are never completely taken in by the artifice of film . . . and then it wraps up: 'Structurally, technically, stylistically, it's deeply flawed; but at the end, you cry, goddammit, real tears.'

I remain looking at the little cut-out rectangle of newsprint on the video-cover; I read quickly, so I've got a few surplus seconds before Dina would expect me to look up anyway. 'At the end, you cry, goddammit, real tears.' Goosebumps swell on my arm at this perfect rendition of what it's like to feel sentimentality breaking through your heavily encrusted force-field of cynicism. He or she is right: sometimes, often, you fight it; and when you give up, the catharsis, the liberation, is greater for knowing that you probably shouldn't be crying at this tosh. It's so mimetic of the experience, in fact, that, pitifully, I feel a lump begin to form in my throat, and my eyes grow moist. Oh no. *Beaches* must be a good weepie; I'm about to fucking cry at a *review* of it.

I hold up the video like Neville Chamberlain held up Hitler's piece of paper.

'This sounds just the job,' I say hoarsely.

On the way back, just outside the big Iceland, I say, 'Did you notice those kids?'

She walks on in her brisk, challenging step, face forward. 'Yeah,' she says. 'They got out *Suburban Sex-Slaves.*'

'Yeah,' I say, a bit taken aback. We walk on a bit in silence.

'It's just a crappy documentary,' she says after a bit. 'That cover's a bare-faced lie.'

Back at my flat, Fran is still on the enormous sofa, stroking Nick's sleeping head on her lap. She's been here for a day and a half. When we come into the living-room, she smiles at us in a way that makes my insides droop. I spent ages deliberating whether to do this video night here, knowing that Fran was likely to be in residence – she's hardly left Nick's side since that night at Casualty; God knows how the pharmacy's coping – or at Ben and Alice's. I could even have asked Ben if he and Alice could go out for the night, but at the moment, that would've felt like a teenage boy asking his dad to take Mum out for the night so that he can shag his girlfriend. Then again, we could've gone out to see a film. If either of us had any money.

Fran's smile makes my insides droop not just because it is her, and she is smiling, but because the smile is combined with something of a nod and a sigh, meaning, 'I told you so.' Nick's head lies amongst the folds of her purple flowery dress like an exhibit in a trial – a civil case, about chlorpromazine. He has basically been out cold since he started the course. I've even considered popping a few of them myself of a bad night.

'How is he?' I say. Dina goes straight into my bedroom, having already given me my orders: get her out of the living-room.

She does the same smile again, slightly more pained. 'Well

. . . he woke up for a few minutes about an hour ago. He was very thirsty.'

'Is that another side effect?' She nods, nodding implying, more than saying 'yes' would've done, that she has this knowledge at her fingertips. I scratch the back of my neck. Fran continues her stroking. I get the impression she is playing the part of the humble sage, waiting quietly for the tide of thinking to turn her way, as of course it must.

'Well, presumably . . . they *will* start to work differently as he takes more of them? I mean,' I say, aware of how much I sound like the incredible shrinking man '. . . he can't be asleep for the rest of his life.'

She shrugs and shakes her head (Fran, it seems, is never content with one action; not meaningful enough). I think the shake is meant to read, no, obviously they won't start to work any differently, and the shrug, what do I know, I'm just a humble sage.

'Anyway,' I say, feeling the pressure of Fran's terrible seriousness flush against the triviality of my approaching entreaty, 'the thing is, me and Dina wanna watch a video, so is there any chance that you could . . .' her over-blue eyes widen, so as to make herself more of a target, a victim '. . . take him into his bedroom?'

She looks at me as if I've just wisecracked about her mother dying of cancer. She holds this look until it becomes clear that I'm not going to say 'I'm sorry, what on earth was I thinking about?', and then, communicating disappointment so clearly no words are necessary, makes to move. She is, however, unable to do so because of the weight of Nick's head; a couple of feeble shuffles of the shoulders and a shake of her non-existent arse, and she lies back on the sofa, perplexed.

'Can't we wake him up?' I say.

She raises her eyes, amazed that I'm persisting.

'Well, I suppose . . .' she says, like an expert medic preparing to consider some lay suggestion as a last resort.

'NICK!!' I shout. 'NICK!!' Then, 'WAKEY-WAKEY!!' Wakey-wakey? I'm turning into Billy Cotton. Fran, rather surprisingly joining in the spirit of things, slaps him lightly and repeatedly on the cheek.

'Hmftgh?' says Nick, opening one eye.

'Nicholas?' says Fran. 'How are you feeling?'

He moves his eye up and round to see who is speaking, and then, perhaps because the drug *is* having a curative as well as a sedative effect, closes it again quickly.

'Oh, for God's sake,' I say. 'We'll have to carry him.' I slip my hand under his skull, heavy with sleep or madness or both, unfortunately pressing my knuckles down rather forcefully on Fran's upper lap. Her eyes blaze in blue fury. 'Give me a hand, then,' I say, trying to defuse the situation.

She tuts, but does shift along, moving Nick's head slightly further down her legs and allowing her to grasp him by the shoulders. Together we raise him into an L-shape, like Frankenstein and Igor helping up the monster. He's still fast asleep.

'OK, hold him there,' I say, and go round to the far end of the sofa to get hold of his legs. There are still two cushions between the end of his feet and the end of the sofa, and I crouch on these with my hands wrapped round his ankles; Fran, keeping his back straight with her hand, twists herself up and round into a kneeling position behind him, all the time giving off an air of having been tricked into this.

'Right,' I say when we are both facing each other, 'One . . . two . . . three!!' I swing his feet up. Fran does nothing, so Nick's body crumples into a legs-in-the-stirrups-for-a-gynaecological-examination shape.

'One, two, three, what?' says Fran, her big-earringed face framed by the soles of Nick's DMs.

'One, two, three – lift him up!' I say exasperatedly.

'Wouldn't it be simpler if we stood up first?' she says.

'But then we can't get any purchase on him!' I say, knowing she is entirely correct and resorting to the word 'purchase' to try and muddy the situation. 'Oh, all right then,' I say, with an element of 'clearly you can't appreciate the complexity of the manoeuvre I had in mind.'

Holding my sanity-less flatmate in what is now a V-shape – it occurs to me that we could sell this whole episode to *Sesame Street* – we get up together and, from a standing position, swing him off the sofa. He sways between us for a couple of seconds like a hammock.

'OK,' I say. 'Tell me if he becomes too heavy.'

'Don't worry. I . . .' she says, '. . . can *carry* Nicholas.'

I move backwards, extending his legs, and she gets the message and moves forward, holding his hands. If, as her intensely stated metaphor suggests, her spiritual support of Nick is indeed informing her physical support of him, I'm impressed: he's a fat bastard, Nick, who hasn't allowed his progress towards ethereality to arrest his corporeality.

'Shall we put him down for a bit?' I say, as we get to the living-room door.

'My arms,' she says, 'are fine.'

We've just got him out of the door and into the hallway when he wakes up. But really wakes up: as if the drug has wiped out the limbo between sleeping and waking. I mean, last time I looked his face was shut and snoring, suddenly he's staring at me like someone injected his face with guaraná.

'*Love is like oxygen*,' he sings, at the top of his voice, swinging his body in time to the music, '*You get too much, you get too high – not enough and you're gonna di-ie*.'

And, with a clunk of his head on his shoulder, falls asleep again. Dina, who has come out of my bedroom, fixes me with hard, questioning eyes, like a teacher demanding an explanation.

'The Sweet,' I say, nodding.

Two seconds after we lie Nick in state on his duvet – 'Why on earth is it so *stiff*?' Fran is saying concernedly – the doorbell goes.

'Who the fuck's this now?' I say, going out of the bedroom door, my hopes for the night deflating quicker than The Hindenburg. Approaching the front door, I recognise the shapes – a hulking dark mass and a shimmering willow – as refracted through the inside pane.

'Hello!' say Ben and Alice together, chirpily, as I open it. Alice, wearing a large red polo-neck jumper and a black leather jacket, leans forward and kisses me on the cheek, and even though my mind is harassed and swirling, I reflexively find a corner in which to record the feel of her lips on my skin. She drifts past me, towards the stairs. Ben, carrying a bottle of wine wrapped in blue tissue paper, moves to kiss me as well, but I put up a hand to stop him.

'What's happening?' I say.

'Sorry?' he says.

'Why have you come round?'

'That's very welcoming of you, Gabe,' he says, passing me to follow in the footsteps of his wife. 'Dina invited us.'

He goes up the stairs, in pole position behind Alice.

'What?' I say.

'I phoned . . .'

'When?'

'About an hour ago. Just to remind you that the second article needs to be in by Friday. And Dina suggested we come round. Didn't she tell you?'

'No.'

'The thing is, when I thought about it, I thought it was a good idea. There's no reason why we shouldn't see each other as a foursome. Anyway, she sounded like she really wanted to see us.'

'Did she?'

'Yeah. I don't think I've ever heard her sound so positive about anything.'

I can't work this out at all. Then, when we go through the flat door, Fran is in the hallway, smiling again.

'Hello,' she says, doing her customary hand-twist before extending an arm towards my brother. 'You must be Ben. I'm Fran.'

He takes her hand, smiling blankly.

'We just spoke on the phone?' she says. 'By the way, Gabriel, you really must get someone in to sort out the line.'

'*Buckaroo!*'

'*Haunted House!*'

'Wicked Wanda drops it down the chimney!'

'*Crossfire!*'

'*Ratrace!*'

'*Flight Deck.*'

It is a truth universally acknowledged that when three or more people over twenty-five spend an evening together, at some point they will start listing board-games they played when they were kids. Either this, or they will try collectively to remember the theme tunes to various children's TV programmes of the 1970s, principally *Wacky Races*, *Top Cat*, *Screen Test*, and *Follyfoot*.

'*Flight Deck?*' says Dina contemptuously.

'Yes,' I say, in a somewhat detached manner, it being the only game I've proffered (the listing has made me spiritually don my smoking-jacket). 'Well ahead of its time. It was a flight simulator.'

'Oh yeah,' says Ben. 'I remember it. You used to play it all the time.' He turns to the non-ugly sisters. 'Mum and Dad used to get really pissed off, because . . .' now back to me '. . . you used to have to tie a huge thread or wire or something all down the hallway to play it, didn't you?'

'Yeah,' I say. 'And the plane would fly down that to a little model runway, controlled by a little plastic joystick thing.'

Once it became clear that Ben actually spoke to Fran and not to Dina, no opportunity presented itself for me to say 'oh well, you'd better go home again then.' Mistaken identity aside, Ben clearly had psyched himself up to the idea that the four of us should spend some time together, and there seemed nothing else to do but go along with it. So the four of us are sitting in the living-room, with cups of tea and coffee, playing *Waddingtons Back Catalogue*; Fran has gone back into Nick's bedroom, pumped up with earth motherly spirit.

'Gabe,' says Alice. 'What happened to the yucca?'

'Oh,' I say, repositioning it upright in the soil, 'I think Jezebel used it as a scratching-post.'

Dina and Alice sit on the sofa, me and Ben on the Turkish rug, a zig-zag of wine-filled tumblers forming a border on the coffee-table between us. It is too intimidating for me to look at Dina and Alice together for too long; the urge to compare cannot be stifled. My sense of Dina, in particular, suffers. In the video shop, she was a separate entity; this close, she is again a satellite. Nonetheless, as I tell the yucca lie, I meet her eyes, inside which a shutter opens upon her greater knowledge; and our looks thread together along a path of superiority bred of resentment.

'What video did you get out, then?' says Ben. '*Ghost*?'

'No,' I say, prising open the plain white Blockbuster cover. '*Beaches*.'

'Oh, I wanted to see that when it came out!' says Alice.

'Gabriel and Alice?' says Fran, poking her head through the living-room door, her face open, neutral, as if she's about to ask if anyone wants a cup of tea. 'Nick would like to talk to you. In the kitchen.'

'When did he wake up?' I say.

'A couple of minutes ago.'

'Why us two especially?' says Alice.

'I don't know,' says Fran, with a sense of patiently dealing with the pedants. 'He thought about it for some time.'

She goes off, delivered of her message. I look at Alice, who shrugs. Somewhat overdoing a sigh, I get up.

Walking alone with her along the hallway, the thought comes to me: 'Wha— Alice! Hey! Let's *fuck*!!' Probably not the moment.

In the kitchen, Nick is standing over the sink, unpinning the Polaroids of himself from the corkboard and throwing them into the swing-bin; some of them have already slid off the top layer of rubbish into a small pile on the floor. He's in his black dressing-gown; who undressed him, I wonder? Fran sits, arms folded and inscrutable at the kitchen table.

'Yes?' I say, adopting a matching tone to Fran's in the living-room.

Nick turns, all Darth Vader meeting Luke Skywalker at last.

'"Yes,"' he says, smiling to himself. '"Yes."'

'What?'

'I knew you were going to say that.'

'Oh.'

'I've become telepathic.'

'Yes, I thought that's what you meant. As you probably already knew.'

The joke does not register. That's something about madness, it's got no time for gags, no matter how antic the jester. Suddenly breaking into a bit of a stride, he comes towards Alice and grasps her by the shoulders. *Steady*.

'Alice,' he says, looking deep into her eyes, an action I've never quite been able to do, in case she spotted some specks of love, 'I know what you're thinking. I know your innermost thoughts.'

'How can you?' says Alice, deeply troubled, sympathy coming out of her every pore. Not that she has ever been close to Nick, not even in a Beauty and the Beast kind of way, but her natural instinct is to nurse. And, of course, she hasn't had the induction period; it must be pretty shocking, seeing him transformed like this. It didn't even occur to me that she must have been nervous on the way from the living-room.

'Because I know the truth,' he says. 'All truth. I know *your* truth.' He smiles beneficently, Jesus forgiving Judas. 'Sit down,' he says. She looks at me, helpless; now I shrug. She sits down at the kitchen table. Nick paces two small circles.

'Think of an object,' he says. 'Any object.'

'Look, Nick,' she says gently, 'I'd rather not.'

He stops pacing. 'Why not?'

She digs her bottom teeth into her upper lip, leaving a faint higgledy-piggledy mark. 'Because I'd rather not . . . play along with this.' His gaze is unbreaking, demanding greater explanation. 'I don't think it's good for you,' she says.

I don't even have to look at him to know how he's going to react to this. Let me guess: another smile, one that says, ah, poor innocent, how ironic that *you* should think to know what is good for *me*? I look up. Yep.

'Alice,' he says, with studied softness. 'There's no need to be frightened.'

'I'm not frightened. I just don't want you to think that I think this kind of behaviour's OK.'

'Just one object.'

'Look, Nick,' I say, 'if she doesn't wanna do it . . .'

'All right then, Gabriel,' says Fran, piping up at last, claiming the umpire role, '*you* do it.'

All eyes are on me. If I say yes, Alice will think I've let her down. But Misrule in me rises at the challenge.

'All right,' I say, with a look to Alice meant to convey that I'm only doing it to get her off the hook. *I am your saviour*.

'Right,' says Nick, with a 'to business' air. 'Think of an object. Just think of that one object, for a minute.'

I look round. Still in the fruit bowl, although now about a third of its original size, is that one manky orange. Orange – brainwaves are supposed to be ultra-receptive to colour. Even though, in terms of wresting Nick back from Lalaland, it'd be best for him to get it wrong, I decide to give it my best shot. Don't ask me why.

Orange, I think, as much as I can. Orange orange orange orange. ORANGE. Johan Cruyff. Mobile phones. No, the fruit, specifically the fruit. An orange. An orange. A great big Yellow-Submarine style hallucinatory orange, livid in the sky, outshadowing the sun. The Man From Del Monte he fucking come in his pants.

I open my eyes. Nick is studying my face, calmly; his hands are together, the points of the fingers forming a small roof. 'Well?' he says.

'Shouldn't you write it down and put it in a sealed envelope or something?'

'*Gabriel*,' he says expansively, his palms open. I sense that actually, he probably won't cheat; he's that sure of himself, or at least, of this self. Alice and Fran, my love–hate relationship, wait on me.

'All right,' I say, taking a deep breath, 'it was "orange".'

'Oh,' he says, crestfallen. 'I thought it was "cat-bowl".'

'Shall we watch the video then?' says Dina, in a conversational lull. Ben checks his watch, making an arithmetical judgement in which the point minus to now is the time he will get into bed with Alice. It is 10:23.

'Oh, come on,' says Alice, giving me a buffer against that thought. 'It's Sunday tomorrow.' *Dozing in each other's clasp, drifting on a tide of shared semi-consciousness, the only pressing need each other.* Blast. The steady drill of Nick's deep snore reverberates through the partition wall of the living-room; he dealt with the vortex of spiritual uncertainty his telepathic shortfall spun him into by falling instantly asleep again, necessitating more awkward carting of his fourteen-stone frame around the flat.

'Oh, all right,' says Ben. 'Only I'm sure it'll be crap.'

'Well, no one's forcing you,' I say, as if indignant at my choice being rubbished, but actually because a thought has suddenly occurred to me: I don't know if I can take watching a crying film in this company. Being with all three of them tugs triangularly enough at my emotions as it is; if they (my emotions, not Alice, Ben and Dina) go into freefall, as indeed they must if *Beaches* turns out to be half as tear-jerking as its review, God knows what might happen. I cannot predict where I might flow once I'm reduced to liquid form.

'I quite fancy that, though,' says Alice, pulling her jumper down over her knees. 'I haven't seen a good crap film in ages.'

A flutter of repulsion passes through me; whatever Dina may think, I hate self-conscious kitschiness, all that 'so bad it's good' shit. Strange when Alice says something that irritates me. You might think I'd forgive her, in a way that I wouldn't others, because . . . well, you know why. But actually I don't; if anything I deliberately pump up my own sense of irritation, I go over and over the irritant in my mind, in the hope, I think, that I'll fall suddenly out of love into a light fluffy freedom of mind.

'Oh, don't be so bloody post-modern, Alice,' says Dina, picking up the tape and slipping it into the Mitsubishi's rectangular mouth. Alice looks at her complacently. 'Either it's good or it's crap.'

The tape emerges again from the VCR like a slow vomit. Perhaps it's trying to tell us something: or perhaps it's just very taken aback – 'Hold on: this *isn't* porngraphy!'

'This is great wine, Ben,' says Alice, deliberately avoiding her sister's aggression. I take a sip from my glass. It fucking is as well.

Dina literally punches the tape back into the slot; the VCR decides it's best maybe to swallow it this time.

'Should we call . . . what's her name again?' says Ben.

'Who?' I say.

'Nick's friend. Shouldn't we ask her if she wants to watch it?'

'*Fran?*'

'Um . . . I think we may as well give ourselves at least a chance of enjoying it, don't you think?' says Dina, falling back into the sofa next to me, pressing the FF button on the video remote and '5' on the ordinary remote at the same time: the screen bursts into life. Rushing silver lines quarterise an explosion, a river chase, a kiss, the words 'NO QUARTER': the usual set of unheard-of movie trailers. Swinging her legs up, Dina drops her head into my lap, in what seems an ostentatious display of affection, directed more to Alice and Ben than to me.

'Oh, she's not *that* bad, is she?' says Alice. Dina raises her eyebrow up at me, and I return it, as best I can; we're congratulating ourselves on our knowledge-surplus again. Alice turns away from us to Ben. 'I mean . . . she means well, don't you think?'

He juts his lower lip out slightly. 'Yeah, seems so.'

'Mussolini probably *meant* well,' I say.

'Is she . . .' Alice pauses, and flicks her eyes at Ben uncertainly '. . . Jewish?'

Dina laughs out loud. 'What, are you blind? What other genes could be responsible for *that* nose?'

'Dina . . .' I say, a bit uneasily.

'Her features are Jewish to the point of deformity,' she continues definitively. Now I too look at Ben, the defender of the faith. To be honest, it's a very accurate description of Fran's face; but even *I* think she may have gone a bit far. I feel my breath hold as Ben, using Alice's shoulder for leverage, silently gets up and goes to the door.

'You off?' I say, desperately trying to lighten the mood.

'Fran?' he says loudly, standing at the door. 'Fran!' I hear a click, and then a slight creak as she opens Nick's bedroom door. A short pause. She must be looking at him significantly.

'Yes?' I hear her say, with just a tiny hint of Florence Nightingale disturbed at her duties.

'Do you want to come and watch a video with the rest of us? You know, if Nick's asleep or whatever,' says Ben.

The breath exhales from my lungs on a wind of relief. For a second, I thought he was going to ask her into the room and invite Dina to repeat herself. Meanwhile, I get a feeling that Fran's eyes are filling with tears.

'*Thank* you,' she says tremulously. '*Really*. But I think I should stay with him.'

'OK,' says Ben, and closes the living-room door. I sense that

Fran is still standing on the other side of it, slightly miffed that he didn't persevere.

'Oh, for God's sake,' says Dina, 'how many of these trailers are there gonna be?'

I look at the screen: a rape, Brad Pitt and Geena Davis in a bedroom, a convertible in a sweeping American desert.

'Fast-forward it out of vision,' says Alice, something which, because of my usual choice of viewing, I haven't done for so long I don't think it would've occurred to me. Dina shuffles the remotes; the screen switches to John Kettley and a satellite map of London. The astral cameraman cannot see us for storm-clouds.

I look at Ben, who has sat back down on the floor and composed himself, with, judging by the redness of his cheeks, a certain amount of struggle; Alice is rather self-consciously stroking the back of his neck. Dina, oblivious, estimates that the tape has fast-forwarded enough, and hits PLAY. In the split-second before the film kicks in, my brain floods again with images of myself bawling like a bairn, infantilised through and through, with a crying child's confessional drive, telling all, all. Crying will pull my guard down, just as I need him to be on all-night sentry duty.

'Actually,' says Fran, coming through the living-room door, 'he really is fast asleep. I wouldn't mind watching a tiny bit.' We look fourways at each other as she perches herself on the arm of the sofa. 'What is it?' Jazzy film music pulls our attention round.

Dina's overrun, missing the first minute or so. Against a black screen, the white words: *God, she's beautiful* . . . It cuts from there to Barbara Hershey standing in a doorway. I settle down into the sofa, and relax my critical faculties, as you have to to cry. A voice I'm sure I recognise speaks over her as she moves through a crowded party room: '*God, she's beautiful. She's got the prettiest eyes. She looks so sexy and so sweet. I just want to be alone with her, hold her and kiss her, tell her how much I love her.*'

The voice-over pauses for a tiny second, and the slight nagging feeling of déjà-vu I've had since the first image came up becomes a rushing panic.

'*Stop it, you idiot,*' says the voice-over, Michael Caine of course. '*She's your wife's sister.*'

'Isn't this . . .?' says Alice, turning round to me confused and not a little anxious. Let me finish Alice's sentence: isn't this a film about men, love and sisters-in-law? Isn't this the most awkward film the four of us could watch together? Isn't this *Hannah and Her Fucking Sisters*?

'Oh, for Christ's sake,' says Dina. 'That dozy git in the video shop . . .'

There is one way out. 'Well, I've seen it,' I say.

'So have I,' says Ben quickly.

'Yeah, me too,' says Alice.

'And me,' says Dina.

'I haven't,' says Fran, with all the predictable tact of the self-consciously sensitive. My intense hatred for her at this point in time is tempered somewhat by the vengeful joy of watching her slide off the arm of the sofa and settle luxuriously into the cushions of the matching armchair. The story, with its hundred points of relevance, begins. Suddenly, the room feels hot as a sauna, the TV spooning the film like water on to the coals. *On white horses, snowy white horses, let me ride. Away.*

Then, suddenly, the film wobbles, as if Manhattan Island itself was shaking, perhaps – who knows – from some vast aerial explosion. A second later, the colour mutates to black and white, and a white glaze like a poltergeist drifts across the images, doubling them up and creating fairground-mirror style reflections of Woody and Mia and Michael. The sound bends, too; maybe the VCR, still confused, has decided to show *Hannah and Her Sisters in the style* of a porn film. Then, video snow begins to fall, covering the screen gradually from the bottom upwards just like the real stuff does; and next moment, it's gone: Peter Sissons is talking about Bosnia and the videotape ejects with a soft whirr, completely out of kilter with the heavily allergic reaction the visual symptoms seemed to suggest it induced in the player.

'It's eaten it,' says Dina, kneeling down and pulling the cassette out, yards of brown tape spewing from the black box.

'Oh, *bugger*!' says Fran, an uncly swearword I've always hated. 'I was just getting into it.'

Palpable relief fills the air like an end-of-term bell, and for the first time I begin to see the advantages of owning gadgets that prefer to make their own life-style decisions.

16

I think Dina might be on to my secret desire. I did a stupid, stupid thing. Last night, in the passion, in the moment of sex, I said, softly, without thinking, the A-word.

No, not Alice, you berk. I'm not that stupid. *Anal sex*. Or rather . . . *anal sex?* That's how I said it; with a hopeful, inquiring, 'have you ever considered . . .?' air.

Now some of you, I know, will be thinking by now: oh, for heaven's sake, that's the third reference, he's anally obsessed. And you'd be right. When I look through a book of quotations, I come across only very few epithets that really speak to me, that pluck the strings of my soul, words which make me feel that, in my strangest core, I am not alone. 'Old age should burn and rage at close of day' maybe; 'The expense of spirit in a waste of shame Is lust in action' perhaps. But the piece of poetry that really did it for me, the lyric which rang most loud the bell of synchronicity, which confirmed that somewhere in the universe there exists another version of me, was when once, in the old London listings magazine *City Limits*, from a book I've never found called *Transgression*, by an author I've never heard of called James Havoc, they ran the quote 'I feel closer to heaven the nearer I get to a woman's anus.' Isn't that terrible? That that should be the one?

Sometimes, you see, I'm not even sure if it's anal *sex* that I'm all that bothered with; I'm so enamoured of the female anus it seems only a pity to block a possible view of it with my penis. 'Shy as a gathered eyelet/Neatly worked in shrinking violet', says Craig Raine in his poem *Arsehole* (a wholly laudatory work, although quite obviously written without any thought towards its discussion in future Modern British Poetry seminars: 'Well, if we look closely at Craig Raine's *Arsehole* . . .') and he's right to express the anus in terms of timidity, for therein lies its erotic charge, as a space most reservedly revealed. I like showing, as part of sex: I especially like it if it's accompanied with a certain embarrassment, or coyness, and, believe me, asking someone to show you their anus will almost always generate a bit of both. It's all power, I suppose; the shattering of the private space of the object of desire with my patriarchal gaze and all that. And the seeing of the arsehole is the great transgression of privacy; I particularly love the fact that the buttocks have to be parted to allow a view of it, like a stage curtain, making the showing of it even more of A Show.

But sometimes, it is fundamentally sex that I want. Anal sex, more than any other, is the sex of ideas: the eroticism lies in knowing what it is you are doing. And beyond that local, immediate hit, another knowing. All sex is essentially a quest for knowledge, knowledge of the other person; penetration is exploration, the penis a searchlight (I speak of course only for the male, because, as far as women go, I don't, despite all my searching, have *the knowledge*). Somewhere deep inside the body lies her uncluttered secret, but often the most obvious route seems not to lead there, whereas the other route, maybe for childish reasons linked with darkness and danger, seems like it must go right to the centre of The Other. With Dina, I felt an especial urge, because there hangs around her at all times an aura of enigma, and although enigma is often nothing more than an assumed air to make oneself seem interesting, or at least worthy of investigation, I sense that her mystery has an actual engine.

It might seem a bit early on in our relationship to try and climb to the top of what I know represents for many people the top of the sexual peculiarities tree, but Dina's pretty experimental. Throughout the night, she was saying 'Tell me what you like. Tell me what you like.' Sausages, I said, eventually. The Carpenters. Dina thought this was a poor joke, a result of inhibition on my part. She wants me to talk to her during sex. I don't know what to say. This may be something to do with having watched too many people talking during sex. I know what *they* say: 'oh yeah, baby', 'do it to me', 'do you like that? huh? my cock in your ass, you like that?', 'ooo! ooo! ooo!', '*ja, meine Titten, ficken Sie meine Titten*', 'hahahaha!' I can't say that stuff: not without growing a moustache and repainting the flat purple. So when she demanded a proper answer, I just went for the flat response: anal sex.

It's what I've always wanted, I said, like someone had just given me a jumper for Christmas.

'Ye-es . . .' she said, turning round to lie on her back.

'What's the matter?'

'I'm not sure that's a good idea.'

'Why not?'

'Why not? Perhaps if you'd care to turn over . . .'

'Women are more resistant to pain than men.'

'Right,' said Dina, raising her eyebrow.

'Obviously, we'll stop if it hurts.'

'I feel,' she said, turning on to her side to look at me, 'that these are *well-rehearsed* arguments. You wouldn't, by any chance, have asked this of anyone before?'

I stuck my lower lip on top of my upper as if trying to remember.

'D'you think Alice and Ben seem a bit . . . funny at the moment?' she said, drumming her fingers on the pillow.

'Are we not talking about anal sex any more, then?'

'No. They seem tense, by their standards. Although not as much as my buttocks in the last five minutes.'

'You'd know better than me. You see more of them.' It began to occur to me that not only were we no longer talking about anal sex, but that we weren't now involved in any form of sex at all. I lowered my fingers, and felt them sink for a second into her mallowy thigh before she brushed them away. 'It's difficult to tell. I thought at first it was just that they weren't comfortable being with . . .' she paused for a second, a before-a-parachute-drop pause '. . . us.'

I let the word go. 'And now?'

'Now I think . . .' her mouth moved as if she was chewing imaginary gum '. . . I was being big-headed. Something's bothering them that's nothing to do with us. Because I've noticed the same sort of tension at their house. Not all the time. Now and again.'

'Why don't you speak to Alice about it?'

Dina made a face. 'We don't . . . speak about emotional things much. Well. We don't speak about *her* emotional life much. Mainly because it's been so smooth. Nothing to talk about.'

'But you do talk to her about you . . .'

'A bit,' she said, rocking her face from side to side. 'But it gets kind of tiring, being counselled by someone who never needs it herself.' She smiled, more to herself than to me. 'You want to hear someone else's dirt if you're gonna tell them all yours.'

A short silence ensued. 'So no one's ever asked it of *you* before?'

Dina looked at me uncomprehendingly only for a second. 'Might have done,' she said, her features resettling into ironic.

'. . . Miles?' I said, after a short internal debate about whether this was an entirely appropriate subject in which to involve one of the dearly departed.

She looked a bit uncomfortable, something I took to be a response simply to the mention of Miles.

'Sorry, I . . .'

'No, it's OK.' The pupils in her eyes contracted to the point where it seemed she couldn't possibly see anything in this light; she appeared to be weighing something up. 'Oh, take me up the arse if it means that much to you,' she said, turning over and somehow extending a sigh throughout the sentence.

The choice was clear to me. On the one hand, Dina's apparent disinclination; the fact that any gentleman worth the name would have had no hesitation in saying 'no, forget it'; the immensely strong possibility of post-coital self-loathing. And on the other: anal sex. No contest, I'm afraid. I'd have preferred a bit more in the way of foreplay – I dunno, some women, they just don't know how to take their time with a man – but that preference itself had to be balanced against the sudden rush of feeling to my groin, inspired, I think, by the sheer flatness of Dina's offer: there is something intensely erotic about matter-of-factness in sex, the prostitute's production-line mentality, the groupie's get-it-over-with-ness as she unzips the security man's fly, the displacement of sex's mystique perhaps the deepest form of stripping.

Luckily, I keep a jar of Vaseline handy for just such emergencies. I went to the bathroom and got it; when I came back, Dina was still lying on her front in resigned expectancy. I took a large clump out of the jar and spread it liberally over my penis; then, exploiting the licence she had granted me, I parted her buttocks with the index and third fingers of my right hand and looked at her anus. Impelling my eyes to drink in as much light as possible, even amongst the lattice of shadows created by the turning of my bedside lamp against the wall, I could tell it was beautiful, classical: inward-rushing, brown-bruised, although going pink on a wider splay, reasonably hairless, and as near as possible a perfect asterisk. This may sound fairly standard, but ani have this similarity to belly buttons, in that some actually protrude, and I don't go for this at all, partly because it seems to me part of the erotic delight of the anus that it points *in* to the body, like an invitation, and partly because it reminds me of a poodle.

'Get on with it, then,' said Dina, still a bit of the sigh left even now. I placed my greasy tip lovingly into her cleft and slid off immediately like the worst skater in the rink; she tutted, and I replaced myself. Though lubricated more than a baby seal, there was, as ever, a moment of total resistance, a sense that we had come to the point at which the body shuts its gates; and then, through into waterworld. 'Uh,' said Dina, with no hint of whether she meant either pleasure or pain. Gripped in the stern anal lock, I realised straight away I had applied too much Vaseline to be in contact with anything except, well, Vaseline, really, a dark cylinder of it, but no matter; I could still feel the soft yielding, the particular feathery give of the rectal passage as it opens backwards, and besides, as I've said, anal sex happens mainly at the other end, in the head. So I was about to frame the words myself, to play them in time with my movements over and over again in my mind, when Dina prompted me, saying, in a narrow voice, 'Tell me what you're doing.'

'Fucking you up the arse,' I said, the words so much on the tip of my brain's tongue that even my considerable inhibition about speaking during sex didn't have time to get in the way. And at least I didn't have to make anything up; I think the problem I have with talking while on the job is that I'd always assumed that what Dina expects me to whimper is fantasies, and, call me unimaginative, but a) I don't fantasise during sex – if I think about something else it's most likely to be Mr Hillman's nose-hairs, and I'm sure you know why that is – and b) if I did, the spelling out of my fantasies in words would, I know, reveal them as the stale pornographic clichés they are, what's not already dead about them killed off by self-consciousness, making me feel, perhaps the truth, that I've just said something really embarrassing. But this – this just saying what you're doing – I could manage that; and in the case of anal sex, no further elaboration is required.

'Up the arse,' I repeated mechanically. 'I'm fucking you up the arse.'

Priding myself as I do on my articulateness, I felt I had never been more articulate than this; never closer to the *mots justes*. That's all that was needed: a clean, stark prose-style, telling a simple, easily understandable story. And, for once, words had an immediate, a chemical impact; Dina moaned, and said, 'Tell me again.'

'I'm fucking you up the arse. Up your little tight fucking little arsehole.'

Admittedly, I was getting a bit experimental now. And although they did come straight from the heart, these words, I did suddenly catch myself saying them, and felt very stupid indeed. But this didn't seem to bother Dina, who was starting to make all the right noises. With some difficulty, I reached round her circling hip and managed to locate her clitoris with a fingertip; her pubic bone bit sharply into my wrist.

We continued our work, now in silence, now in words. Then, Dina's body started to move from side to side, the basted skin on her back gliding against my chest like a silk scarf. At first, I thought this was just to further my pleasure and inspire another repetition of my illicit mantra, but as it became convulsive, I realised it was involuntary. Virtually noiseless, just the odd soft gasp breaking what seemed like desperate concentration, it grew to a great shaking, almost a struggle, as if I was a pillow placed firmly upon her face; and then it ended, as that would too, in a sudden reversion to limpness. I came at the same time, having perfectly timed the moment at which to relinquish my mental hold on Mr Hillman's nostrils.

When Dina came back from the bathroom, I said, 'Look, I'm sorry I mentioned Miles before.'

'I said it was fine,' she said, propping her pillow up vertically against the wall behind the bed. Turning slightly away, she leant down and rummaged in her doctor's bag, eventually pulling out a packet of Silk Cut and some mock-Zippo lighter I've not seen before.

'*He* was very keen on it,' she said, her buttocks moving backwards through the air as she resettled herself into bed.

'What?'

'What we've just done.'

Sitting up, she opened the lid of the Silk Cut packet and flicked it from underneath, making one cigarette head poke out from the pack. She appeared to be gearing herself up to talk about Miles, like a paraplegic on parallel bars about to take a first few steps.

'It represented something for him,' she said, leaning back against the wall. The overlarge flame of the lighter blinded me for a second in the semi-darkness and hid her face, and everything smelt of petrol; then she clipped the lighter lid shut and exhaled smoke. 'A pinnacle of some sort. Or, like, a symbol of his domination over me. Whatever.'

'Yeah, well, I suppose it could be seen as way of affirming your machismo . . . So was it like a permanent fixture in your sex-life, then?'

She shook her head; smoke came out her mouth zigzaggedly. 'No. We never did it.'

'Huh? I thought you said he was very keen . . .?'

'We *tried* it quite a lot.'

Lying on my back with arms underneath my crumbling pillow, I felt sure I saw an abstract shape on the ceiling suddenly pull itself into a pattern, like a kaleidoscope.

'But never actually did it because . . .?'

'Gabriel,' she said, stubbing her cigarette out on a saucer by the side of the bed with her left hand and stroking my neck with her right, 'let's go to sleep.'

'No, wait a minute . . .'

But it was too late. In seconds, she was lying on her side with her eyes shut, breathing deep and rhythmically. Perhaps she was faking it, but sleep, even a somniac's, is too sacred a thing to risk destroying.

That's why it was a stupid, stupid thing. As if I don't have enough on my mind already, because it's 5:32 in the morning, and that's when I always have enough on my mind, *all* toss, *all* brain-babble at the best of times, now I've got a new piece of flotsam to bob against the jetsam, a rampant Miles Traversi, kindly drawn for me by Aubrey Beardsley, the phallus that reaches from his groin to just below his salaciously smiling lips alternating in shape between an obscenely purple penis and a massively complex, twenty-first-century-looking paint-gun. I mean, I'm not even that bothered if her previous boyfriend *did* have a bigger penis than me; what would you rather be, well-hung or alive? But I'm bothered that she thinks I might be bothered, so much so that she chose to avoid the subject with the total *fait accompli* of falling asleep. It bothers me that she thinks of me as so shallow, so likely to conform to that tired old male paranoia. In fact, as a result of her thinking I might be bothered, now, I kind of *am* bothered; I've thought myself into it, because 5:32 in the morning places your thoughts into a microwave, a brand spanking new one with no fly living in its clock, which forces the thought molecules to oscillate wildly and reform into patterns and structures totally alien to themselves, just to pass the fucking time. So I begin by being maybe slightly, I'll give you slightly, concerned about having a smaller penis than Miles, but then, because I can't go to sleep, I wonder what it must be like to be *very* concerned about it, and then I move from that into an overstated reminder that six and a half inches is really quite enough, thank you very much, well above average, not because I need reassurance, but because I know that's what someone who was worried about it would do, and I'm into it now, acting out the whole persona, and we go straight from there to the grinning satyr himself.

'If you move again, I'm going to scream,' says a muffled voice from the other side of the bed.

Shit. I've woken her up. 'I'm sorry,' I say, scooping the plugs out of my ears and wanting to add: *look. Thoughts like this cannot be accompanied by stillness. And who's responsible for these thoughts?* But I don't, probably correctly.

'Every single time I've started to drop off,' she continues in a whisper designed less to keep her voice than her temper down, 'you've moved. Every single time I've begun to really fall asleep, I've been snapped out of it by feeling you do this!' Dina spins herself around violently. 'Or this!' She jerks the duvet cover roughly over to her side, exposing my increasingly flabby nakedness to the dawn. 'Or this!!' She raises her fists in the air and pounds her pillow like a sane man unfairly shut in the asylum would the pads of his cell.

She sticks on this. She is, of course, exaggerating – she has slept soundly for at least three hours, only possibly being woken by my movements, which I've tried as best I can to minimise, during the last half an hour, when she would've been going through a period of light following deep sleep – but I know that good sleepers can never judge the night; a couple of abnormal wakings and they think they've had no sleep at all.

'I said I'm sorry. It's not my fault.'

'Well, whose fault is it then?'

'What d'you mean? It's no one's fault. It's just one of those things you can't ascribe blame for.'

'Yes I can. I fucking blame *you*. Because it's *you* who can't fucking stop moving.'

'But no position is comfortable,' I say pleadingly. 'I get into a new position, and for a second, it feels comfortable, and then two seconds later it feels like I'm on a fucking rack. So I have to move again. The only comfortable position is moving.'

'Can't you do it a bit more quietly?'

'I was doing it quietly. I didn't mean to wake you up.'

Outside, a bird begins the cheerless chirping. I've been here before, and will again.

'Well, look,' says Dina, sitting up on her haunches, her hands flat on the mattress, 'you can't . . . what's that on your head?'

'What?'

'This,' she says, grasping it and pulling it backwards, almost breaking the elastic.

'It's my blindfold.'

She lets it go; it rebounds on to my brow. *Doiyoinnnggg*, says Fred Quimby in my head.

'Can you not do that, please?' I say. 'If the elastic gets too slack, I have to tie it in a knot round the back, and then sometimes I can't get to sleep because I can feel the knot like a big lump against the back of my head.'

'You look like a nutter.'

'I know. That's why I always wait until the light's off before I put it on.'

'Where d'you get it from, an airplane?'

'Yes.'

She lets her supporting elbows fold, and falls back, her head crashing into the pillow.

'I'm not sleeping with you on a regular basis if it means no sleep,' she says, in a definite, decided tone, staring up at the ceiling.

'It's not always as bad as this.' *No: sometimes it's worse.*

'Can't you take anything for it?'

'Kalms?'

'Very funny. Proper sleeping pills.'

Sighing over-wearily, I get out of bed, go over to my desk and pull open the second drawer down. 'What d'you think?' I say, plunging my hand into it in such a way as to deliberately create the loud and distinct sound of rattling plastic. 'Mogadon?' I hold the small half-full bottle up to the clearing light; then I put my free hand back into the drawer. 'Nomission? Amitryptiline? Temazepam? Zopiclone?'

Dina looks at me neutrally. 'How about all you've got, at once?'

I drop the pills and close the drawer. 'Thanks very much.' She watches me with an unchanging expression as I cross the room, crushed; as I get to the side of the bed, I notice a momentary down-flicker of her eyes to my groin, and curse internally my decision not to set the heating to go on this early.

'Aren't you going to take one, then?' she says as I resettle myself into bed, somewhat ostentatiously turning away from her.

'I can't take one now,' I say, speaking towards the bedside table. 'It's quarter to six.'

'So?'

'So if I take one now, I'll be groggy all day tomorrow.'

'Why didn't you take one earlier then? You *knew* you probably weren't going to sleep.'

I'm starting to feel extremely badgered. 'Look!' I say, raising the stakes by being the first one to speak at a normal, non-whispery level. 'I know I'm probably not going to sleep *every* night. If I took a sleeping pill every night, I'd be fucking *Elvis* by now.'

I feel a hand spider over my side and come to rest on my abdomen, fingers outstretched. 'The impersonation's not going too badly as it is,' she says, patting my belly drowsily. Her aggression has started to melt as sleep, easy sleep, unlooked-for sleep, turns her brain to blancmange. 'But you *should* see someone about it.'

Prompted by her change of mood, I turn round so that our faces are close; her eyes are half closed and her breath smells thick and misty.

'I have. I've tried it all. Acupuncture, herbal remedies, flotation tanks, aromatherapy – I even once went to bed with wet socks on because a woman who wrote in to the *Daily Mirror* health section said it always worked for her.'

'Hiploterrapin,' she mumbles.

'Sorry?'

Her eyes open, green in this light. 'Hypnotherapy,' she says, pulling herself awake for what I know will only be a little while. 'Have you tried that?'

'Yes. It didn't work. And it cost a fortune.'

'I've got a friend, Alison. She's a hypnotherapist. I'm sure she can do something for you. And she'll see you cheap.'

'Well . . . thanks, but I don't think it'll work. The one I saw . . . I didn't go into a trance. I think it's probably something to do with being an insomniac.'

'Alison's better.'

'Right.'

Dina's eyelids close like two falling feathers.

'You . . .' she says, reaching out from beneath the covers and touching my face gently, the tips of her fingers pulling my blindfold down over my eyes '. . . you're so *proud* of your insomnia, aren't you?'

'No, I'm . . . I'm . . . well, OK. I'll go. But, y'know . . . you should come with me and watch. You'll see. I really don't think it's possible for me. I don't think I can be talked into sleep.'

But Dina can.

17

Alison Randolph's flat is in Streatham, and had I known that when we had the original conversation I'd never have agreed to go. Streatham, you see, is in South London, and since I spent my entire childhood growing up in the green North, I've got a physical aversion to crossing the bridges, not helped by the fact that the first time I did venture below the Thames, at the age of thirteen, I got beaten up. I was on the river-bank waiting to meet a friend at the Tate Gallery – yes, I was *that* poncy, even then – when, realising I had half an hour to spare, the urge to travel, to see the world, overtook me and I crossed Vauxhall Bridge. I saw my mistake as soon as I hit dry land: I wasn't in London any more, I was in an episode of *The Sweeney*. There were no houses, only vast rusting railway bridges and alleyways; the traffic seemed no longer to move in two directions, but in five; what pedestrians there were, and these were very few, scuttled in and out of the shadows in beige draylon suits, all of them, apparently, on their way to somewhere else; and it smelt like . . . like Steven Moorer, a kid at my school who was the unfortunate victim of some gene bypass – not Down's syndrome, nothing with a name, just someone who had been built indefinably wrong, and was bullied every day as a result – it smelt like his house. I hurried back over Vauxhall Bridge to Pimlico like a suddenly spotted lost toddler to his crying mother's arms, where, on the way to the Underground station later that afternoon, me and my friend got viciously attacked by a gang of skinheads.

So technically, yes, I was beaten up in *North* London. But I didn't blame that ground, as I felt the tip of my nose press hard against it under the weight of a sixteen-hole DM. I was being punished for straying; I carried with me the taint.

Since then, I have been forced to go south often enough to realise that my impressions of the place garnered on the dark end of Vauxhall Bridge were maybe a bit unfair, a bit the result of a pounding thirteen-year-old heart feeling itself suddenly very far from home. But as me and Dina trundle bumpily over the Thames in one of those strange BR trains that seem to operate in a parallel universe to the Underground, I still sense, I am sure, the sky begin to lower and the distant sound of the music from *Jaws*.

'Why is the river that awful grey colour?' says Dina, looking down out of the narrow sliding window. 'I'm sure it wasn't that colour when I went away.'

'I'm not sure it was that colour when we first started crossing the bridge,' I say unhappily.

'Just listen . . . listen to the sound of my voice, and relax. Nothing else matters. Just listen to my voice, and feel the weight of your body sink slowly into the couch. You're safe, you're warm, you're away from harm.'

How can she say these things when *Streatham* is just outside? Alison's flat is above Poundsavers on the High Road, and although she's done much to create a sense of cocoon – warm, reddish lighting, wall-to-wall Turkish rugs, a tropical fish tank in one corner – the tinkle of New Age music from some concealed CD cannot plug the jarring bellow of the traffic outside.

'Now, keep them closed – but try and look into the lids of your eyes. Look into the darkness.'

She speaks, as I knew she would, in the hypnotist's metronome, underpinned by a slight Scottish burr, which intensifies as she becomes more confident that I am entranced: perhaps, she thinks, her voice is like whisky, intoxicating. When she greeted us at the door adjacent to the shop, Alison was a chubby, red-haired woman, with a raucous laugh that opened her mouth very wide and threw her head back like a seal, who made us lemon tea and ironically swung about an old pocket-watch; now she is all inner calm and measured tones.

'And staying relaxed the whole time, feel your tongue come

away from the roof of your mouth and just loll, gently, behind your teeth. Feel the tips of your fingers begin to slide away from the rest of your hand. Feel the point at which your head rests on the pillow lift, and your mind lighten with it, rising in the air, free of thoughts. Like a balloon – imagine your mind is a balloon. And your thoughts are like weights, thrown one by one over the side.'

Dina sits on a tri-coloured – brown, red, and orange – Victorian armchair by the fish tank, watching. She and Alison were schoolfriends, and have kept in contact by letter, something I've never managed to do with anyone; the letters must've been good, because not only did they greet each other effusively, which is only to be expected from pen-pals, but, once all the hugging and kissing and *geshrie*ing about how fantastic the other looked was over, they continued to share the same space without awkwardness, unheard of for pen-pals. As we stood in Alison's tiny, *A Taste of Honey*-style kitchen, doing the standard questionnaire – how much do you sleep normally? what do you eat? what do *you* think the problem is? have you tried Kalms? – glances as pass between friends who know each other well enough to have dispensed with speech would pass between them; perhaps that's what happens when correspondence works.

'You're resisting it, aren't you?' she says, still in her tick-tock rhythm.

'No,' I say, keeping my eyes shut.

'You are. Don't worry about how well you're doing. Don't try and calibrate how relaxed you are. Would you prefer it if Dina went out?'

Alison had from the start been uncertain about Dina staying in the room during the session itself, as indeed had Dina, but I've got a point to make.

'No. It's fine.'

Opening my eyes ever so slightly, like I was frightened of being caught doing it, I saw through the thinnest strip of light the two women exchange one of those glances.

'OK,' she continued. 'Remember to breathe. Clear your head of everything but the sound of your own breathing.'

That I've done many times before, in bed: created a mind-vacuum and listened to its sound, my own breath, like the swirling wind in a ghost-town. But, like all the other mind-games, if it doesn't work, i.e. if it doesn't send you to sleep, it kind of makes things worse; you end up fighting a desperate battle of will against your own consciousness, which starts throwing thought-missiles at the brick wall you've built within your brain until it knocks it down. Something inside doesn't want you listening to the sound of your own breathing over long periods of time, maybe because, with no other thoughts to act as a block, eventually the monster-thought will hatch, the one about the time when it stops.

I have to give her credit, though. I *am* feeling a bit more relaxed inside. Perhaps a bit *too* relaxed, actually.

'So now, you have no thoughts. Imagine you are a stone . . .'

'Alison?'

'Yes . . . ?'

'Look, I'm sorry about this, but I really need to go for a piss.'

'What, now?'

'Yes, now.'

She sniffs. 'OK. Slowly . . . slowly . . . come out of the trance . . .'

Come out of the *what*?

'. . . feel your muscles revive . . . then gradually lift yourself up into a sitting position. I'm gonna count to three and on three, I want you to open your eyes. One . . . two . . . three.'

From a sitting position, through my open eyes, I see Dina looking at me somewhat smugly.

'What?' I say.

'Nothing,' she says.

I swing my legs off Alison's blanket-covered couch. 'How else am I supposed to get up except by following those instructions?' I say.

'Turn right out of the door and it's at the end of the corridor,' says Alison. 'And . . .' (this she calls out at me as I walk perfectly capably out of the room) '. . . I know you think you've not been affected, but be careful – you might be a bit dizzy.'

She's wrong. I make it to the end of corridor completely steady on my pins. Half a minute later, I come back.

'There's only a bedroom there.'

'Right, I said. Turn right.'

'Oh.'

I can't utterly deny a certain level of psychological displacement, because going to the toilet is not as mundane an experience as usual. You know that scene in the British comedy film after the stereotypical stupid husband has tried to use the washing machine, and then later, someone opens the kitchen door and gallons of soapy liquid floods out on top of them? That's what this piss feels like: it also reminds me of throwing up 200 magic mushrooms at the age of fourteen, crouching over my parents' toilet and thinking, clearly and precisely: *I am a waterfall.*

But then I never thought the hypnosis would have *no* effect. I just know it's not going to have deep structural effect. And anyway, unless she actually talks me to sleep, all bets are off.

Back on Alison's sofa, she tries to click back in where she left off.

'You comfortable?' I nod. 'OK, remember what I said about not trying to gauge how it's going?'

'I remember.'

'Imagine you are inanimate. A stone. No thought. Not even the possibility of thought. Stay like that for a minute.'

'Good. Now slowly, let some thought trickle back into your head . . . only this time let it be subconscious thoughts.'

Let. Slow. Flying on a seesaw. By night, by night. Don't come. Along hard wind and then it takes two paths and my grandfather dead have you got the time? Wrench the rust from the nails from the wood. Hap hap happy talk. A way a long a last and all that, I suppose – level of irony even at this level, spirit. Hacking into the mother bored, a cough.

Sorry, lost it for a moment there. Fuck, the subconscious talks *bollocks*, doesn't it? Shame, because I was happy drowning for a moment, but I had to wrench myself back up when I realised that all that's waiting at the bottom is a bloody Adrian Henri poem.

'Now . . . of those subconscious thoughts . . . select the ones that stop you from sleeping . . . whatever they are. I don't want you to confront them. I want you to let them go. Like those weights we dropped earlier from the balloon. Just let them go.'

'I have . . .' My voice appears to come from some other part of the room.

'Yes?'

'. . . to go to the toilet again. Sorry.'

I sense a terrible deflation in the room.

'Is this normal?' I hear another distant voice say. Dina.

'It's happened once before,' says Alison, speaking at her unhypnotic speed. 'Various sphincters relax, I suppose. Or it might just be an elaborate way he's got of blocking the whole process.'

'Excuse me. Hello. I *am* still here.'

'OK,' says Alison, breaking a principal rule of hypnotherapy by starting to sound quite pissed off, 'I'm going to count backwards from three and just listen to my words. Three: without completely coming out of the trance, feel control flow back into your body. Two: staying relaxed, regain independent use of your muscles. One: open your eyes.'

Some time and four visits to Alison's postcard-stuffed toilet later, resettling on to the couch I say, 'Alison? Do you want to try actually hypnotising me to sleep?'

'I'm not sure Alison wants her sofa wetted,' says Dina flatly.

'Is it my fault? My bladder loosening?' I say, looking to Alison.

'No,' she says, not very convincingly. 'Of course not. But I've got someone else coming at five . . .'

'What time is it now?' says Dina.

'Twenty to.'

'Can you do it in that?'

'I dunno. Not if he has to get up and go to the bog again.' The Scottish burr has gradually mutated to fucked-off Glaswegian.

'No, I think I'm OK now,' I say, feeling a bit sorry for myself in a three-year-old-about-to-cry kind of way. 'I don't think I'll need to go again.'

'Ever?' says Dina.

'Well, let's give it a try, anyway,' says Alison, rolling up her sleeves both physically and metaphysically. I close my eyes and rest back my head.

'Relax again, to the state you were in before you got up last time,' she intones. 'Find it in your mind and body . . . and let yourself slide straight back into it. Are you there?'

'More or less,'

'OK. Stop there.' I feel her hand, rougher than Dina's, slide under my open palm and lift my arm at right-angles to my body. 'Now I want you to think of this arm as a lever. And as I pull it down . . .' she begins to move my arm very slowly '. . . I want you to feel it bringing you further and further down into relaxation.' She drops my hand on to the couch. 'Sleep now. Sleep now.'

I feel the spin of sleep; being touched helps. Alison seems to sense this, because next I feel her hand again, this time on my forehead.

'Let go,' she says. 'Imagine a feather bed so comfortable you fall into it endlessly, sinking further and further into its mattress, an infinity of softness. Sleep now.'

Drawn down though I am, something in the circular movement of her hand on my brow makes me feel I could go further.

'Dina,' I say, from some other part of the world.

'Yes?'

'You touch me.'

'Sorry?'

'Alison, keep talking. But *you* touch me.'

There is a pause, and, for all I know, more glancing, this time uncertain. Then, the removal of Alison's slightly dry, sandy palm and its replacement three seconds later by what seems to be myrrh, poured on my forehead: Dina's hand, moving gently down over my eyes like a blindfold from heaven.

'Think of Dina as a guide, her hand leading you down into the safe, safe dark. Sleep now. Remove yourself from all responsibility; just follow her. There is no danger.'

Alison's voice, confident though improvising, sounds thin and boomy, like I'm only hearing the echo of it, the original lost in some far-flung valley. In the graphic equaliser of my soul, sight, sound and smell have all been turned down, leaving me sensate only of touch. I feel Dina's hand move off, and cry internally for my skin-fix to return; a second later, it does, alighting on my neck like a butterfly. Then, a different handling, the softest of skin grafts, her cheek against mine, full with something not that far from love, at least for now; thank you.

'Sleep now. Sleep. Sleep.'

Dina's beautiful hands move together under my head, cradling it, and then, I sense, gravitationally, her weight next to mine. She's climbed on to the couch. And now, a total enveloping; she holds me, and we fall together down the ventilation shaft of the mind.

'Sleep now.'

The command brings me close to my impossibility, knowing the moment of sleep. I can almost see sleep, just a bit further down. Something lifts, something goes. Then, right on the edge of blackness, I hear Alison's voice say, 'And *all* sleep, from now on, will be easy. You will go to sleep as easily as you . . .' she struggles momentarily for a comparison '. . . go to the toilet.'

Sadly, even from the encasement of hypnotic trance, this makes me laugh, and the laughter reels me quickly out of the deep like a scuba-diver heedless of the bends.

Dina and I do not exchange a word on the walk back along Streatham High Road to the BR station; it is not until we go through the collector-less barrier to the platform steps that I break the silence.

'Look, I'm sorry I started laughing.'

She doesn't say anything, just wraps herself a bit more fully in her dogtooth coat and carries on down the stairs.

'I know what you think,' I say, staying put for a moment

and then, feeling rather ridiculous shouting after her receding back, moving on down myself. 'You think I just started laughing deliberately to shake myself out of the trance.'

I catch up with her by a half torn-down poster for Clorets, and grab her arm.

'I didn't. I just thought it was funny.'

'OK,' she says quietly, and lifts my hand off her arm, before continuing on to the platform.

For a while, we stand some distance apart waiting for a train to Cricklewood. The station clock, like most of them, is wrong.

'That can't be right,' I say, pointing at the numbers 6:13, more for something to say than for any other reason.

Dina looks at me, then at it; her face is red, and it occurs to me that she may have been crying. What for, for heaven's sake? At the end of the day, it's my lookout if I still can't sleep. She checks her watch; then, after some sort of inner calculation, whether moral or numerical I can't tell, she turns to face me for the first time since I gave Alison Randolph £15 outside Poundsavers.

'No, you're right, it isn't,' she says. 'It's only ten past five.'

I look around me. Near the defunct chocolate machine in the centre of the platform, two black kids in clothes so baggy it looks like their bodies have shrunk inside them are laughing loudly at each other's jokes; beyond them stands a green peeling bench, along which some Streatham version of Mental Barry lies asleep; and, at the other end of the platform, I think I can make out a 1960s city gent, complete with umbrella, bowler hat and pin-striped trousers, but my eyes can't quite tell from here.

'See?' I say. 'It even gets darker earlier in South London.'

18

Today was not so good. I knew something had to go wrong, because my life's been on an upswing this last month and a half. Incredibly, I actually have started writing a regular column for *Over The Line*, and people seem to like it, which, to be honest, is why it's now regular; people seeming to like it, much more than Ben upbraiding me, or pressure from the dole office, or, worst of all, reliance on my own self-discipline, is what has spurred me on to do it properly, and I am: for the first time in my life I'm meeting deadlines. Ben doesn't give me much – £130 a column – but the response has been so good, next issue he's upping it to £150. Last week, I was able to bring the Dolomite home, which was lucky, as I get the impression that I walked into Moran's SuperDrive just as the mechanic was on the phone to the scrap merchant. Driving it, it feels a bit Paul Gascoigney – it's been fixed, but it'll never be quite the thing it was; nonetheless, I was still able to ride it in triumph to the Willesden DSS and tell an astonished Mr Hillman where to stick his Peek Frean factory tins. Actually, of course, I didn't do that, I just fantasised about doing it all the way there; although I did manage to get in a final solemn 'Goodbye, John', which he could only counter by walking away and leaving me with my ironic hand outstretched.

Dina's moved out of Ben and Alice's and found a flat in Finsbury Park; unfortunately, she found the flat before getting a job as a design assistant in a small fashion house in Balham, so has a nightmare journey to work every day. There's been an element of compromise in our relationship: she finally has come with me to Loftus Road, and I've been with her to *The Ministry of Sound*. I'm not sure who enjoyed which outing less: QPR lost 1–0 to Southampton, courtesy of Matthew Le Mesurier, and she walked out of *The Ministry* in a strop halfway through an extended *A Guy Called Gerald* track when she discovered I was wearing my wax earplugs, but a narrowing of boundaries was still achieved. I feel more and more that I respond towards her without reference to her sister; that, weighing up the matter rationally, taking into account her complexity and her sarcasm and her secrecy and her skin, I am probably more compatible with tight and wound-up Dina than with slack Alice. Of course, the employment of rationality is surely the biggest cliché of romance: we all know that there is no better indication that the lovelorn hero really wants to be with X than telling himself that, rationally, he is better off with Y. But in reality, calibration can be made, and, in this case, the calibration *is* the difference between reality and fantasy; I know now that it's stupid to try and compare my feelings for Dina with my feelings for Alice because they live in different emotional compartments. When I see Alice, I will always feel a huge rush, always want to burst immediately into tears; but I'm not an idiot: I know the fact that that doesn't happen with Dina has a lot to do with the fact that I am *with* Dina. In some respects, at least.

And we finally got a video out successfully. Frightened off by the *Beaches* disaster, we went for *While You Were Sleeping*, which turns out to be about a woman in love with a man, and then in love with his brother, and so would probably have been as potentially troublesome to watch in Ben and Alice's company as *Hannah and Her Sisters* anyway; but it's perhaps an index of how far we've come that the relevance of the plotline didn't even occur to me until well after Dina had dried my eyes and said 'There, there.' The only blot on the horizon of our relationship is that her gynaecological problems have recurred, causing a cessation of sexual activity, something I can't be doing with very long. But even this love-cloud might transpire to have a silver panty-lining, in that we've been having sex fairly regularly now for three months, and were probably just about to come up to the point where novelty, play, and the excitement of discovery curdle anyway; and a small halt now may stave that off.

Most extraordinarily, I'm sleeping a bit better, and, difficult though I find this to admit, I think I can trace the improvement back to the session at Alison Randolph's. Don't get me wrong, there's no *like a log* stuff going on, but the early morning wakefulness has receded – it now happens only one morning in four, as opposed to all the time – and I think I'm *getting* to sleep slightly quicker as well: I'm not sure because I don't feel the urge to try and calculate it to the second any more. The other night, though, I have a sneaky feeling I went to bed about one, got to sleep about two, and woke around ten: the magic eight hours. It's really weird to wake, though, feeling refreshed, your brain all scrubbed and serviced. I'm not sure I can handle it; I think I only know how to make coffee from within a somnolent smog.

So the first inkling I got that life might have kind of peaked for me *yesterday* came, wouldn't you believe it, from Nick. He, too, seemed to be improving. He's taken himself off chlorpromazine, on Fran's advice, of course; at first, I was very pissed off about this, but came round somewhat when I realised that it would mean considerably less fetching and carrying of his comatose body. Until today, I would've said it was the right action for his mental health as well: it's difficult to tell with Nick, because you can't really talk about him gradually returning to cogency, as cogency for him represents knowing the Bradford reserves' entire results for the last ten seasons, but he did break a day's silence last week by frowning and saying softly 'Cec Podd . . .?', which I took to be at least an acknowledgment of his former existence. And then this morning he said to me, 'Do you want to take me to the psychiatric hospital?'

Now, this *sounded* very positive. It *sounded* like Nick was finally admitting that he was not so much the Messiah, as ill. But watch what happened.

'What, now?' I said, putting down my bowl of Branflakes.

'Yes, now.'

'I've got my dressing-gown on.'

'Well, get dressed then. You think I should go, don't you?'

'I'm not sure . . .'

'You're the one who thinks I've gone mad,' he said, with a straight face.

Me and most of North London, I thought, but let it pass. So I was just about to get into the shower – I had paused for a moment in front of the mirror to try and confirm a conviction that my belly was ever so slightly flatter than it had been – when he opened the lockless bathroom door.

'What are you doing, you nutter!' I said, scrabbling a towel round myself. I've run out of euphemisms for 'mad'.

'Get on with it,' he said. 'Can't keep the loony-bin waiting!' And walked out.

It was then that I realised that a week off chlorpromazine had just landed him straight back in the same frame of mindlessness as when he melodramatically blubbed his lips in front of Dr Prandarjarbash. Nick Munford was once again SuperLaing, his mission, to avenge free-thinkers everywhere for the mislabel 'maniac', a walking satire on society's ingrained assumptions about sanity and insanity: this was confirmed when I came into the kitchen dressed and ready to go and he was wearing a tiny red striped bobble hat and a far-too-tight orange bri-nylon suit.

'Where did you get those clothes from?'

'Oxfam,' he said.

I knew what tiresome point he was trying to make, so didn't ask him why. Instead I said, 'I dunno if we should bother going now.'

'Why?'

''Cos you're just being stupid.'

'I'm not. I'm being—'

'Mad. Yes, I know. How incisive of you.'

My irritation, I could tell, made no dent on Nick's purposefulness.

'I know what you're frightened of,' he said, twirling a spoon between his index finger and the table.

'What?'

'You're frightened of seeing the "lunatics".'

I was about to dismiss this, then realised it had a certain truth. I am frightened of seeing the lunatics: I'm always petrified in films when it turns out there's one hidden in an attic room. But what Nick meant was, I couldn't face the world-shattering revelation, obviously apparent if I were to meet any *en masse*, that they're all really geniuses; whereas of course I'm just frightened of contorted faces and screaming.

'You're right. Let's go.' I've had it, I thought. Maybe once we're there, he'll fucking stay there.

'Fine,' he said, and put on, from round the back of the kitchen chair, a polka-dotted ladies' mac.

In the car, Nick sat in the back with his window wound down. Every so often, he would lean most of his body out and shout at passers-by, 'Hello! I'm a loony! I'm a nutter! I'm on my way to the madhouse!!'

I tried going faster, but it didn't seem to bother him, and anyway, the new, resuscitated Dolomite can only do forty-three. At least no one paid him any attention, apart from Mental Barry, who smiled and waved supportively.

Park Royal Psychiatric Hospital is a vastly spread-out red-brick complex in industrial estate country somewhere round the back of Harlesden; most of the buildings appear to be bungalows, and so, from the road, it could easily be mistaken for a very badly located Butlins. Harlesden itself is perhaps the worst place in the universe, and it soon became apparent that the Psychiatric Hospital is its living, beating heart. The first thing we saw on going through the security-encoded glass door to the reception area was a topless old woman dancing in the corridor beyond; and after an orderly had typed a code into the digital lock to get us into that area, we could hear that she was singing as well, the dying swan music from *Swan Lake* only not to 'la' or 'da', but to the word 'Sybil'.

'Sy-*billll*, sy-bilsy-bilsy . . . *bill* – sy-bil, sybilsybil, sybilsybil!' she sang, hopping round us as we walked. I looked at the orderly.

'It's her name,' he said.

'Did she used to be a ballet dancer?'

'No,' he said, looking as if he was well used to people making such easy connections. A ridiculously tall black man in striped regulation pyjamas, apparently blind, came out of a door in front of us with his arms stretched out directly in front of him: it looked for all the world like he was about to say 'Heal me, Jesus! Heal me!' but instead he walked straight into the opposite wall. I glanced through the door he'd come out of as we went past him, stuck fast against the red brick like a massive spider, as if he refused to believe the wall was even there; inside was one of those large institutional living-rooms, a bit like the one at Liv Dashem House, only with even less emphasis on the living. Five or six people, some in dressing-gowns, some in hospital whites, and one, bizarrely, in a suit and tie, sat in a completely still circle around a TV blaring out the twelve o'clock news at about five times the necessary volume, as if it knew it was going to have its work cut out to get the message through here: it was like looking in on a meeting of Catatonics Anonymous. We stopped at the end of the corridor, outside an office-like area with a one-way window blocking our view in, where the orderly knocked on the door and left. 'Coming!' said a voice from inside; I looked at Nick, who'd gone white.

'Let's go,' he whispered.

'Why?' I said.

'Look what they've *done* to these people.'

An intensely anorexic woman, probably about thirty-one but with the body of a ten-year-old, came round the corner and strode towards us confidently, as if we'd planned to meet her there at exactly this time.

'Do you wanna fuck me, Ian?' she said, staring at me incredibly piercingly for someone who was clearly seeing someone else. Her eyes were full of anger. 'You can if you like. Here!' And lifted her shift, to show legs and pubis like those you see shovelled into pits by Allied troops that so disorientate the libido. I felt suddenly ashamed of everything I am. Then, luckily, the office-door opened and she ran away.

'Hello?' said a hassled-looking, acne-scarred man in a white coat and Christopher Biggins red glasses.

'Hello, my name's Gabriel Jacoby. This is my flatmate Nick Munford. You should have been contacted by Dr Prandarjarbash at the Royal Free . . .'

'I know Dr Prandarjarbash, yes.'

I paused. Feeling a bit like a schoolboy and his naughty mate asking an adult for something they know they're not meant to have, I nudged Nick with my elbow.

'What?' he said.

'Tell him, then.'

'What?'

'That you want to be admitted as a voluntary patient.'

Nick looked at me like a frightened rabbit. 'I don't,' he said, in a small voice, and sat down on an orange plastic chair butted against the wall. It was at this point – as the doctor began to evaluate him and his clothes, and looked about an inch away from concluding that we'd just come in to take the piss – that I completely lost my rag.

'Yes, you do!!' I shouted at the top of my voice. Various heads poked out of various doors in the corridor and looked at me like I was, well, mad. 'These are *your* people, aren't they?' I indicated the inhabitants of the corridor with a sweeping arm gesture. 'With the same gifts as you? Who can hear and see things off-limits to the rest of us? You *must* want to stay! You and them have got so much to talk about!'

Nick stared resolutely at the grey-carpeted floor; even through the mist of my rage, I noticed the carrot-coloured smudge still muddied his crown.

'Excuse me,' said the doctor. 'Would you mind . . .'

'Where else would you want to be, Nick? You've found your home!'

'. . . not raising your voice. It disturbs the patients.' He put a gently restraining hand on my fervently gesticulating arm; I shrugged it off – all that latent Jewishness within me must've built up my shrug muscles – accidentally slapping him round the face and knocking off his glasses. A second later, and his fist connected with the side of my face, thankfully not very accurately. I turned, and punched him as powerfully as I could under the chin with my right hand: and it occurred to me, in the midst of it all, that this behaviour was intensely out of character, probably as much for him as for me, but that this was what happens when two men who cannot even *see* their tethers any more unfortunately collide. He tried, unsuccessfully, to nut me, missing my forehead by a couple of inches; thanking God that I'd begun by knocking off his glasses, I threw my entire fat weight against him, smashing his back against the one-way window, and shattering it into a thousand pieces. He didn't go through it, thankfully, and next thing I knew,

I was being pulled to the floor by a hundred hands, most of them belonging to orderlies, although I'm sure I saw Nick's nicotine-stained fingers among them; then, a sharp pain in my thigh, and the world swam, just like I always want it to, and I knew the moment of sleep, definitely, because I can remember, as I went down, a large crowd of inmates gathering to look curiously in on a window that before had only given out their unrecognisable-to-themselves reflections.

In the evening, I was back in the flat, having my wounds dabbed at by Dina with balls of cotton wool soaked in iodine.

'But what the fuck where you thinking about?' she asked me, for the third time.

'I've told you. Nothing. That's just the point. Ow. Can you be careful?'

'Yeah, right, *I'll* be careful.'

'If I'd stopped to think, obviously I wouldn't have got into a fight. *Obviously*, if when he hit me, I'd stopped and thought "oh, of course, he's only doing that because he thinks I knocked his glasses off deliberately, and besides, he's clearly got a very stressful job", I wouldn't have ended up coming round with four policemen standing over me about to charge me with assault. But I didn't.'

'How much will the window cost to replace?'

This lowered my spirits still further, as I hadn't even thought about it.

'I dunno. Will I have to pay for it?'

'Should think so.'

She lined up a ball of cotton wool with a particularly nasty cut on my right cheek. My face contracted into a tight flinch. Through my squeezed eyes, I saw her smile, put down the soft white ball and replace it with her softer face, moving towards my cheek with her lips theatrically pursed. It was ironic, of course, done with the knowledge that a girlfriend kissing her man's cuts is a well-rehearsed couply action, but still, when her mouth landed, the gentleness was so genuine, so actually healing, that irony, and the thick coat it can lay on actions of love, was left emasculated, like a smart-alec wishing he hadn't made that last remark.

Her face moved away; her eyes were smiling, but not in a way that blanked out concern. Maybe because of the sudden irony-amnesty, maybe because it had been a long day, or maybe just because it was true, but I was surprised to feel within me the beginnings of that surge, the one that forces out irresistibly the words 'I love you.' I opened my mouth, and the doorbell rang. Dina looked at me.

'You expecting someone?'

'No,' I said.

'Don't worry, I'll get it,' said Dina, with a sense that I was somewhat overdoing the injured soldier act.

When she returned, she was with a policeman and a policewoman.

'Mr Jacoby?' said the man, slightly built for a policeman, maybe twenty-two years old.

I got up quickly, fastening my dressing-gown. 'Look,' I said, 'I've given you all the information you need. It was an accident – a misunderstanding.'

'Sorry?'

I paused. 'The fight. Breaking the window. At the mental hospital.'

'I don't know anything about that, sir,' he said. I frowned, and felt the drying iodine crack slightly on my forehead.

'Is it Nick?' I said. 'What's he done now?' There'd been no sign of him when I woke up, which hadn't helped my attempt to explain the incident to the police. He hadn't yet come back to the flat.

'I'm afraid I don't know anything about a Nick either, sir.'

It occurred to me to say 'what about the one you've got the keys to?' but thank heaven I suppressed it, and stood there instead trying to frame my brown-spotted face into an expression that might be called open and encouraging. An absurdly long silence set in: he took off his helmet and fumbled with it, looked like he didn't know what to say, and eventually lowered his eyes to the floor, at which point the policewoman, an imposing, freckled-faced woman, told me in a broad Midlands accent that Mutti died today.

19

Dina and I arrive late for the funeral; as the Dolomite revs angrily round the corner of Pound Lane and up through the reproduction antique gates that lead to the Jewish end of Willesden Cemetery, I can see family and friends in various shades of black waiting by the hearse, and Rabbi Louis Fine looking over and tapping his watch. 'It was *her* fault,' I desperately want to tell him: she spent ages worrying about not having the right sort of hat, and then, when we finally got going, claimed never to have been told that the car can now only manage twenty-eight. That's the thing about funerals: you still have to get up, dress, have breakfast and drive through oblivious traffic to get to them, all of which activities seem oddly inappropriate, oddly reassertive, in their mundanity, of your life carrying on as normal: almost as if they were happening at the deceased's expense.

Anyway, I think, as I slam the door shut and glare reproachfully at Dina – *see, I told you they'd all be waiting for us, see* – five minutes isn't gonna bother Mutti: not with all eternity on her hands. It's funeral weather: grey, slight drizzle, a wind that seems to be colder than it is blowing up the sleeves of my scratchy black suit (£12 from Help The Aged – it's always best, on these occasions, to wear something that someone's died in, don't you think?) I walk over to the funeral party briskly, partly to compensate for being late, and partly because I am anxious to be enclosed in their mourning bosom. My family is arranged centrifugally, with the fringe contingent on the fringes: Auntie Bubbles and Auntie Edie, both wearing black frilly dresses and black hats with purple netting, stand on the outer ring talking to Simon and Uncle Ray, in Paul Smith and Burton suits respectively, the circle conjoined at the other end by Tanya and Maurice, their tightly linked hands poking symmetrically out of identical buttoned-up black capes. As we approach, the adults all turn as one, as if the talking was purely staged, and in fact one of them was saying 'OK, here he comes. One, two, three . . . conciliatory expressions!'

'I'm sorry,' says Uncle Ray, holding out his hairy-knuckled hand. 'Your grandmother was a marvellous woman.'

'Marvellous!' says Auntie Bubbles.

'I know,' I say, taking his hand, and, having glanced round at the group, restraining myself from saying 'where's Avril?' 'This is Dina, everybody: Alice's sister.' She has been hanging back behind me, obstructed, I sense, half by sullenness and half by awkwardness; Auntie Edie bestrides the gap between her and us instantly with a quite magnificent waft.

'Hello,' she says, making to kiss Dina on the cheek; I have a sudden nightmare vision of Edie getting her baggy under-chin skin out of the way by swinging it up and over her head like bald people do with their remaining strands of hair. 'Sad to meet on such an occasion, but . . .' She shrugs.

Dina smiles supportively; I take her hand, and my relatives part to allow us through to the next level of grief, although not before I notice Simon ostentatiously moving his eyes from Alice to Dina and back again, a gesture I'm meant to catch. Within the inner sanctum are Ben, Alice, my mother, my father, and Rabbi Louis Fine; instinct wins over religion and lust, and my eyes go first to my mother.

'Oh, *Gabriel*,' she says, and her eyes are raw. Bursting into tears for clearly not the first time today, she comes and throws her arms round my neck, and I, useless fucking shithead that I am, do not know how to respond, because there is a wall between me and my mother, and so, unused as I am to her displaying genuine emotion, I stiffen, at a stroke reinforcing that wall with concrete. While her form trembles on my shoulder, I see my dad, dressed entirely inappropriately in a burgundy flannel three-piece suit that Oliver Tobias would have refused to wear in *The Stud*; a stranger might assume that he'd chosen it deliberately to upset my mother's family, but then they wouldn't know it's the only suit he's got. His eyes fidget away: he is never comfortable with any emotion other than anger.

'What happened to your face?' says Alice, immediately concerned. She is wearing a black mid-length silk dress and a matching fake-fur Russian pillbox hat: she looks fantastic, incredibly sexy.

'I'll tell you later,' I say. My mother backs off, and tugs a tissue from the sleeve of her blouse, something Mutti used to do: she dabs her eyes with it, but it's too wet from previous tears to dry them.

'I'm sorry you had to find out from the police,' she says, through sobs. My mother had been away at a Zeppelin convention in Hanover when the news came; I don't know where my father was – he may have already heard from private sources and been out celebrating – but Liv Dashem House couldn't get in touch with him either, and so they told the police, who mistakenly came to me as next of kin.

'That's OK,' I say, and go and stand next to Ben: Dina mirrors the action with Alice. Rabbi Fine, a short, stocky man with, like all rabbis, a beard and glasses, coughs and puts his hand on my mother's arm.

'We'd best begin,' he says. She nods, and we set off in slow procession through the graves, hundreds of them, swelling on the face of the earth like an allergic reaction.

There is a tradition at Jewish funerals that, after the coffin is lowered into the ground, the shovelling of soil on top of it is actually inaugurated by the closest relatives. I'm not sure whether this is a therapeutic act or not, but I know that nothing makes you aware of your own mortality like a good spot of grave-digging: as I take the shovel from my father, I can almost hear the rooks in my soul cawing. Bending down to take a hefty chunk of earth from the mound, however, my attention is distracted away from gothic contemplation by something on top of the coffin, something that looks like writing. It is: in stark black Magic Marker across the pale pine, the words 'Eva Baumgart'. That can't be right, can it? I mean, obviously it's better than burying the wrong person, but surely someone could have scrubbed it off with a wet cloth before now? Something about this petty scrawl makes me angry: I see the undertaker's assistant's hand, checking the meaningless name against a list, writing it on the lid, and then forgetting to rub it off before the coffin was put into the hearse, and I'm not angry with him, but with death, for happening so often that we have to employ people to become professionally inured to it. Quickly, I throw the earth off the blade down into the ground, and watch Mutti's name cover over with dirt; meanwhile, the real grave-diggers, lolling by some nearby stones, watch bored, waiting for this silly tradition to be over so that they can begin their work in earnest.

I hand the shovel over to Ben and get down from the mound, the turn-ups in my suit overflowing with dust. He should really have taken his turn before me and not just because he's older: he's the one who believes in all this ritual, or, at least, who's come to believe in it in recent months. When we said Kaddish, the prayer for the dead, he knew it by heart, whereas I had to read mine from a scrap of paper with the words printed phonetically. The Reverend Fine, standing far enough away from the grave to avoid any fine spray of dust falling on to his black robes, intones, '*Baruch Hashem Halevi Hashoah Adoni*.'

Ben finishes his shovelling, and the immediate family stand in a line, in order for the rest of the funeral party to come up and shake hands with us. 'On *Simcha*,' they say, one by one: 'On *Simcha*', 'On *Simcha*.' It means 'on a feast day/joyous occasion', i.e. that's what I hope it is *next* time we meet. I like this typically Jewish sense of deferred happiness, of accepting that now is bad but soon things'll be better – and not in the next world, but here, in Willesden, in Buchenwald. I don't know the names of all the old men and women shaking my hand, but then one comes up who I do recognise, even though, judging from his enormously magnified eyes, he can't recognise me: Mr Fingelstone.

'On *Simcha*,' he says, and looks very sad. 'She was a good woman.'

He looks thinner than I remember him, shrunken within his brown demob-style suit like those black kids on the platform at Streatham BR. His hand grips mine with all the ridiculous strength that people who have virtually no strength left seem to reserve for handshakes; then he drops it and moves on. His presence reminds me that someone is missing; I look up and scan the cemetery.

'On *Simcha*,' a small German voice says.

'193 Cloister Road. Just off the A40,' says a very similar voice. I look down: Lydia and Lotte Frindel, zimmer- and chair-supported, wait for my reply. Then I see who I'm looking for, about a hundred yards away, underneath a statue of a trumpeting angel.

'Excuse me,' I say, and run away from them, which I feel is what Mutti would have wanted.

The grass underfoot is damp and easy to crush as I swerve through the graves towards Millie Gildart. As I get close to her, I can see that though my run transgresses her line of vision, she is staring steadfastly past me, at the burial. Her eyes are so fixed it looks like she's taking aim.

'Hello, Millie,' I say breathlessly, slipping slightly as I come to a halt.

'Gabriel . . .' she says, with a nod, not breaking her hundred-yard stare. I suddenly become aware that although I darted over here as if possessed, I actually have nothing in particular to say.

'Um . . . why don't you come over and join the rest of us?' turns out to be the best I can manage.

'I'm not very into funerals.'

'Who is?'

She turns round; her eyes unsquint with the change of focus. 'Your Auntie Edie. She *fucking* loves 'em.' And her whole being radiates a dark rage, convulsed into the swearword: she is living out Dylan Thomas's moratorium.

'Even her sister's?' I say, deliberately containing my inner amazement at hearing an eighty-two-year-old woman swear.

'Some people have dislocated themselves so far, not even death can bring them back.'

'Yeah, well . . .' I say, not sure how to respond to Millie being quite so undistilled.

'She was very sweet, your grandmother,' she continues, speaking to the air, 'very sweet.' She blinks. 'There's many really bad things about growing old, Gabriel. Loads of them. Your body goes and your wits dull and so on and so forth.' She sighs heavily. 'But the worst thing, I think, is that you have to spend all your time with *old* people. I mean . . .'

I know what she means. 'Really old people,' I say, nodding.

'Yeah,' she says excitedly, 'people who have given in to it. Eva was about the only one left who hadn't.'

I raise my eyebrow slightly at this.

'Well, obviously she had a bit,' says Millie, tutting. 'She was very interested in biscuits, I grant you. And she would insist on bloody dyeing her hair blue. And it really mattered to her whether or not you and Ben married out. Which, yes, is all a bit old. But beyond that – and maybe you didn't see it because she would always . . . *grandmother* it up when you were around – you know . . . she was still . . .' Her eyes begin to falter. 'She'd clap her hands when she was pleased. When it snowed, she'd still look out of the window with wonder.'

Her ice face thaws a bit; she reaches out two fingers, that at first appear curved into a claw by arthritis, but when she clamps my badly shaved cheek in between them, I realise she's just doing that affectionate Jewish thing.

'I'm glad you came over,' she says, vibrating her hand back and forth. 'I'm particularly glad it was you and not . . . I don't know, Simon, or the rabbi, to tell me how it's all right, we'll all meet up one day.'

'No.' I look over to the burial site. 'It's not all right, is it?'

Millie shakes her head, and I, who cry at the most meaningless Hollywood machination, who, on a good day, will cry at *Neighbours*, feel my throat catch for the first time since my grandmother died. An aeroplane passes overhead, and I jerk my neck back to look up at it. It must seem like I'm looking away, using gravity as a last recourse against tears, but I'm not, I just want to be on that plane: not to be going anywhere in particular, just to be travelling, endlessly floating, above the clouds, not arriving, just moving, drifting, looking out of the window at the Antarctic of the sky.

'Hello, Ben,' says Millie, over my quaking shoulder.

'On *Simcha*, Millie. Gabriel? Can I just have a word?'

* * *

Ben and I walk round the gravelly path which circumvents Willesden Cemetery; the path is flanked by a row of trees – no idea what type they are, sorry – and a six- or seven-foot wooden fence, which together do their best to screen the dead from the living.

'How do you think Mum's taken it?' he says after we've walked in silence for about a minute.

'Not very well,' I say, recognising immediately that this banal question cannot be what he wants to say. We scrunch on a bit further.

'No grandparents left, then . . .' he says eventually.

'No.' *Next time 'grand' will go, it'll just be 'parents', and then after that, no word.*

'She's the one I'm really gonna miss.'

'Yeah, well, we were too young when the others went.' More aimless walking: from here, we can see the mourners gathered round the grave. The drizzle-clouds have lifted a bit, burnt out by a tentative April sun, and so they've begun chatting and circling, enjoying the day out.

'Look at that gravestone,' I say, pointing at one about three graves down; the stones in this section are new, black and glossy and engraved in gold. '*In loving memory of Brian Flan*. How on earth could he have spent . . .' I squint at it '. . . seventy-three years on this earth and never made it to the deed poll office?'

Ben stops, but looks the other way, towards the road.

'Gabriel. How serious are you about Dina?'

'More serious than I was. Why?'

He does not turn my way. 'I've been having an affair,' he says, as if it's not a non-sequitur.

My insides lurch. I've fantasised about this moment many times, of course. Not exactly like this. Not at my grandmother's funeral, for a start. And normally, it comes via Alice: she calls me, breaks down over the phone, says she's convinced Ben's seeing someone else, I go over there to comfort her, badabing, badaboom. I've not been troubled by it for a while, though. And even when it was a regular part of my daydream-scape, I never paid it much attention. You know how you give some of your fantasies a certain amount of credence, like they might actually happen? The out-of-work actor who dawdles over his big film role, the Sunday Leaguer lifting the cup in his living-room, Steven Moorer on his own at break-time mulling over what it must be like to have a friend: all done with just a fraction of possibility, just a hint of you-never-know. I never bothered with that with mine; it was purest conjecture. Why, after all, would someone want to cheat on the most beautiful woman in the world?

'Did you hear what I said?' Ben is saying.

'I'm not sure,' I say. 'Can you just run it past me again?'

He looks at me hard. 'Don't piss me about, Gabriel. I'm serious.'

'No, you're not,' I say. 'You're very, very foolish.' I swallow: I fear I may be about to give myself away completely, and although a blessed time has suddenly hovered into view when that may be the right thing to do, now is not it. 'What do you *mean*, you're having an affair?'

'I've *been* having an affair. I'm thinking of calling it off.'

'What's to think about?'

He swings away, kicking a pebble off the gravel with the outside of his right foot. Always a better player than me, it swerves in a sweeping parabola to the right, just nicking Brian Flan's gravestone on the corner, scratching the words 'loving wife Doris'.

'Now look what you've done,' I say. Continuing his sulky three-year-old behaviour, he starts to walk off by himself.

'Who is she?' I say, trying to build an image in my head of a woman more beautiful than Alice, and failing: it whirrs repeatedly back to Alice.

'No one you know,' he says, without looking round.

I remember his initial question, about Dina. *How serious are you about Dina?* Seriousness, so difficult to gauge, and yet I felt I was on my way to doing it, I had the ruler out and everything, and now it's all had to go back in the drawer. The slow deliberate tortoise of my feelings for Dina has been lapped and lapped again by the sudden remergence of the Alice hare.

'What's it got to do with me and Dina?' I say.

Now he turns round. 'She's not Jewish.'

My head spins with irrelevance. 'So?'

'Look,' he says, heaving an enormous and rather stagey sigh,

'I know you think it's ridiculous, but I've become concerned recently about losing my religion.'

'The REM song?'

'No! I *knew* you were going to say that. You're so predictable.'

'Sorry,' I say, feeling genuinely upbraided. 'Carry on.'

He breathes out through his bulky nose. 'I've been feeling it increasingly for the last six months. I even talked to Alice about converting.'

'What did she say?'

'That she would if it really meant that much to me. But, y'know, it takes two years, and if her heart's not really in it, then she probably wouldn't get through the tests.'

'So, anyway, me and Dina . . .?'

'Yeah. Well. So. My wife isn't Jewish. I never thought that'd be a problem when we got married. But suddenly, it was. And then you started going out with Dina. Like, seriously.'

'*And . . .*?'

'And I thought: that's it for the Jewish Jacobys. That's the end of the line.'

Wow. The starting-point of his thinking is so far away from anywhere I might ever end up that I don't even bother to oppose it, I just sweep to a conclusion on the helter-skelter of his logic.

'So . . . I presume this woman you're fucking is Jewish, then?' He doesn't answer. 'And what . . . you're thinking you might have a child with her, and then he or she will carry on our glorious Judaic dynasty? Very religious, Ben. Really. Oh, hold on . . .' I click my fingers repeatedly '. . . what does that commandment say, the one about adultery? I'm sure it's "Thou shalt *not*."'

'Look . . .'

'Or are you just dressing up having a bit on the side with a load of religious *bollocks*?'

I'm getting too angry now, years of longing readable in my irritation. And besides: what am I doing? What do I want here? Do I want Ben to sort it out, or do I want him to travel further on down his uncharted Semitic path, leaving Alice lost and in need of a guide home – perhaps one who looks comfortably like the one she set off with? We stare at each other in silence for an appreciable amount of time.

'You don't understand . . .' he says finally.

'No, I don't. Since when were you so fucking concerned about lineage?'

'Ben! Gabby!' My mother's voice sails gaily over the prostrate dead. 'We're going to the *shivah*!'

I look over; the funeral party is trudging slowly off like some lumpy black dinosaur. Perceptible in its centre are Alice and Dina, both looking this way, reproachfully, I would guess, at our respective desertion: they don't know the half of it. Millie, I notice, is nowhere to be seen.

'You're right,' says Ben suddenly, coming over and putting his hand on top of my head, causing my black yarmulka to slide jauntily to one side. 'I've been very stupid. I'll end it.'

I nod, and grasp the back of his neck with my hand, and feel my life's central options closing.

'Does Alice know anything about this?' I say as we begin walking back across the cemetery.

'No! No,' says Ben, looking rather scared. 'I mean, she knows things haven't been quite as good as they were – but, no. I think she'd probably leave like a shot if she knew I'd ever had an affair.'

Right.

20

The problem with current attitudes towards forced sexual intercourse is that, at some point, *everybody* has forced someone else to have sexual intercourse with them. Thankfully, only a few have done it using physical violence; but unthankfully, we have all done it using psychological violence. My preferred method is to say 'Fine. No, honestly, that's fine. If you don't want to do it, we won't do it', turn over without saying good-night, and then follow that up with some elaborate tutting and sighing, culminating in a series of ultra-irritated twists and turns, all meant to imply 'I can't get to sleep now – and whose fault is *that*?' It's not just a male thing either. Early on in our relationship, Dina once dropped round as a surprise, all horned-up and panting (honestly); unfortunately, I'd just dabbed the sperm off my chest for the fourth time that day – not a lengthy process by that stage – and although I could probably, if pushed, have masturbated a fifth time, sex, with its much more implosive effect on the undercarriage, would have felt like squatting in acid. So I feigned disinterest – well: I didn't feign it, I *wasn't* interested, but I played it as 'no reason, I just don't fancy it' disinterest, rather than 'sorry, I'd love to, but my prostate might fall out' disinterest – and the narrative of her consequent reaction ran, basically: genuine confusion, followed by disinterest rather better feigned than my own, followed by a second, more raucous assault on my trousers (still repelled), followed by irritation, a moment of pathos – 'don't you fancy me any more?', emotional blackmail – 'well, don't expect me to perform next time *you* want to have sex', and finally the big walkout, including a shouted threat about finding someone in the street who did want to do it then.

Tonight, though, as it has done for the last three weeks, Dina's reluctance stems from something gynaecological, and, politically, that puts me in a very difficult position. It's the litmus paper of relationships, really, affairs of the womb; the mention of them invariably signals a customs-officer-level search of your internal new mannishness. You remember how, a few years ago, if you wanted to test that your phone was working – always the last resort of the lonely night – you dialled 175 and then the last four digits of your number, and a taped female voice would say 'Start test. Start test.'? That's the voice I hear in my head every time Dina says her womb hurts.

So I've *tried* to stop myself going into my usual rejected boy-sulk, in a way that I probably would not have tried to stop myself were Dina to proffer any other reason for her continued abstinence; I've *tried* genuinely to reassure her and to listen sympathetically to her fears about infertility and inflammation; but – and it's a big if extremely immature but – it's been going on now (have I mentioned this before?) *for the last three weeks*.

'Fine,' I say, rolling off her stomach. 'No, honestly, that's fine. If you don't want to do it, we won't do it.'

There is a silence, broken only by the odd tut and sigh from my side of the bed. I feel a warm hand on my dramatically turned back.

'Gabriel, I'm sorry,' she says, I sense looking up at the ceiling. 'I know it's been a long time now. But I'm still getting these terrible womb pains.'

'OK,' I say, mumbling, as if I'm already near sleep, I'm that unbothered about it.

'Don't pretend you're asleep.'

'I'm not pretending.'

Now it is Dina who tuts and sighs.

'I'll toss you off if you like . . .' she says.

'It's OK,' I say quickly, although I bank this anyway.

'It's just . . . you hurt inside me.'

'I said OK.' There is a part of me that wants to claim comparison with Miles Traversi here, but it is the worst part of me.

'What were you saying to Ben at the funeral? When you went off?'

'What, you want to talk now?'

'Yes. What's wrong with that? Are you not speaking to me because I won't have sex with you because my womb hurts?'

Start test. Start test.

'No,' I say, turning over. 'Because it's two o'clock in the morning.'

'So? A minute ago, you were obviously prepared to stay up for . . .' she pauses '. . . at least another three minutes.'

'Ha ha.'

'And since when was two o'clock in the morning so late for you anyway?'

'You've got to go to work tomorrow.'

'Something else that didn't seem to be worrying you a minute ago.'

I know when I'm beaten. My underarm skims across the top of her breasts as I reach over to turn the bedside lamp on.

'What was the question again?' I say, blinking at her.

'What were you saying to Ben at the funeral?'

'That was two *days* ago!'

'Well, I've only just thought about it.'

I haven't. I've thought about it long and hard, in all senses of the phrase. It has, to some extent, reignited, in my many spare moments, a complacent dwelling on the subject of Alice, her face, her body, except now with me actually in shot as it were, rather than just holding the fantasy camera. To some extent: because although it took a bit of a knocking in the two or three minutes immediately following Ben's revelation, now, away from the first impact, my affection for Dina has got up, dusted itself down, and, as is its wont, quietly set about reestablishing itself in my thoughts like an undertone. And, perhaps more than thinking about Alice, Ben's news has made me think about Ben. I mean, we all know that even those of us with the most coveted partners stray. Desire after all is driven by novelty and discovery and revelation; it is the commodity that most perfectly demonstrates the law of diminishing returns, and a diamond mine will run out of ore as quickly as a tin one. But I don't think this has been the issue with Ben, even though I sort of accused him of it at Brian Flan's grave. I think it comes back to his questionnaire mind, his method of choosing women by ticking off their attributes. Perhaps he wasn't searching for perfection, as I've always assumed; perhaps he was doing the opposite, searching for flaws – for something to allow him to continue the search. Except then Alice came along, and she was perfect, and so he had to stop; until it suddenly occured to him that there was one category that she didn't fulfil, one qualification that she could never have – Jewishness – and settled on that *because* there was no getting around it.

'Oh, nothing,' I say. 'Football.'

Dina looks doubtful. 'He didn't say anything about Alice?'

'No. Why?'

'She's worried about him. This Jewish kick he's on, apparently it's like a really big deal between them now. And you know what she's like, thinks she should do more . . .'

'How?'

'I dunno, go to synagogue, learn Hebrew. Who knows? But it's like now she thinks it's her fault that she's not Jewish.'

I look at her elegantly rounded, perceptive features, and, not for the first time, wonder why I bother about Alice. I feel, unsurprisingly, an enormous urge to tell her the truth, but I think that really would be a mistake; unselfishly, because she may tell her sister, and that would be a terrible thing to do to my brother, and, selfishly, because if anyone *is* going to tell her sister, it's going to be me, however terrible a thing that is to do to my brother. My hand wanders absent-mindedly under the duvet to her nipple.

'Well, he did go on a bit about Mutti and the funeral service and whatever,' I say, my thinking being that going halfway along with her will be convincing, 'but he didn't say anything about Alice.'

'Right,' she says, and grabs my wrist, now lowered to her belly button, in an iron grip.

'What?' I say.

'*Gabriel . . .*'

'What?'

'Five minutes chatting doesn't mean that my womb pains are cured.'

I release my hand and settle back on to my side of the bed, although less ostentatiously than previously, still looking at her.

'What does your gynaecologist say?'

Her eyes move away. 'He says I have to go for a scan. That that's the only way they'll be able to tell if something's really wrong. But I haven't made an appointment.'

'Why not?'

'Because I'm scared.'

I feel my heart dip, and reach for the side of her face; she buries her cheek in my hand. I resolve to put my frantic imaginations about Alice back in a box marked DO NOT OPEN and am free again to love Dina, as I do most when she does this – suddenly admit vulnerability – something she has come to do more as she has grown to trust my own admissions of it. It's perhaps a banal equation, but I think my affection spurts faster as a result of her previous aggression; having worn a suit of armour, she now seems more in need of a blanket to cover her nakedness than if she'd only ever worn a bikini.

'It's better to know,' I say.

'Yeah . . .'

Her eyebrows lift together in the middle, giving her a troubled, slightly pleading look which makes my chest ache. I've learnt, now, that the range of Dina's eyebrow movements extends far beyond ironic arching. They can bend to indicate interest, dive together for concern, flip for amusement, and much more: they are two synchronised swimmers on her forehead. Much of the beauty of her face, in fact, lies in its mobility, a mobility which is happy to run the risk of occasional ugliness, as opposed to Alice, whose face is constantly beautiful, but constant to the point of stasis.

Outside, a car door slams and a male voice shouts incomprehensibly.

'Will you come with me?' she says, looking and sounding like someone too young to have these problems.

'To the scan . . .?'

'Yes.'

Now *I'm* scared: four parts having to deal with bad news, one part entering the off-limits lair of the feminine.

'I came with you to the hypnotist,' she says, sensing my disquiet.

That hardly balances, does it? She was your friend, for a start: and you were hardly likely to have to cope with discovering anything awful about me, either. What kind of scales are you working with?

'OK,' I say. I have my reasons.

She kisses me gently on the forehead; then reaches behind her and switches the light off.

'Dina . . .' I say after a moment's silence.

'Yes?'

'You know you said that thing about tossing me off . . .?'

So I'm sitting in my bedroom, typing out an article on Laurie Cunningham, Number Five in my series *Boots From Beyond*, when Nick bursts in and tries to kill me. Obviously, this has been on the cards for some time, but it's still come as a bit of a shock.

'You bastard!' he shouts, pressing his thumbs hard into my Adam's apple, easy enough for him to do from a kneeling position on top of my chest. 'You fucking wanker!'

'What's the matter?' I say, or try to. I remember, through a mist of fear and increasing soreness, that some people use strangulation as an erotic aid, and wonder how.

'You had to get rid of her, didn't you?' He's moved his hands off my throat now, thank God, but only so that he can grab hold of my hair and use it to pound the back of my head repeatedly down on to the floor in time to his words. *A danger to himself and/or other people*. 'My only real friend in the world! The only one I could talk to! Just 'cos you were threatened by her!'

I'm too busy trying to breathe back lost air – difficult while your head's being knocked about – to concentrate on what he's saying. Huge gulps seem not to fill my lungs. For the third time in recent weeks, I am privileged enough to see the point, not far away, where unconsciousness begins.

'Why?!' he cries, lifting my pinging skull up to meet his face. I think I can feel a trail of blood tickle down the back of my neck, but who knows? It may just be the first symptom of brain damage.

'Why what?' I say, noticing that his breath smells strange, a mixture of citrus and offal.

'Don't pretend you don't know,' he says contemptuously.

'I don't. All I know is you've attacked me.'

He jerks my face even closer to his, a movement that, I'm sure, comes from buried memories of Bradford.

'You've driven her away!'

'Who?'

'*You* have!!'

'No! Who have I driven away?'

He looks at me incredulously. 'Fran!' he says, as if it was the most already established thing in the world; and lets me drop back to the floor, banging my head *again*. This is starting to piss me off.

'She was crying,' he says, and his own eyes grow moist at the thought. 'Crying down the phone.' He sniffs. 'Said she couldn't come and see me any more. She couldn't come round, because . . .' and here his eyes land on me again with their studs out '. . . *you* were here.'

'Well, look—'

'She said it was so stressful here that it even made her come out in a rash. Lumps all over her body.'

Hmm. Well done that chair.

'Look, Nick,' I say, 'I know me and Fran haven't exactly got on, but I never said she couldn't come round any more.'

He ignores me. 'I'll move out,' he says, and above his head, I see the switched-on light-bulb.

'Oh . . . if . . . if you want to . . .' I say, and thank heavens his knees are still pinning me down or my fists would by now have punched the air in celebration.

'Yes. I think it's best.'

'Perhaps you're right.'

He gets up and off me with a dignified air, as of someone who has used the process of strangling and head-pounding in order to come to an intellectual decision.

'I'll pay what I owe in rent, of course.'

'Of course.' Of course he fucking won't; he hasn't paid any rent for four months. But anything rather than avert the present direction of his thinking.

Dusting his arms down completely unnecessarily – he has no dust on him whatsoever – Nick turns to leave. As he swings open the bedroom door, I, staying on my back on the floor – it suddenly doesn't seem worth getting up – say, 'Nick?'

'Yes?'

'What did Fran say I'd done?'

He turns, frowning. 'Huh?'

'What did I do that upset Fran so much?'

It may seem strange to ask for a reason from a man who has lost his, but there's a part of me that cannot abide anyone hating me, even someone I hate. Pathetic, isn't it? He scratches the top of his head, making his nails go carrot-coloured.

'She said . . .' he says, apparently straining to remember – short-term memory loss appears to be one of the features of cannabis psychosis, rather like it is of cannabis usage '. . . she said . . . that she couldn't come round, because you were aggressive and sarcastic and unloving and didn't give a fuck about anybody but yourself – just like your brother.'

'Pardon?'

'That she couldn't come round, because you were aggress—'

'No, just the last bit.'

He looks at me with an expression that is vague but willing to help, this man who just tried to strangle me.

'About my brother,' I say.

'Oh yeah! That's what she said. That you were just like your brother.'

'Nothing else?'

He frowns.

'About my brother . . .?' I say gently.

'Oh! No.'

Nick's mind is a Kafkaesque information centre – asking questions of it leads nowhere. My mind, however, feels overloaded, toxic with information.

'OK,' I say, anxious now for him to go. 'Shame about you leaving, but . . .'

He stiffens. 'Yes, well: I've been stuck in one place for too long anyway. It's time to move on.'

Thank goodness he hasn't forgotten about that, at least.

* * *

As soon as Nick's gone into his room to pack – I dunno – whatever will *fit* into a handkerchief knotted on the end of a stick, I run into the kitchen and reach for the phone. I don't even stop to wipe the blood off the back of my neck.

'*Over The Line*?'

'Can I speak to Ben, please?'

'He's on another line at the moment.'

'It's his brother.'

'I'll see if I can get his attention.'

The voice disappears and is replaced by *Sunderland Are Back In The First Division* by Crystal Air, which sounds remarkably good on my phone. It clicks off.

'Cunt?'

'No, *you're* the cunt.'

'I'm sorry?'

'You really *are* a stupid cunt.'

'Really, Gabriel, I'd love to chat all day, but—'

'It was Fran, wasn't it?'

He goes quiet. And amazingly, perhaps because it can't believe it either, my phone is silent too.

'In a minute,' he says, away from the receiver. 'Yeah. No, tell him to hang on.'

'Ben?'

'Sorry, everyone's trying to talk to me here.'

'I'm right, aren't I?'

His breath comes heavily down the line. 'Yes.'

'No one I know then . . .'

'Hold on a minute . . .'

Another click, and once again I hear in song about Sunderland's triumphant return to the top flight.

Then, 'Gabriel?' His voice is more in the foreground of the phone: he's gone to a smaller room.

'Could you put it back down again – I just want to hear the middle eight about beating Burnley . . .'

He laughs, mainly because the joke signals to him that I'm not as cross as I initially sounded.

'Why?' I say.

'Why what?'

Why did you swap the most wonderful woman in the world for the worst?

'Why Fran?'

'I dunno. These things happen.'

'Well, all right then, how? I thought you only met her the once – that time the video shop gave us the wrong tape . . .'

'No, I saw her again.'

'Obviously.'

'She works in a chemist in St Johns Wood. I just stopped off there one day, because I had to get . . . something for Alice.' I don't know if the pause is because he's trying to remember or because the mention of his wife holds him up. 'I didn't know she worked in there. In fact, when I came up to the counter, I couldn't remember who she was. I knew I knew her from somewhere, but that was all. But *she* was really, y'know . . .'

'Like you were her oldest friend in the world?'

'Sort of,' he says reluctantly. 'Anyway . . . I remembered who she was then, and then I remembered something else from that night. You remember Dina saying that Fran was ugly 'cos she was Jewish?'

My recall loops. 'Jewish to the point of deformity. It's not quite the same thing.'

'Yeah, well. It suddenly came back to me as I was looking at her. And – this was what I was going through at the time, God knows why – it really outraged me. I thought, how *dare* she. How *dare* Dina say that.'

'This is a beautiful woman, you thought.'

He pauses. 'I was going through something. She did seem somehow beautiful to me then,' he says quietly.

The pieces are fitting together. 'What day was this?'

'I dunno,' he says. 'About two months ago?'

'No. What day of the week was it?'

Another pause; he knows what I'm driving at. 'Oh. Saturday.'

'You wouldn't have just been to the United Synagogue, by any chance?'

He sighs. 'Yeah. I probably was a bit . . . full of fervour.'

Neither of us say anything for a moment. Then, with a sense of having relieved himself of the worst, Ben continues, 'So I ended up going into the pharmacy quite a lot over the next couple of weeks, and then eventually we started seeing each other – y'know . . .'

'Round the back of the United Synagogue.'

'No. It only happened a few times. At her place.'

'And all to prove that one can look very Jewish and still be sexually attractive.'

He laughs again. 'No, that was just what kicked it off. But what kept it going was . . . everything I said at Mutti's funeral.'

I look out of the window. An old lady with a shopping trolley stands in the road sticking her hand out at full stretch for the 31B, like catching it means everything to her, like this is the only bus home ever.

'Did she tell you?' he says.

'No. Nick did.'

'*Nick?*'

'In between trying to strangle me.'

'What d'you mean?'

'Well, you obviously kept your word about breaking it off . . .'

'Yes.' Within the space of that very small word, he conveys all the horror of telling someone who, at the best of times, thinks of themselves as oppressed, victimised, helpless and man-abused that you don't want to see them any more.

'And now she doesn't want to come round here any more. Too painful, I suppose.'

'You must remind her of me in some way.'

'Let me count them: sarcastic, aggressive, unloving, and not giving a fuck about anyone else but yourself. That's what we have in common, apparently. How could she miss black hair?'

The windows in the hallway reverberate as the 31B moves off.

'And Nick took it very badly, then . . .'

'Yeah. All my fault, he seemed to think. Next time, I might just point him in your direction.' I have a sudden Jewish instinct and remember the other hand. 'However, it has made him think about leaving, thank fuck.'

'Where will he go?'

'I don't care,' I say, but my stomach shifts somewhat, and I look round towards his bedroom, because I can't completely relinquish responsibility for him. Down the phone, I hear a door open, and a muffled voice.

'Yeah, OK. Be there in a minute,' he says. 'Look, I gotta go.'

'All right . . .'

'Oh! Have you written that *Boots From Beyond* yet?'

'No, I had to put it on ice. It's difficult to type when you're being strangled.'

'True. Well, soon as you can.'

He hesitates before going into full winding-up mode.

'Gabe?'

'Yeah?'

'You don't think Nick might take it upon himself to . . .' His voice drifts away, into crackle; the phone has gone back to sounding like my percolator should.

'Tell Alice?'

'Yeah.'

The thought hadn't occurred to me. Nick's hardly likely to run into Alice, in the normal course of events, but then he isn't running in the normal course of events any more.

'I don't think so. I'm not sure if he knows.'

'I thought you said . . .'

'No, all he knows is that Fran doesn't want to come round here any more and it's got something to do with you. Or rather, with me being like you.'

'But he might guess.'

'I don't think so. Well. The old Nick would've guessed straight away. He'd just've assumed immediately that it was something to do with sex, because that was what he assumed was behind everything. But now, he's too confused.'

Something ruptures in the receiver.

'Sorry?' I say.

'I said, I hope you're right.'

'Hm.'

'I'll see you soon, anyway.'

'OK.'

He pauses, momentarily; he's wondering about whether or

not to say something, which, if it's what I think it is, is not really worthy of sustained internal debate.

'Cunt?' he says hopefully. Sure enough.

'Cunt,' I say, after a pause just long enough to make him worry. He puts the phone down, I imagine smiling to himself.

21

I was sleeping soundly until about ten minutes ago – that's right, soundly – when a sound woke me up. For some time, the soundtrack of my dream – about trying to tame an underwater horse – had included an occasional rabid scuttling. My subconscious had done its best, but, gradually, it became clear that the scuttling was not down to a sea-gnome driving a little buggy in fits and starts around the coral, but because something was in my bedroom. When I actually woke up, the noise seemed to have gone, but noises that wake you up always do that: stop for ages, as if the bogeyman/axe murderer/monster cockroach has seen you sit up and is just waiting for you to hit the pillow again. I looked for a full four minutes into the hatching light, my heart beating faster than some terrible Jungle record, but nothing took shape; fell back into the pillow again, and straight away *ffffffffscccrrrrrrdddrrrttt*!

I got up and turned the light on, which of course is what these noises want you to do: they're not happy until you're truly disturbed. Again, nothing at first. Then, seconds later, Jezebel darted out from underneath the bed chasing a mouse.

I shouldn't really sleep with my bedroom door open. I only do it because of a truly vain hope that, one day, Jezebel will come and sleep on my bed. That's what I wanted, a cat that would come into my room during the night and nestle on top of my duvet, warm, comforting, softly purring, a rope to slide with down the slope to easy sleep. It hasn't really worked out like that. I've tried squashing her on the bed, holding her underneath the duvet, putting Go-Cat on the pillow, but nothing will convince her to sleep with me. Normally, I'm left watching her char-grilled arse rush out of the room and wondering whether we've got some Elastoplast.

Jezebel resurfaces from beneath the wardrobe with the mouse hanging out of her mouth. I grab her by the scruff of her neck, which brings up memories of her as a kitten carried by her mother, and it upsets me, like when you see a bag lady and wonder what she hoped to become as a child. Shaking her head from side to side does not make her release the mouse; but it does make her growl, or, rather, emit one ridiculously elongated growl that varies in tone from very high to very low like someone's jiggling her pitch control. I can see the mouse still alive in her mouth, but this, Jezebel's only gentleness, is double-edged: she will hold something in her teeth with great delicacy, with just enough force to keep it there without damaging it, because she wants, when she puts it down, to torture it, and torture's no fun if your victim's already dead. I try to pull it from her teeth, but she increases her grip, and I realise she will kill it before letting go.

'Let it go!' I say. 'Leave it!'

'*Woorrrrhhhhgghhhhhhhaaaaaa*,' says Jezebel suspiciously.

The mouse's black pinhead eyes look at me oddly unperturbed. *Why are you bothering?* they seem to say. *It's the cycle of nature*. But then, suddenly, she drops it, and it just sits there, patiently, waiting for the bat of paw or claw. Jezebel, overcome with lust, has forgotten I'm here; quickly, I sweep the tiny brown creature into my hand, and she looks up at me, appalled. With my free hand, I unhook my dressing-gown from its peg on the door, slip it across my shoulders and go. As I walk down the hall stairs, I hear the bleakest, most despairing yowl, like I've heard her do only once before, when she came round from the anaesthetic having been spayed. But then she was crying for her lost children, for goodness' sake: this is a fucking *mouse*. Has she no sense of proportion?

It's raining outside, a misty morning drizzle; cold on flesh I thought was covered makes me look down and realise how much of my body is available for the view of milkmen and paperboys, if such things existed in Kilburn. I can't retie the gown, because the mouse is forcing me to clasp my hands in a 'here's the church, here's the steeple' shape so I crouch quickly into our mixture of weeds and brickwork that disgraces the name patio. A blue Vauxhall Astra comes piling round the corner at 'there'll be no other traffic on the road at this time of the morning' speed, and the driver sees me, but pays no attention to the sight of a half-naked man apparently praying to his house. I put my hands to the ground and uncup them. The mouse stands on its hind legs and wiggles its nose, an action so absurdly mouse-like I begin to worry that the animal kingdom too has become infected by self-consciousness. Then it's off, probably to find some cheese and go blind with two mates.

Back in the bedroom, Jezebel is sniffing manically around the area she last saw the mouse.

'I took it outside. You saw me do it!'

She carries on sniffing. I turn round to switch the light off and get back into bed, thinking that perhaps, exhausted by sadism, she might condescend to join me, and, immediately, she bites my ankles. Ow! Fuck! The sniffing was just a ruse! I whirl round to try and slap her, but she's gone: already I can hear the crash of the cat-flap and the pelting pawsteps receding.

What warmth my sheets retain from the sleep-heat I was lying in fifteen minutes ago escapes out the side of the duvet as I get back into bed. I spend a good three minutes searching for my blindfold, before I realise that it's on the top of my head (and must have been so while I was outside). Oh well. I draw the dark visor down, and kind of over-ensconce myself in the sheets. This, a different action from pure insomniac tossing and turning, involves drawing myself up past the foetal position into a tight ball, and pulling the sheets over my head, repeatedly; to a casual observer, it would look like someone trying too hard to snuggle. Then, I hear a clump. Then, another one. *Clump*.

What? What is it now? I uncurl my body and fumble for the bedside light. 'Jezebel?' Nothing. She's still outside. My black bin-liner bin rustles in the corner, and clump! Out pops a sweating frog, a vein in its neck bulging and unbulging sedately. Our eyes meet and it freezes.

Two minutes later I'm back in bed, having left the frog far enough away from the mouse to feel it's got its own space; as it hopped away, I thought for a second that I spotted some flecks of red on its warty back, but it might just have been spots on my exhausted retinas. Going back into the house, I caught sight of Mental Barry, staring at me from the corner of the street, calmly, as if he'd been watching me for some time; and maybe because it's the only time of day he's sober, I don't know, but his look was readable, it did not gibber. It said: *where am I supposed to put all these mice and frogs?* And I felt like I should apologise, because, after all, I was dumping them on his doorstep.

Amazingly, sleep feels like it's still just about redeemable – there's still a bantamweight lump of it somewhere in my bones, and if I can only fix on it . . . and then Jezebel starts yowling again, and scratching frantically at my bedroom door: when I look over – no need to turn the light on any more – her leg, so outstretched the bone seems to be straining through the fur, waves back and forth between the frame and the floor like an overwound metronome. I get up to let her in, even though I know full well that all that yowling and scratching *doesn't* mean 'please, I want to come and nestle on your duvet and softly purr you to sleep.' She flips off her back like an acrobat, goes past my feet, and, for a second, does appear to be heading towards the bed, only to dive underneath it, resurfacing a scrabble or two later carrying in her mouth an enormous dead rat. She drops it at my feet, and looks at me, like: *there you are – the whole range.*

What is the matter with this cat? Three things she's brought in, just tonight, just while I've been asleep! What is she trying to prove? I look down. The rat is about a foot and a half long; its neck has been twisted round so its head rests on its spine, the only sign of leverage a tiny red nick in its off-white fur. Its eyes are closed, but its mouth is open in one corner, one long spiny tooth exposed in a 'you can't hurt me' sneer. I wonder why she has brought it in dead, but then it occurs to me that alive, a rat is probably too strong to carry in her mouth for any distance: I know I wouldn't like to try it. Jezebel gently pokes the corpse with her paw.

I don't really know if I'm supposed to pick it up – rats, don't they give you bubonic plague or something? – but I don't think it's a great thing to leave lying around in the bedroom either, so I pinch the tip of its tail in between my forefinger and thumb and lift it up with a view to throwing it out of the back window (I'm not going into the street again: Mental Barry might draw the line at this). As it slides limply up off the floor, Jezebel cuffs it with her paw, and it swings to the right; I move it higher and she leaps up at it like a kangaroo. For a while, I let it swing in the air; her neck cranes to follow the movement, her pupils engorging with black. She makes for it again: I jerk it out of her reach, and, for a second, she is level with my head, all paws forward, before unfurling back to the floor. This is incredible. Jezebel is actually playing with me. The dead rat is working as a toy. Forgetting all my fears about ending up on the back of a 'Bring Out Your Dead' wheelbarrow, I clasp the rat in my right hand and run into the kitchen to open all the drawers.

String, I'm sure we've got some string somewhere. Drawer after drawer though reveals only random house-detritus: a tin full of drill bits, five empty video-cases, a plastic bag mountain, a packet of chocolate digestives with one left, a bakelite egg-cup, a huge roll of gaffer tape, the nameplate – *Gabriel* – that I had on my bedroom door as a kid, a Glenfiddich miniature, *A Souvenir From Nick*, a broken electric clock, a Bunsen burner (how?), and *Frampton Comes Alive* on eight-track. Giving up, I slap the rat on its back on the kitchen table and tie the red ribbon from the Glenfiddich miniature in a knot around its stomach, lumpy with beetle-bits never to be digested; pressing my finger down to hold the ribbon in place, I think 'why not?' and make it a fairly ornate bow.

In the bedroom, Jezebel is waiting for me demurely, behind the door. I produce the dead rat from behind my back and jiggle it in front of her like it's a special treat Daddy's bought for his little girl after a long trip away.

'*Weiu*,' she says interestedly.

I put the rat down on the floor, Jezebel's eyes tracking it. I crouch down and jerk my end of the ribbon. The rat moves clumsily backwards, its legs splaying out at grotesque angles, rolled by its upper body: Jezebel spurts a paw towards it, then another, but I pull the ribbon sideways, and the rat becomes a corpse possessed by The Dodge, feinting and sidestepping, double-jointed by death. Jezebel leaps over it, trying to cut it off at the pass, but things have really worked out for the rat since dying, it can fly now as well, and she stares confused but excited as it rises into the air and hovers there like a rodent angel. Then she goes for it again.

For twenty minutes we play, as the wee small hours grow large, cat, man and dead rat in perfect harmony. Then, suddenly bored and tired, Jezebel walks away from the gyrating cadaver, and I begin to wind the excess ribbon round and round the rat in preparation for its mummification in the swing-bin; but then my attention roots, my weaving hand freezes, as I see her leap up on to the bed and knead the duvet with her front paws, purring. *Purring*, for God's sake. And then she falls into the tenderised space and curls her tail round past her head in a perfect cat-circle, asleep in seconds.

I look at the half-wrapped rat in my hand. I go over to my desk, open the second drawer down, and place it carefully in a clearing in the centre of the sleeping-pill bottles: it is a shrine to unconsciousness.

22

The scanning-room of the Gynaecological Wing of the Royal Free Hospital is on the fourth floor, accessible only by one of those enormous hospital lifts. Myself and Dina lean against the grey back wall as it rumbles slowly skywards, not really looking at one another: the atmosphere between us on the drive here was strained, laced with silences, with deliberate misdirection from our present objective.

'Do we go through Obstetrics?' I say.

'That's what she said,' says Dina, face forward, set, like I haven't seen it since we were waiting for the Green Flag man on Westbourne Park Road. The lift stops at *1*, Psychiatric: the huge metal doors part, and, in amongst a large group of student doctors, walks Dr Prandarjarbash.

'Hello . . .?' he says, after noticing me and starting slightly.

'Gabriel Jacoby. I brought in my flatmate a few months ago – he's got a cannabis psychosis.'

'Yes, yes, of course.' He looks up. 'You remember, Steve – the apparent schizophrenic . . .' Steve, a thin blond whitecoat of about twenty-three, nods keenly, although his eyes betray a certain bewilderment. The lift moves off.

'How's he getting on?' Dr Prandarjarbash continues.

I shrug my shoulders. 'Difficult to tell.'

He nods. Then, a strip of suspicion bisects his eyes, and he points an index finger at me. 'Oh, hold on a minute – you were involved in that fight at Park Royal.'

Steve looks at me with renewed interest, maybe even a certain respect. 'Yeah,' I say, with, sadly, just the tiniest hint of pride. 'Don't worry, I'm not going to smash the place up.'

His expression is inquisitive, as if he's prepared to give me a hearing.

'It was a stupid thing,' I continue. 'I was under a lot of stress. Nick forced me to take him there . . .'

'Nick's your flatmate . . .'

'Yeah, sorry. And then he wouldn't check himself in as a voluntary patient, and I sort of lost my rag a bit. The doctor there tried to calm me down and I brushed him off a bit too strongly and next thing you know everyone was piling in.'

'So what happened in the end?'

'I got charged with assault.'

The lift has been stopped again, at *3*. A young Arabic man with sunglasses, pushing a bearded geriatric in a wheelchair, goes out.

'Well,' says Dr Prandarjarbash, leaning over and pressing *10*, 'I seem to remember there was some trouble when you were here as well.'

'Yeah . . .'

'It wasn't his fault,' says Dina, breaking her silence; I had thought she was too preoccupied to be listening. 'Here *or* there.'

Dr Prandarjarbash studies her intent face with detached curiosity. The doors open at *4*, our stop. As we make to go, he says, studying his long, possibly manicured nails, 'Yes, well, you don't seem to be a violent sort. I'll have a word – see if I can't get them to drop the charges.'

'Thank you,' I say, trying to catch his eye and show him I really mean it, but it's difficult to do on the move, and I only catch the lift doors narrowing on an image of him and Steve in animated discussion of something else.

'And Gabriel is your . . .?'

'Boyfriend,' I say, feeling the absurdity of the word, not being a boy any more, and having done things to Dina that a friend would never do. Dr Levin, a reassuring-voiced man with stuck-out, gappy front teeth and a Bohemian shock of crazy grey hair, nods attentively, and scribbles something down on his notepad.

'We've been regular partners now for about three months,' says Dina, her hands inside the bottom of her tight red acrylic jumper, pulling the neck down.

'Fine . . .' he says, still writing. The blinds on the long window behind him are half-shuttered, backlighting him in streams and motes; he lifts his Bic off the pad and asks me, 'Have *you* experienced any problems? Any discharge, pain during urination, impotence, NSU?'

How *dare* you ask me such questions?

'No.'

'Of course, some of the bacteria that cause womb damage can be carried by males without showing any symptoms . . .'

'Yes . . .?' I say. He has this habit, Dr Levin, of breaking off his sentences, as if their conclusion is too obvious to voice.

'Oh! So perhaps it's best if you come and get checked out anyway. We'll make an appointment for you at the Marlborough Clinic. It's on the seventh floor.'

'Um . . .' I say, as he scribbles a number on a new leaf of paper '. . . does that involve – y'know – little umbrellas and stuff?'

'No, Gabriel, you're thinking of cocktails,' says Dina.

I know what cock I'm thinking of, thanks.

'It's just a swab,' he says, handing me the note. 'Ring them and they'll . . .' He waves his hand in the air.

'Fix up an appointment.'

'Yes.'

I'm not very happy about this. I did once get a check-up at a Sexually Transmitted Diseases Clinic, a few years ago, when, for various reasons, some of which you may be able to guess, I became convinced that I had prostate trouble. *That* was called a swab; it was the most painful experience of my life. And also, the nurse operating the little umbrella was called Edwyn. I'm not saying anything. Just that. He was called Edwyn.

But Dina looks at me with that face which means I'm still on test – I'd say there was even a part of her pleased that I now had to undergo my own bit of reproductive organ pain – and I fold the piece of paper and put it in my pocket.

'So let me just recap,' he says, moving his attention back to Dina, 'you've been getting these pains on and off now for over two years.'

'Two and half.'

'Which was when you first experienced inflammation of the pelvic area . . .'

'Yes.'

'Have you been given doxicyclin?'

Dina sighs. 'Yes. Three times now. But it never seems to completely clear things up, and . . .'

She trails off, but in her case, not because the conclusion is obvious, but because she doesn't want to say it: that, as a result, she's probably infertile by now, at the very least.

'When did these last pains begin?'

'About two months ago.'

He jots another note down on his pad, and then jerks the Biro off it, indicating finality.

'OK, then, let's have a look at you. If you wouldn't mind just slipping your things off through there, and I'll get the scan ready.'

Dina nods, and reaches for her handbag, but it's on the other side of the chair, my side. I get it for her, aware that such absent-mindedness is unlike her: it must be due to stress. Our eyes meet as I hand it over, and I really try to dispense with everything in mine but love. The shield in hers, on full at the moment, drops for a second, just long enough to see something I don't quite understand, some destroyed hope, some given-up-on longing; then she gets up and goes through a door in the back of the room.

There is more than a smidgin of awkwardness as me and Dr Levin wait together in the room; the only-to-be-expected tension is not helped by the fact that here we are, two guys who've only just met, and already one of them knows whether the other ever gets any penile discharge. I look aimlessly around, as, for a while, does he, until with an 'Oh!' he remembers where he is and goes over to the white-sheeted couch in the corner. He hums a non-tune to himself as he switches on some buttons on the adjacent machinery.

'Dr Levin?' I say.

'Yes?'

'Is there anyone who works in the Marlborough Clinic called Edwyn?'

His bushy eyebrows knot together. 'Edwyn? Hmm. Edwyn. Edwyn, Edwyn, Edwyn . . .'

Dina comes through the door in a white shift and gives us both a worried smile.

'Ah! Just hop on to the couch, then!' he says.

Dr Levin's distracted briskness reminds me of something. Then I remember: the way the man who came to do medicals at my primary school would, after a cursory once-over with the stethoscope, say 'OK, drop your shorts then!' before inexplicably asking me to cough. Perhaps it's a tone that everyone who's involved in the daily demystification of the intimate has to adopt, for their own protection.

Dina lies back stiffly on the couch, the white of the ceiling reflected in her eyes. Dr Levin smacks his rubber gloves on and picks up a small white plastic probe.

'Now this might be a little cold . . .'

She grimaces slightly as the probe enters. Dr Levin throws another switch on the ultrasound: a grey liquid triangle, curved along the bottom, appears on the screen. It looks like a laser in a very cheap light show. As his hand moves, the shape of Dina's womb clarifies, although it remains watery at the edges. I don't feel any great-mystery-of-life stuff: it's too murky, too out-of-focus. Then I notice some sort of little black splodge on the edge of the laser line. On this messy radar it looks like it's probably just a screen blot, but my heart stops nonetheless: let it not be cancer. Let it not.

'So your main concern about these pains is they may be a symptom of infertility, I suppose . . .' says Dr Levin, switching his head back and forth between Dina and the screen.

'Yes. That's *one* of my main concerns,' says Dina, still looking at the ceiling.

'Have you been trying to get pregnant to check?'

Her eyes finally move to him. 'No.'

'Well, you are. About . . . nine or ten weeks, I'd estimate.'

And the world gives way. Dina looks to me, Dr Levin looks to me, the little black splodge looks to me; but a huge liquid triangle has come down from the sky and I am drowning in its grey waters.

* * *

In Hunger, a café in Chalk Farm, Dina over-stirs her black coffee, as if it had loads of sugar or milk in it.

'So, y'know . . .' I say '. . . if you wanna move in with me that's fine – Nick's moving out now after all – and have the kid – y'know – or if you don't, that's fine as well. It's your decision.'

This is the third time I've said this, or something like it; it is the speech I know I'm supposed to give. She nods, but doesn't seem to have listened.

'When could it have happened?' she says.

'Um . . .'

'I mean, we *have* used condoms every time, haven't we? I didn't forget one time?'

'Well, there was that time a couple of months back . . .'

'Gabriel. You can only get pregnant through the vagina.'

'I know that. I was just thinking about condoms.' It comes to me. 'Oh. Hang on. The first time – the very first time? The frog night . . .?'

'Yes?'

'I remember getting up and flushing the condom down the loo. And . . .'

She looks at me demandingly; I smile wanly.

'. . . it kind of leaked a bit.'

She stops stirring at last. 'Why didn't you tell me?'

'I wasn't sure! You should try filling the fucking things up with water for once. Drips come off them all over the place. Anyway, what difference would it've made?'

'There's the morning-after pill!'

'But you told me you couldn't *get* pregnant.'

'I never said definitely!'

A rap-rhythmed gibber-thought appears in my head: *The history of her hystero is making her hysterical* . . .

'Didn't you notice you'd missed some periods?'

She waves a hand across her face. 'Oh, they've been fucked up for ages. Ever since I first started having gynae trouble. I didn't give it a second's thought.'

Hunger is fairly deserted, 3:23 on a Monday afternoon deserted. Along the pink and purple rag-rolled walls hang some artist friend of the owner's amplified stick-cartoons: £72, £83,

£104 – so cool no doubt he thought to resist the conventionalism of the rounded number. A black-legginged waitress sits on a stool by the bar chatting to a man, too hirsute in my opinion to be working with food, behind the small kitchen window.

'Well, look,' I say, sliding my hand across the table to touch her still-round-the-cup fingers, 'it's good, y'know? At least it means there's nothing wrong. You can have kids if you want to.'

She nods, but gently as if to herself, and takes a sip of coffee, which involves moving her hand away. It occurs to me that there is a part of me that really wants her to have this kid. There's a part of me that wants to give it all up, that can see, just across the way, peace, a state of mind unirritated by the constant itch of desire, by next door's gardener's hourly regreening of the grass, by Alice. A part of me.

The black-legginged waitress looks questioningly in our direction; Dina reaches down to pick up her handbag.

'No, it's all right, I'll get it,' I say, feeling that my responsibilities as a bread-provider begin here.

'OK,' she says absently. 'I haven't got any money on me anyway,' and parts the heavy deco clip with her finger and thumb to take out a packet of Silk Cut.

'Um . . .'

'What?' The mock-Zippo comes out of her pocket and her aggressively questioning expression is covered by a mask of flame.

'Should you be doing that?'

She takes out the cigarette in a nicotine mist and looks quizzically at the lighter.

'Only way to get the smoke out of them, isn't it?' she says, bringing her face back round to mine; her eyebrow, for the first time for weeks, is raised.

'Oh, Dina . . .'

'I'm not going to have it, Gabriel.'

A part of me dies.

'Why?'

She stubs the cigarette out in the white china ashtray, its long unsmoked length buckling; the paper tears in two places and dry, brown flakes fall out.

'Because it would be the stupidest possible thing we could do. Because it really fucking hurts when they come out. Because I don't want to spend the next two years talking about colic. Because neither of us has got a proper job.'

I look round embarrassedly at the waitress, catch her pretending to wipe down a table, and look back again, leaning in close to Dina's so touchable face.

'None of that matt—'

'And because you're in love with my sister.'

She says it with just a slight sob in the middle, the smallest give, like Karen Carpenter. As she says it, her eyes lock into mine like a hacker into a mainframe, and I'm so surprised I can't block them, they drain me of information, everything, all that I am rushing out of me at the speed of light; she catches the nano-flicker of guilt and her head goes down.

The occasional clang of china meeting china is the only other sound in the café besides Dina's sobs. For a second, I consider the option of denial, but it's too late, and besides, I want to tell her: she's my friend. Relief is on hand.

'How do you know?'

'You told me . . .' she jerks her head up and her tears back '. . . in your sleep.'

This makes me wish I'd denied it. 'No. Never.' The flat of my hand hits the dark pine of the table. 'I've never talked in my sleep. I don't reach that level of sleep.'

'You did once.'

'When?'

'At Alison's.'

I kill the breath starting in my lungs, the one that was going to shape my next words.

'You think you never went under, don't you?' she continues, fiercely now, with menaces.

'Well, no . . .' I say, falteringly, my emphatic drive dissipated '. . . I know I did a bit – specially just before I came out of it . . .'

She nods, heavily, deliberately. 'When I was hugging you on the couch.' She says the words slowly: I can hear the click of the gun-barrel between each one.

'Yes . . .' A pang, a wish to be back there. 'But it was only for a second.'

The nod turns to a shake.

'It was quarter past six when we left. I lied to you about the time at the station. You were under for over an *hour*.'

I can feel myself frowning. I get the impression I'm *really* fucking frowning.

'What about her other customer?' I say, my brain in its confusion picking out tiny details at random.

'He didn't turn up.'

'Oh.'

What did she do, put me in some kind of confessional coma?

'What did I say?' There seems nothing else I can do but ask the questions here. She does her flicking thing on the cigarette packet and pulls out another one.

'You said your thoughts. The ones that stop you from sleeping.'

'Which came out how?'

Smoke pours from her mouth and nose. 'Gibberish mainly. Ranting. Something about your grandfather.' Her eyes narrow. 'And then you said her name.'

It seems incumbent on me to fill this waiting gap.

'Alice.' The word hovers between us like a spread-winged bat.

'Yes.'

'What, just that? Alice?'

'Basically. But loudly. You were practically screaming it. Oh, and "please".'

'What is it?'

'No, you said please. Alice. *Please*.'

I feel my cheeks redden at this pitiful image of myself, naked and roaring like a baby desperate for its mother.

'Right,' I say, churlish now, feeling more than slightly violated.

'Oh, you're pissed off now.'

'Well—'

'You feel you've been abused in some way, do you? Exposed? Humiliated?' She rounds on me, pushing her face close to mine turned away. 'Well, that really *does* make two of us then, doesn't it?'

There is a silence. The waitress has retreated tactfully into the kitchen. I should apologise, of course, but where to begin? If I were to give her the length of apology she deserves, we'll be here till Chanukah.

'Let me tell you something, Gabriel.' She stubs out another hardly smoked cigarette; I feel the cold steel in my stomach about to twist. 'That first night. The frog night. Do you know why I slept with you?'

'Um . . . well, I had kind of thought it might be because you fancied me.'

'No,' she says firmly. *Thanks very much.* 'I'd had a big row with Alice before I came over. *About* coming over. She thought it was a bad idea me getting involved with you. Well, actually, I think Ben thought it was a bad idea, but that was in the days when her and Ben thought the same way about everything.'

Sound blurts into the room. The waitress is supplying us with discretion by putting on a tape of some background band, *Simply Red* I think.

'Anyway, to cut a long story short, by the time I arrived at your house I was pretty bloody certain I *was* going to get involved with you, just to piss her off. Mature or what?'

'You didn't seem that certain.'

'Well, I'm not that see-through. But that's not the point I'm making.'

'The point you're making is that I shouldn't think, for a second, that you got into this relationship because you liked me. Yes?'

'Well, who did *you* like when you got into this relationship?' she says loudly. 'Not me, I think. Someone who looks a bit like me in a bad light doesn't count as *me*.'

The waitress turns up *Simply Red*. The bell on the door clatters, and with a rush of cold five para-booted crusties come in, smelling of mobile homes.

'And that isn't my point either,' says Dina, lowering her voice. 'My point is, the whole thing, our whole relationship, has been about Alice – for both of us. You because you love her, me because I hate her.'

'You don't *hate* her,' I say, shocked.

'Sometimes I do,' she says, raising her jaw. 'I did that night when I came over, and . . .' her head falls again '. . . I do now.'

Simply Red ends; one of the crusties coughs, much too violently for someone under eighty-five.

'Why didn't you just get rid of me after the hypnosis session?' I say.

She shrugs. 'I'm used to men fancying Alice more. But I've won some over in my time. Maybe I thought you'd grow out of it. But this . . .' she pats her stomach '. . . this is too big a step to take with that knowledge.'

I feel this is my cue.

'Look,' I say, 'you're probably not going to believe this because – well, because you probably don't believe me now anyway – and because you've got such low self-esteem you never believe anything good about yourself, but I kind of think I *have* grown out of it.'

'Right,' she says, looking away and smiling sardonically.

'*You've* grown me out of it.'

'Oh, *please*.'

'You have. OK. I'm prepared to admit that there have been times in my life when I've been obsessed with your sister. And, yes, that may have had something to do with my initial attraction to you. But people get together for loads of reasons, not all of them the right ones.' I reach over and put my hand on hers again, and this time she does not move away. 'The starting-points don't matter now. We're in it. And I never think about Alice any more.'

'Never?'

'Well, less and less.'

Judging from her eyes, 'Never', plus a firm headshake, would have been the better answer, but I'm on the honesty helter-skelter now.

'Do you love me?' she says, mounting me on the pin of her stare. 'Me, that is.' She frees her hand and points to herself. 'This one.'

This is always a tough one. I know I *have* loved her, from time to time; and I know that sounds shit, but that's how love works, doesn't it, in moments? I'm not sure any of us love constantly. We love in spurts, on sight of softness, or sadness, or sex: love-lines run along the parabolas of buttocks and tears. I loved her last week, when she told me she was scared about going for a scan; and I loved her last night, when she rested her head on my chest in bed; and there's a part of me that loves her now, because I know I may be about to lose her. Will that do?

'Yes,' I say, but she is too black and white, and translates the hesitation as 'No.'

'You don't.'

'I do.'

'Not really.' She sighs; the waitress brings the crusties a selection of cakes and cappuccinos; I wonder how often men and women will have to have this conversation. 'You know what you're in love with, Gabriel? Missed opportunity. That's what Alice is to you. A permanent missed opportunity. You're only able to love what might have been.'

She gets up, putting the cigarette packet and lighter back in her handbag.

'Where are you going?'

'Back to America.'

'Pardon?'

'Back to America. I need friends, someone to talk to. Who can I talk to about this here? Not my sister.'

Some phrases that end with 'then' come to mind: *So that's it then . . . I guess this is goodbye then* . . . and one not resigned to it, *no, please no, say you'll stay forever*, but it all feels tired, oversaid, and I'm overcome by weariness, by the effort required to respond to this situation originally. And underneath, a certain gladness, that at least she isn't going to tell Alice: my cover is safe in the bosom of her bitterness.

'What about . . .?'

'I know a gynaecologist in Manhattan that I trust. He'll take care of it.'

Her cut-and-driedness makes me suddenly very sad.

'Oh, Gabriel,' she says, putting her hand into my hair, 'don't look like that. If it had your genes it would end up fat and insomniac and if it had mine, it would end up . . .' she rotates her fingers, still held in a V-shape from the cigarette's ghost 'oh, I dunno . . .'

'Beautiful,' I say, chancing my arm with the movie-script line, and I mean it, I really fucking mean it, but although her eyes liquefy, she shakes her head, and her face says *it's no good*.

'No,' she says. 'I don't think you can inherit genes from your auntie.'

'And Miles?'

'He's dead.'

'There'll still be all the fall-out from it, though.'

She smiles. 'Gabriel, a few people got killed. In *America*. They'll have forgotten about it months ago.'

I look up to her, standing in her dogtooth coat, ready to go; her mind, I can tell, is made up. She bends over and kisses me, on the cheek, and I kiss her on the cheek back. A kiss on the cheek usually reads as the end-note of a relationship, a signal that the mouth is now out of bounds, but this is where I *want* to kiss her, here where the surface area of skin to skin is largest, where I can bend my face around and fuse our cheeks as one, gulping down, like a man about to swim under the reef would air, as much memory of her texture as I can. She responds by pressing her cheek back against mine, and for a second, there's no Hunger, no Chalk Farm, no London, no world but her skin; and then I feel her face move away, and open my eyes to see her back moving away, out through the clanging door and into the street.

There's a moment when I think about running after her, but as the door shuts, another creaks ever so slightly ajar, and I hear the distant din of the futures and options market reopening. Because although a part of me, the part I've been going on about, wants to cry, and cry hard, another part is already turning over what this means in terms of the information I possess about Ben and Alice, and about the freedom I now have to act on it, and so I don't run after her, I order another coffee and sit there, shrinking out of all that spiritual growth I told her I'd achieved, oscillating, vacillating, contradictory as a rapist's kiss.

23

'Let's ask your mother. Irene? What's for dinner?'

'One of your stews, darling. A big pot of Stu's Stew.'

'That'll be lovely. Can't wait!'

'Well, you'll have to!'

Is this my father's house? 22 Salmon Street this Friday evening is suffused with a completely alien air of homely indoor calm, of safe bourgeois tranquillity. It's like walking into an advert.

'What's going on?' I say, low enough not to be heard in the kitchen, offering my father the chance of being conspiratorial, but he looks at me blankly, as if the idea of him ever speaking nicely to my mother *wasn't* ruled out in their marriage vows.

'Something to drink, Gabriel?' he says, after my question has withered in the air.

'Don't mind if I do,' I say, before wincing inside, and telling myself I meant it ironically, I really did: I was just momentarily thrown by his manner. He goes over to the nasty 1970s drinks cabinet they appear to have had since the 1950s and opens it by the gold handle.

'Scotch? Gin and Tonic? Vodka? Wine? Or we've got some soft drinks in the fridge . . .'

'Wine, please . . .'

'Red or white?'

'Red,' I say suspiciously. He gets out a bottle and a tinted blue glass as my mother comes in, her lower half surrounded by an apron on which you can see only a small central section of The Hindenburg.

'Hello, stranger!' she says, and kisses me on the cheek. I think if I moved in and followed her around the house all day like a spaniel, my mother would still address me as if I hadn't bothered to visit for ages. 'What have *you* been up to?'

'Not much.'

'Oh, come on. I hear your column's been a big hit in Ben's magazine.'

'Yes,' says my father, handing me the glass, 'he seemed very pleased with the way it's working out.'

What *is* happening? Not swearing at my mother is bad enough, but taking a fatherly interest in my career is bordering on the ridikalus.

'And Tina? How's she?'

'*Dina*, darling . . .'

A momentary flicker of rage passes across my father's eyes, indicating he's still in there somewhere.

'I'm positive you said Tina,' he says, with restraint.

'Does he *ever* get anything right?' she says to me, laughingly. I'm sure I can hear the bubble and hiss of boiling blood.

'She's gone back to America,' I say, rather killing my mother's mood.

'Really? Oh, for a short holiday . . .'

'No, I don't think so.'

A blanket of I Don't Know What To Say-ness falls into the room.

'Oh,' says my mother, and looks for a second as if she is about to cry. Since Mutti's death, I've noticed, the membrane between her and her life, the one that keeps reality out, has become stretched and porous. If it breaks, she will undoubtedly have a nervous breakdown; perhaps that's the reason for my father's transformation . . .

'Oh well,' he says, taking the initiative, 'plenty more fish in the sea.'

I look at him unbelievingly – no one says that *surely* – but then remember he's only just begun speaking normally: I suppose he'll have to go through all the clichés, the rubbishy crust on top of language, before arriving at some kind of original self-expression. It's a shame, 'cos he had so much of it when he was swearing.

'I shouldn't think Alice is very pleased about that . . .' says my mother, pulling herself together.

'She isn't. Ben thinks she was just starting to appreciate having her sister in London.'

'Ah well,' says my father, going over to his wife, *putting his arm round her*, and pouring her a glass of wine as well. 'I propose a toast. To Gabriel. And his fortunes in love.'

'Oh, fuck *off*,' I say.

'Gabriel!' he says loudly, strictly, like a father. 'Not in front of your mother!'

He recorks the bottle; my mother turns and smiles at him thankfully, like he's just made some domestic dream come true.

'I think it's a lovely toast, Stuart,' she says gently, and raises her glass. 'To Gabriel. And his fortunes in love.'

'To Gabriel. And his fortunes in love.'

'To me. And my fortunes in love.'

I'm not sure it's possible to say it any more sarcastically. Resonating irritation, I clink my glass with theirs and raise it to my lips. I'm so childishly exasperated, in fact, that I hardly notice the liquid passing across my tongue; but the aftertaste is so . . . so . . . oaky buttery spicy and mature, it knocks me sideways.

'Are you going to throw this in with all the rest, then?' says my father, plucking at my mother's apron.

'Oh, I meant to talk to you about that,' she says.

Hurriedly, I take another sip, more like a gulp actually. God. It's like a completely different drink. It's more like a *food*. You know how wine writers are always going on about *body*? Well, that's what this has got. It's like something three-dimensional in your mouth, a beautiful taste cube. I've found it. I've found it.

'I'm not sure I want to sell the whole collection any more . . .' my mother is saying.

'WHAT!!'

My father's sudden return to his normal volume snaps me out of myself.

'Don't start, Stuart.'

'Oh, for fuck's sake!! You heard what the man said: he'll give us over eighty thousand for the whole lot!!'

'He'll give *me* over eighty thousand for the whole lot.'

'Well, you know what I bloody mean.' This a bit quieter.

'And *I* think he undervalued it. I mean, Kapitan Lehmann's hat alone must be worth about three thousand. And as for my father's model . . . I just think perhaps it's best to wait a bit.'

'Oh no. I know you. You've just found a pus-bucket of an excuse!! You'll never fucking sell it ever now!'

'Dad . . .'

'WHAT!!!'

'Where did you get this wine?'

'I DON'T FUCKING KNOW!!'

'Well, let me just have a look at the la—'

'You've planned this, haven't you?' He's turned back to my mother, and moved his face close to hers. 'You hold it in front of me like some arse-pissing paradise – a house free of The *cunting* Hindenburg – eighty thousand quid in the bank – and then you snatch it away.' He looks away, breathes in very deeply, and then out the same way. 'I know why you did it. Because you couldn't get to me any more. I'd reached rock bottom. So you had to raise me up a bit and then drop me again – just to push me down that little bit further.'

My mother has shut her eyes and is trembling slightly, her arms folded across the numbers LZ 129. I feel my dad gearing up for some final atrocity.

'The Hindenburg crashed, Irene. Do you hear me? It wasn't air-worthy. It fucking crashed. BOOOM!!' His arms widen and circle. 'So how about we stop celebrating its fucking memory?'

He's gone too far.

'Dad. Would you . . .?'

'HERE YOU FUCKING ARE!!' He throws the bottle in my direction, far too fast for me to catch it, although I don't think he meant it primarily as a missile: it whizzes past my head and smashes, or seems rather to burst, like the sugar-glass ones do in cowboy-film fights, against a glass cabinet on the far wall containing five models of The Hindenburg and some miscellaneous ephemera: tickets, a passenger's passport, the route-map to Manhattan. The wine trickles down the cabinet door like the blood of all those brave experimental travellers.

My dad, realising that he's gone a bit far, tuts and marches out of the room. I look at the floor just long enough to realise that the label has been rendered completely unreadable before I turn my eyes to my trembling mother.

'I can't believe it was for the money,' I say, handing her a cup of tea. I wanted to put lots of sugar in it, like you're supposed to when someone's had a terrible shock – I don't think it matters if the shocking event itself happened fifty-nine years ago; news travels very slowly to some – but my mother insisted on having it as she always does, weak and black. She wrings soapy wine out of the wet cloth into the kitchen sink, moving a corner of her mouth sideways and raising her eyebrows.

'Eighty thousand pounds is a lot of money. We could've done with it. I'm not sure how much longer your father's going to be at Amstrad.'

'Really?'

She wipes her hands down on her apron and takes the cup, and makes another face, halfway between resignation and exasperation. 'He had a big row with Brian Goldring.'

Brian Goldring, amazingly, is a name I know; it's my dad's immediate superior.

'That must've been on the cards for a while . . .'

She nods, and takes a sip of tea, in that way of hers, pursing her lips well before the cup reaches them.

'Aaaaaah . . .' she says, after swallowing. 'But you're right, of course, there was more to the decision to sell etc than just the money. Since Mutti died, it's not the same.' She looks at me like she's come to the end of a long course of therapy. 'Do you know, Gabriel, I think that there's a part of me that kept it all going just for her. Just so she wouldn't think I'd forgotten my father. Do you know, I think there is.'

Even though the tone is still daytime TV, there is a hint of truth and tragedy in all that, perhaps the first genuine facing-up to those two my mother has ever done, so I decide to press home the advantage. She has started absent-mindedly to dry a breadknife from the washing-up rack.

'Mum?' She looks up, slightly startled, but clearly doesn't know why; it's because I haven't directly addressed her – that is, called her mother – in years. 'Are you ever going to work it out with Dad?'

She blinks into the middle distance. 'I don't know, Gabriel. I really don't.' We have moved on, then; time was when she would have said 'work out what?'

'You know how it is, Gabriel,' she continues. 'You've just lost someone who you cared about. It's difficult. You have to get on with the choices you make. I mean, I was watching the TV the other day, and two words came up on the screen which I think sum up what I'm trying to say: Love Hurts.'

I search my head for a possible response to this. 'Isn't that that show with Adam Faith in it?'

'Yes.'

And I'm just about to dismiss her as usual, as fatuous, as someone who dissipates any kind of difficulty into platitudes, when I look at her eyes, and they're desperate: they're a trapped person's eyes, a very trapped person's eyes, because, I realise, she is trapped twice – once in her marriage, and once in her discourse. The words may be naff and unreal and not follow any logic, but the sadness and the rage and sense of injustice aren't. What else is she supposed to do, when these are the phrases that offer themselves in her head? Imagine Yeats, disabled of poetry: imagine most of us. I've put too much store on words, on what you can be told.

'You're right,' I say, and put my hand on her shoulder – the most genuine physical contact we've had since breast-feeding – 'it does hurt.'

She touches my hand. 'I'm so tired, Gabriel. It's so tiring living without an emotional life. Your father, he . . .' She trails off.

'Well, if it's between him and The Hindenburg . . .'

It's a joke, but she looks at me ultra-seriously. Her eyes move in an arc around the kitchen, overloaded with pine; it was a present, the new kitchen, from Mutti, one of a number of bestowals brought on by a desire to get rid of all her money before she died. They end, eventually, on a vista through to the dining-room, and her father's prized model revolving obscenely.

'He's right, though, isn't he?' she says, her eyes refusing to move on. 'It did crash.'

'Mother!'

'Well, it did!' Suddenly, I see purpose in her face; if I was a counsellor, I'd be concerned that she was progressing too fast. 'Don't you know? Look!'

She throws the dishcloth down and quick-steps through the door, knife forward, a menopausal avenger. I'm getting a bad feeling about this, not dispelled when she hikes up her apron and climbs on to one of the four chairs around the laid-for-dinner dining-room table. For a while, I can see the back of her head, all Autumnal Auburn, rotate slightly, as she watches the great fat tin balloon continue its oblivious circling, like a force-fed goose granted a last fly.

'Hold on a minute . . .' I say, feebly.

She turns slightly to profile. '*This* is what happened!' With one hand she pulls the string above the model taut, and with the other, slices through it with the breadknife. It could be just a consequence of my own panic, but, for a moment, the Zeppelin seems to hang in the air, like Tom after he's chased Jerry off a cliff, like God has granted it an 'Et tu, Brute?' moment; and then it comes crashing down, only this time not into the waters of Hudson Bay, but nose-first into a big pot of Stu's Stew.

I come through from the kitchen, slightly ducking, still frightened by the possibility of being hit in the face by one of the bits of meat: I haven't been trained how to face a nail bomb. The tapering back end of the model sticks out of the casserole-dish like an obese ladle.

'It's broken,' I say, picking up the centre-piece of the Irene Jacoby Hindenburg Collection and scraping odd bits of stew off its sides. 'You won't be able to sell it now.'

Looking down at me from the chair, her gravy-spattered face smiles, and I get the impression that that was what she intended, that this was an act of defiance not just against her father, but against her husband as well; perhaps the bloody thing was a phallic symbol after all.

24

Little Venice, so-called because it is so little like Venice: there are no houseboats in the city of canals, and you don't have to wear blinkers to avoid seeing the Westway. But that's what London's like, untrustworthy – every so often, you might find a genuinely nice part of it, but Don't Look Now: round the corner there'll be some terrible urban *Ungeheuer*. Greenwich is back-to-back with Woolwich, Finsbury flush against Hoxton, there are no buffer zones. London never lets you relax.

I've already gone through what might be considered the pleasant, the Venetian, part of Little Venice: it took me about fifteen seconds, and bear in mind that the Dolomite is now down to about eighteen miles an hour, tops. Puttering alongside the canal up Delamere Terrace, on my right I can see water, boats (more sparsely moored than further back), a block of white stucco houses, and, on my left, the elephantine graffitied legs of the A40 (M), and beneath them, some asphalt five-a-side pitches and an impromptu rubbish dump. I'm just about to stop, feeling that if I go any further I may be about to enter some kind of inter-universe black hole, when I see him, crouching on the deck of a tiny sky-blue tugboat.

'Nick!' I shout, winding the window down. He looks up from whatever it is he's doing, something mock-nautical, some unnecessarily complex knotting of a stupidly thick piece of rope, and waves at me. He's wearing a sort of Cultural Revolution outfit, a blue boiler-suit with a little Casey Jones hat.

I park the car with some difficulty – I'm not sure it's got enough power left for reverse – at the point where the terrace curves down to the Harrow Road. Nick's boat is moored half under a bridge across the canal, but the position of the late afternoon sun throws the shadow of the bridge completely over it. I walk down the steps cut into the canal walls to the towpath. We're far enough into summer for the water to smell fairly rancid, although, remembering Nick's citrus and offal breath, that may be why he feels at home here.

'Hello!' he says as I approach, his hand still fretting at his piece of rope. 'How's things?'

'OK,' I say. I remain standing somewhat awkwardly on the tow-path, uncertain whether it's all right for me to make the leap on to the boat. 'So this is it then . . .'

He looks up again from his knotting and smiles. 'Yeah. *Wanderlust*.'

'What?'

He nods to the side – port, starboard, I don't fucking know: the one nearest the bank; in black letters near the prow is painted the boat's name, *Wanderlust*. Nick had pronounced it with no regard to the German language.

'It means "a need to travel",' he says. He looks somewhat thinner than last time I saw him, on his way out of the house three weeks ago; and, in a sense, less mad, although still, obviously, barking – just more settled into his madness than before.

'I know.'

'That clinched it for me. That's why I bought it.'

I nod, unchallengingly.

'What do you think?'

I think: £9,000? Seems to me *Wanderlust*'s previous captain has ripped you off. It's a very small vessel, with some sort of wooden tower-cum-steering post (look: I don't know much marine vocab – I'm *sorry*) at the far end, and an expanse of tarpaulin covering the rest; there is a manhole in the middle of it that must lead down to some cabins below. But then when Nick rang me up, from God knows where, and said he knew what he had to do – buy a boat – it really was the next unscrupulous boat-salesman to come along's lucky day.

'Very nice,' I say. Of course the thing I really couldn't believe was not that Nick was going to buy a boat – buying a boat, a sex change, opening a cheese factory, moving in with Princess Margaret, it could've been anything – but that he had £9,000. Can you believe it? Next time someone with a bucket and windscreen-sponge approaches you at the traffic lights, don't be intimidated: either stop them before they've lifted your wipers, or let them carry on until the lights go green and put your foot down, taking their arm with you.

'Come on board,' he says, extending a hand. I hesitate for a second, and then grasp it; he pulls me away from the sure footing of the tow-path and on to the rocking one of the boat. We stand faces close together on the narrow deck, and I become anxious that Nick's next visionary realisation may be that he has to push me overboard, until he looks away and says, 'It's great, isn't it? The river.'

'Great, yeah.'

'To feel that you're always moving. Even when you're still.'

'. . . Yeah.'

'That way you can never get stuck.'

He releases my hand. When he looks back to me, I do my best to make it look like I've learnt from his words.

'Let's go downstairs,' he says.

He lifts the manhole cover, and unhooks a half-extended stepladder underneath so that it stretches all the way below (aft, is it? midships?); grabbing the top of the ladder with both hands, he swings himself around, lands on the third rung down, and begins to walk into the boat, all done with more than a little 'I'm very much at home at sea'-ness to it. I follow him cautiously, happy to play the part of landlubber.

Down below, virtually no light can penetrate through the two small portholes positioned on either side of the boat. A sudden smell of gas makes me feel oddly sad, until I realise it's reminded me of Dina's mock-Zippo, concretely, in the way that only smell, the memory-sense, can; and then, an aura of light extends in a small radius from a hurricane light held in Nick's hands, allowing the dark wood walls of the cabin to come into view, but not much else: the slight but continuous side-to-side movement makes the shadows hop, skip and jump around the inside of the boat.

'Sit down,' he says. 'There's a sofa behind you.'

I take him on trust, and sit on something rather wet. As my eyes adjust to the light, I become aware that the cabin is tiny, and my 'sofa', a plastic camping-cushion on top of a chest.

'Not as big as the one you're used to . . .' I say.

He doesn't answer, presumably because he sees that as a typically negative assessment of his new surroundings. I don't particularly like being in a position where I can't clearly see his eyes; they're the only gauge I've got.

'Is there a toilet?'

Nick nods, and leans to the side: it becomes clear that the side wall is in fact a door, which judderingly opens. He lifts his arm and puts the hurricane lamp inside, lighting up not only the smallest room in the houseboat, but probably the smallest room in the world: it contains one of those nasty chemical toilets, and I don't look away fast enough to miss the three or four stools floating in the blue liquid. The room is so small it is perhaps best not to think of it as a toilet, but as a chemical-toilet case.

'How do you get rid of it?'

'There's a big waste-system for all the boats halfway along the canal. I carry it there.'

The thought of Nick madly humping his spilling shit along the tow-path is almost too much to bear.

'How's Dina?' he says, shutting the toilet door with some difficulty.

'Gone back to America.'

'Ah . . .' he says, irritatingly, as if he always knew that would be the outcome. *Hold on: not yet.*

'I always quite fancied the idea of a boat, myself.'

'Did you?' he says, with a sense that I am sadly mistaken, not being one of the chosen.

'You gonna go anywhere in it?'

He coughs, a phlegmy rattle from somewhere deep in his chest, which may have something to do with the fact that although it is warm outside, it is irredeemably damp in here.

'Yes,' he says, once he's recovered. 'I've got to do a bit more work on it. The engine needs a couple of new parts.'

'Oh, it's got an engine . . .'

'Yeah. And I'm going to get a sail up as well. Then I'm going to head east.'

'Southend?'

'Indonesia,' he says, and starts to cough again. *Now*.

'Do you ever see Fran?'

Silence sets in, apart from the mild lapping of the canal against the boat; the thought wanders across my head to come down here and record the sound for use as a relaxation tape. The bluish light flickers across his face, covering his stubbly chin with a second beard of shadows.

'She came down once,' he says. 'But she didn't stay. She was pleased I'd got the boat and everything – pleased I was away from the house – but she said it was still too painful to see me. Brought back too many memories.'

'What memories?'

He brings the hurricane lamp closer to his face, allowing me to see his eyes, doubly reflecting the gas flame.

'You know . . . memories. Of that time.'

'No. I thought it was a great time for the two of you. You were discovering all sorts of things about yourselves.'

'Yeah, but then you put a stop to that.'

'*I* didn't.'

'Well, who did?'

I sniff sharply. 'Did Fran mention Ben when you saw her?'

He frowns: mundane thought-processes, like thinking back over a previous conversation, must be difficult to do over a terrible din in your head.

'I don't think so. Why?'

'You remember she did during that phone call . . .'

'Yes . . .'

'I dunno. I worry . . .'

'What?' he says, interested now, caught.

'Just that he might have said something to her. Something to make her go away.' I look up from my trying-to-work-it-out mask. 'I'm only telling you because I don't want you to think that it was me who was trying to split the two of you up.'

Even in the half-dark, I can see he believes this. It's in the character of the psychotic to assume that the universe revolves around him, and all actions of others motivated by his centrality to their thoughts at all times.

'OK,' he says. 'But Fran's too strong for that. She wouldn't have been scared off by anything Ben said.'

I nod, letting him lead the way. Hints and pushes and clues suggest themselves to me.

'Unless . . .' he says.

'What?'

'There was something between them.'

Good old Nick. And I mean: good *old* Nick. He's still in there somewhere, sniffing out sex like a dog in the park.

'I don't think so. Wouldn't she have told you?'

Old and new Nick go into battle. 'Well . . . yeah. I mean – I would've thought I'd just've *known*. We were so close. But now I think about it—'

'I can't believe it. Y'know – why should he want to cheat on Alice?'

He looks up defensively; pieces of my jigsaw click into place. 'Alice isn't Fran,' he says definitively.

'I know that.'

'I wouldn't expect you to understand this, but Fran – Fran has an inner beauty, and when you begin to see that, no amount of surface looks can compare with it.'

It's become important to him, now, kind of as it was with Ben, to defend Fran's attractiveness as a human being. The boat pitches rather further towards my side than usual, and something hard and pointed slides across the floor and hits my foot. I bend down and pick it up; it is the steering-wheel, a classic, *Mutiny on the Bounty*-style wooden spoked circle.

'Shouldn't this be attached to the boat in some way?' I say.

'It's not the original,' he says. 'I bought it in an antique shop on Edgware Road. I'm going to work out how to connect it to the rudders.'

I rest it upwards on my lap.

'She was so upset, though,' he continues, and his face hardens. 'He'll have been a complete bastard to her.'

'Well, he shouldn't have got involved with her in the first place.'

His appreciation, moving in large planes, will not include my sudden movement from dubiousness to certainty.

'No,' he says, and moves the hurricane light down to the

floor, but I no longer need to see his eyes: my objective has been achieved. It's not difficult to provide a would-be Messiah with a mission. In the darkness, I spin the steering-wheel, and wonder whether it would be too much to remind him of Ben and Alice's address.

An awful thing to do; worse than I have ever done. There can be no moral justification for my actions, not, at least, if you take morality to mean the rules and restrictions which restrain our licence to behave in ways that benefit ourselves but harm others. But there *is* another morality, or rather, another code of being: the 'to thine own self be true' one. Most of the time, the two codes are not necessarily incompatible – you can, in everyday life, be true to yourself without hurting others, unless, of course, you're Dennis Nilsen – but unfortunately, fate sometimes conspires to bring you to a place where selfhood becomes so *rushing*, so imminent, that the only viable action seems to be that which will bring it to the point of total culmination. Whatever the cost.

I can't sleep: hence the tortuous philosophising. I raise my head, and, like scratching an old wound just as it was finally about to heal, check the bedside clock: 3:02. My sleep pattern, as you know, had been improving night by night, until the night following the day Dina left, half of which I spent in debate with myself about what to do, and the other half deliberately holding sleep off as an immature reaction against the obvious 'success' of Alison Randolph's hypnotherapy. Since then, sleep has still been easier to come by than it was, but sometimes I've found myself back on the other shore, desperately needing to feel the soft placement of Dina's head on my inner shoulder to carry me across.

Tonight, though, it's not that. It's not even insomnia as I've always known it, and I've got to know it really well over the years. Because the one thing insomnia *isn't* is guilty-secret driven. That's insomnia for idiots: it's beyond even 'have you tried Kalms?', those people who hear you have trouble sleeping and say 'something on your mind?' No. There's something *under* your mind, something flashing *across* your mind, something hatching like the spider's eggs of urban myth *inside* your mind: but something *on* your mind, something specific that you have done and are aware of and feel bad about – the sort of sleeplessness that induces doesn't classify as insomnia. Because, at the end of the day, or rather, night, something like that can be cast out of your mind easily; you just have to undo it. You just have to go and take the time-bomb out from under the car.

Unless, that is, you've already activated it.

Two hours, thirty-three minutes and two weeks later. Things haven't quite panned out as I would've expected, except in the regard of me being still up at this time. I thought Nick would go straight round to Ben and Alice's and have it out with them – he seemed so impelled, so switched on, when I left. Three days I spent convinced that the next ring of the telephone would be Alice, calling in tears, maybe even needing a place to stay. I listen quietly, patiently, as she tells me the whole story – how Nick had raved about Ben and this Fran woman, how Ben had denied it, and she'd believed him, dismissed it straight away as more madness, but, gradually, begun to worry, heard the silences in Ben's story, and saw the guilt in his eyes. And now she didn't know what to do, who to turn to: and then, at last, I start to speak.

But nothing of the sort. I saw them a few days ago, and they seemed more infuriatingly content than ever, the sandpaper of religious neurosis that had for a small time rubbed between them worn down to nothing, the only awkwardness in the air not between them at all, but between them and me, because no one was going to mention Dina. Troubled, I returned to Little Venice to see if I couldn't prod Nick a bit harder – perhaps, I thought, it's just that memory thing again, he just needs reminding – but the boat had vanished. No trace of it. I spoke to some of his neighbours, but none of these non-Vietnamese boat-people seemed to remember *Wanderlust* at all, although the owner of a houseboat about five hundred yards up the canal, a quaint old sea-dog in a Nicole Farhi suit, told me, between interruptions from his pager, that he remembered seeing 'some guy in a hat carrying a toilet about' who he'd assumed worked for Thames Waterways.

I suppose he must've got the engine going, which really puts paid to my little plot. I can't see Nick, silhouetted against an enormous Pacific moon, the junks of Jakarta in sight, the smoke from *Wanderlust*'s funnel mingling with the smell of frying parrot-fish, thinking 'oh hold on – I forgot to go and confront Ben about Fran! About stern!' (or whatever it is). The slight ache of lost friendship mingles with the greater pain of being no further forward than ever I was in love: next time I come up with a dastardly plot, I'll see if I can't get lessons from Iago or someone.

I throw the duvet off my frayed body. I'm too hot, but my fucked body-clock fucks up my body temperature too, so I'm too hot, yet clammy and cold-to-the-touch; within seconds of lying there uncovered, the pool of sweat in the small of my back feels like iced water.

File *this* insomnia under 'Unresolved'. I don't know whether to leave the whole business alone now, or to hope that Nick hasn't gone East and may yet come good – bad, if you like – or, the third and most terrifying option, to go and tell Alice about Fran myself. It's unfortunate, because the way I planned it, I'm clean – in my scenario, when asked, Nick had come up with the conclusion himself and nothing I could say was going to stop him coming round and delivering the truth. I'm in sleeping-pill limbo as well, that time of the night when you know you can't sleep but it's too late to take a pill because there's not enough time to sleep it off, and you don't really fancy a wool-stuffed skull until early evening tomorrow.

Sod it. I've made a decision. Better that than never sleeping again. I haul myself out of bed and over to my desk. Pausing there for a moment, through a gash in the curtains I can see, not sunrise, just the fact that the sun has risen, in the a priori way it does in London, because there is no horizon, no mountains in the distance for it to rise from, so therefore, no such thing as a London sunrise, not as tribesmen in the Serengeti or farmers in the Yorkshire Dales or Nick standing in his boat in the Indonesian dawn understand sunrise. Still looking at the bright blue air – it's going to be another hot day – I delve my hand into the second drawer down in search of temazepam, the pill with the least length on it, and feel my fingers sink into something warm and soft and moving. The memory-centres of my knackered brain are too slow, and I bring my hand up to my face a split-second before I put two and two together, thus denying myself the opportunity of running into the bathroom, screaming, vomiting through my nostrils, but at least facing hard away from an open palm coated with maggots and decaying rat-pieces.

'Hello!' says Alice, prepared to open the door now I've given my identity. 'What are *you* doing here?' She is not dressed for visitors. Her hair, unusually, is down, and as she bends her face forward to reach mine on the lower steps, I catch the luxuriantly heavy swing of her breasts through the hanging V-neck of her grey mohair jumper, and the pale of a bikini-line where there is no bra.

'Oh, I was just passing,' I say, and cannot believe that in all the rehearsing I've done for this, I forgot to think about an excuse for the basic fact of turning up. I kiss her proffered cheek, and the skin bulging round my lips reminds me of Dina's, only less absorbing. 'I'm on my way back to that garage. The car's dying a slow death.'

Ben appears from behind her, his hands first, beefy and gripping around her delicate waist. The mohair jumper becomes kite-shaped.

'Don't tell me you've finished the Peter Houseman piece?' he says, resting his chin on her left shoulder.

'I have, actually,' I say, and go back to the car, delighting inside that my visit has been given an ostensible purpose. It's on the back seat of the Dolomite somewhere, I'm sure: I've been driving around with it for days intending to drop it into *Over The Line*'s offices. When I open the door and look in, though, there's no sign of it amongst the old newspapers, old cinema tickets and old unpaid bills.

'It'd be great if you could get it to me in the next hour,' Ben's voice, coming from the pavement behind my crawling-about arse, says. 'Only I'm going into the offices for a meeting now, and I can get it subbed.'

Looking away from him, up through the left-hand back window, I – I don't exactly smile to myself, but my face registers an inner satisfaction. Across the road, I can see Ben's car, a red Volkswagen Polo.

'You're going in now?' I say, as if I didn't know. 7:30 I believe was the time the receptionist had told me was set for this evening's meeting, when I'd phoned to ask if she knew what time Ben was coming in.

'Yeah. We've got a lot to catch up with.'

'Here it is,' I say, turning round and flicking a triangular piece of Dime bar off a couple of sheaves of stapled-together A4: it leaves a golden smear across the words 'quiet industry'.

'Have you got time for a cup of tea?' Alice calls from the house.

I look at Ben, holding his hands out waiting for the essay, a knowing but affectionate smile still on his face from seeing the Dime bar shoot into the gutter. He looks warmed, as from a log-fire, by the rusty light of early summer evening, the sort of light when sometimes you look up and see hundreds of birds clustering together in search of air-borne insects: it is too dim clearly to read the words on the page, yet the street-lamps still bide their time. I get up from my half-in, half-out of the car posture, and pass him the piece; and then, on an instinct, I kiss him on the cheek, even though I always hate it when he does that to me; it is rough, pin-pricked with stubble.

'Thanks,' he says, about the pages rather than the kiss, but still a little shocked, unsure how to process its significance. Perhaps if he ever moves on from the *Old* Testament . . .

'Well?' says Alice, opening the door further.

'I think I can spare five minutes,' I say, and walk slowly enough up the garden path to hear the sound of Ben crossing the road, opening his car door, slamming it shut again, and driving away.

A man could swoon in Ben and Alice's kitchen from the overpowering smell of herbs. Basil, thyme, oregano, sage, parsley and sweet marjoram compete in a scent riot, from tens of different strategically placed racks, and that doesn't even take into account the spices. Every drawer and fitting is wooden, as well, which seems to soak up the almost medicinal aroma and give it out again with an extra hint of tree, as if it wasn't enough of a forest in there already. I wonder if she's noticed that I'm jumpy.

'Everyone's well pleased with your column, then,' she says, forcing my tea-bag against the side of the cup with a spoon. This seems to be what people say when they're warming up for a conversation with me.

'Are they?' I say, fishing.

'Yeah!' she says, pouring in the semi-skimmed and bringing the cup over to the table, where I'm seated, absent-mindedly flicking through the *Guardian Guide* and its endless wittering on about *Frasier*. 'Ben says it generates no end of letters every week.'

'Not all of them complimentary, though,' I say, and try to smile bashfully. It's difficult. My actions with Alice are always slightly self-conscious at the best of times, but now I'm watching my every move.

'What about you?' I say. 'What you working on?'

'Oh!' she says, colouring somewhat. 'I haven't done anything for *Sight And Sound* for weeks.'

'Really?'

'Not since April.'

She doesn't seem to want to explain why, which I take to be an example of how little I am in her confidence. Instead, she sits on the chair at right-angles to mine and pours herself a glass of orange juice: I feel her closeness like static, and the fact that it is just me and her in the house. But then, she says, 'Gabe . . .'

And I catch my breath, because *I* was the one who'd come here to make an announcement.

'Yes?' I say, after a couple of seconds silence, making me wonder: could it be she already knows?

'I'm sorry about Dina.'

'Oh,' I say, palpably deflated. 'Yeah. So am I.'

'I don't think – I'm not sure me and Ben did our best to help, really.'

'Well . . .'

'No, we didn't. It was stupid of us. We felt a bit weird about it – I dunno why, because we're mad in some ways, paranoid – and when she was living here I think we probably put some pressure on her about it.' She looks at me keenly; it's all I can do to listen and not simply wallow in our intimacy. 'I don't know if that had anything to do with why she went back to America . . .'

'She didn't talk to you about it then . . .'

'Not properly.' She sighs, an affection-inspiring coo. 'It really upset me, actually. She might've told you, we've had our sisterly problems over the years, me and Dina. And they got worse, if anything, when she first came back. We *were* getting on each other's nerves. But lately, I thought we were really sorting it out – y'know, once she moved out and we gave each other a bit of space and all that stuff, and me and Ben accepted that you and her were an item and there was no problem with that . . .' She trails off, lifting her glass with both hands to drink her orange juice. Her lips land on the rim. I don't say anything.

'But then,' she continues, putting the glass back down on the table, 'when she told me she was going to go back to America, she'd just closed off again. She wouldn't explain her reasons at all. And I told her I'd really like her to stay, but' – she shrugs – 'it didn't seem to make any difference.'

Her precise and complete face, like an Identikit picture drawn from information supplied by my heart, looks out from its surrounding frame of black curls inquiringly. She wants me to explain. She looks tired, but I think that may be just because she has no make-up on; even Alice wears make-up, although what exactly she's improving on I'm not sure. Looking tired I don't see as a deficiency, more a condition of being.

'Do you not want to talk about it?' she says, snapping me from dreaming into her face. I can feel the memory of my love for Dina batting like a moth against the great light of her beauty.

'No. Yes. I mean – I don't know what there is to say. It didn't work out. I don't think you should blame yourself.' Although perhaps she should, because it may be no bad thing for her to feel beholden to me at this time. She leans into her chair and reaches up her svelte hand to hold the back of her neck, for which I have no adjectives, none of them will do.

'I know you think me and Ben never fight,' she says, apropos of nothing, her curvaceous eyes looking at me searchingly. 'But we do. There was a point recently when it got quite bad.'

Alice seems to think that we are at some sort of personal information swapmeet; that if she opens up to me more than usual, I will eventually tell her why Dina left. Or maybe she just wants to talk. I burn for the unT-shirted heaven locked inside her mohair jumper.

'I got a feeling something was not quite . . . as it usually is,' I say, nodding.

Alice looks surprised, as if she hadn't expected her and Ben to be so readable, but then she doesn't know how closely they were being read; and perhaps a little put out, from a trading of secrets standpoint. She leans forward, however, both elbows on the table, and pulls her hair back from her brow with both hands: a let's-do-some-serious-talking posture if ever there was one. Her hair spills out from and around her fingers like black rain; along the line where it meets her forehead, the skin is paler again.

'Yes, well . . . it wasn't. D'you remember when you came round for dinner that time and he told you he'd gone to synagogue?'

'Yes.'

'It became a massive issue with him. His Judaism, I mean.'

'I know.'

She purses her mouth. 'Well, I suppose he made that kind of obvious. But then . . .'

'It became a problem between the two of you that you're not Jewish.'

She starts again, and sits up, folding her arms. Her hair swathes back over her ears.

'Did Dina tell you?'

'No. He did.' Well, Dina did tell me, but I knew by then already, and, anyway, I feel we're going in the right direction here – if she thinks that Ben has already, in a small way, betrayed her trust, she may be prepared, later on, to believe he's done so in a much more comprehensive way as well. Alice blinks rapidly, three or four times, almost a flutter: clearly, she is taken aback – she'd gone into this expecting to talk, only to discover that much of the talking has already been done.

'Oh well,' she says, 'I suppose if I'm going to talk to Dina about it, there's no reason why Ben shouldn't talk to you about it.'

'No. And there's no reason why you shouldn't talk to me about it, now.'

Above her right eyebrow, the muscle twitches evanescently, but there is no perceptible upward movement of the finely curved line. It is a response, nonetheless, which indicates an understanding that what I've just said is in a sense flirtatious, not sexually but emotionally. Perhaps the first flirtatious thing I've ever said to her.

'No . . .' she says a touch uncertainly; and then, more definitely, 'But I'd still like to know what happened between you and Dina.'

Oh, for heaven's sake. Why is she quite so bothered? It's getting in the way of my progress, this tit-for-tat heart-pouring.

Stalling, I take a sip of tea. Bleeurgh. Again, she's forgotten. Coffee without, tea with. Above the rim of the cup I see her brown like sugarless tea eyes, innocently interested, wrapped up in her need to know, to discover this knowledge – knowledge that will compress even further the tiny space in her thoughts given over to me, to me alone, rather than to me as I relate to her through her sister, or through her husband: me as someone who takes sugar in his tea but not in his coffee. I feel suddenly impelled, suddenly driven to throw out this softly-softly approach and come out with it, tell her that her husband has had a fucking affair. Fantasies of a future together after she's left Ben aren't even in the frame any more – just to move her, to touch her deeply in some way, even this appallingly selfish and destructive way; just to make some dent in her life.

'Alice . . .' I say.

'The thing is, Gabriel,' she says, but I'm only half-listening to her, the sentence '*I think you should know Ben's had an affair*' plastered on the front of my consciousness like the titles of a film, ready and waiting, ready and waiting, 'I probably shouldn't tell you this – although for all I know Ben's told you already, even though he's the one who seemed to want to keep it quiet – but . . .' she looks at me studiedly, and takes a breath, sucked grittily through her zigzag teeth, '. . . I'm pregnant.'

Ahhaha. Ah ha ha ha.

Of course you are. Of course. Because God must have his pattern, mustn't he? His awful symmetries. Women, when they live together, their menstruation synchronises, I remember. All those eggs and blood released at the same time. Must be doubly synchronic for sisters; a fertility tandem. My mind's arms circle like those of a man running towards the edge of a cliff and stopping at the last minute.

'I really, really wanted to make Dina the godmother.' Alice scratches her head violently, making her volcanic hair spray out in all directions – an action designed, I think, to stop her from crying, crying in front of this person who, all things considered, she doesn't know very well. 'I thought – this may have been wrong, but it's what I thought – that it would really consolidate our relationship; the fact that it had got better, I mean.'

Her delicate chin wobbles marginally, and I focus there to try and keep my mind still, but it races. Ben and Alice were out when I first rang Dina: at the doctor's. He was at Fran's pharmacy getting something for Alice. And all that anxiety about lineage – terrified like all us Jacobites of closure, he drove himself via Jewishness into Fran to avoid facing that unequivocal map of the future called having a child. She looks down and puts her hands in her lap, a recovery position, and I realise that I still urgently have something to say.

'Congratulations.'

She looks up and gives me a watery smile, like a sin wave, a curve on a graph charting the stress her marriage must've been under until very recently. Inside me, the death of hope mingles with relief; it's very stressful trying to live out your dreams.

'Thank you,' she says, and then, moving up from her chair, she throws her arms around my neck and hugs me. Reality, littered as it is with details, conspires to make this not quite the moment it should be: the edge of the table is kind of in the way, and her half-standing posture is not conducive to enveloping me in my chair, not that a reed like Alice could envelop an elephant like myself anyway, and she has to bend awkwardly. But, as my hands join behind her mohair back, her slim then full body feelable against mine, that gap in my soul closes slowly again like the two halves of Tower Bridge. A taste of paradise, I think, and then feel a bit stupid because that's the slogan for the Bounty advert.

Her face moves from its position in profile on my shoulder,

backing away to create the same space between us as in that optical illusion where the eye sees two faces and then a glass. Oh. She is so beautiful. For a split-second, it occurs to me to take the short-cut and just kiss her, and, for a second split-second, I'm sure I see the reciprocal thought flit across her eyes – we are in that pause, that moment of looking at each other for infinitesimally too long – and then the doorbell goes, and instantly I know that for the rest of my time I will look back on that split-second as the pivotal missed opportunity of my life. But perhaps it's OK, I think, as, frowning, she straightens up and arches her neck to look down the hallway: I knew the moment of heaven.

'Who on earth is that?' she says, and goes off, after giving me a quizzical look which means, simply, 'who on earth is that?'; it has no trace whatsoever of 'God, we almost kissed then, didn't we?'

I wait until she has gone and then pour my tea, cold and undrunk, down the sink; I watch it swirl in a vortex down the bright stainless steel plughole like my intended plan of action.

'Oh my God!' I hear Alice cry. Fear shakes me out of self-pity and I rush out of the kitchen and down the hallway. Standing on the steps behind the door and the backed-off figure of Alice is a hulking figure, soaking wet, his face daubed with grime. My fear increases with my speed down the corridor, but then mutates as I realise that this is not just some lunatic who I must protect Alice from – I take that back – it is exactly some lunatic who I must protect Alice from: it is Nick.

'Nick?' I say, my lungs and my senses gasping. 'What happened?'

'*Wanderlust* sank,' he says calmly

'What, with you on it?'

'No, two days ago. I just dived in to try and get back some stuff from it.'

Even though I have much else to worry about, the thought comes to me: *£9,000?*

'God,' says Alice. 'Look, come in, I'll get you a towel, and some of Ben's clothes.'

'No, wait,' he says, and when I hear the purposefulness I

panic, badly. 'I'm not coming in. I just came round to tell you something.'

Alice looks at me, like, *oh no, what madness now*, but I don't think so; I don't think she'll dismiss it so. Across the top of Nick's head, a single piece of pondweed, very like the sort of thing Jezebel used to bring in before the rats and frogs, lies like a combed-over covering for his baldness.

'Nick,' I say, frantically trying to fix his eyes to mine. 'It's fine. Don't worry. Forget it.'

'I've come to tell you the truth,' he intones solemnly, still resolutely staring at Alice. I have to move my head sideways so my face is right in front of his – fuck, he smells *terrible* – but he won't look at me: from a distance it must look like a hard nut trying to start a fight with a stranger.

'Look, if you've been in the river perhaps we should take you to hospital,' I say, and raise my hands to push him out of the door, but he grabs my wrists and with his mad strength pushes me away.

'I'm going to tell her, Gabriel. I have to tell the truth,' he says, and I realise there is nothing I can do. I turn to Alice helplessly, and recognise immediately from her expression that it is me who has given the game away; that there may have been a chance of her rejecting Nick's forthcoming words as mad rubbish, but my crude and obvious attempt to prevent them coming out has stamped them as credible.

'What is it, Nick?' she says softly, her voice never more her own.

She looks prepared, girded, ready to face anything, except, I would guess, the news that her husband's been having an affair with The Herpe.

'Gabriel's in love with you,' he says. 'He has been since he met you.'

And finally, he turns so that our eyes lock, like some sadistic parody of my missed split-second in the kitchen moments before; and in his I see something I've never seen before, not even *before* he smoked the killa bud – a deep, deep sanity, which perhaps does despite everything lie just round the corner from madness. It is not vengeful; he is not getting his own back on me for attempting to use him for my own ends. He is trying to help me, to shut down, once and for all, my eternally glowing tumour. Is that what it takes, then, to bring a man round from madness? Not chlorpromazine, not counselling, not EST, but simply a shatteringly cold dip on a hot day?

I hear this sound in my ears. *Boom. Boom.* Not big and loud, but distant, like background noise in the trenches. And then through it, something else: like sprinkling silver, Alice's laughter. I look at her, her face thrown back, still gorgeous even when distorted; and the opportunity is there to go back, to re-enter my coordinates. All I have to do is laugh with her.

Bollocks to that.

'It's true, yeah,' I say. 'I am.'

In a fit and a start, she stops laughing. In apparent slow-motion, frame by frame her features resettle into seriousness, and on to me.

'What can I do?' I continue, feeling the words coming up from some central point inside. 'You met my brother first. That's just a chance, isn't it – probably because of nothing – a walk in the park, a party you decided to go to after all . . . and you met him. If you'd gone somewhere else, you might have met me. But that's it, then. That note in your diary you made three years ago – "walk in the park" – "go to party" – you may as well have written "end all possibility of happiness for someone I haven't even met yet".'

Alice is looking down now, her brow layered with lines; there is a sense that perhaps it would be better if I left. Nick has stretched out his arm and is leaning his weight against the door-frame, staring tactfully away. That wasn't quite what I wanted to say, of course; you never do, do you, when these times come round.

'That's why Dina left me, by the way,' I say, looking out of the door and seeing the street-lamps haltingly light up, grimly resolved. 'She found out.'

If I was to get the whole thing off my chest, I'd tell her about Dina being pregnant as well, but that seems to me to be Dina's prerogative, whereas this, this really is mine. Alice lifts her head up, facing me, facing this. 'You told her?'

I think about it for a tiny moment. 'Yeah. Basically.'

'Gabriel . . .' she says, in a 'I'd like to help, really I would' tone.

I hold my hands out, palms to her. 'No, honestly, Alice. Don't worry.' I don't – I know this is a tired thing to think, but then again, I *am* tired, very tired – I don't want her pity. With a small flex, I angle my hand sideways and move it forward to touch her cheek; she lets her face rest in it like her sister once did.

'I won't tell Ben,' she says. 'If you don't want me to . . .'

'It's up to you.' I try desperately to record this moment, these four or five seconds of total communion, like a passionate gardener on his deathbed might smell a rose. I have made my dent, after all, and these are its contours. Then I bring my hand back to my side; time's up.

'Bye, Alice,' I say, and walk out of the door. Nick, I notice, seems to have gone, but then I see him sitting on the pavement with his back against their garden wall.

'Coming back to the flat?' I say.

He nods and gets up, picking bits of reed and mud off himself as he stands. 'Should just make it in time for *Endsleigh League Extra*,' he says.

25

The big-haired, big-glasses man on my right says something to me, but I can't make it out over the music.

'Pardon?' I say, digging out the tiny phones from my ears with no small amount of pain.

'What are you going for?' he says. 'As those awful customs people at JFK would say: business or pleasure?'

He laughs, a wheezy accordion laugh, his mouth full of fillings. I look back at the little screen carved into the chair in front of me, showing a series of *You've Been Framed*-style home videos – kids falling off high chairs, people smashing into each other, dancers careering off-stage. Just what you want to see as you're taxi-ing up for take-off A short reminder of the incredible fallibility of man, a quick jolt to the memory, in case you'd forgotten, of how the smallest of human endeavours – the smallest: walking down the road, sitting on a chair, stuff like that, not going up above the clouds in an enormous cigar box, oh no – can end in disaster. Fasten your seat-belts and let's send *this* one in to Jeremy Beadle.

I turn back towards my fellow passenger. It's a good question, actually. Both, I think. I think I'm going for the difficult and often cut-throat business of pleasure.

'I'm going to find Dina,' I say, hoping that the somewhat eccentric response will make him worry that I'm crazy and leave me alone, but the sudden roar of the plane's engines as it turns into the straight of the runway drowns me out.

'What?' he says, thrown back into his seat.

'I'm going to find Dina.' *And maybe those lost five hours.*

'Who's Dina?' he says as our stomachs register the lift into the air, and I remember that blank honesty never puts off Americans. I shake my head, conveying that the story is long. He shrugs.

'Would you mind,' he says, pointing to my lap, 'if I had that?'

I look down. Inside the polythene bag where the earphones came from is a small plastic case, unzipped to reveal a blindfold, all black and taut and unworn, and two foam earplugs.

'Only Louise – my wife – she has trouble sleeping if there's any light at all in the room, so I always try and steal a blindfold or two from the airplane for her.'

I look back at him; behind the fat neighbourliness of his face I sense a certain exhaustion, the result no doubt of so many nights spent soothing Louise. I look back down again, and then out of the window. There it is. The Antarctic of the sky.

'Sure,' I say, handing him the entire plastic case.